A BRIDE'S STORY

10

Kaoru Mori

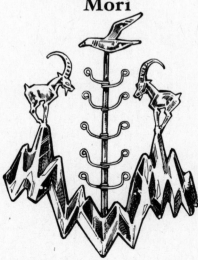

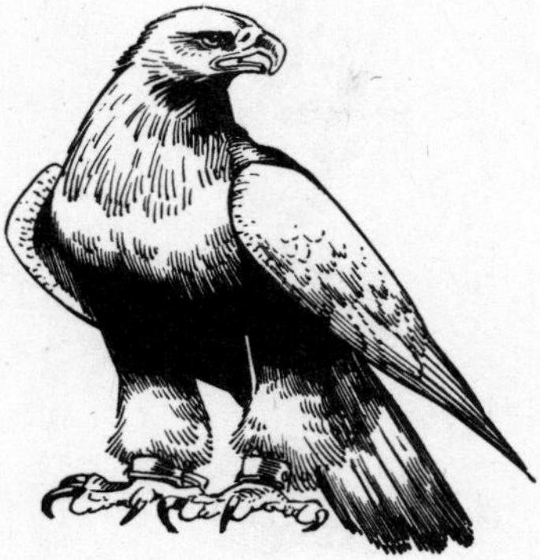

Table of Contents

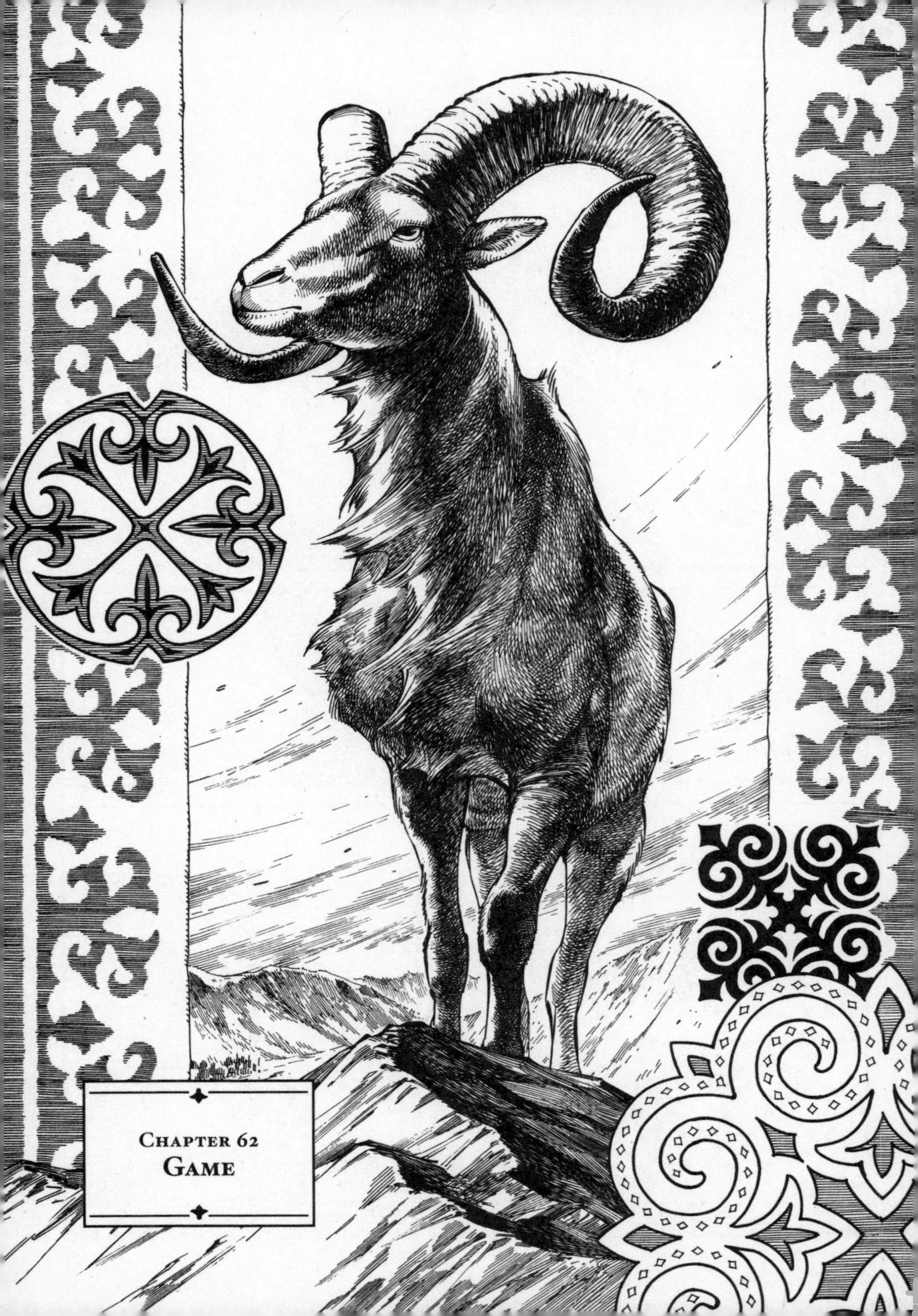

Chapter 62
Game

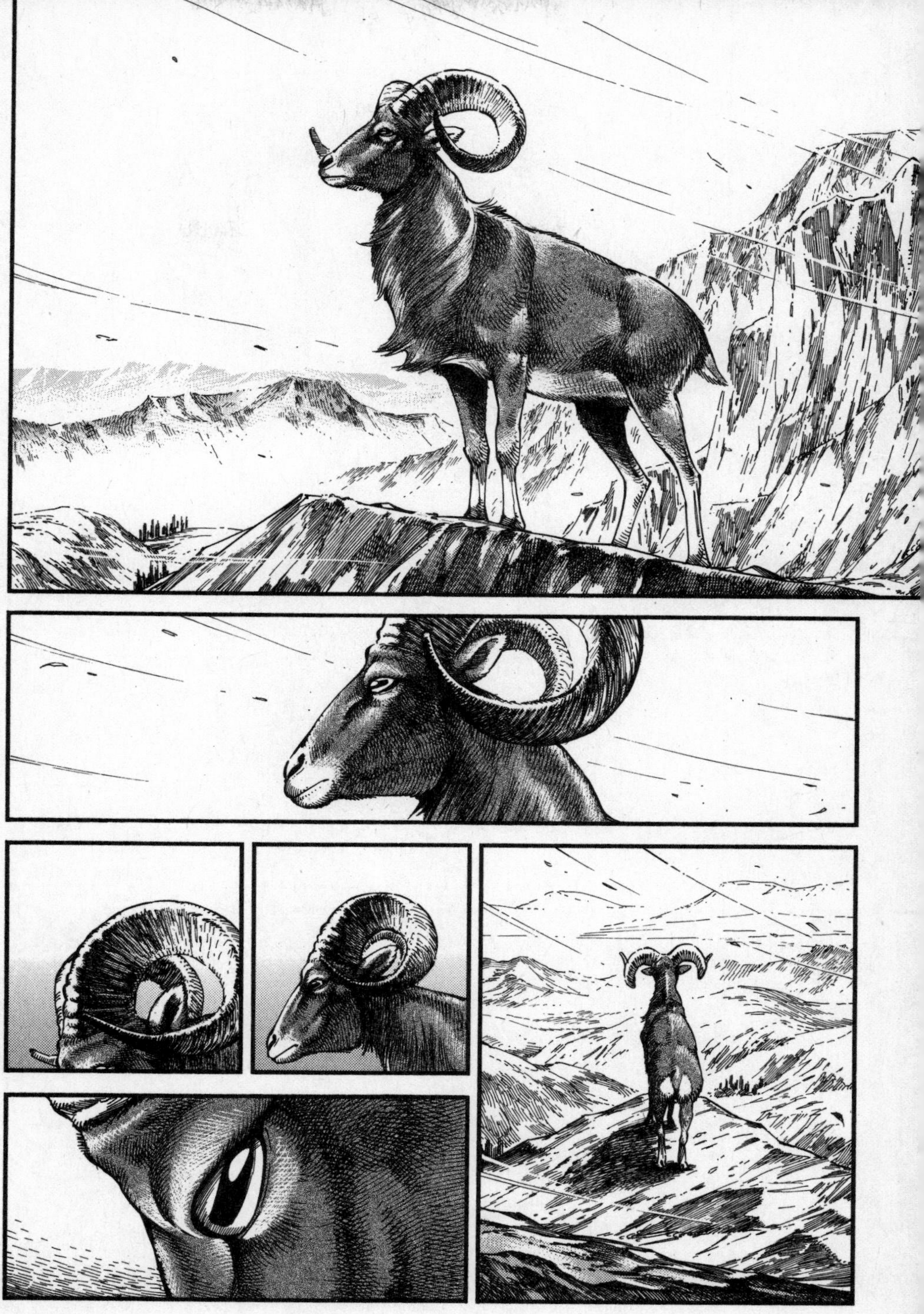

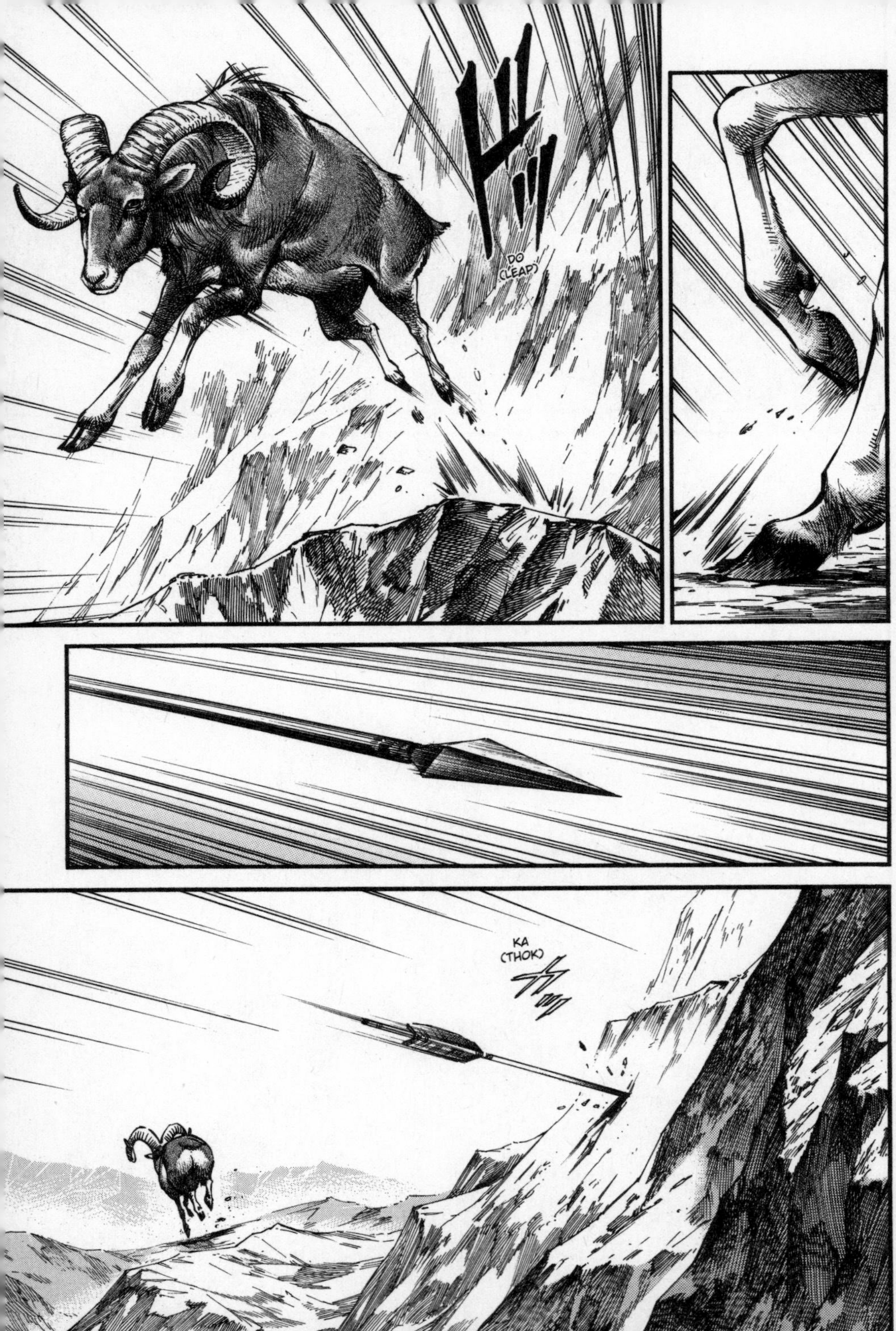
DO (LEAP)
KA (THOK)

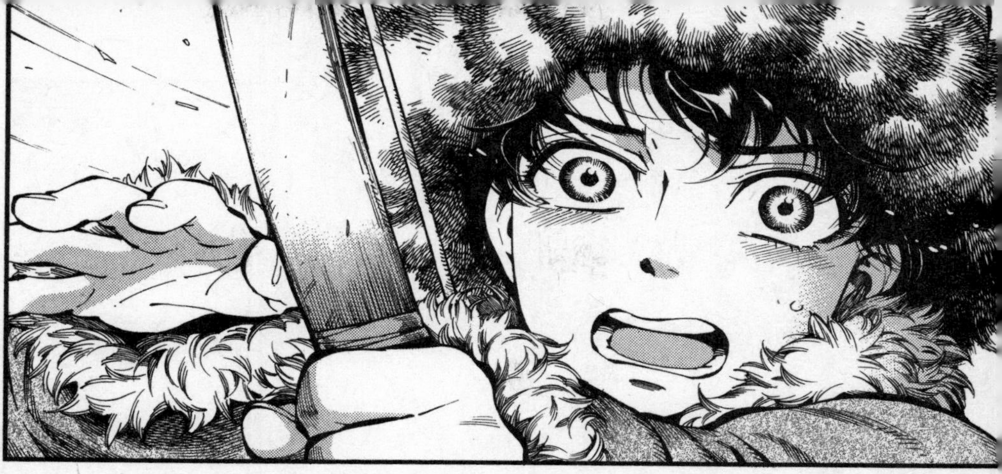

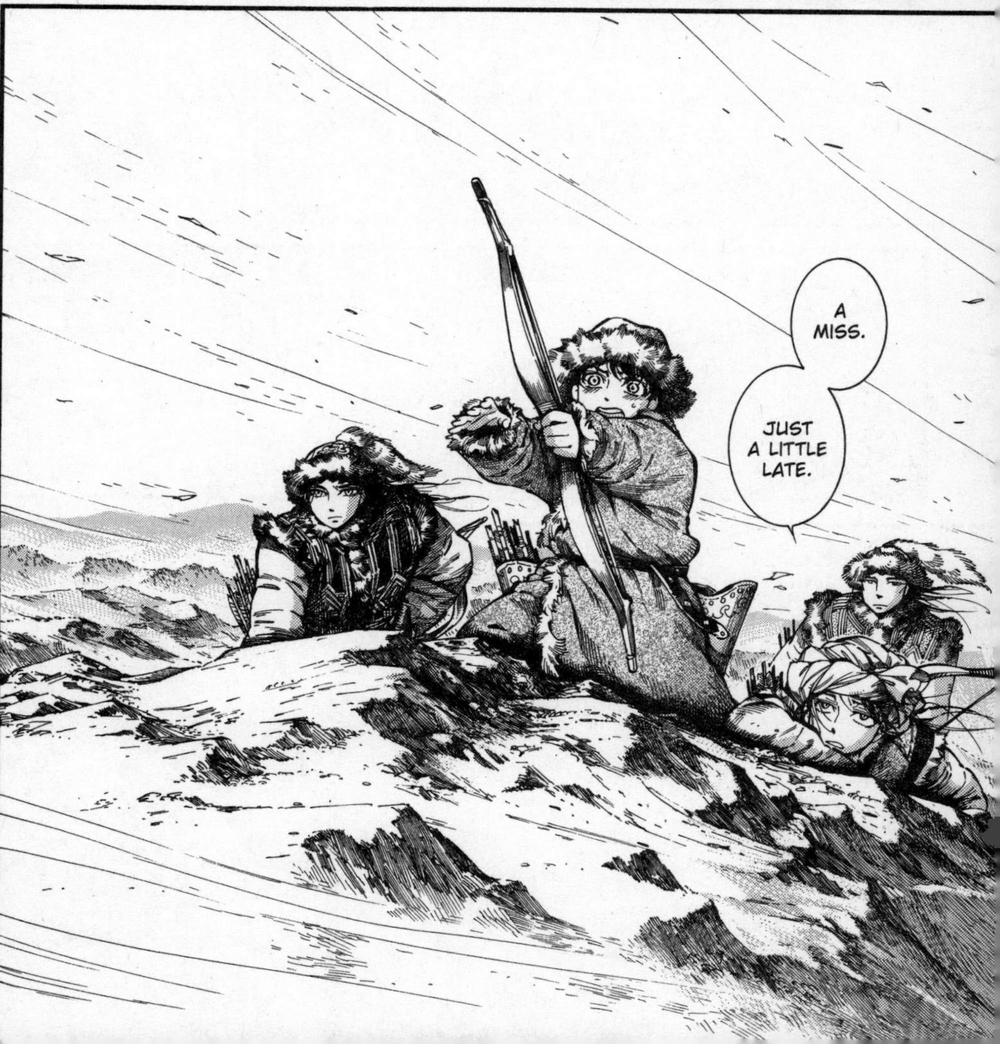
A MISS.
JUST A LITTLE LATE.

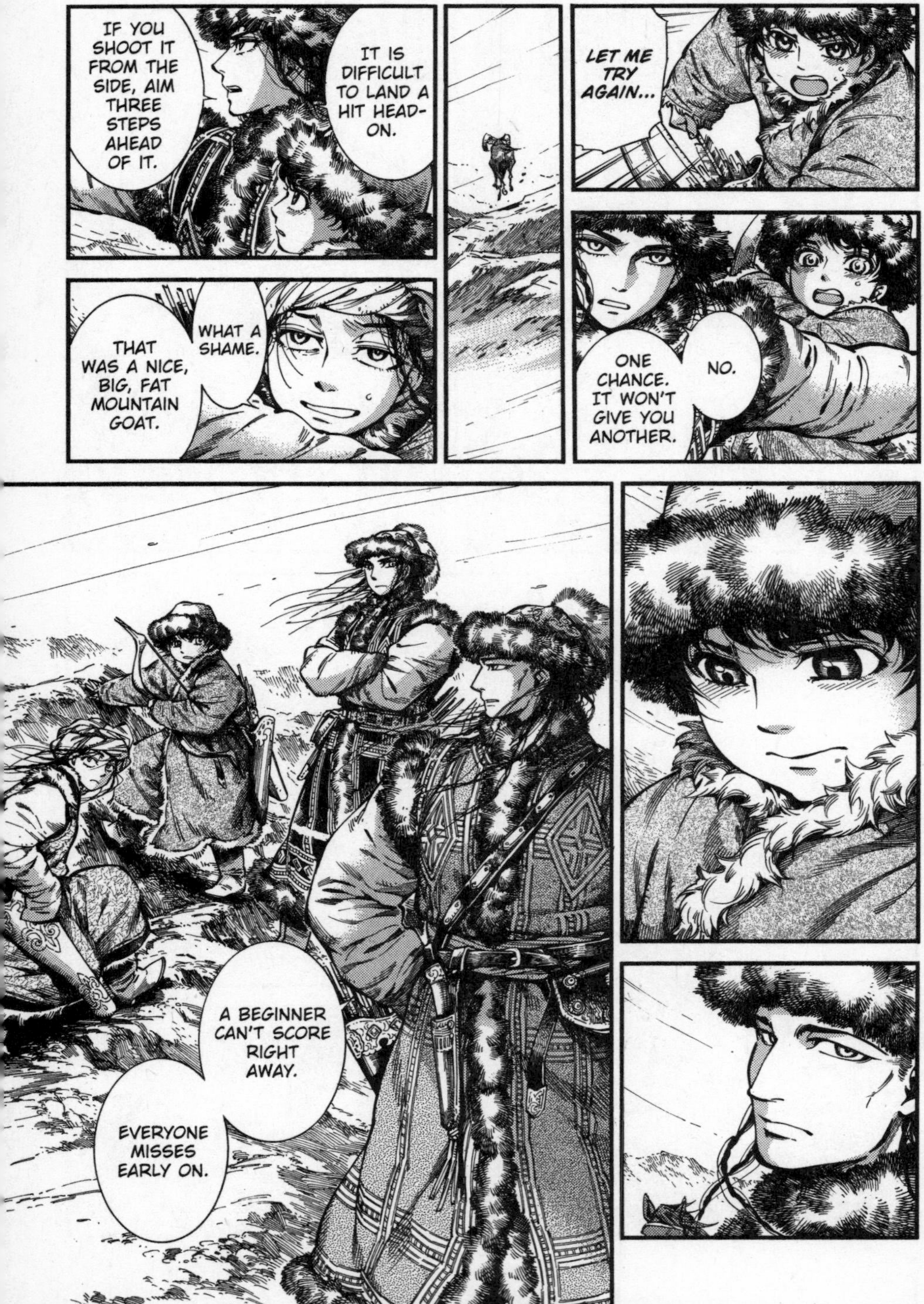
LET ME TRY AGAIN...
NO.
ONE CHANCE. IT WON'T GIVE YOU ANOTHER.
IT IS DIFFICULT TO LAND A HIT HEAD-ON.
IF YOU SHOOT IT FROM THE SIDE, AIM THREE STEPS AHEAD OF IT.
WHAT A SHAME.
THAT WAS A NICE, BIG, FAT MOUNTAIN GOAT.
A BEGINNER CAN'T SCORE RIGHT AWAY.
EVERYONE MISSES EARLY ON.

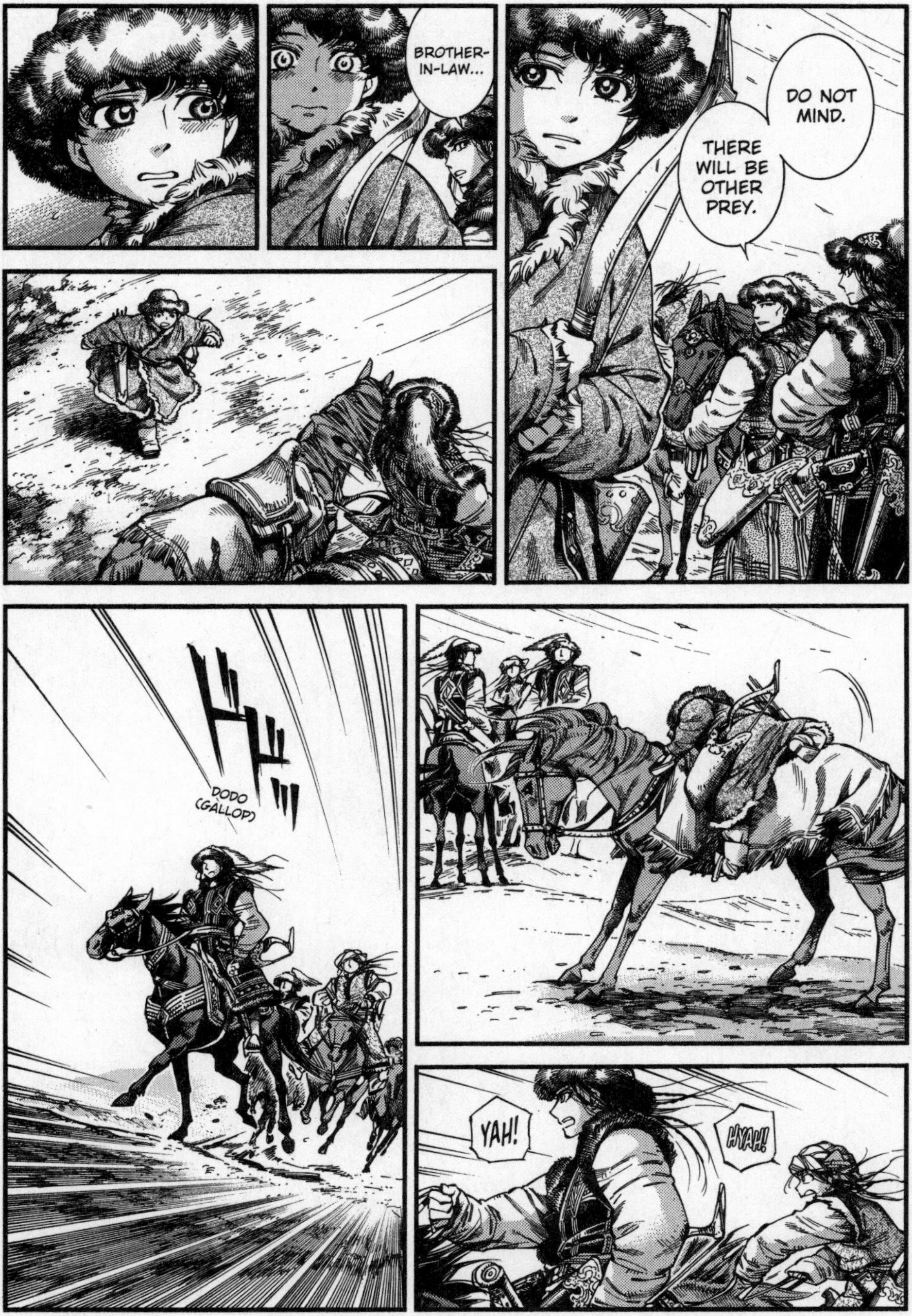
DO NOT MIND.
THERE WILL BE OTHER PREY.
BROTHER-IN-LAW...
YAH!
HYAH!
DODO (GALLOP)

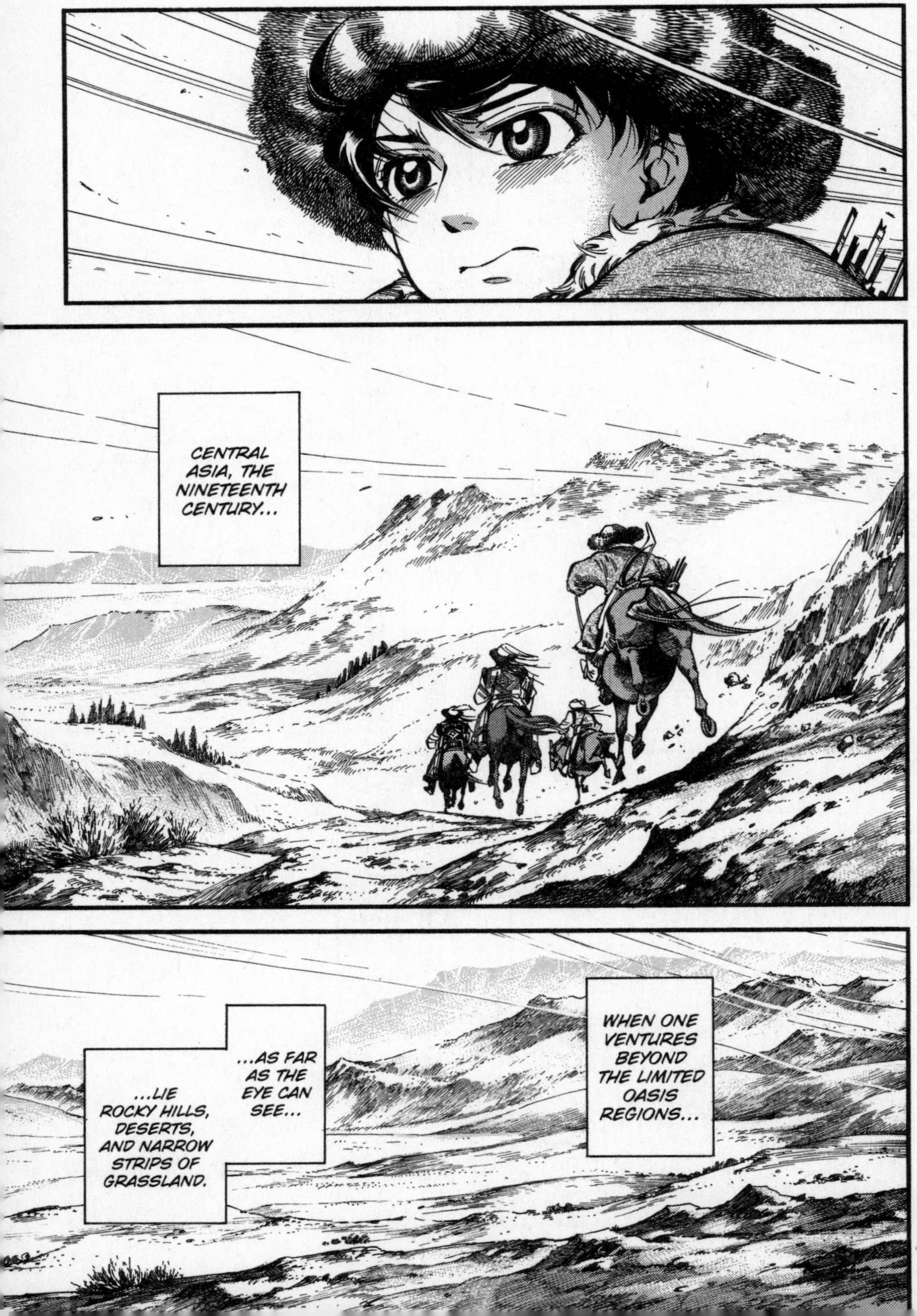
CENTRAL ASIA, THE NINETEENTH CENTURY...
WHEN ONE VENTURES BEYOND THE LIMITED OASIS REGIONS...
...AS FAR AS THE EYE CAN SEE...
...LIE ROCKY HILLS, DESERTS, AND NARROW STRIPS OF GRASSLAND.

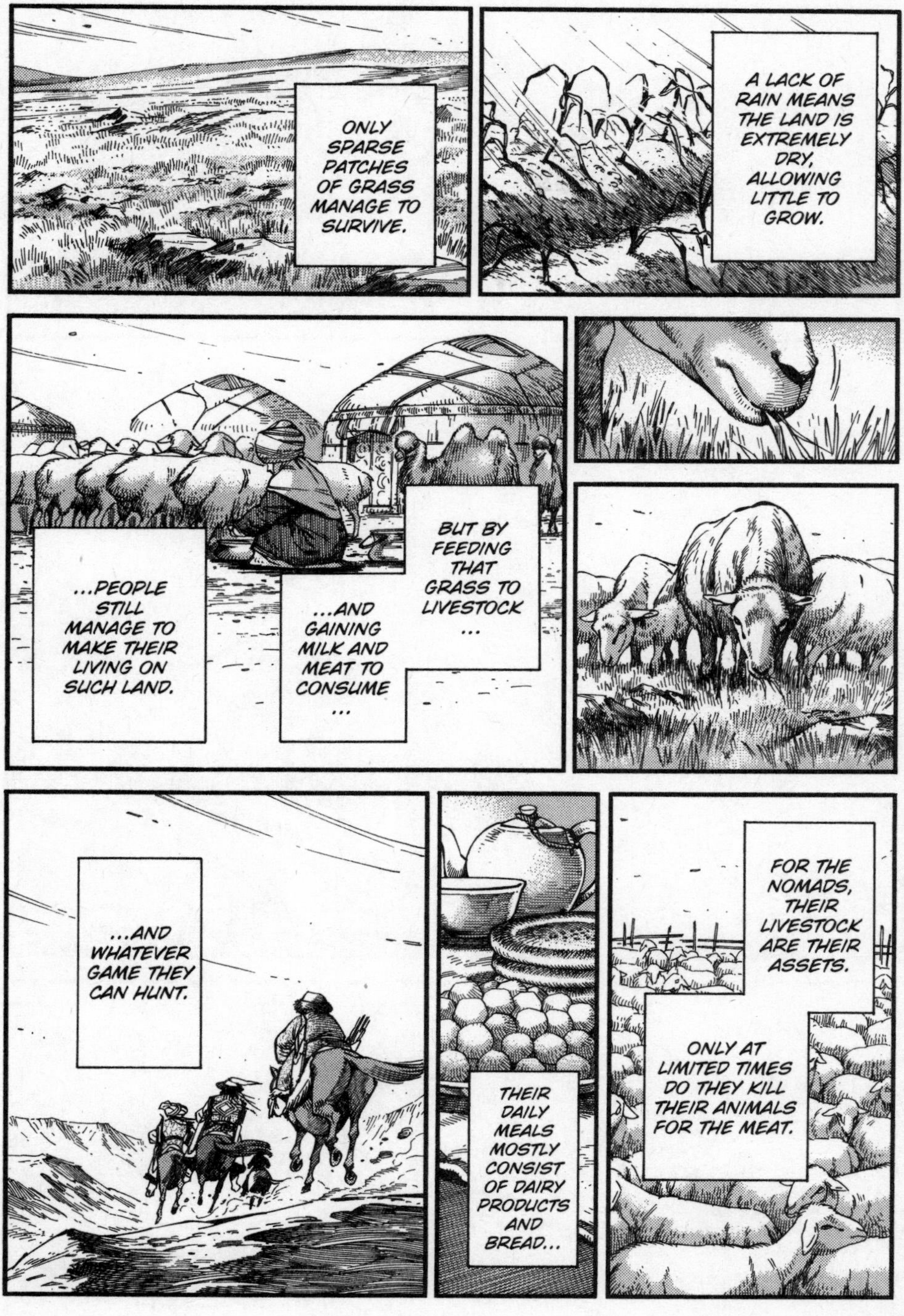
A LACK OF RAIN MEANS THE LAND IS EXTREMELY DRY, ALLOWING LITTLE TO GROW.
ONLY SPARSE PATCHES OF GRASS MANAGE TO SURVIVE.
BUT BY FEEDING THAT GRASS TO LIVESTOCK...
...AND GAINING MILK AND MEAT TO CONSUME...
...PEOPLE STILL MANAGE TO MAKE THEIR LIVING ON SUCH LAND.
FOR THE NOMADS, THEIR LIVESTOCK ARE THEIR ASSETS.
ONLY AT LIMITED TIMES DO THEY KILL THEIR ANIMALS FOR THE MEAT.
THEIR DAILY MEALS MOSTLY CONSIST OF DAIRY PRODUCTS AND BREAD...
...AND WHATEVER GAME THEY CAN HUNT.

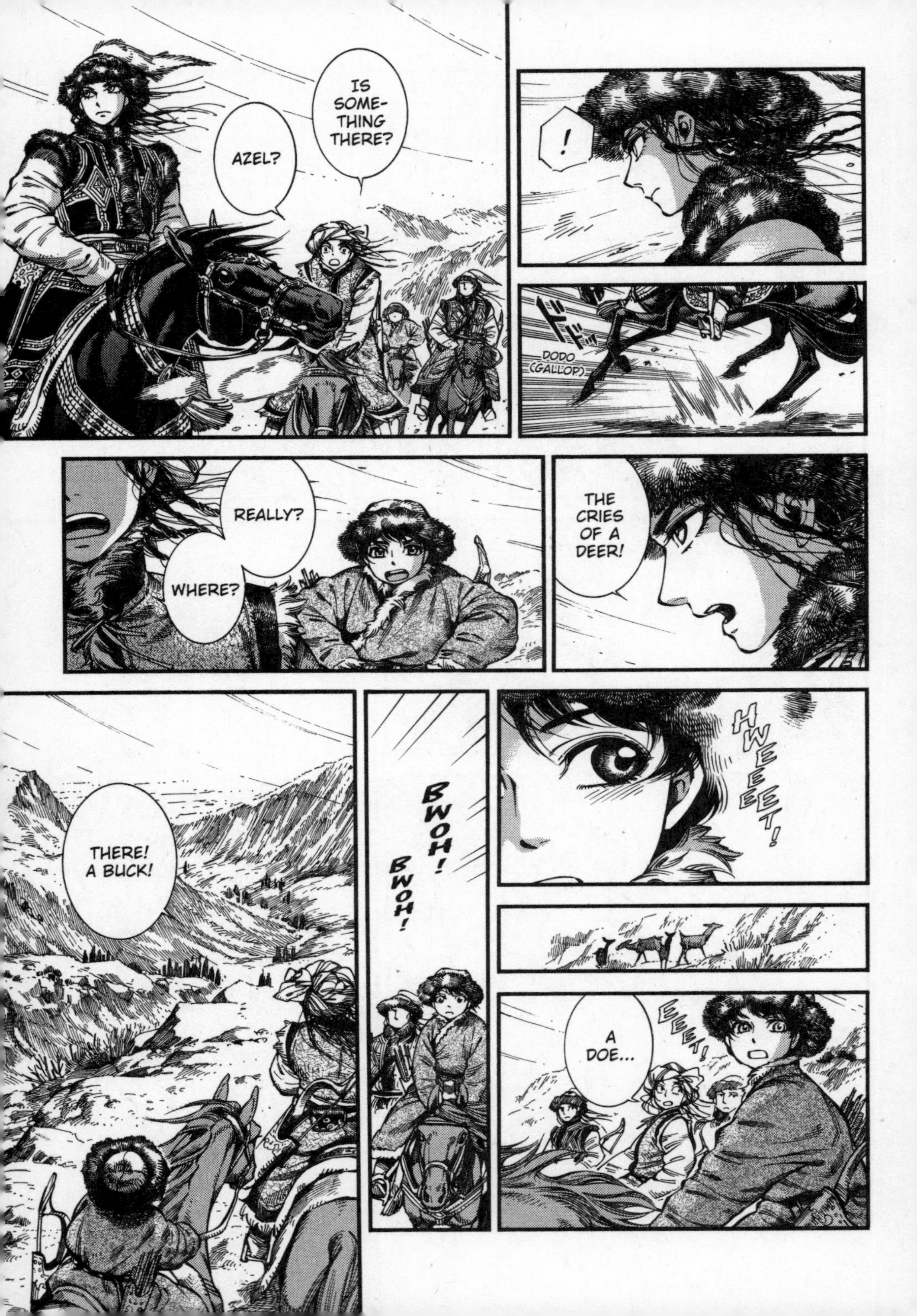
!
DODO (GALLOP)
IS SOMETHING THERE?
AZEL?
THE CRIES OF A DEER!
REALLY?
WHERE?
HWEEEET!
EEET!
A DOE...
BWOH! BWOH!
THERE! A BUCK!

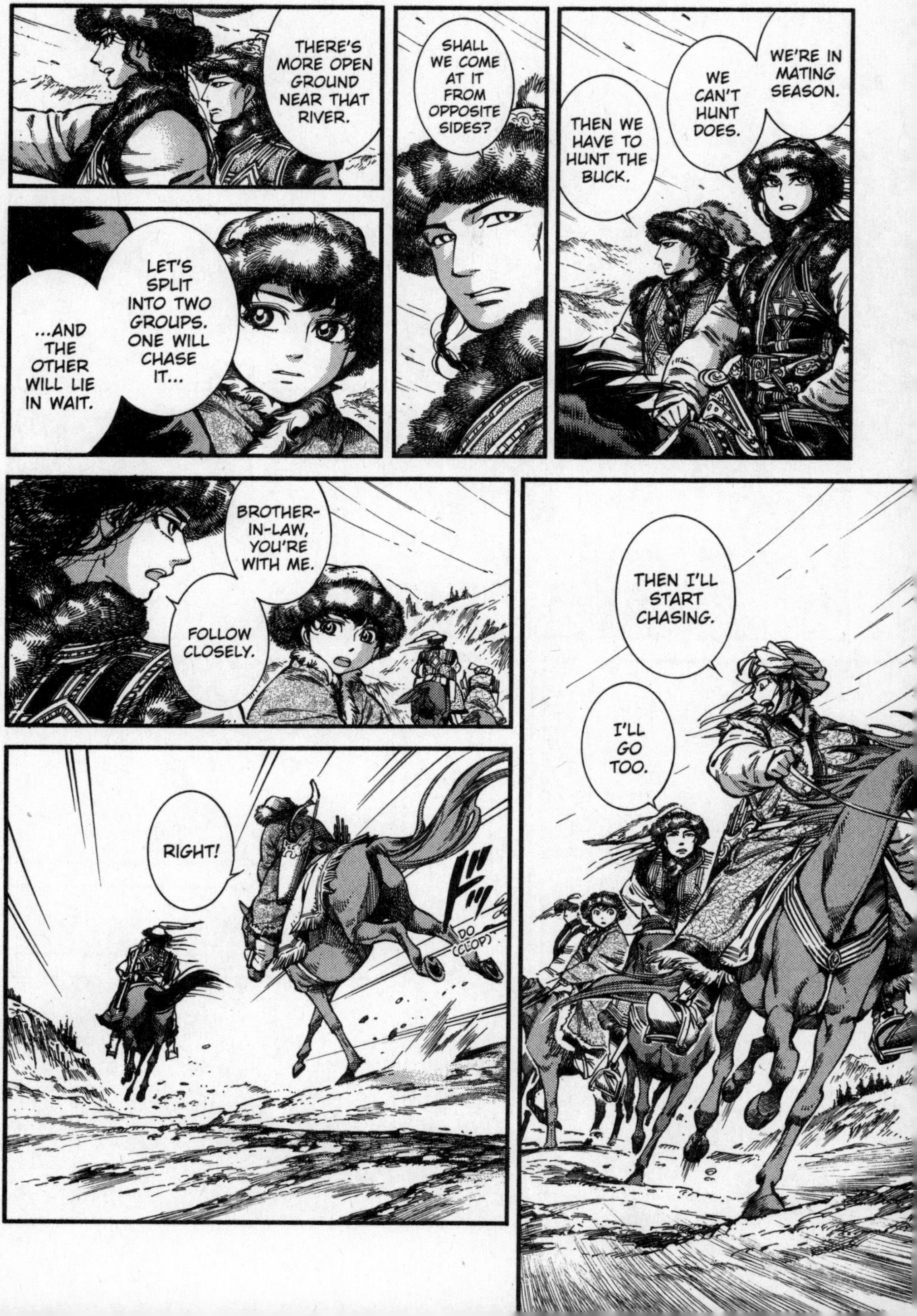
WE'RE IN MATING SEASON.
WE CAN'T HUNT DOES.
THEN WE HAVE TO HUNT THE BUCK.
SHALL WE COME AT IT FROM OPPOSITE SIDES?
THERE'S MORE OPEN GROUND NEAR THAT RIVER.
LET'S SPLIT INTO TWO GROUPS. ONE WILL CHASE IT...
...AND THE OTHER WILL LIE IN WAIT.
THEN I'LL START CHASING.
I'LL GO TOO.
BROTHER-IN-LAW, YOU'RE WITH ME.
FOLLOW CLOSELY.
RIGHT!
ドッ
DO (CLOP)

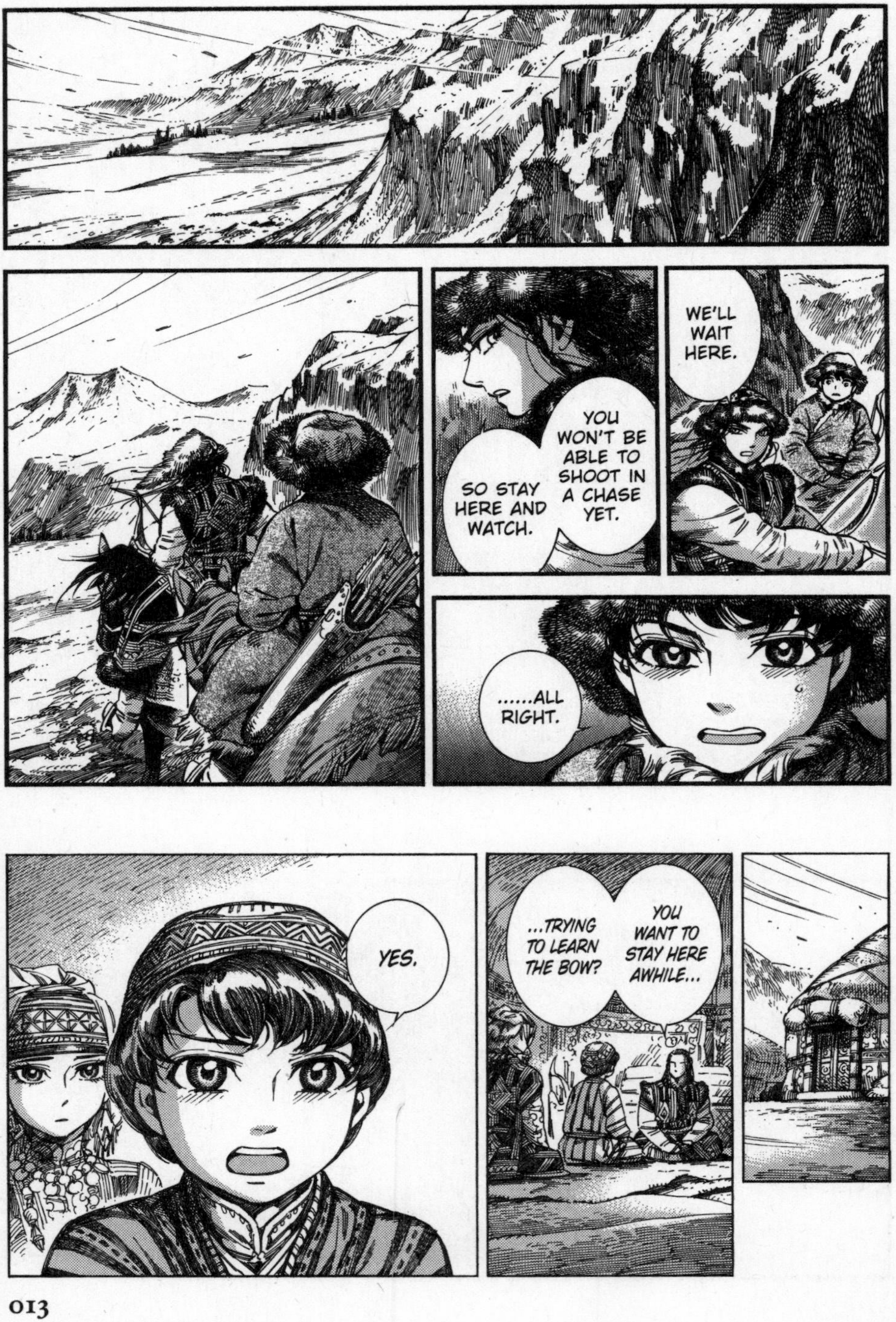
WE'LL WAIT HERE.
YOU WON'T BE ABLE TO SHOOT IN A CHASE YET.
SO STAY HERE AND WATCH.
......ALL RIGHT.
YOU WANT TO STAY HERE AWHILE...
...TRYING TO LEARN THE BOW?
YES.

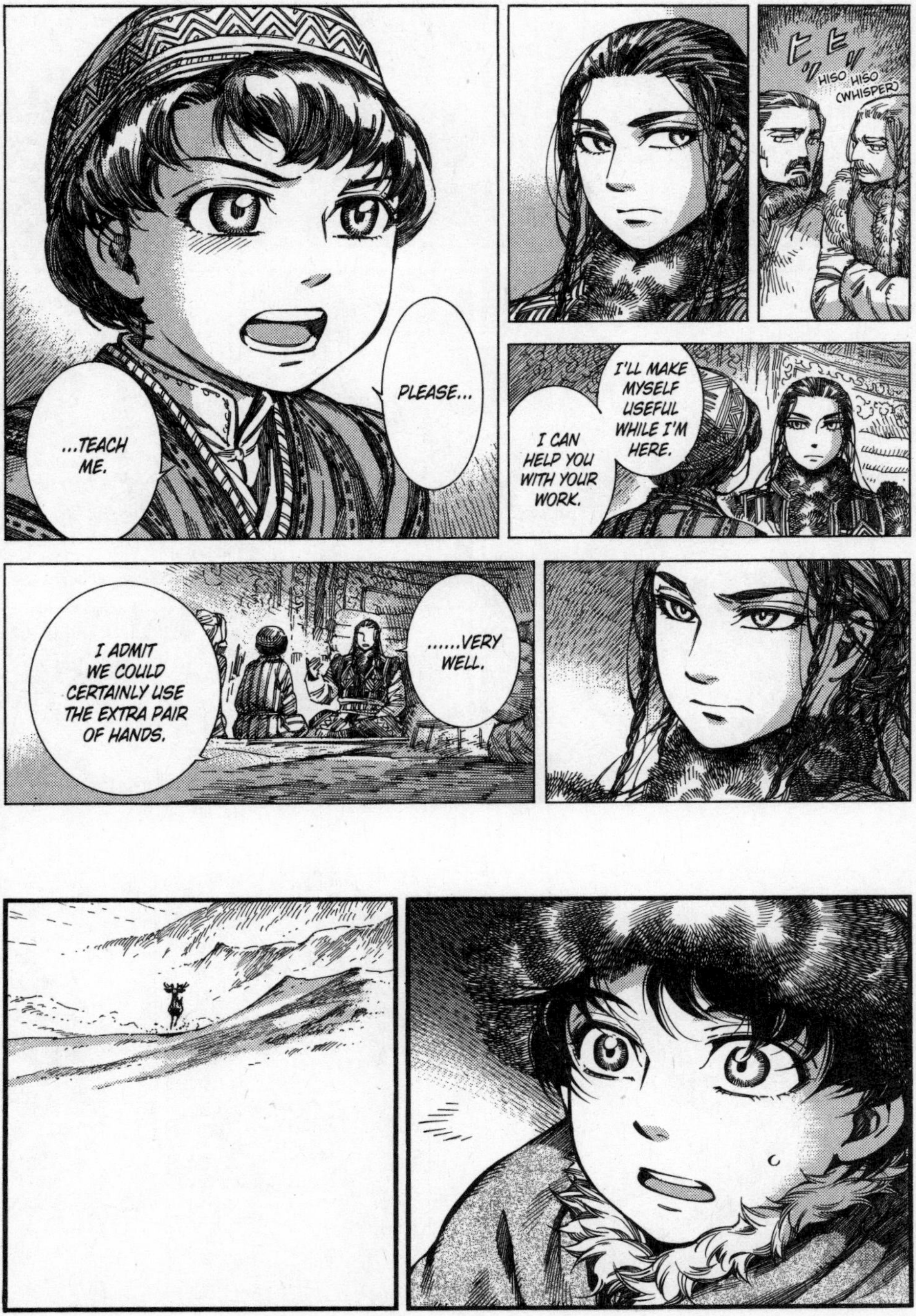
ヒソヒソ
HISO HISO (WHISPER)
I'LL MAKE MYSELF USEFUL WHILE I'M HERE.
I CAN HELP YOU WITH YOUR WORK.
PLEASE...
...TEACH ME.
......VERY WELL.
I ADMIT WE COULD CERTAINLY USE THE EXTRA PAIR OF HANDS.

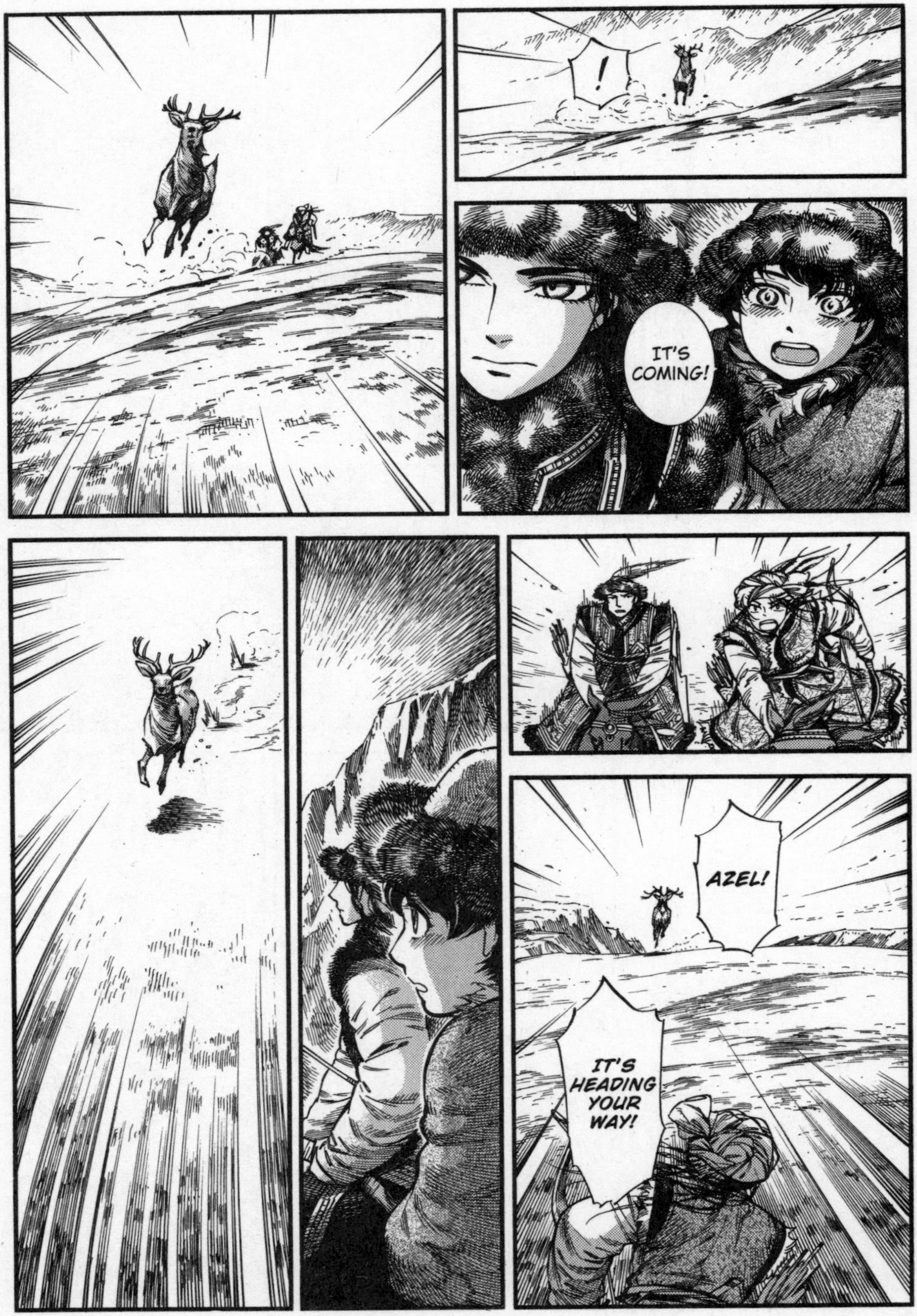
!
IT'S COMING!
AZEL!
IT'S HEADING YOUR WAY!

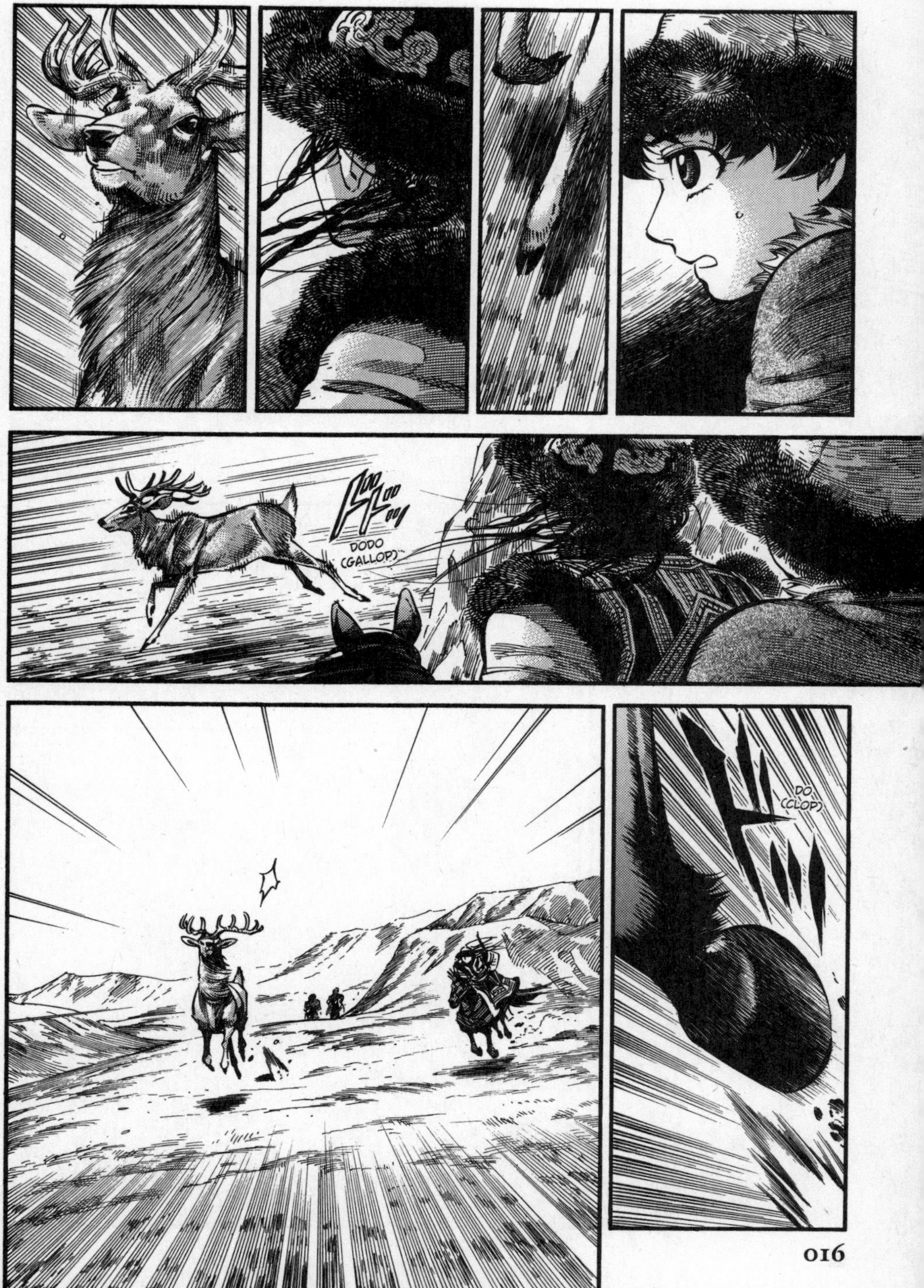
DODO (GALLOP)
DO (CLOP)

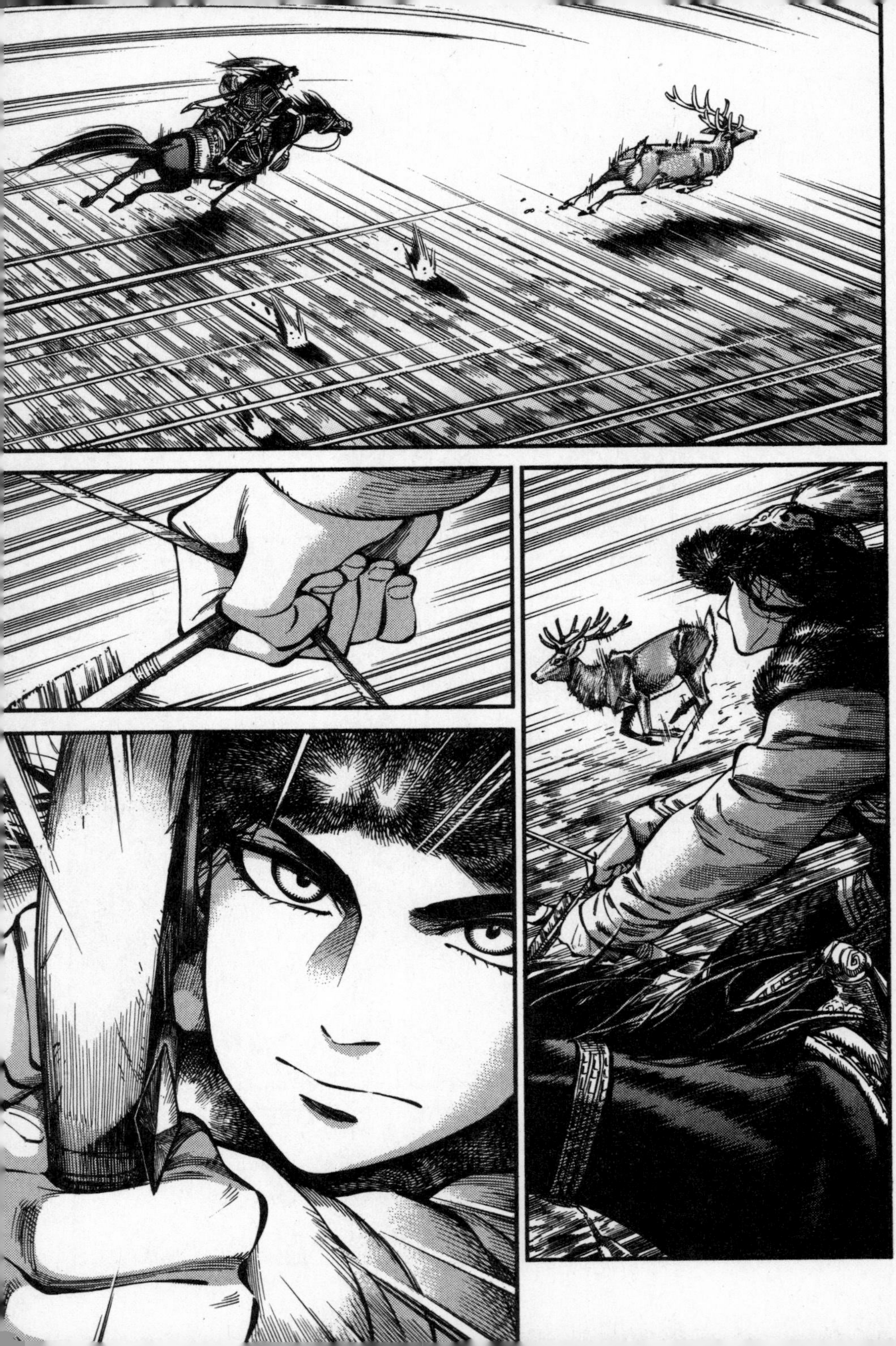

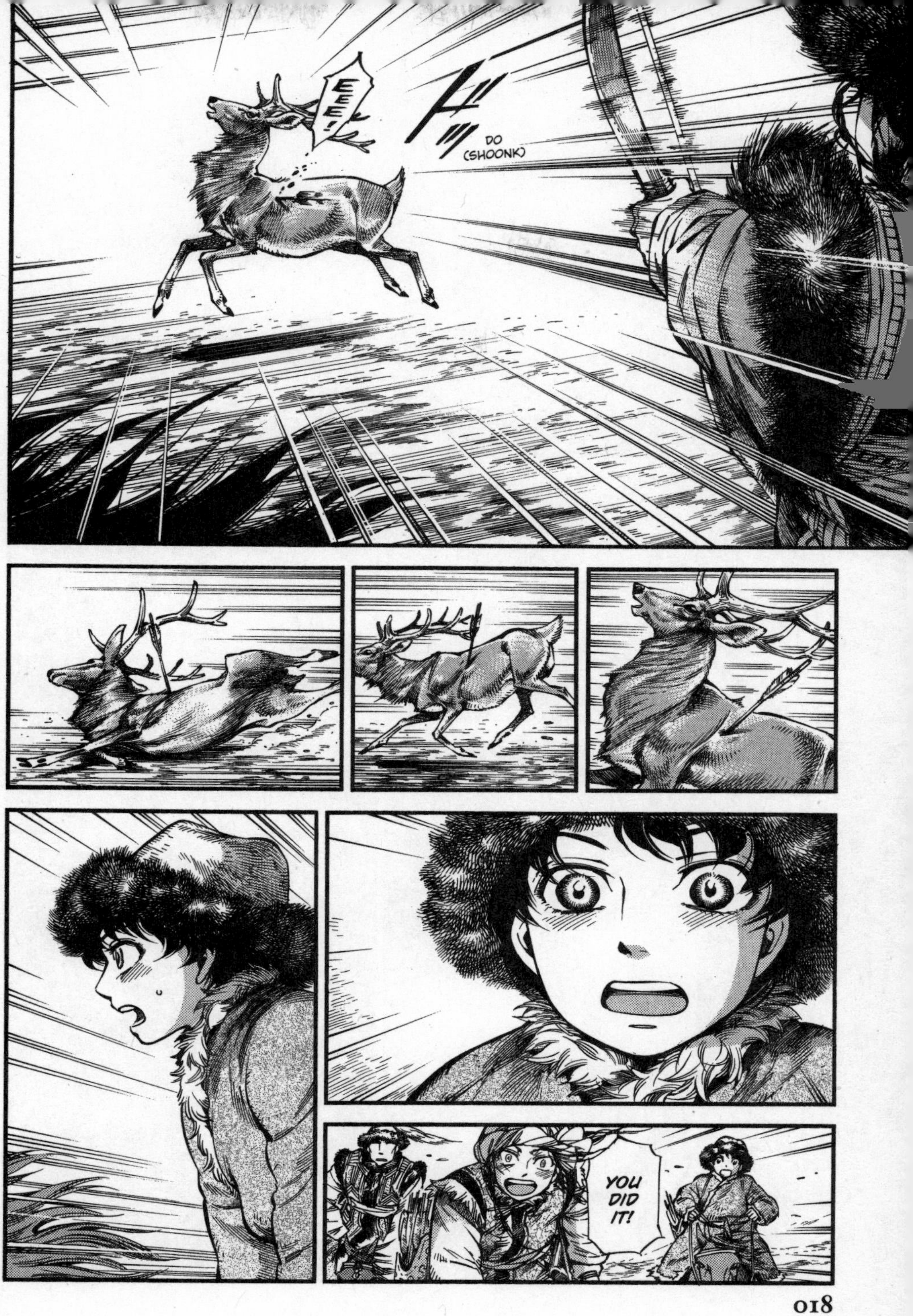

EEEE!
DO
(SHOONK)
YOU DID IT!

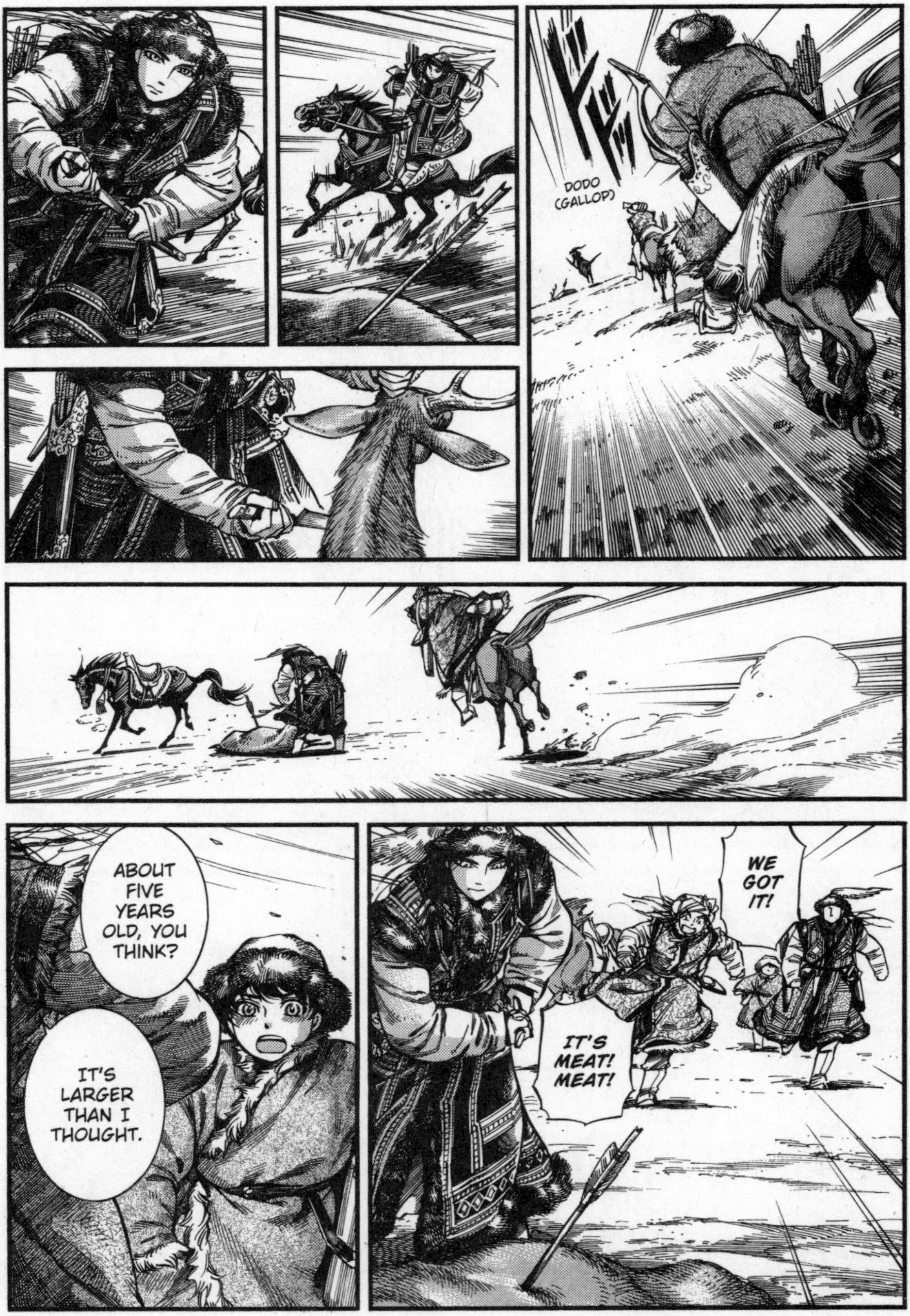
DODO (GALLOP)
WE GOT IT!
IT'S MEAT! MEAT!
ABOUT FIVE YEARS OLD, YOU THINK?
IT'S LARGER THAN I THOUGHT.

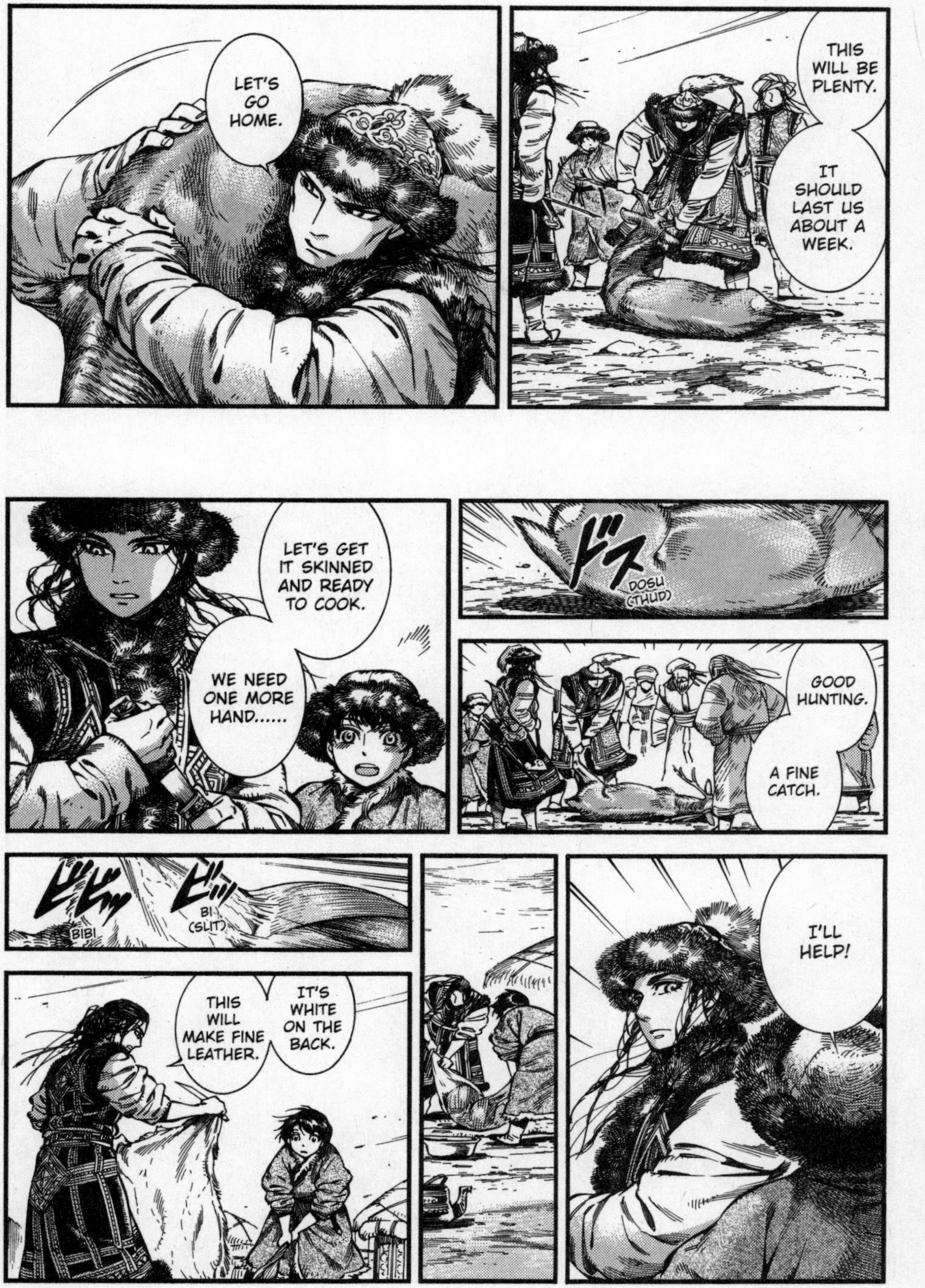
THIS WILL BE PLENTY.
IT SHOULD LAST US ABOUT A WEEK.
LET'S GO HOME.
ドス
DOSU (THUD)
GOOD HUNTING.
A FINE CATCH.
LET'S GET IT SKINNED AND READY TO COOK.
WE NEED ONE MORE HAND......
I'LL HELP!
ビビッ
BIBI
ビッ
BI (SLIT)
IT'S WHITE ON THE BACK.
THIS WILL MAKE FINE LEATHER.

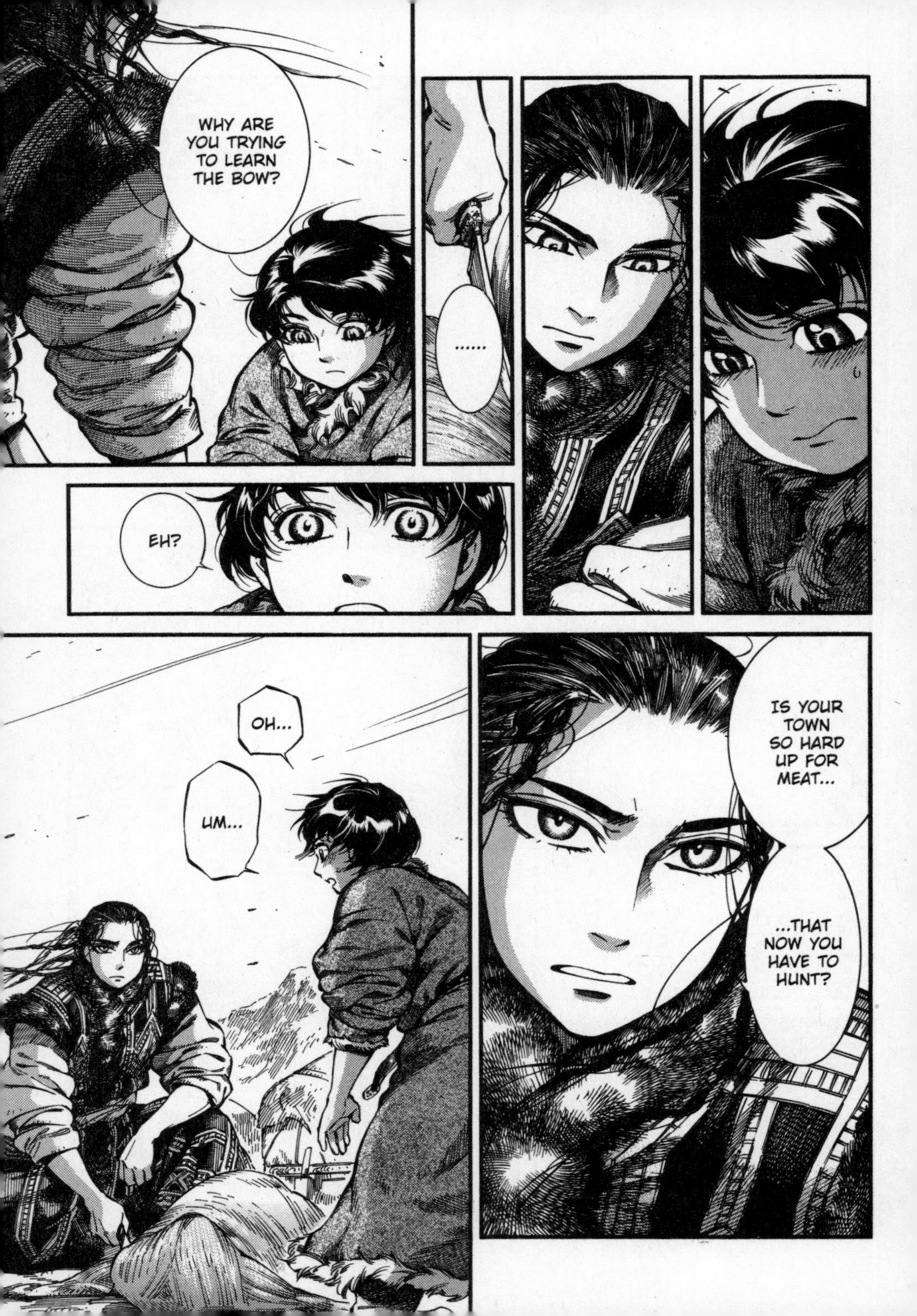
......
WHY ARE YOU TRYING TO LEARN THE BOW?
EH?
IS YOUR TOWN SO HARD UP FOR MEAT...
...THAT NOW YOU HAVE TO HUNT?
OH...
UM...

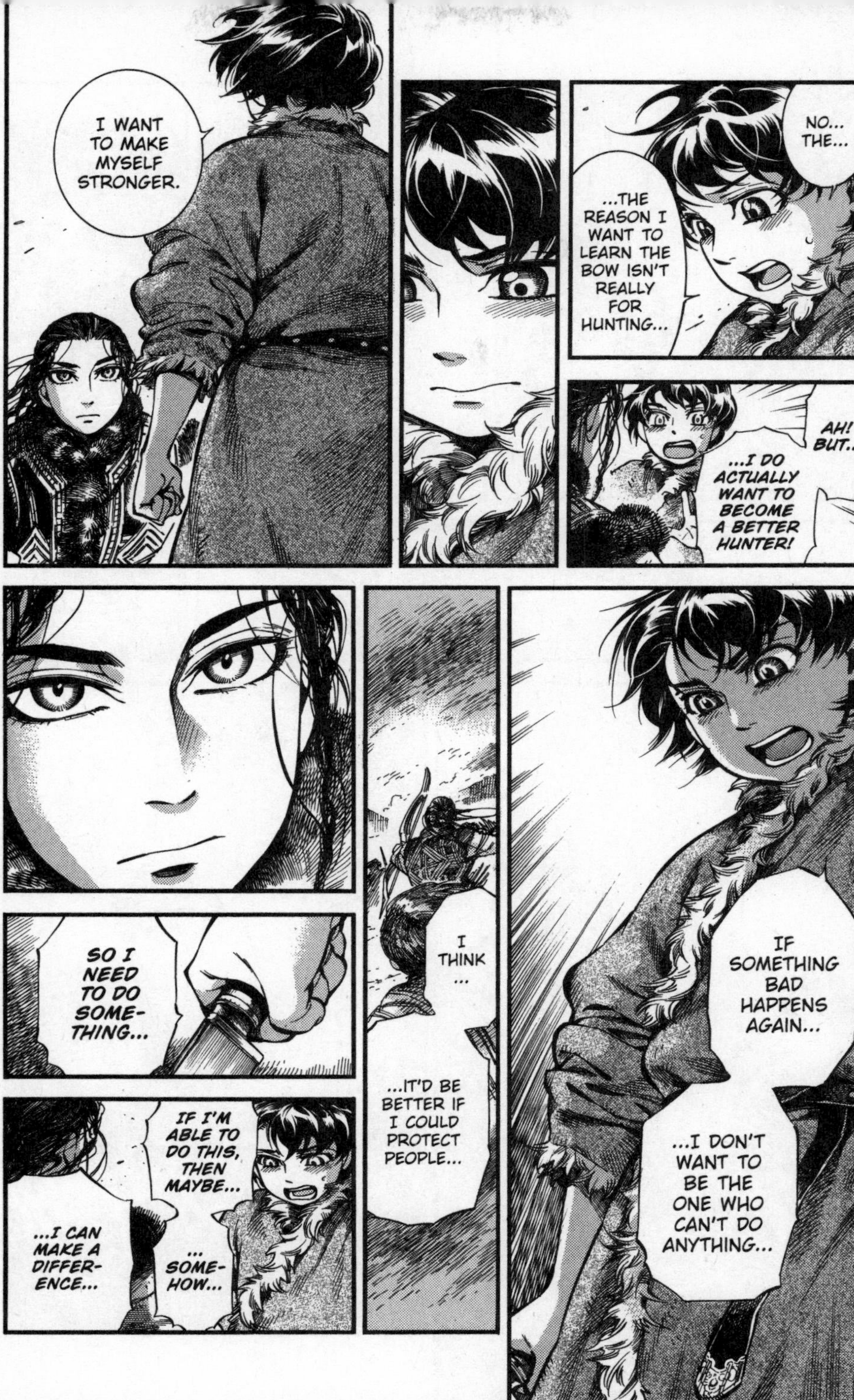
NO... THE...
...THE REASON I WANT TO LEARN THE BOW ISN'T REALLY FOR HUNTING...
AH! BUT...
...I DO ACTUALLY WANT TO BECOME A BETTER HUNTER!
I WANT TO MAKE MYSELF STRONGER.
IF SOMETHING BAD HAPPENS AGAIN...
...I DON'T WANT TO BE THE ONE WHO CAN'T DO ANYTHING...
I THINK ...
...IT'D BE BETTER IF I COULD PROTECT PEOPLE...
SO I NEED TO DO SOME-THING...
IF I'M ABLE TO DO THIS, THEN MAYBE...
... SOME-HOW...
...I CAN MAKE A DIFFER-ENCE...

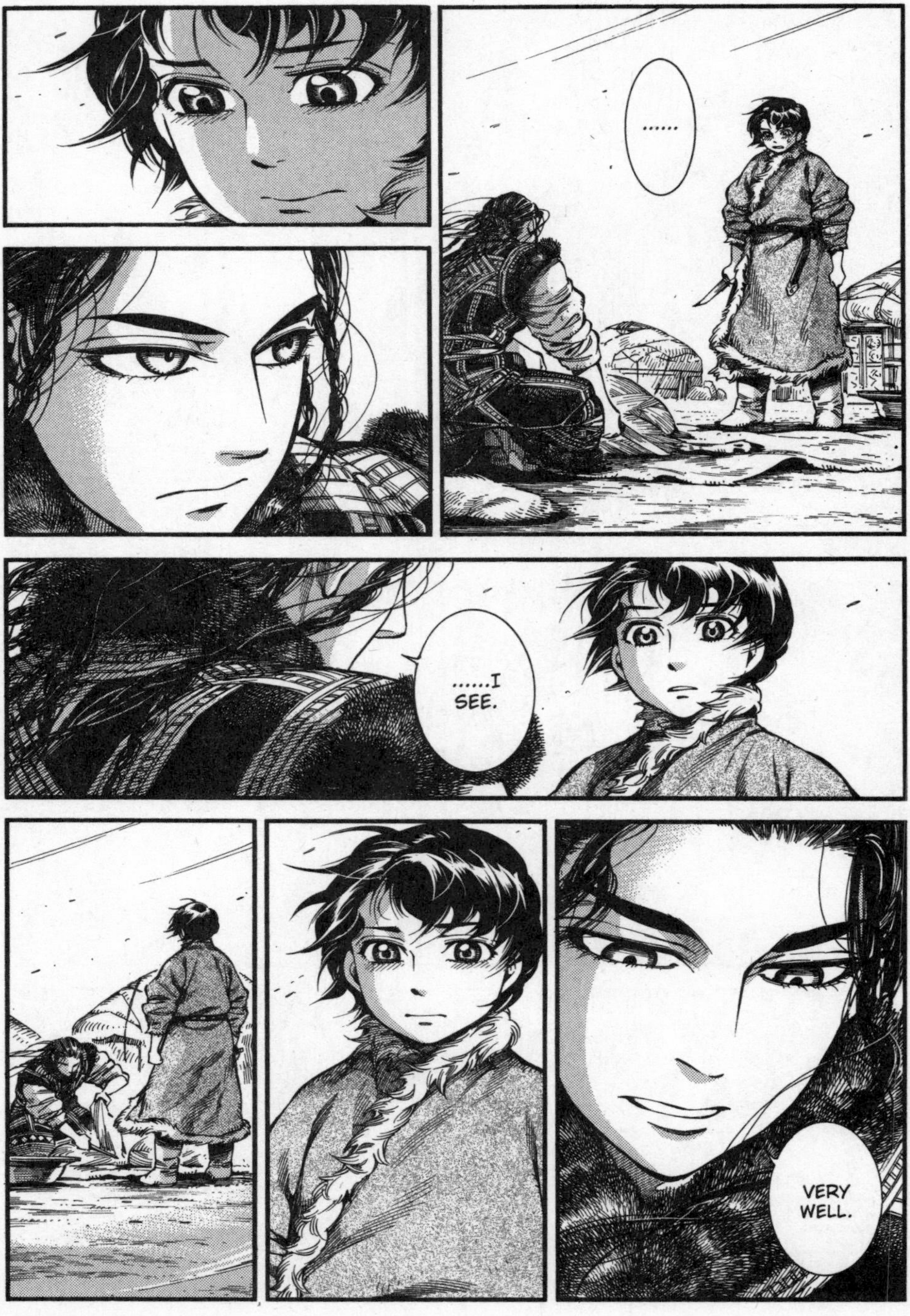
......
......I SEE.
VERY WELL.

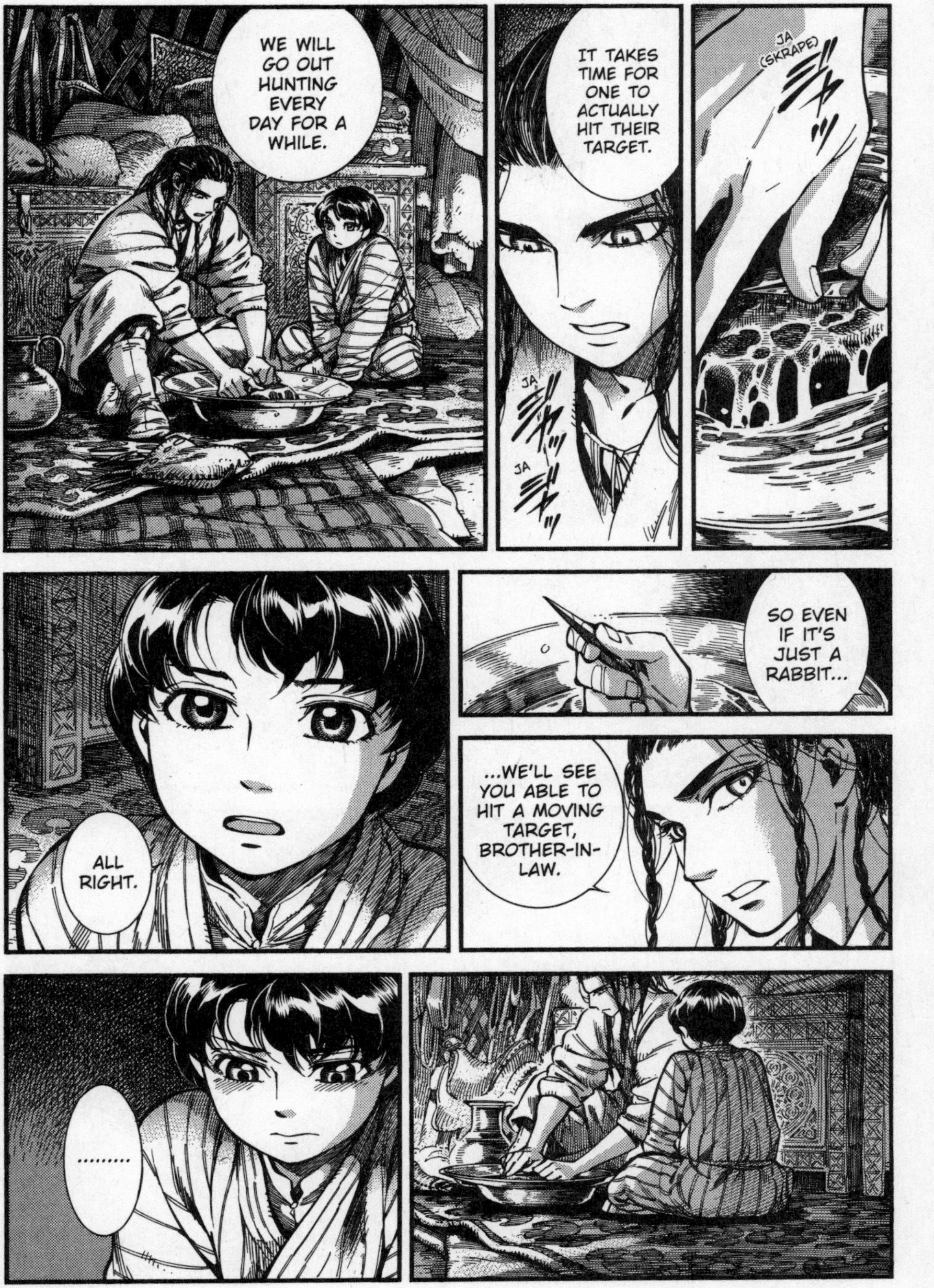
JA (SKRAPE)
IT TAKES TIME FOR ONE TO ACTUALLY HIT THEIR TARGET.
JA
JA
WE WILL GO OUT HUNTING EVERY DAY FOR A WHILE.
SO EVEN IF IT'S JUST A RABBIT...
...WE'LL SEE YOU ABLE TO HIT A MOVING TARGET, BROTHER-IN-LAW.
ALL RIGHT.
....

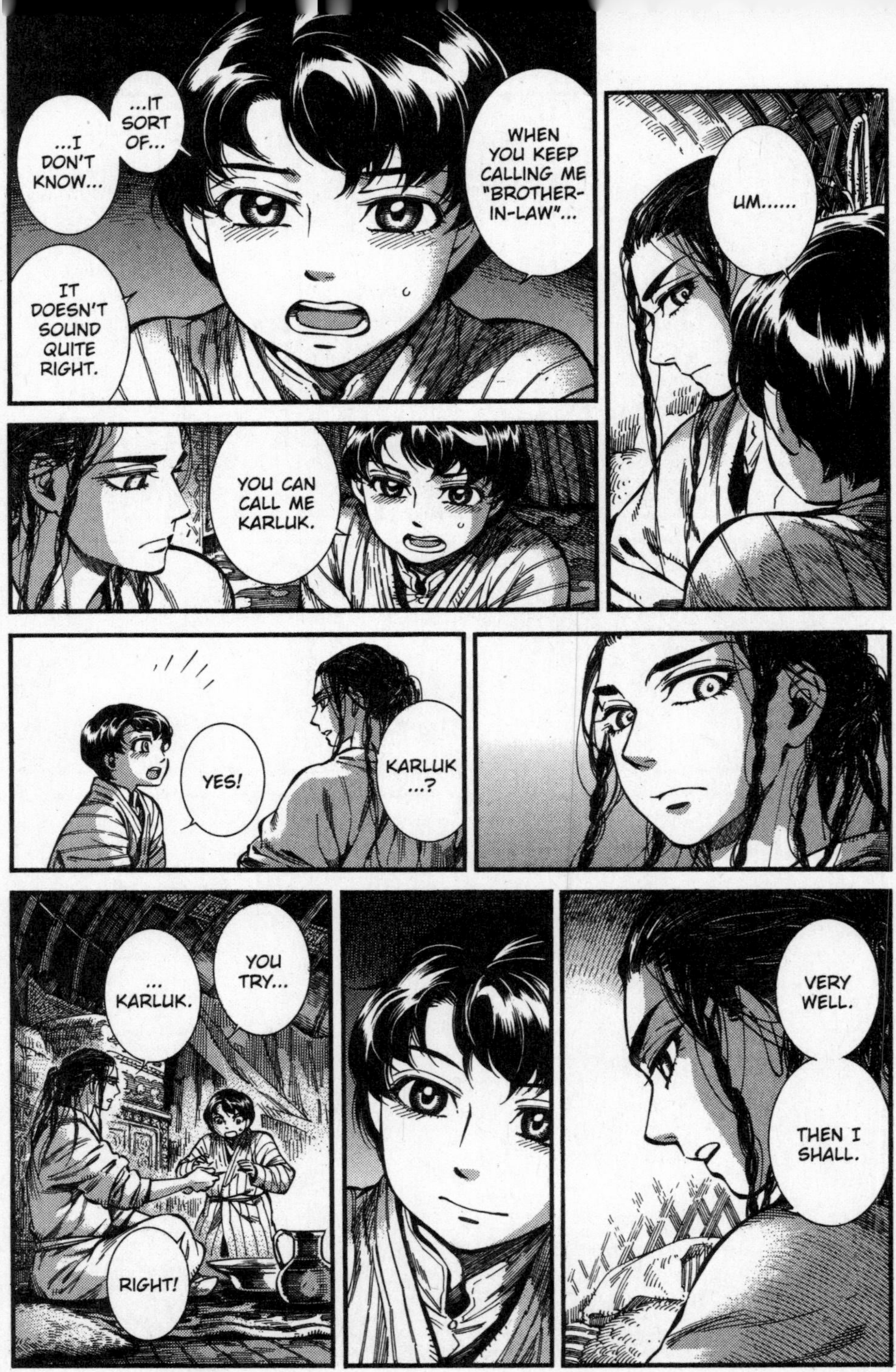
UM......
WHEN YOU KEEP CALLING ME "BROTHER-IN-LAW"...
...IT SORT OF...
...I DON'T KNOW...
IT DOESN'T SOUND QUITE RIGHT.
YOU CAN CALL ME KARLUK.
KARLUK ...?
YES!
VERY WELL.
THEN I SHALL.
YOU TRY...
... KARLUK.
RIGHT!

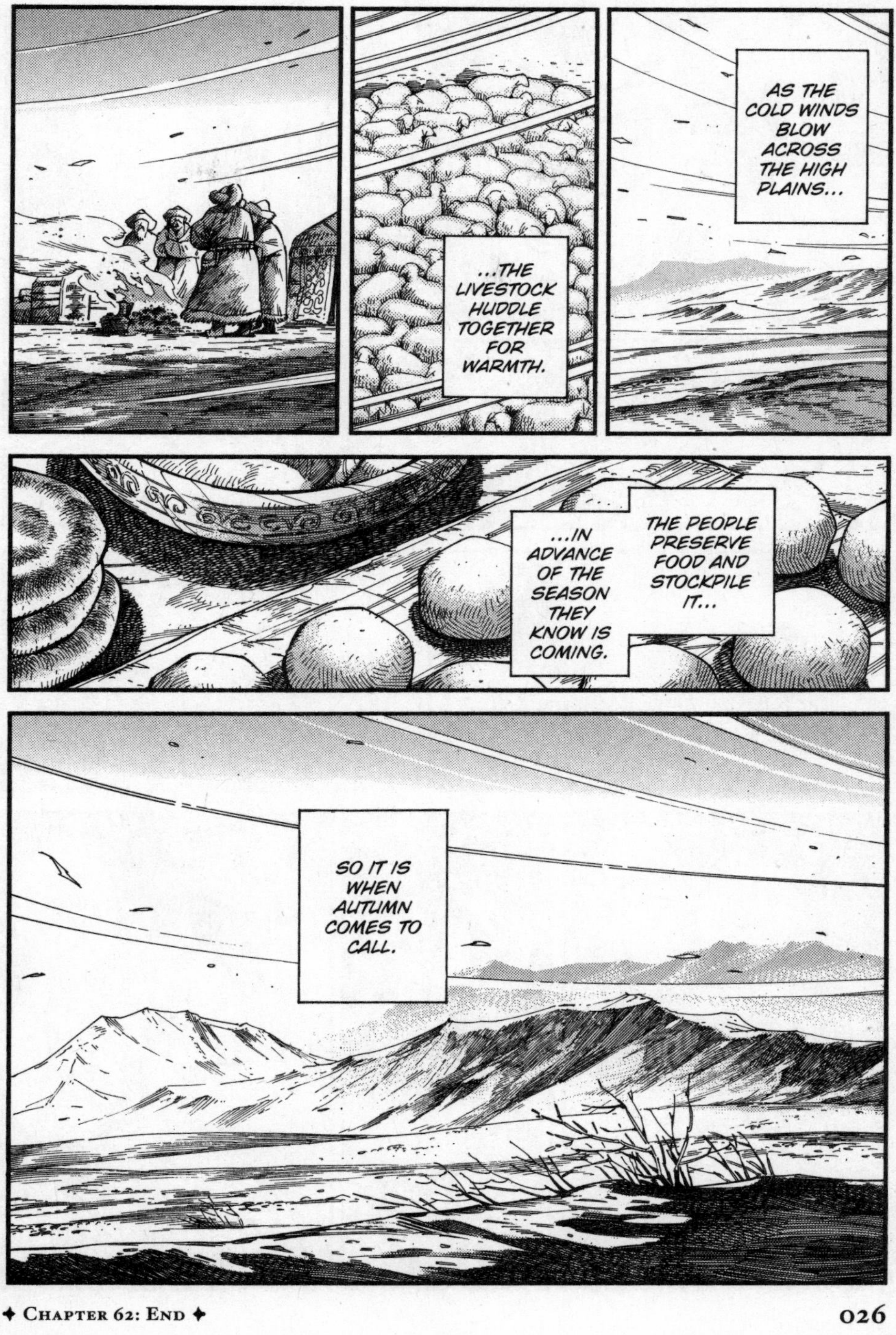
AS THE COLD WINDS BLOW ACROSS THE HIGH PLAINS...
...THE LIVESTOCK HUDDLE TOGETHER FOR WARMTH.
THE PEOPLE PRESERVE FOOD AND STOCKPILE IT...
...IN ADVANCE OF THE SEASON THEY KNOW IS COMING.
SO IT IS WHEN AUTUMN COMES TO CALL.

✦ Chapter 62: End ✦

Chapter 63
Golden Eagle

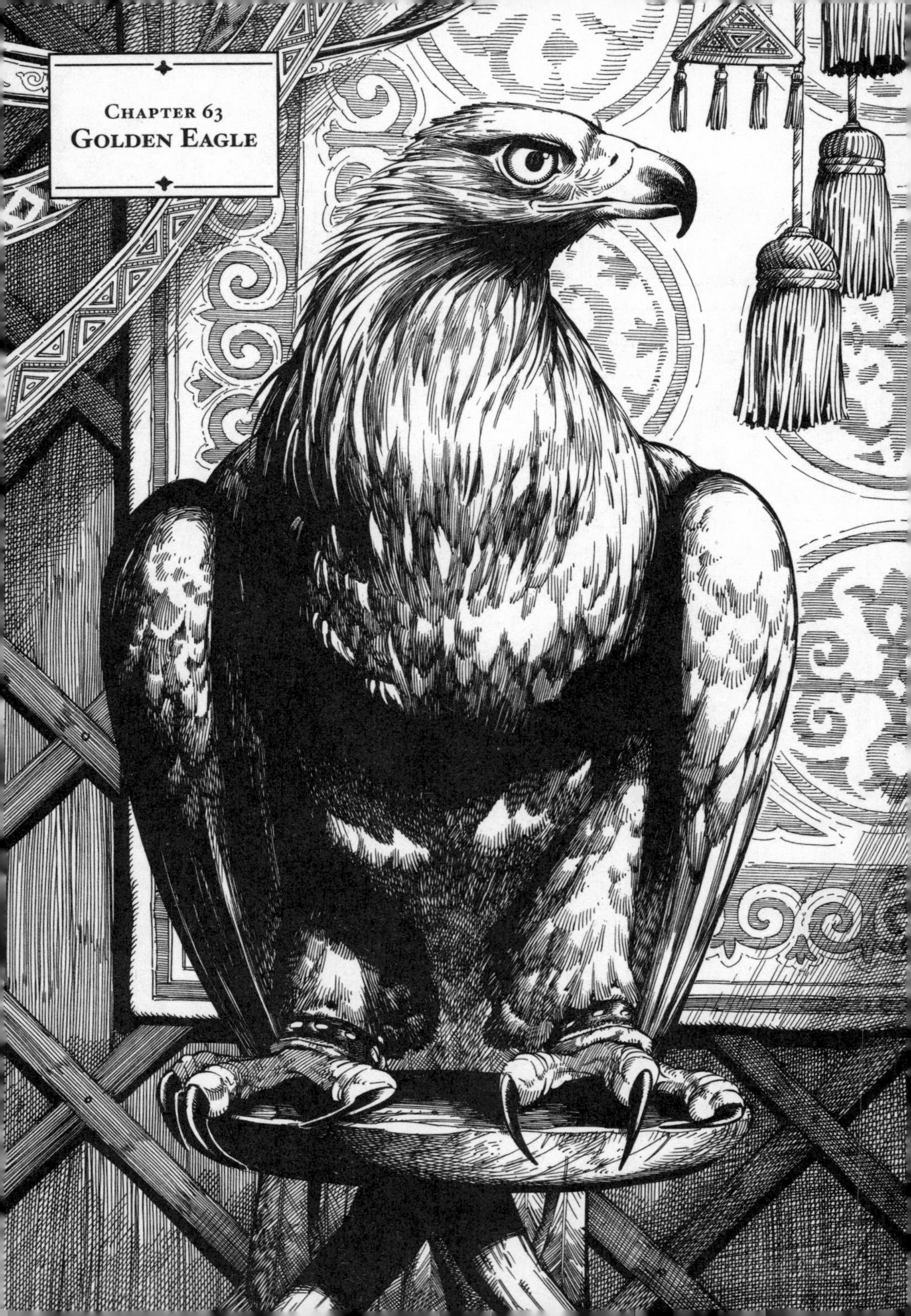

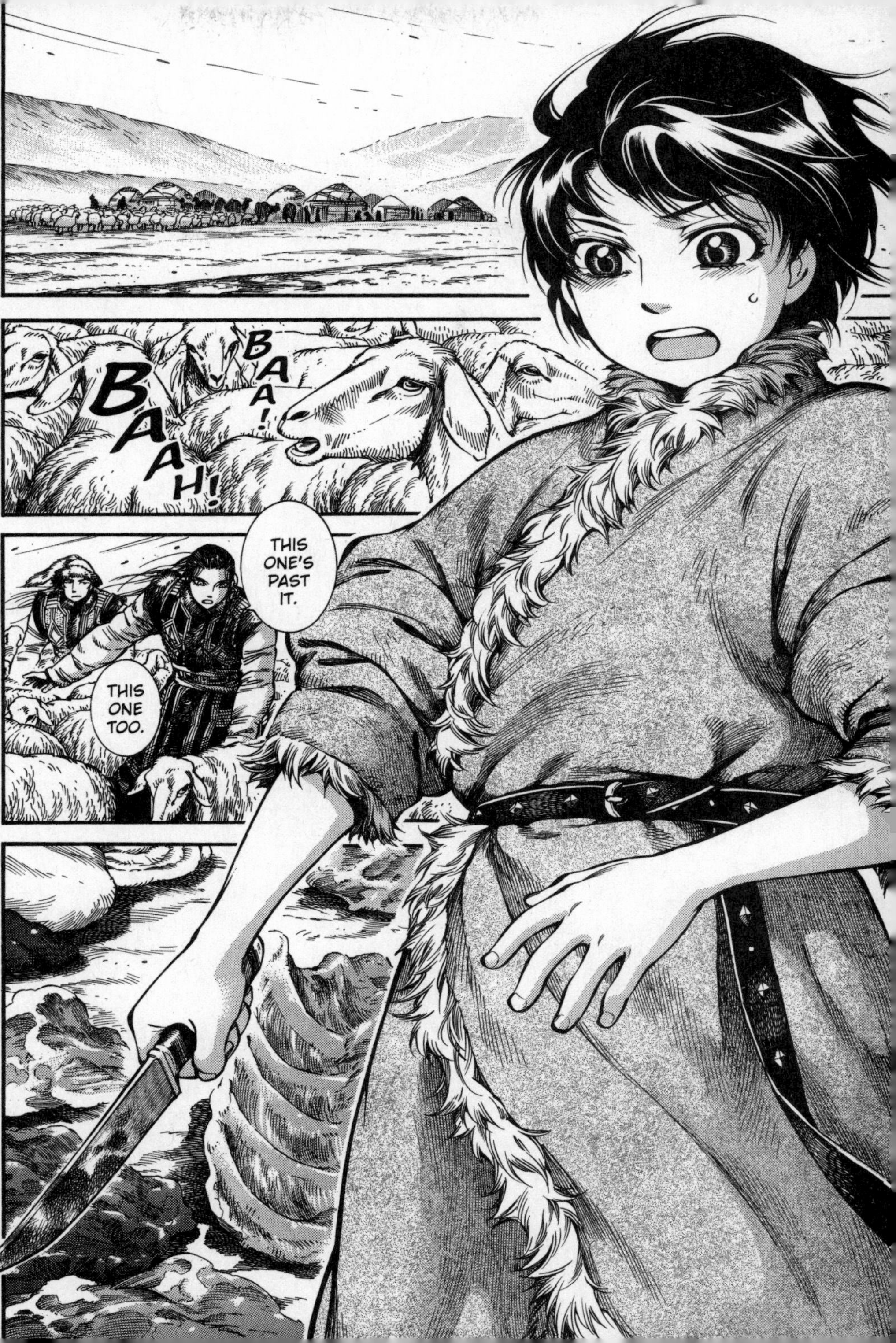
BAAAH!
BAA!
THIS ONE'S PAST IT.
THIS ONE TOO.

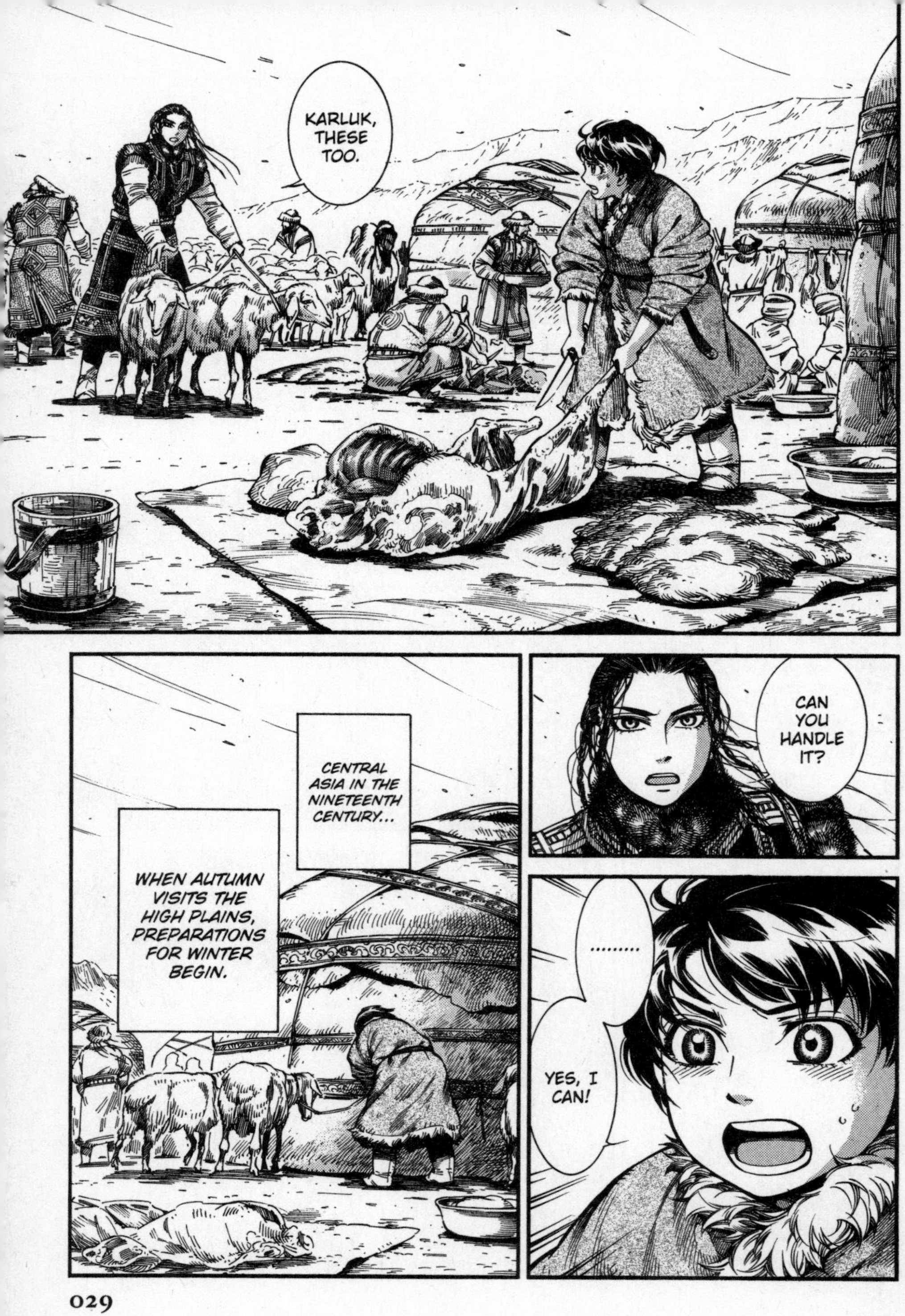
KARLUK, THESE TOO.
CAN YOU HANDLE IT?
....
YES, I CAN!
CENTRAL ASIA IN THE NINETEENTH CENTURY...
WHEN AUTUMN VISITS THE HIGH PLAINS, PREPARATIONS FOR WINTER BEGIN.

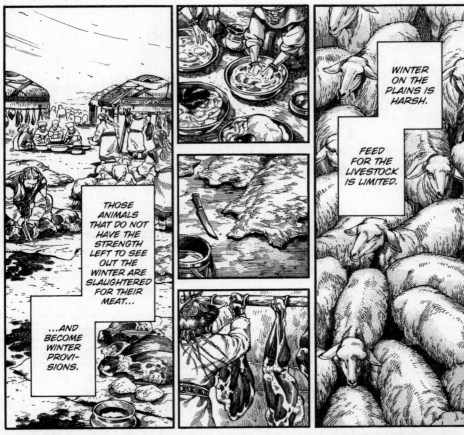

WINTER ON THE PLAINS IS HARSH.

FEED FOR THE LIVESTOCK IS LIMITED.

THOSE ANIMALS THAT DO NOT HAVE THE STRENGTH LEFT TO SEE OUT THE WINTER ARE SLAUGHTERED FOR THEIR MEAT...

...AND BECOME WINTER PROVISIONS.

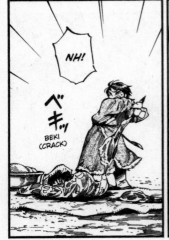

NH!

ベキッ
BEKI (CRACK)

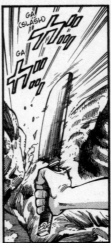

ガ
GA (SLASH)

ガ
GA

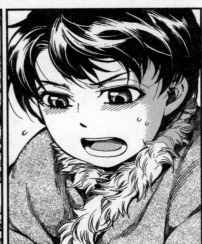

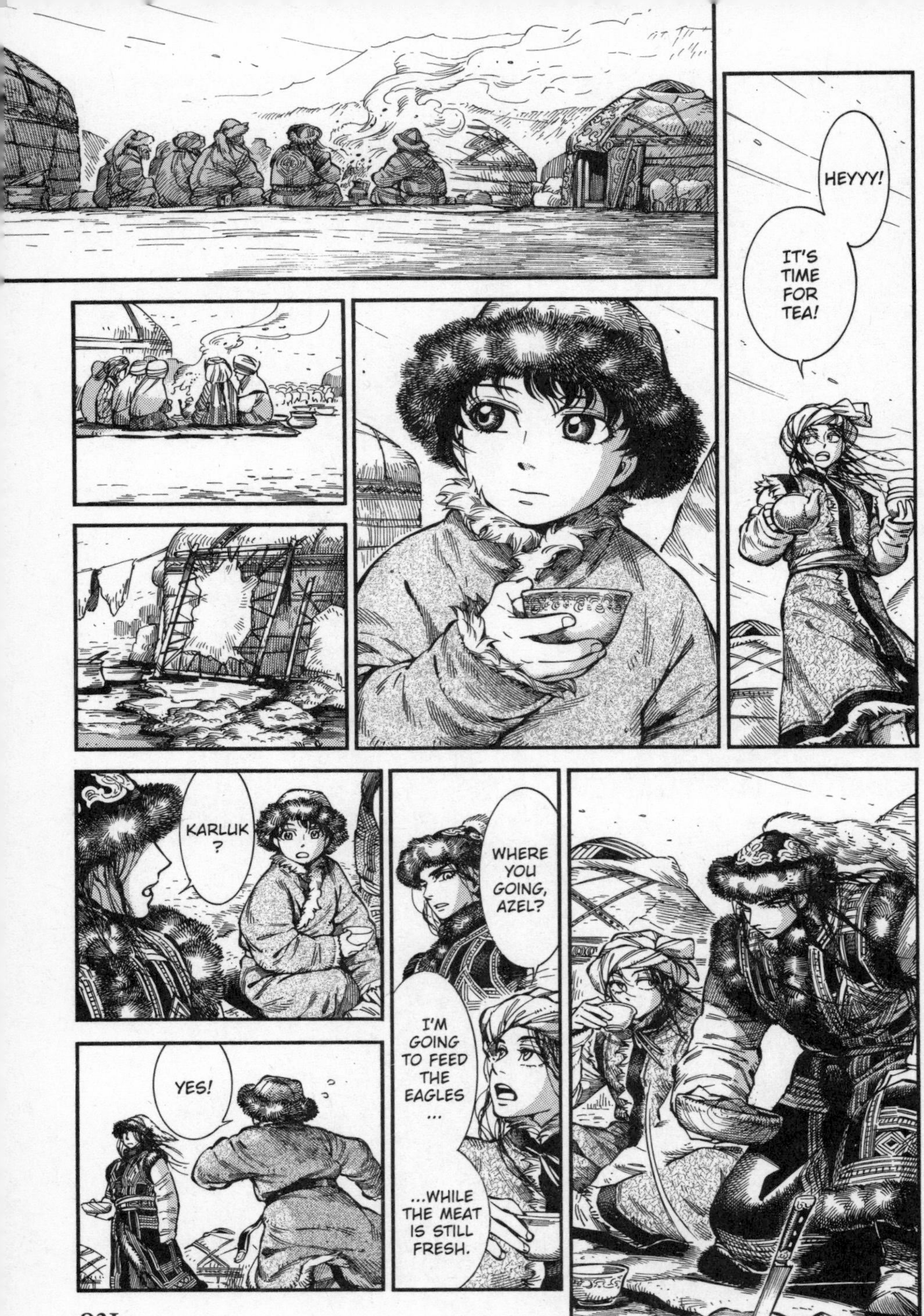
HEYYY!
IT'S TIME FOR TEA!
WHERE YOU GOING, AZEL?
I'M GOING TO FEED THE EAGLES...
...WHILE THE MEAT IS STILL FRESH.
KARLUK?
YES!

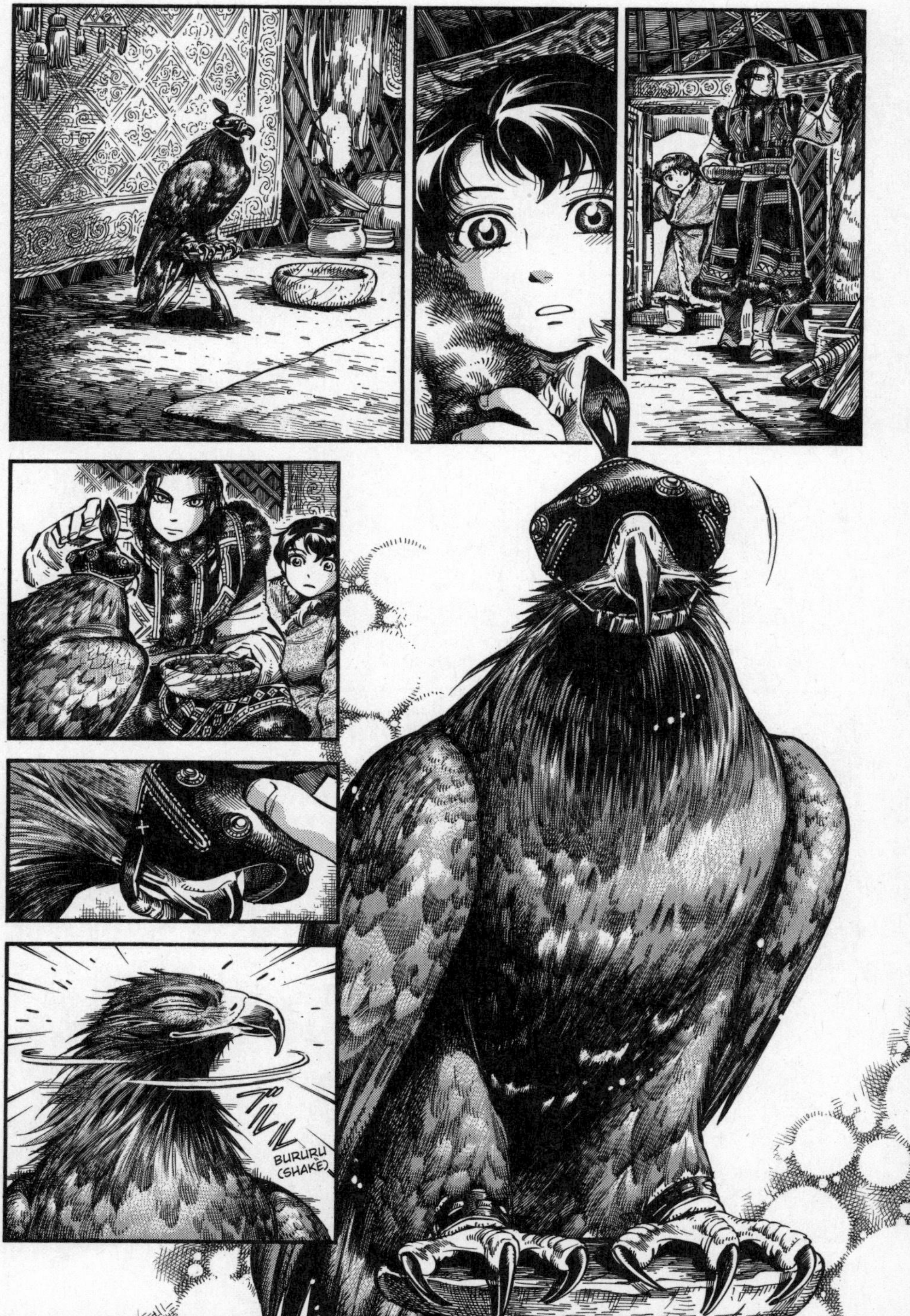
BURURU
(SHAKE)

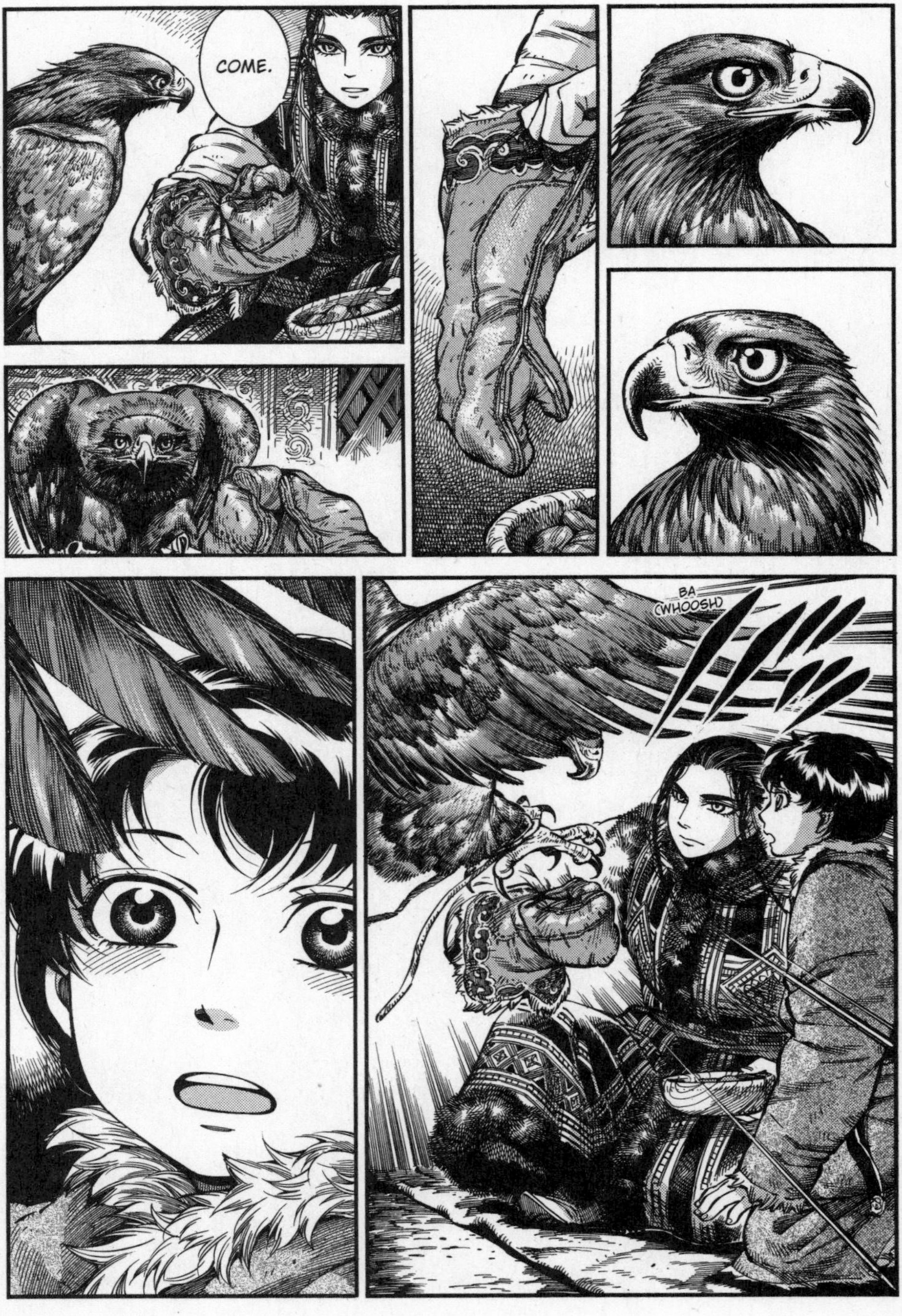
COME.
BA
(WHOOSH)

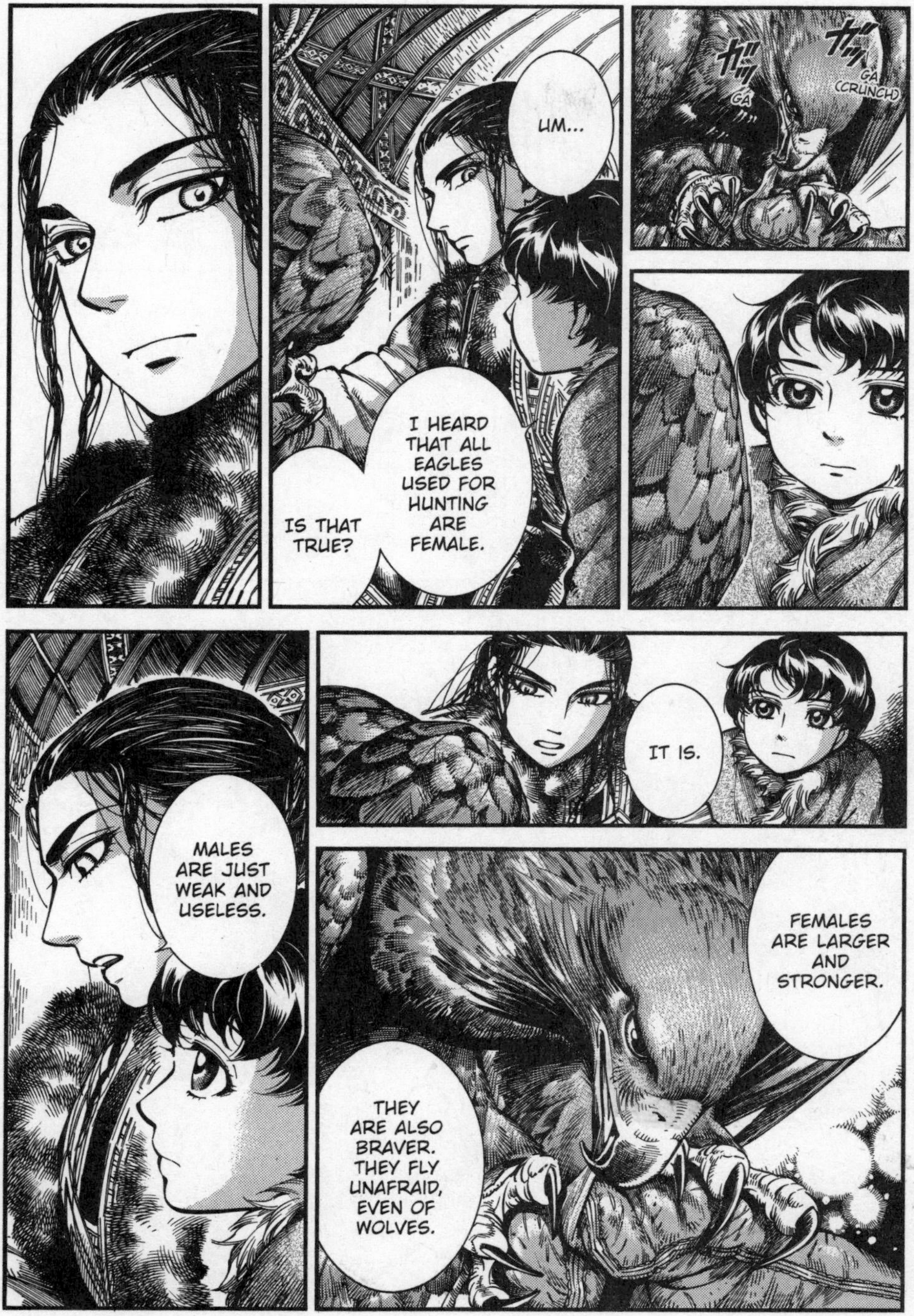
ガッ GA (CRUNCH)
ガッ GA
UM...
I HEARD THAT ALL EAGLES USED FOR HUNTING ARE FEMALE.
IS THAT TRUE?
IT IS.
FEMALES ARE LARGER AND STRONGER.
THEY ARE ALSO BRAVER. THEY FLY UNAFRAID, EVEN OF WOLVES.
MALES ARE JUST WEAK AND USELESS.

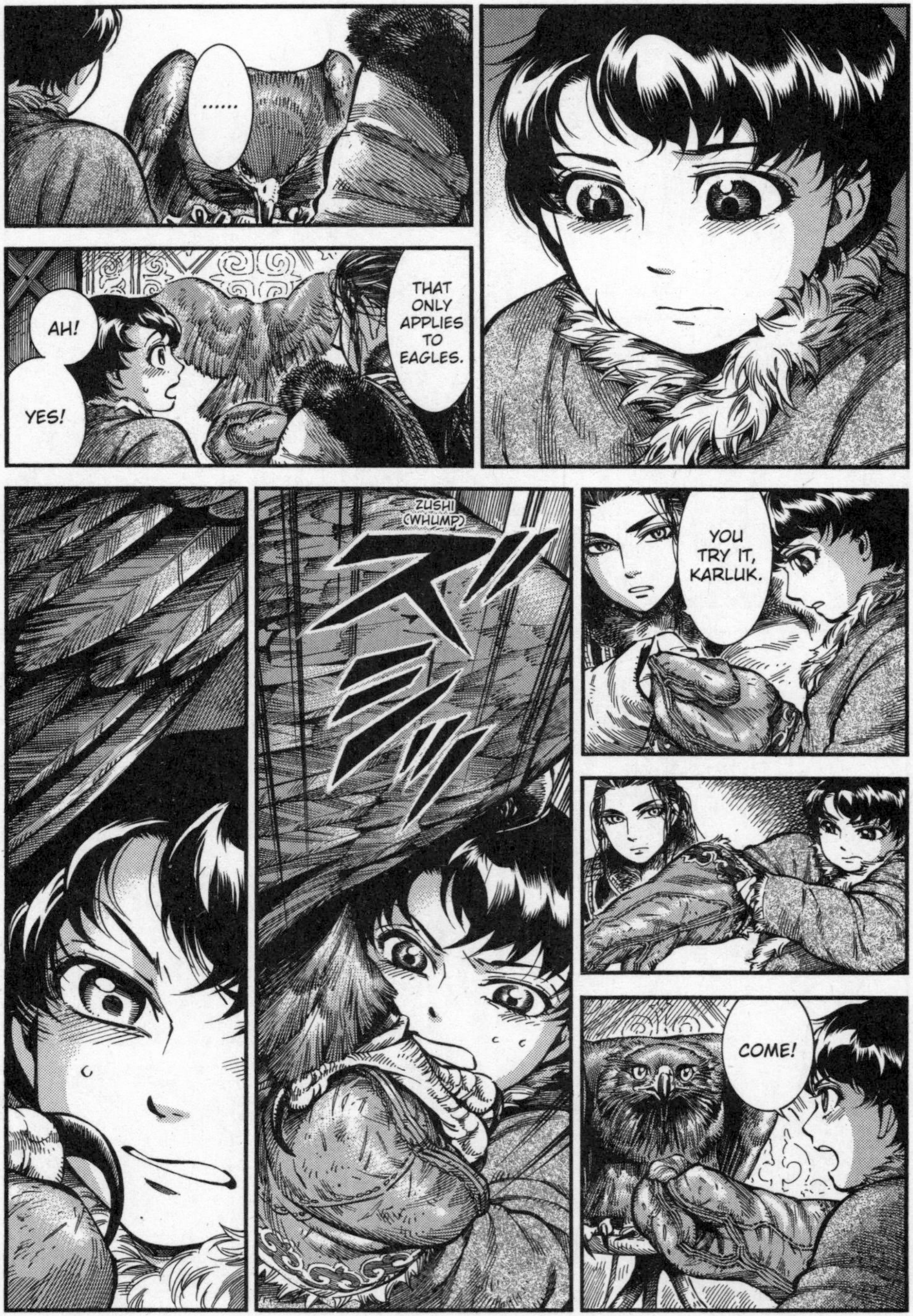
......
THAT ONLY APPLIES TO EAGLES.
AH!
YES!
YOU TRY IT, KARLUK.
COME!
ZUSHI (WHUMP)

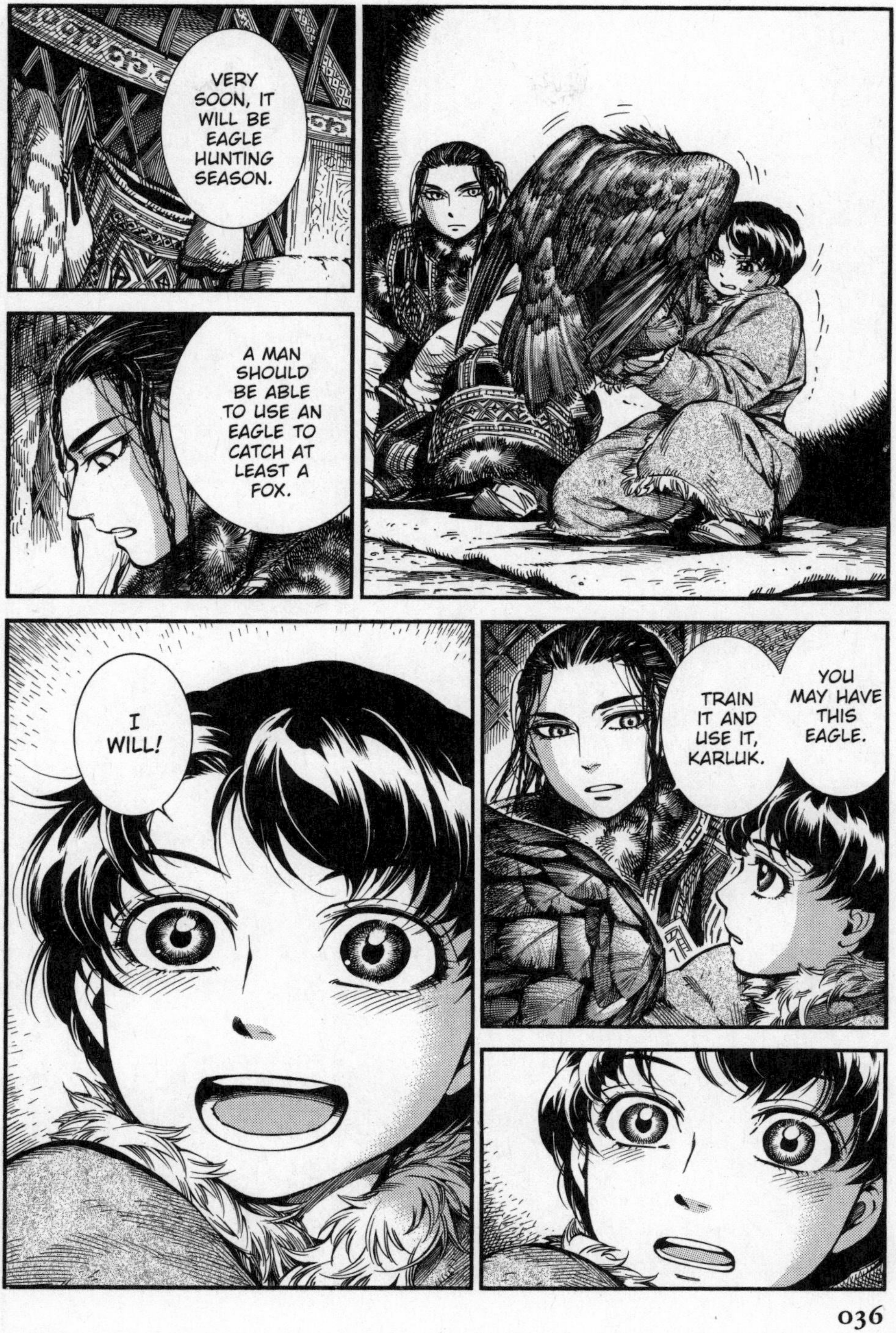
VERY SOON, IT WILL BE EAGLE HUNTING SEASON.
A MAN SHOULD BE ABLE TO USE AN EAGLE TO CATCH AT LEAST A FOX.
YOU MAY HAVE THIS EAGLE.
TRAIN IT AND USE IT, KARLUK.
I WILL!

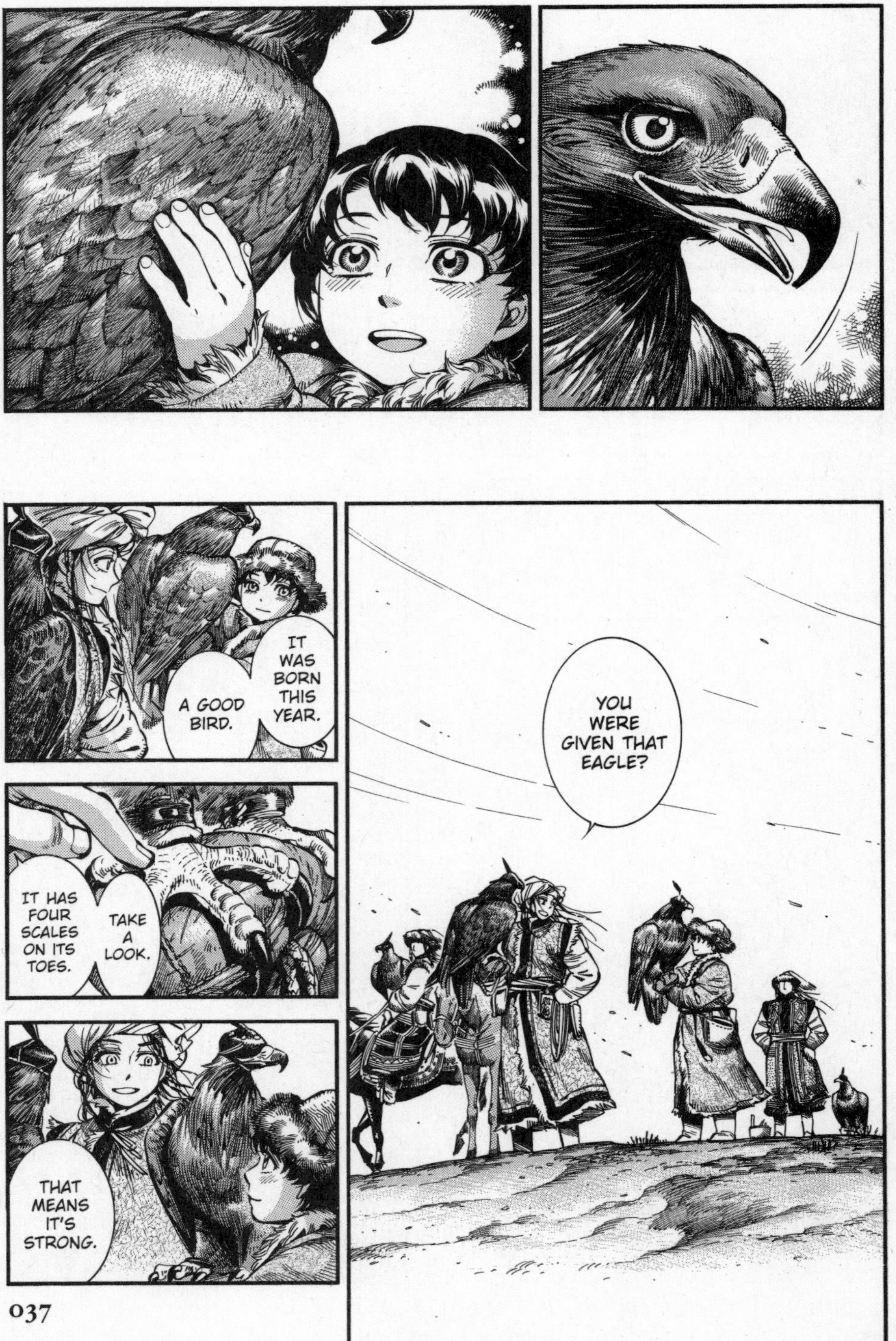
YOU WERE GIVEN THAT EAGLE?
IT WAS BORN THIS YEAR.
A GOOD BIRD.
TAKE A LOOK.
IT HAS FOUR SCALES ON ITS TOES.
THAT MEANS IT'S STRONG.

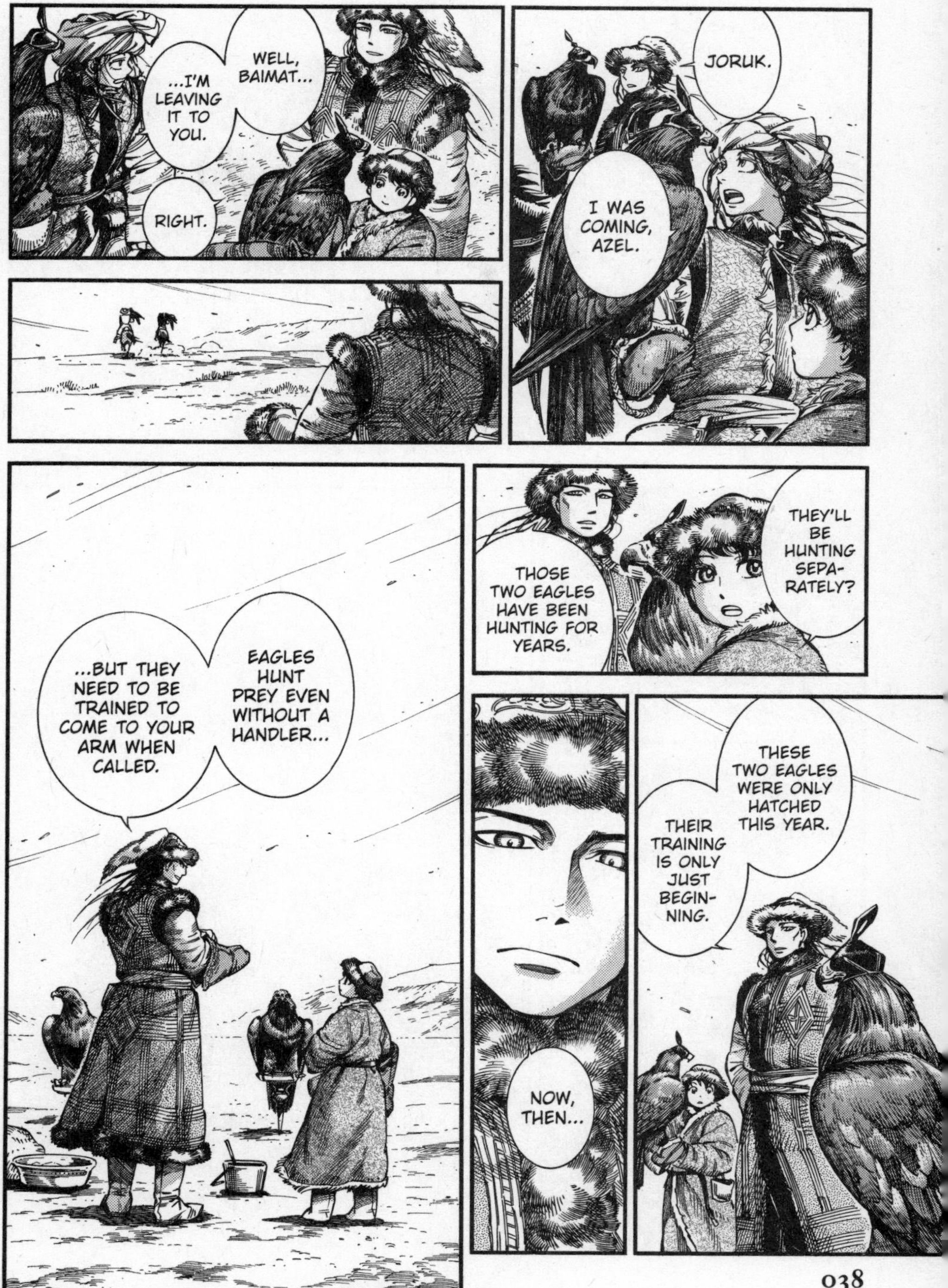
JORUK.
I WAS COMING, AZEL.
WELL, BAIMAT...
...I'M LEAVING IT TO YOU.
RIGHT.
THEY'LL BE HUNTING SEPA-RATELY?
THOSE TWO EAGLES HAVE BEEN HUNTING FOR YEARS.
THESE TWO EAGLES WERE ONLY HATCHED THIS YEAR.
THEIR TRAINING IS ONLY JUST BEGIN-NING.
NOW, THEN...
EAGLES HUNT PREY EVEN WITHOUT A HANDLER...
...BUT THEY NEED TO BE TRAINED TO COME TO YOUR ARM WHEN CALLED.

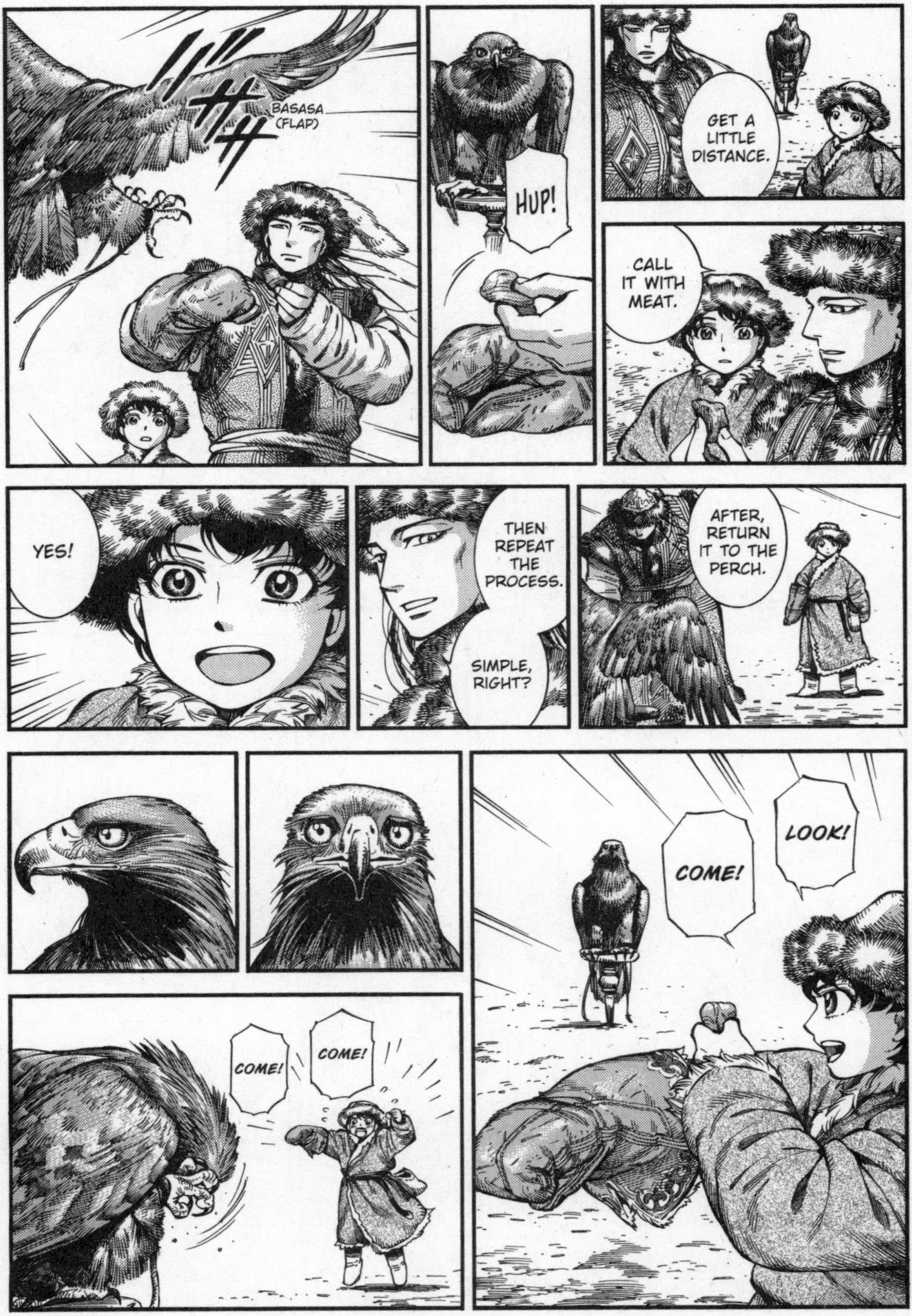
GET A LITTLE DISTANCE.
CALL IT WITH MEAT.
HUP!
BASASA (FLAP)
AFTER, RETURN IT TO THE PERCH.
THEN REPEAT THE PROCESS.
SIMPLE, RIGHT?
YES!
LOOK!
COME!
COME!
COME!

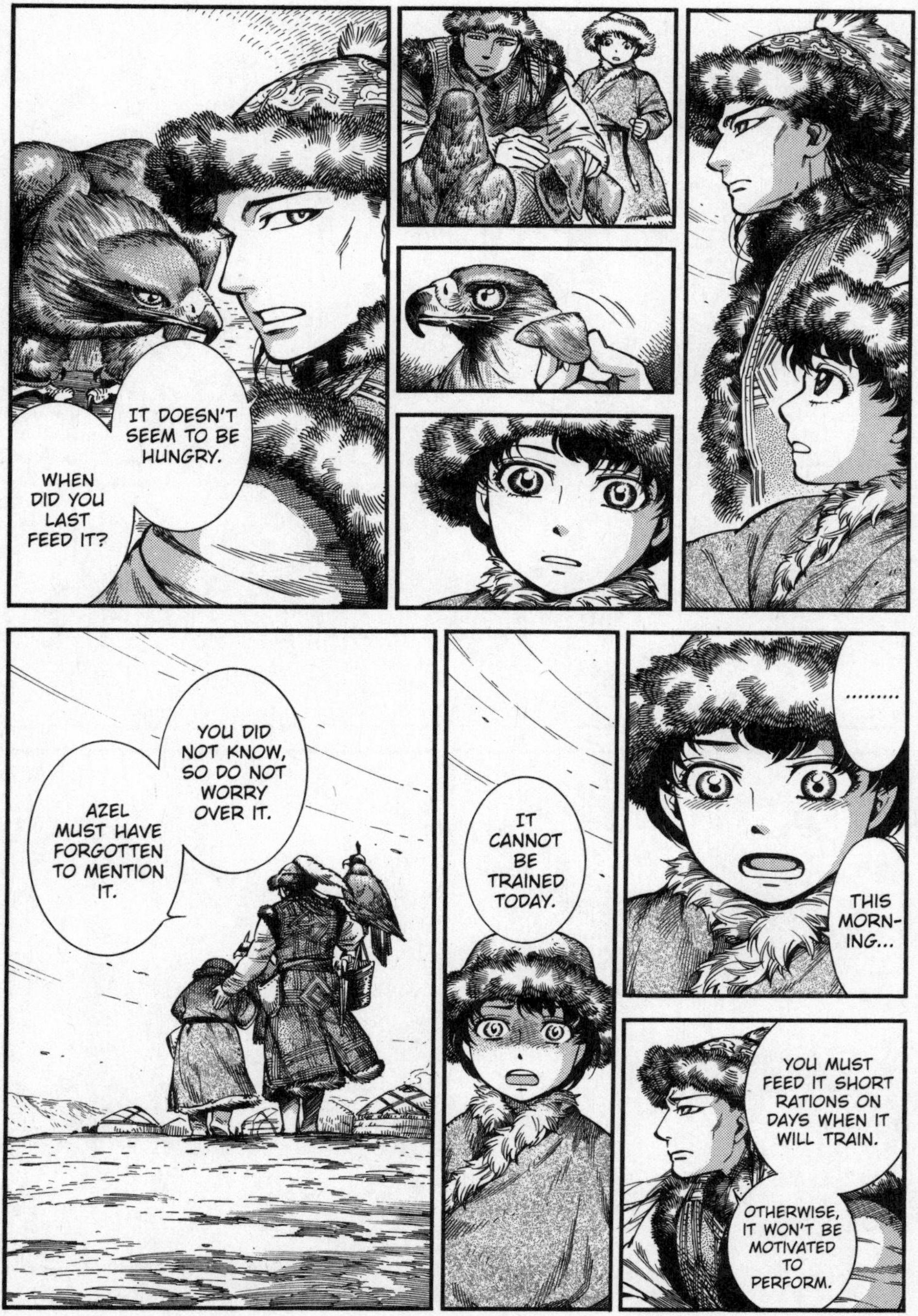
IT DOESN'T SEEM TO BE HUNGRY.
WHEN DID YOU LAST FEED IT?
....
THIS MORNING...
YOU MUST FEED IT SHORT RATIONS ON DAYS WHEN IT WILL TRAIN.
OTHERWISE, IT WON'T BE MOTIVATED TO PERFORM.
IT CANNOT BE TRAINED TODAY.
YOU DID NOT KNOW, SO DO NOT WORRY OVER IT.
AZEL MUST HAVE FORGOTTEN TO MENTION IT.

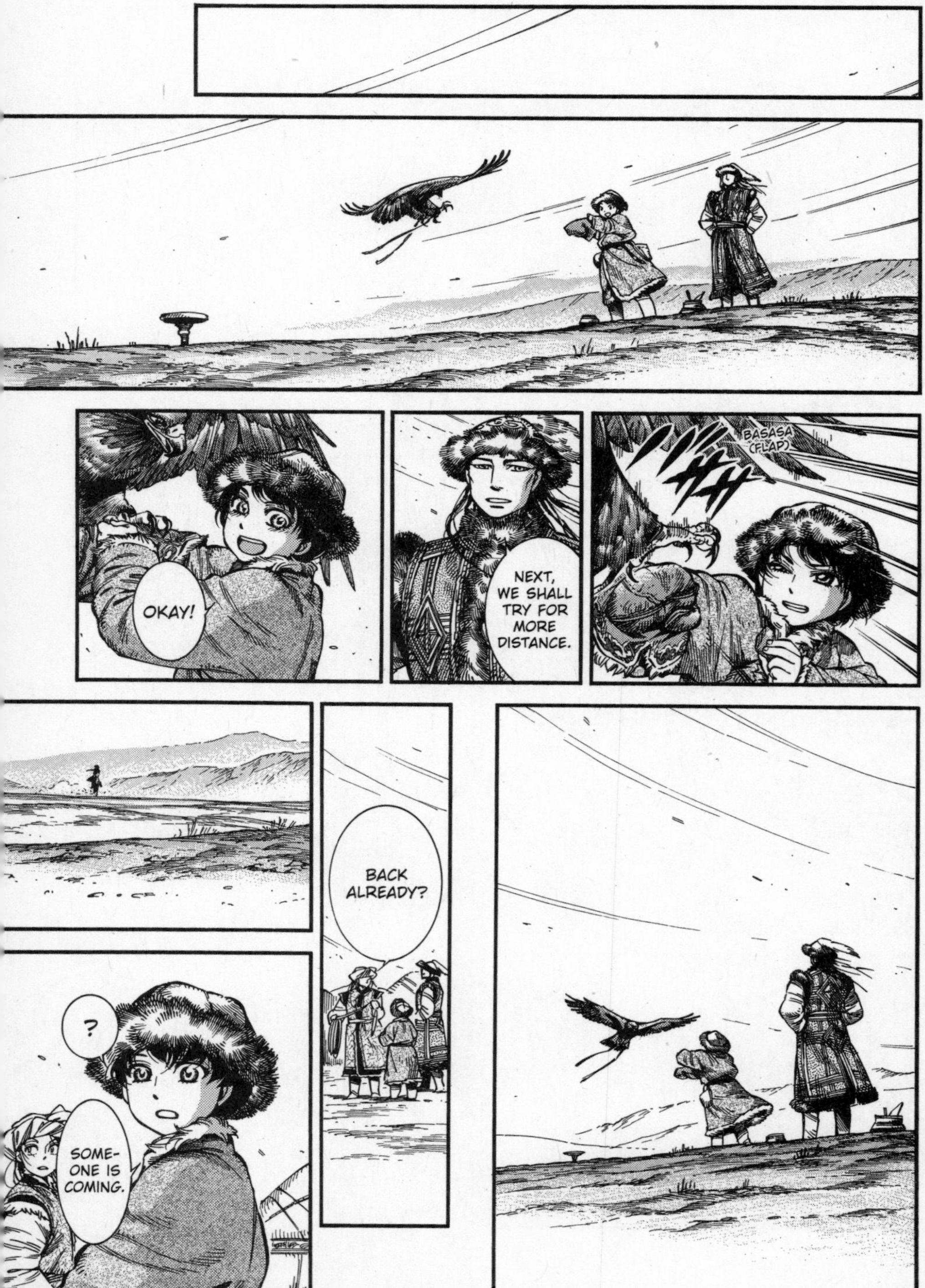
BASASA (FLAP)
NEXT, WE SHALL TRY FOR MORE DISTANCE.
OKAY!
BACK ALREADY?
?
SOME-ONE IS COMING.

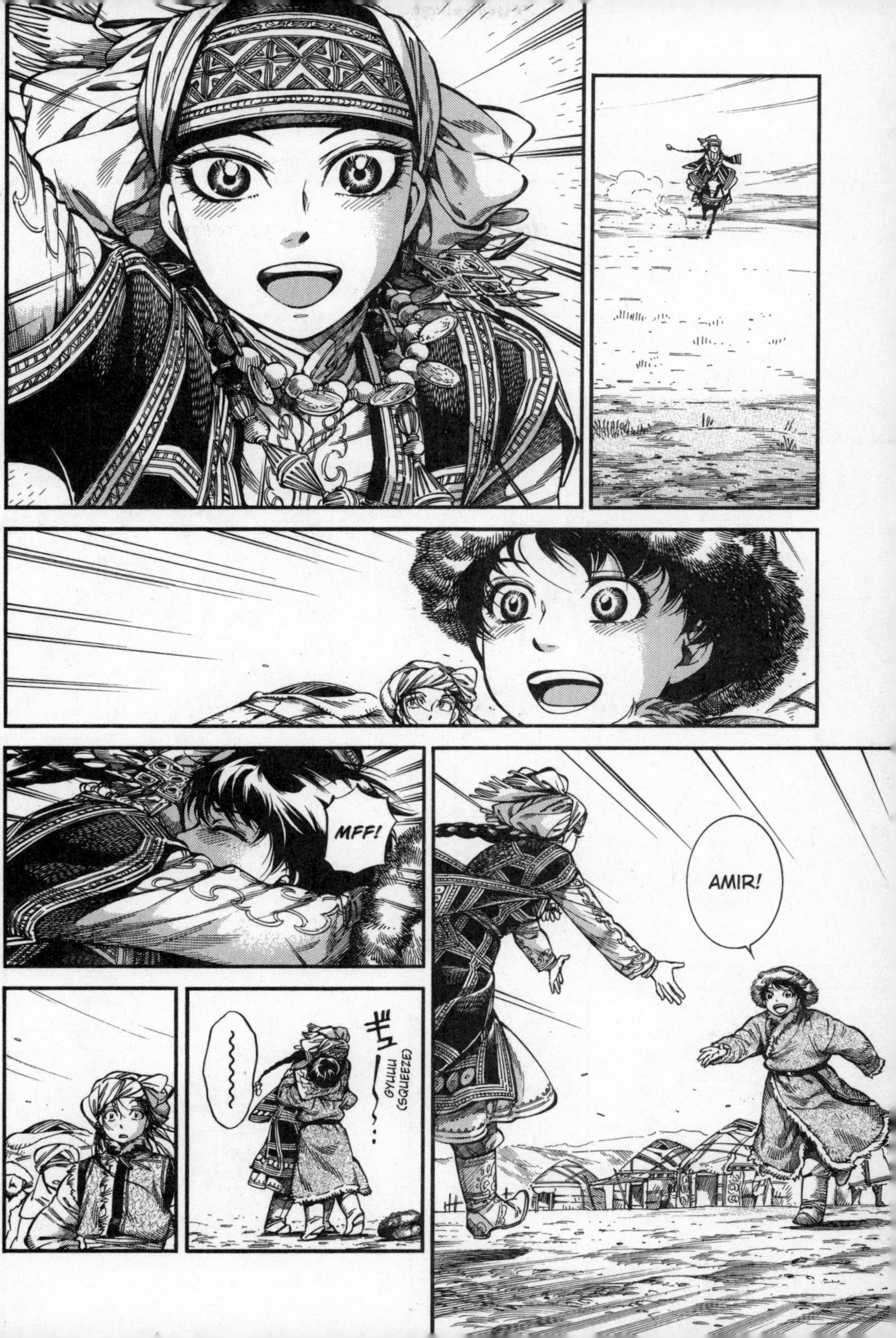
AMIR!
MFF!
ぎゅー…
GYUUU (SQUEEZE)

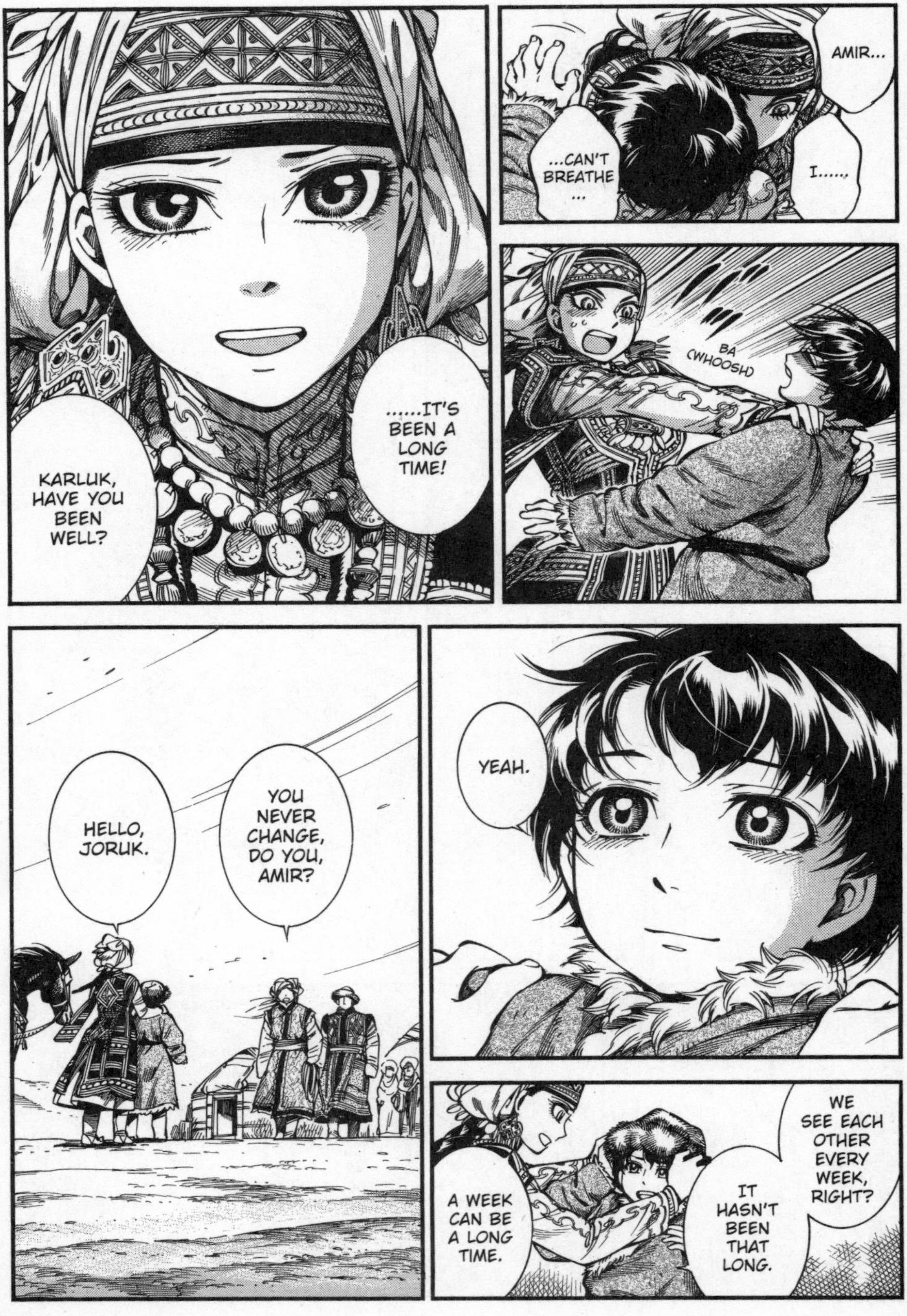
AMIR...
I......
...CAN'T BREATHE ...
BA (WHOOSH)
......IT'S BEEN A LONG TIME!
KARLUK, HAVE YOU BEEN WELL?
YEAH.
WE SEE EACH OTHER EVERY WEEK, RIGHT?
IT HASN'T BEEN THAT LONG.
A WEEK CAN BE A LONG TIME.
YOU NEVER CHANGE, DO YOU, AMIR?
HELLO, JORUK.

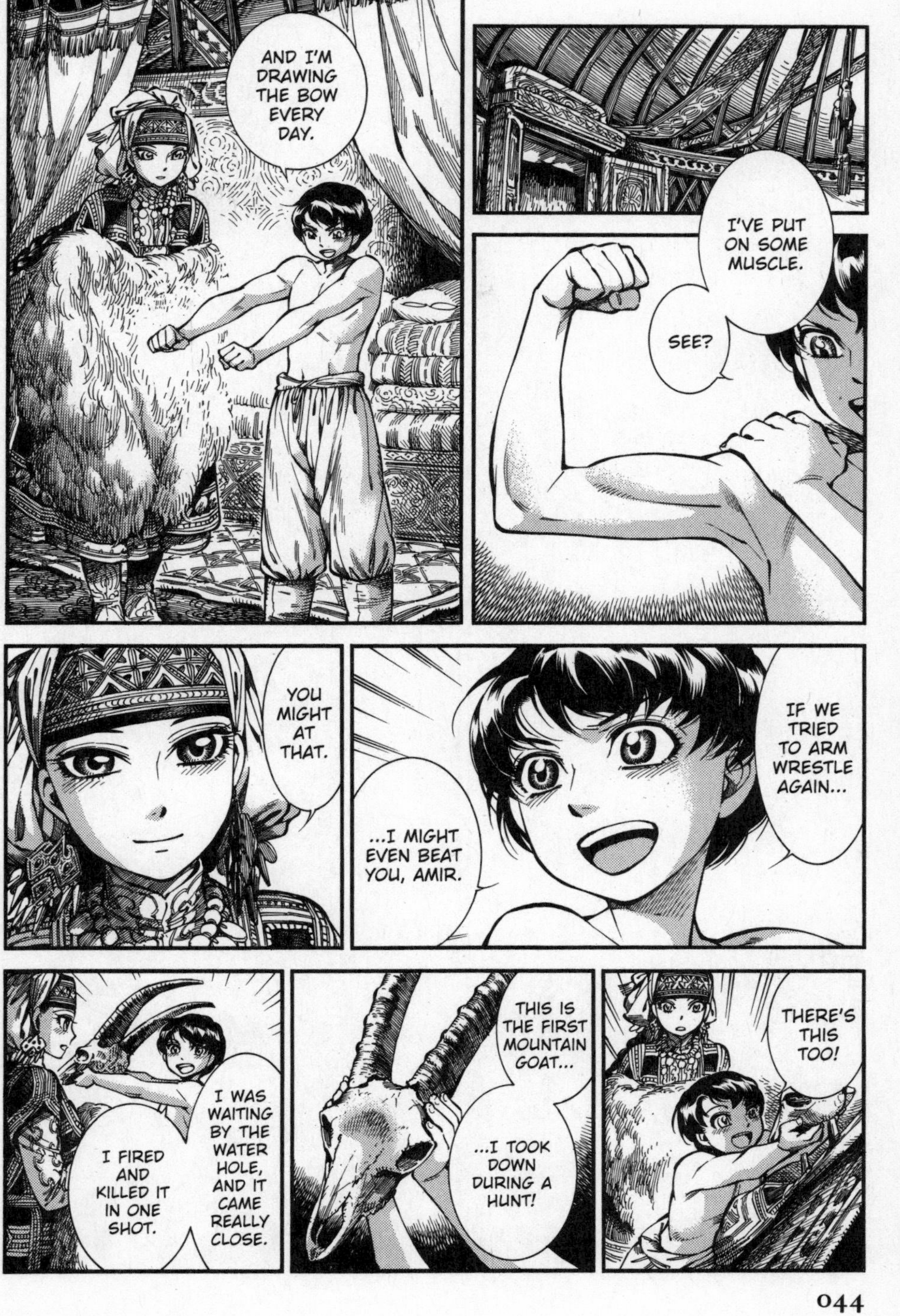
I'VE PUT ON SOME MUSCLE.
SEE?
AND I'M DRAWING THE BOW EVERY DAY.
IF WE TRIED TO ARM WRESTLE AGAIN...
...I MIGHT EVEN BEAT YOU, AMIR.
YOU MIGHT AT THAT.
THERE'S THIS TOO!
THIS IS THE FIRST MOUNTAIN GOAT...
...I TOOK DOWN DURING A HUNT!
I WAS WAITING BY THE WATER HOLE, AND IT CAME REALLY CLOSE.
I FIRED AND KILLED IT IN ONE SHOT.

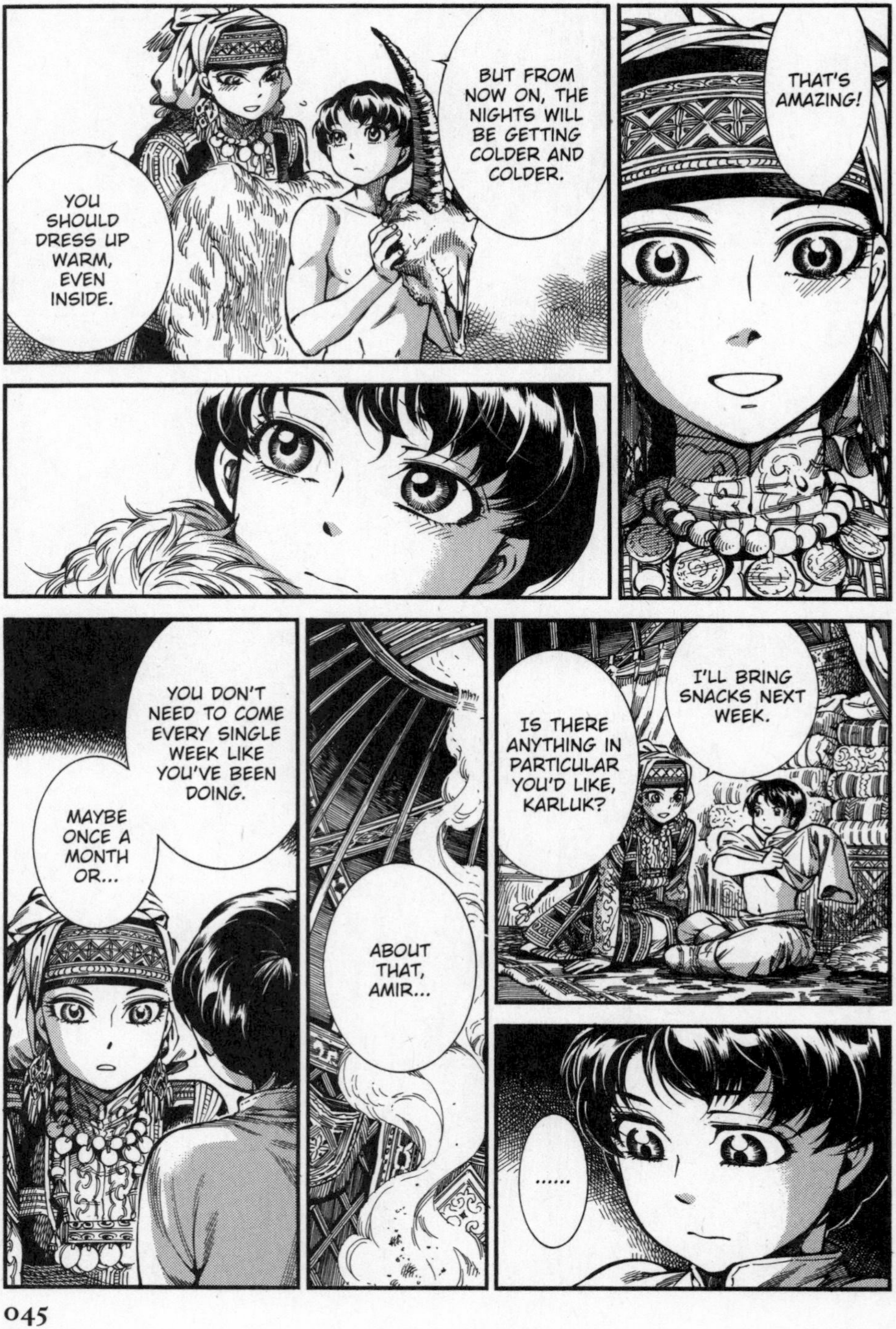
THAT'S AMAZING!
BUT FROM NOW ON, THE NIGHTS WILL BE GETTING COLDER AND COLDER.
YOU SHOULD DRESS UP WARM, EVEN INSIDE.
I'LL BRING SNACKS NEXT WEEK.
IS THERE ANYTHING IN PARTICULAR YOU'D LIKE, KARLUK?
......
ABOUT THAT, AMIR...
YOU DON'T NEED TO COME EVERY SINGLE WEEK LIKE YOU'VE BEEN DOING.
MAYBE ONCE A MONTH OR...

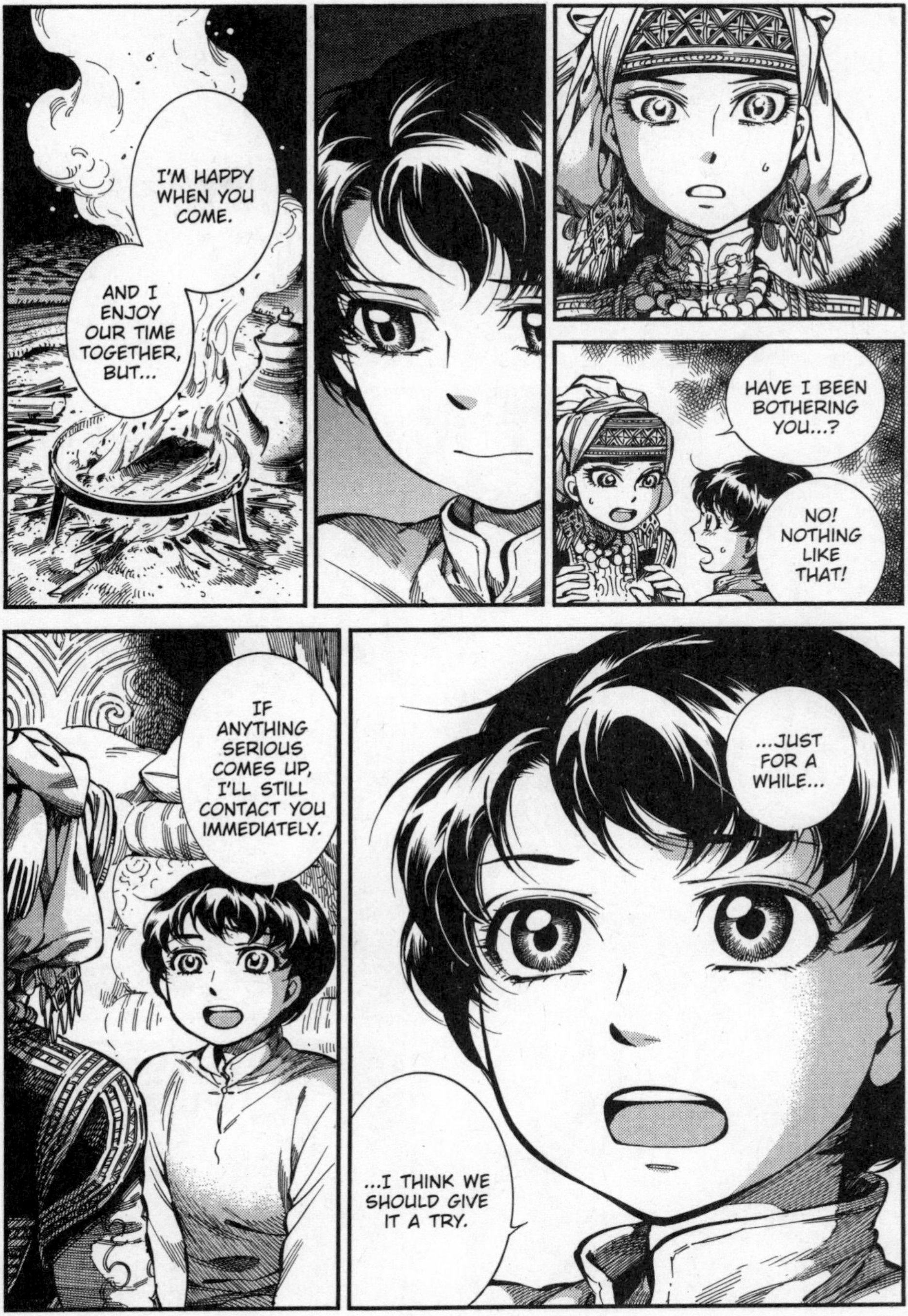
HAVE I BEEN BOTHERING YOU...?
NO! NOTHING LIKE THAT!
I'M HAPPY WHEN YOU COME.
AND I ENJOY OUR TIME TOGETHER, BUT...
...JUST FOR A WHILE...
...I THINK WE SHOULD GIVE IT A TRY.
IF ANYTHING SERIOUS COMES UP, I'LL STILL CONTACT YOU IMMEDIATELY.

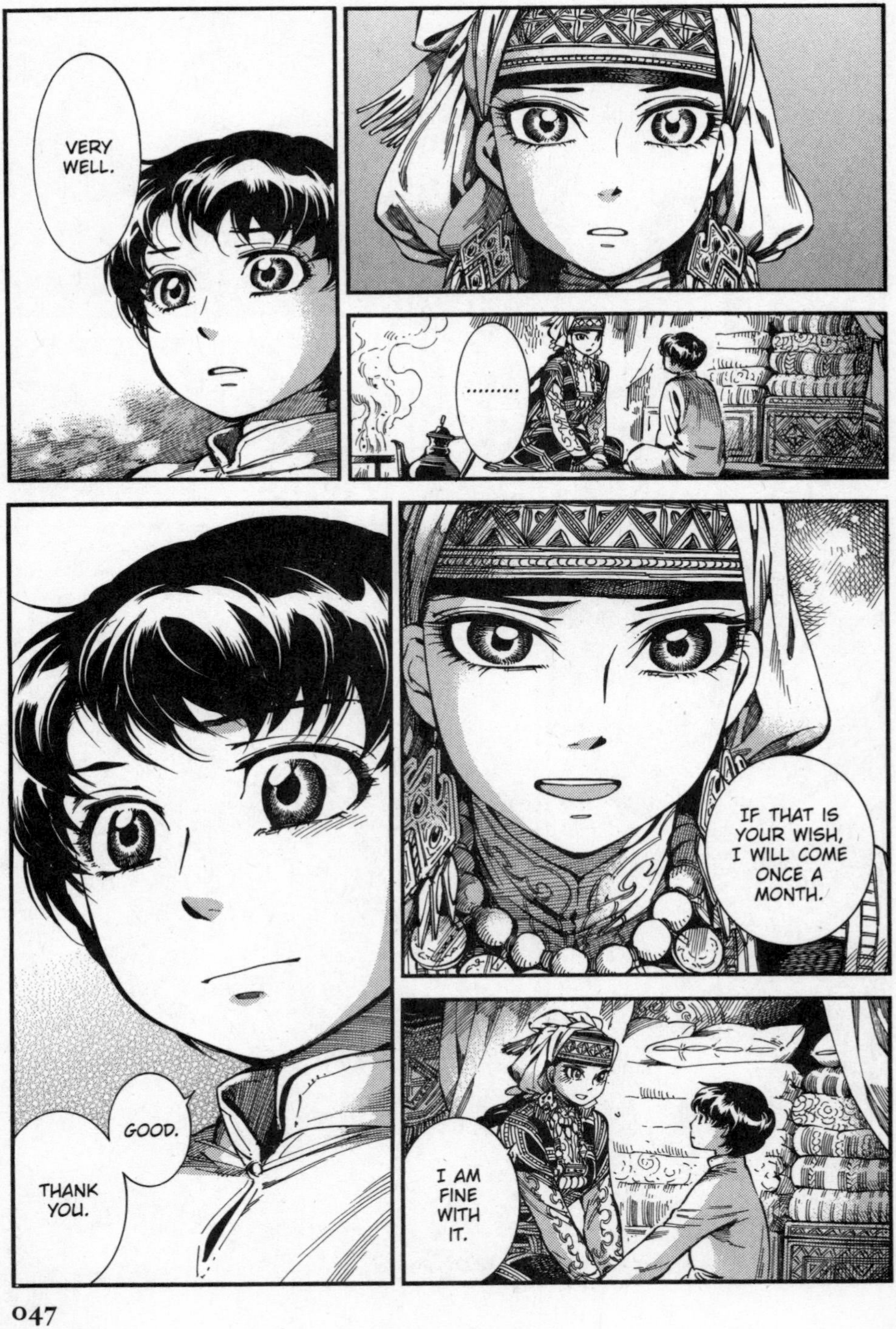
....
VERY WELL.
IF THAT IS YOUR WISH, I WILL COME ONCE A MONTH.
I AM FINE WITH IT.
GOOD.
THANK YOU.

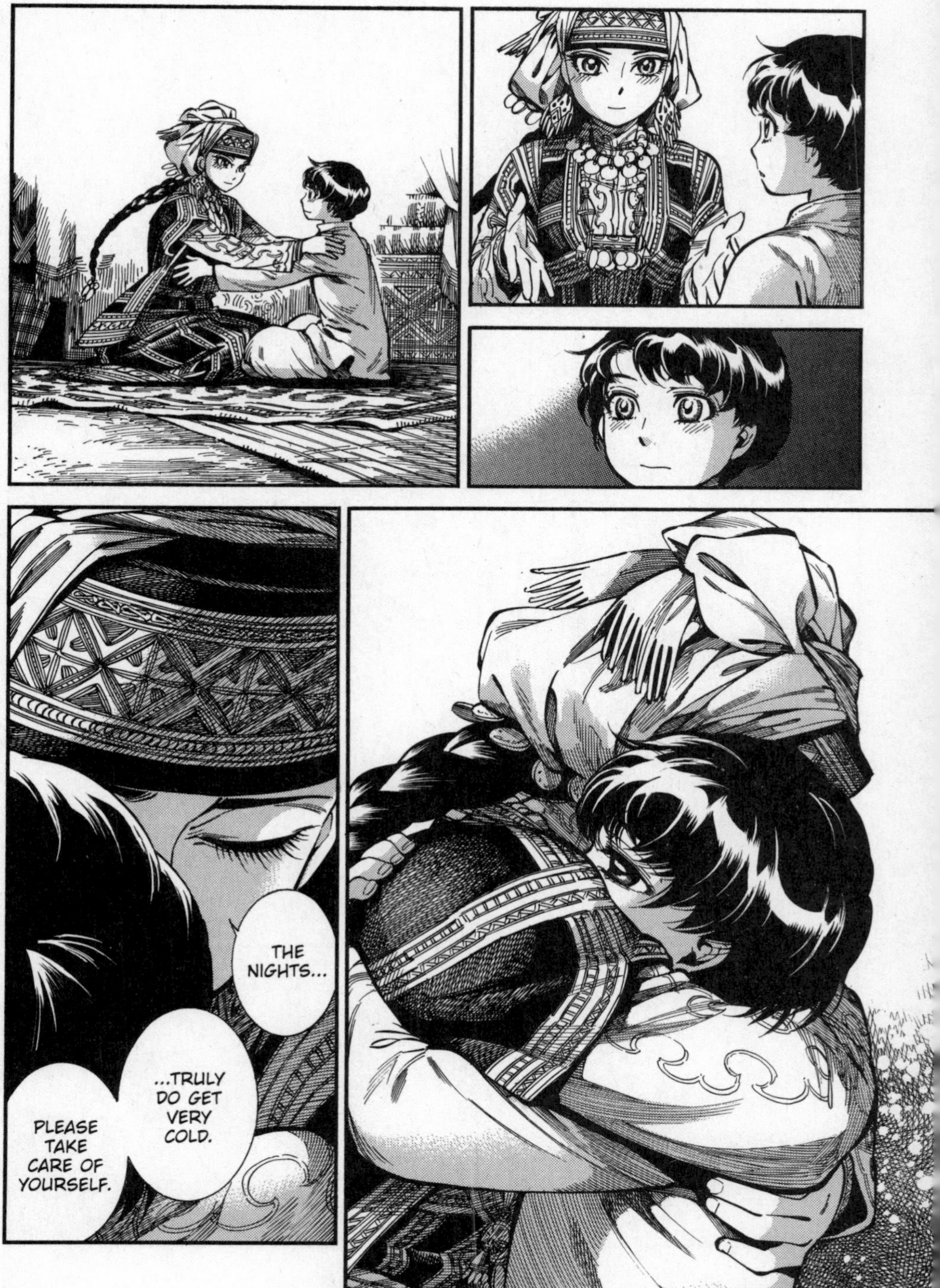
THE NIGHTS...
...TRULY DO GET VERY COLD.
PLEASE TAKE CARE OF YOURSELF.

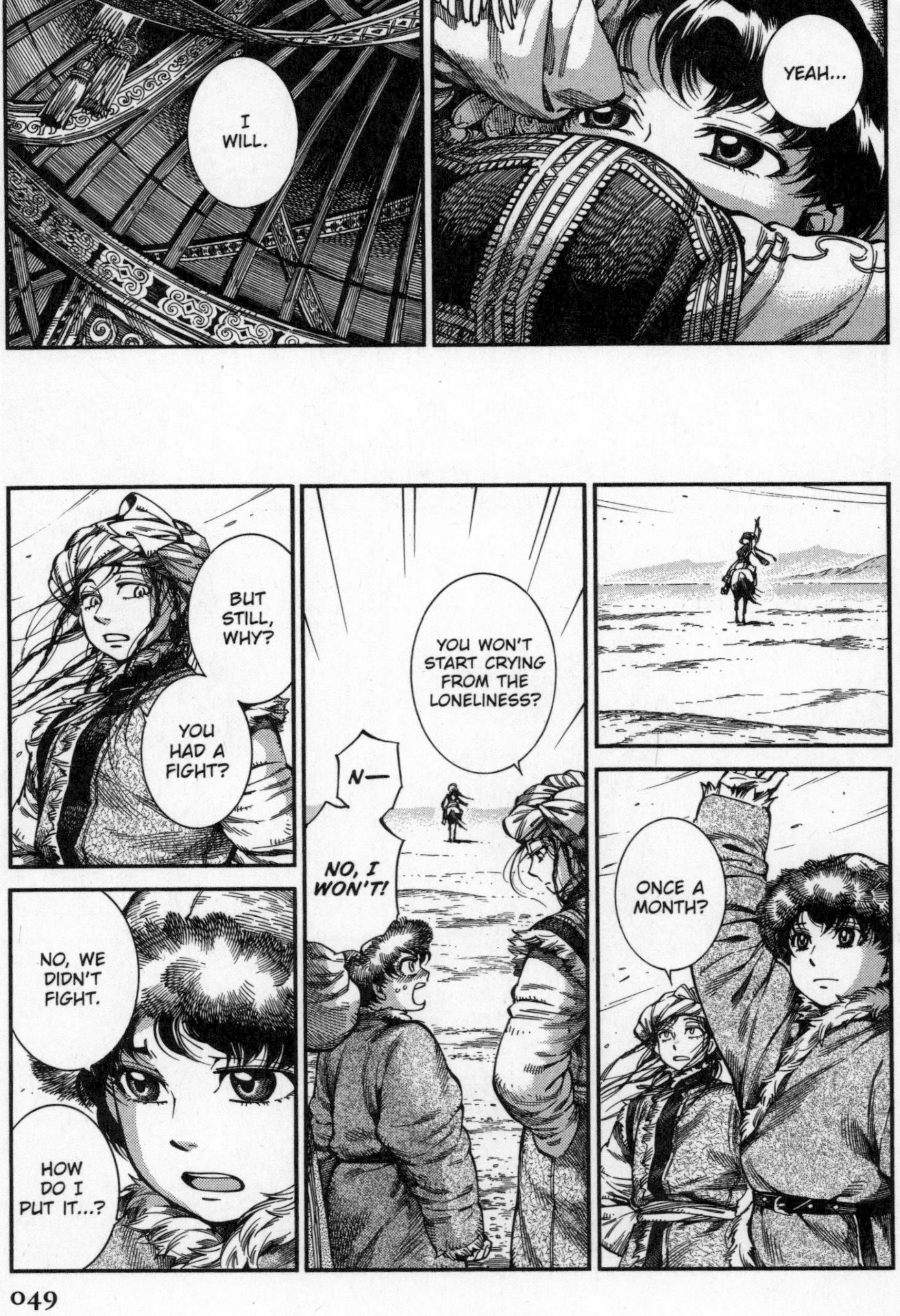
YEAH...
I WILL.
ONCE A MONTH?
YOU WON'T START CRYING FROM THE LONELINESS?
N—
NO, I WON'T!
BUT STILL, WHY?
YOU HAD A FIGHT?
NO, WE DIDN'T FIGHT.
HOW DO I PUT IT...?

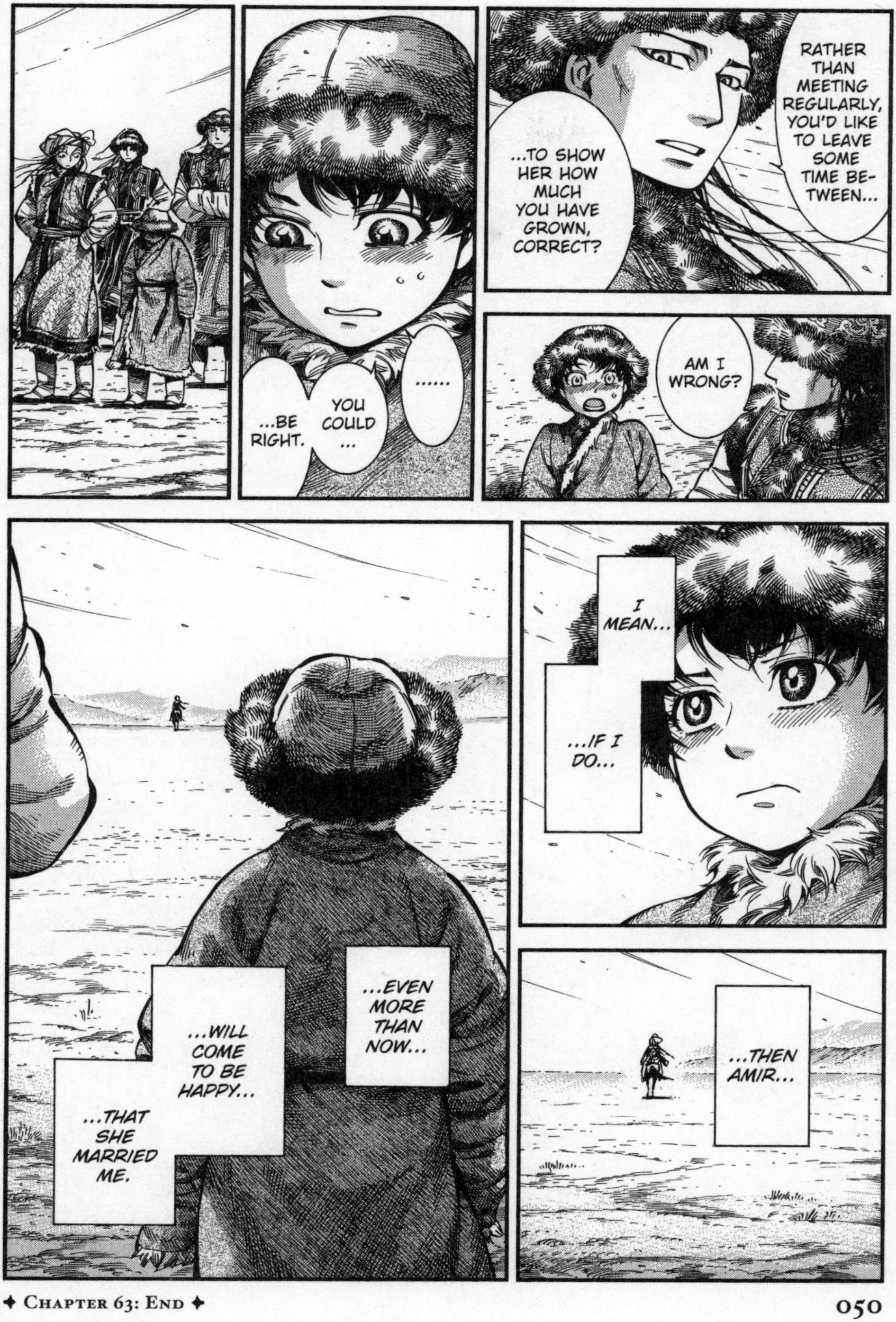
RATHER THAN MEETING REGULARLY, YOU'D LIKE TO LEAVE SOME TIME BE- TWEEN...
...TO SHOW HER HOW MUCH YOU HAVE GROWN, CORRECT?
AM I WRONG?
......
YOU COULD ...
...BE RIGHT.
I MEAN...
...IF I DO...
...THEN AMIR...
...EVEN MORE THAN NOW...
...WILL COME TO BE HAPPY...
...THAT SHE MARRIED ME.

✦ Chapter 63: End ✦

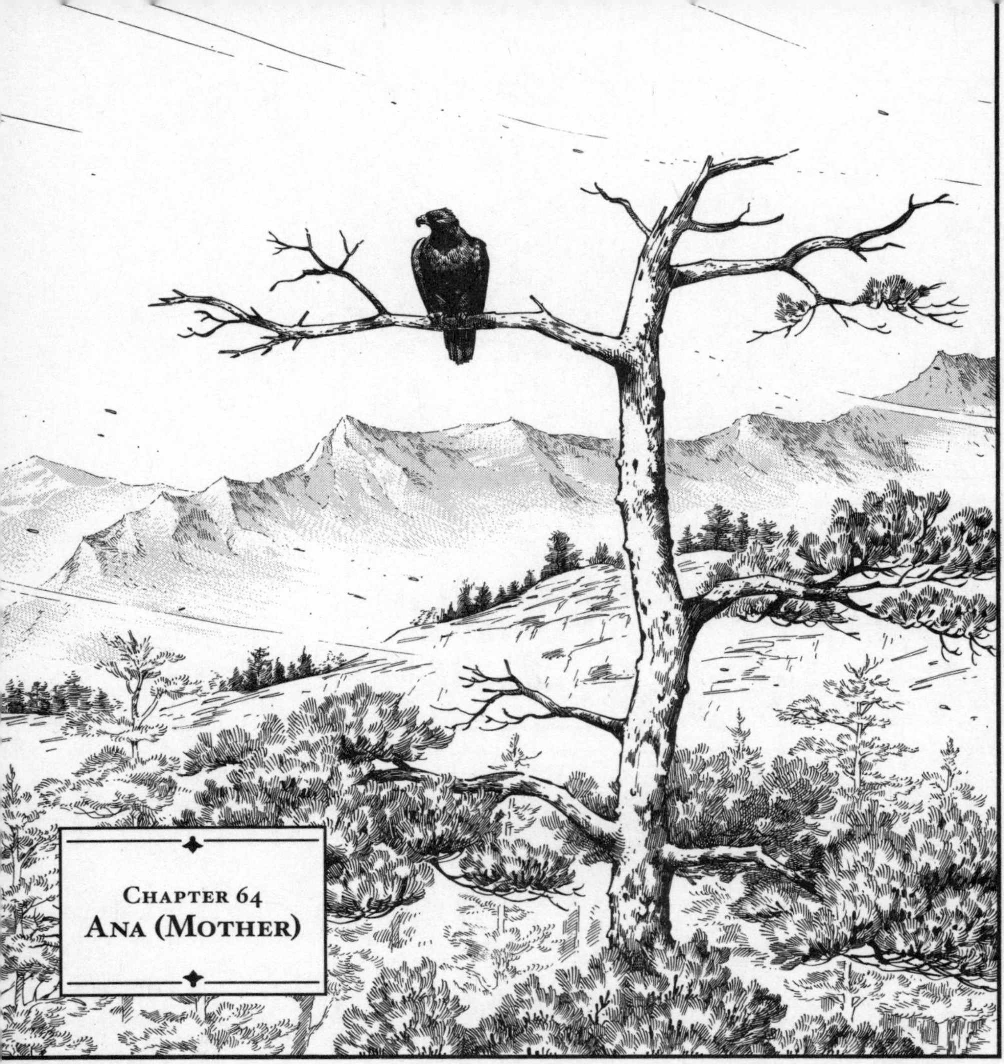
CHAPTER 64
ANA (MOTHER)

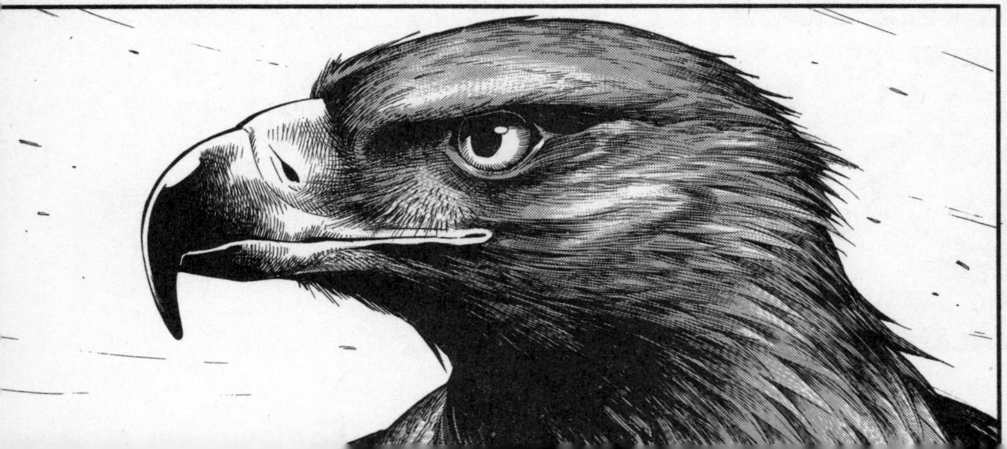

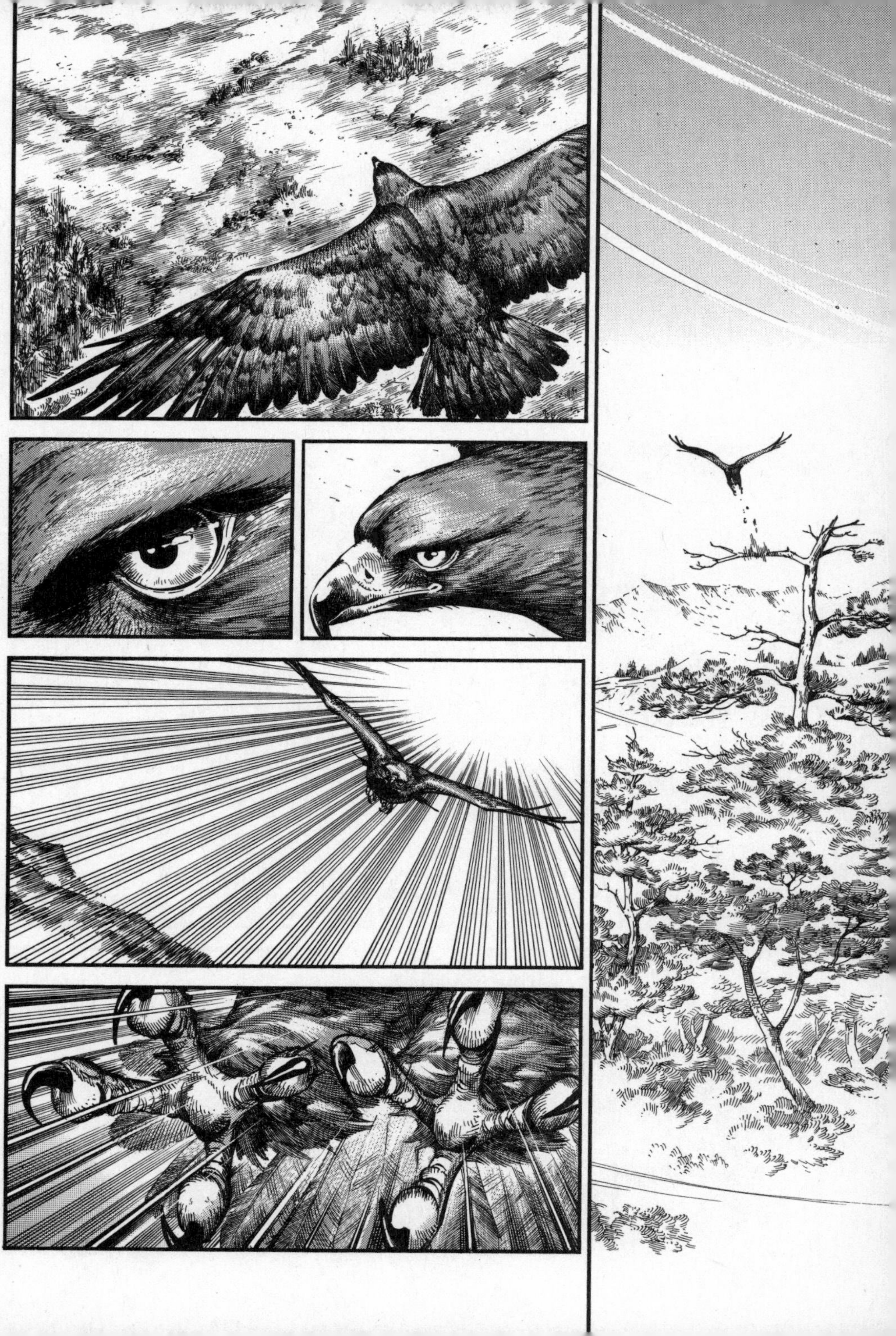

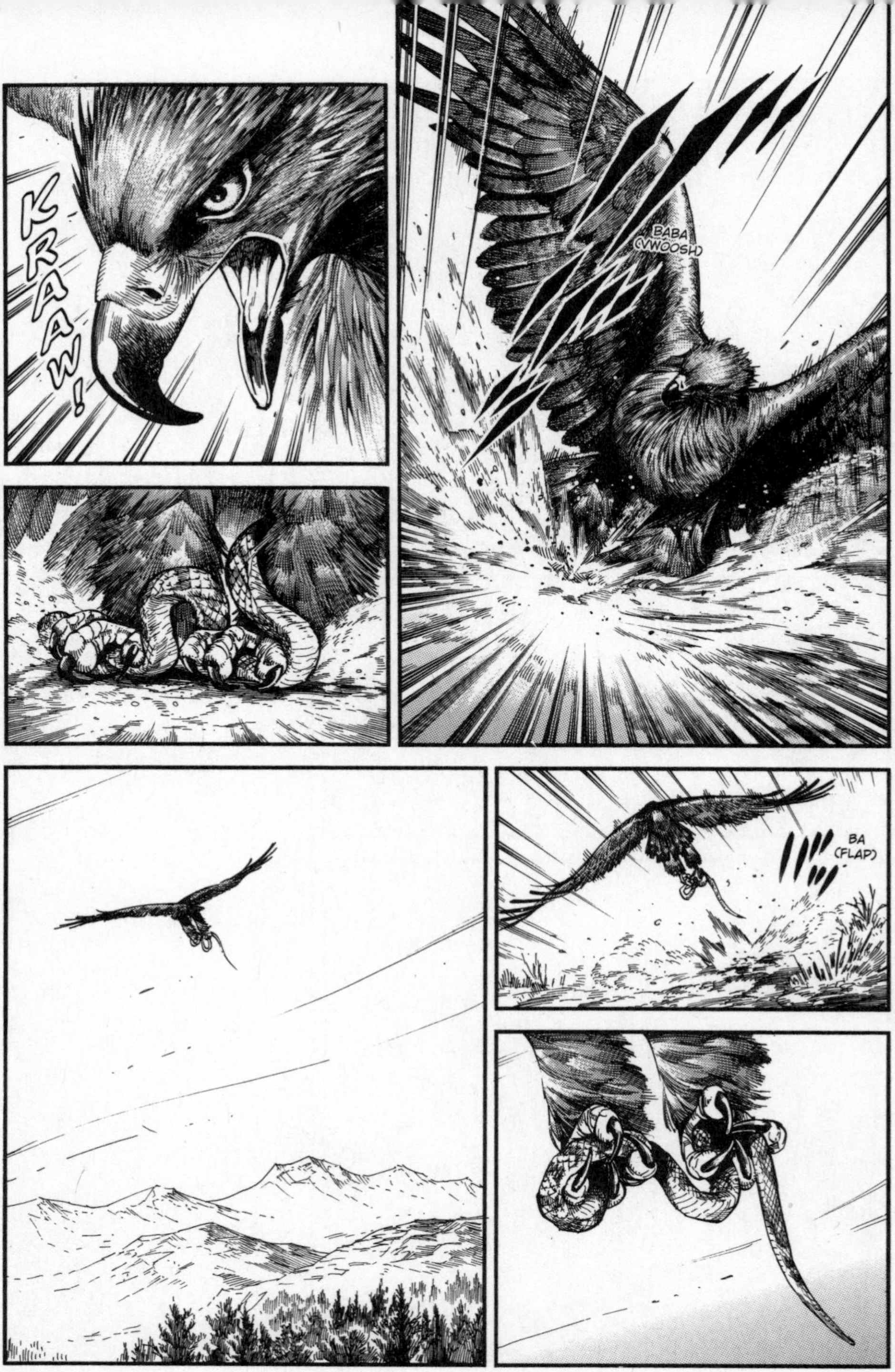
BABA
(VWOOSH)
KRAAW!
BA
(FLAP)

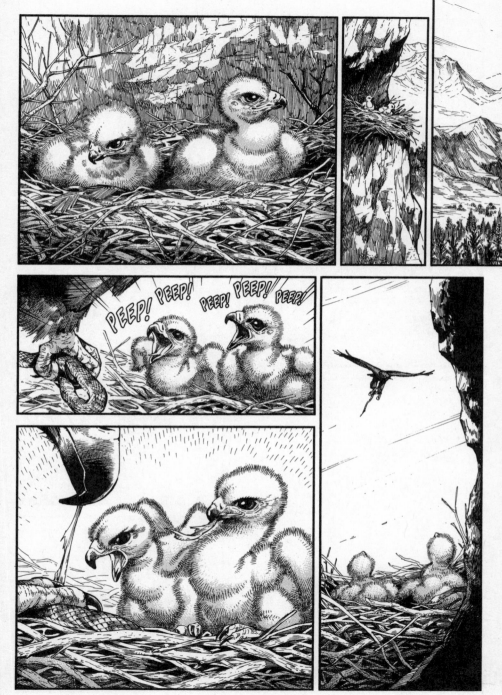

PEEP! PEEP! PEEP! PEEP! PEEP!

054

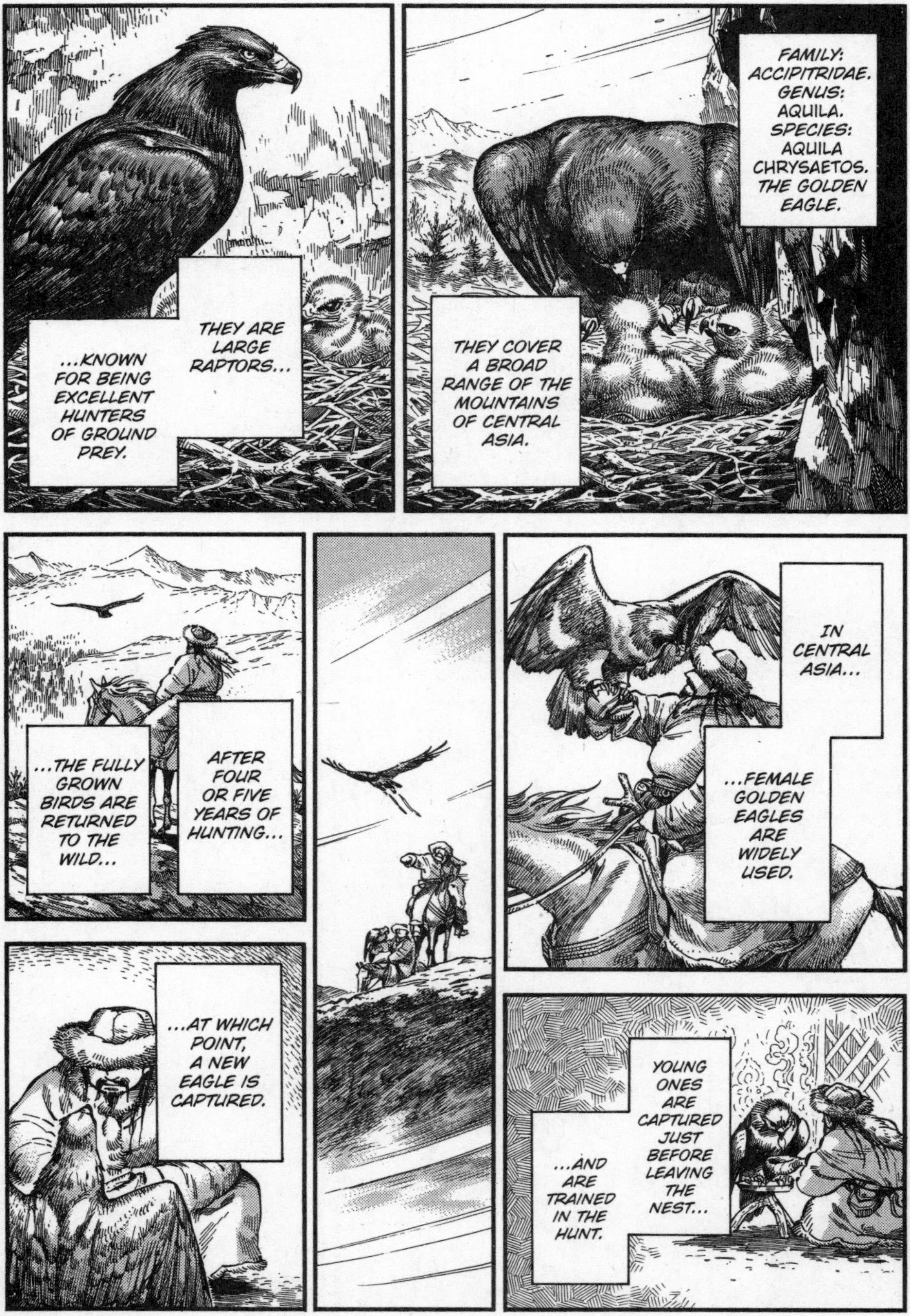
FAMILY: ACCIPITRIDAE. GENUS: AQUILA. SPECIES: AQUILA CHRYSAETOS. THE GOLDEN EAGLE.
THEY COVER A BROAD RANGE OF THE MOUNTAINS OF CENTRAL ASIA.
THEY ARE LARGE RAPTORS...
...KNOWN FOR BEING EXCELLENT HUNTERS OF GROUND PREY.
IN CENTRAL ASIA...
...FEMALE GOLDEN EAGLES ARE WIDELY USED.
YOUNG ONES ARE CAPTURED JUST BEFORE LEAVING THE NEST...
...AND ARE TRAINED IN THE HUNT.
AFTER FOUR OR FIVE YEARS OF HUNTING...
...THE FULLY GROWN BIRDS ARE RETURNED TO THE WILD...
...AT WHICH POINT, A NEW EAGLE IS CAPTURED.

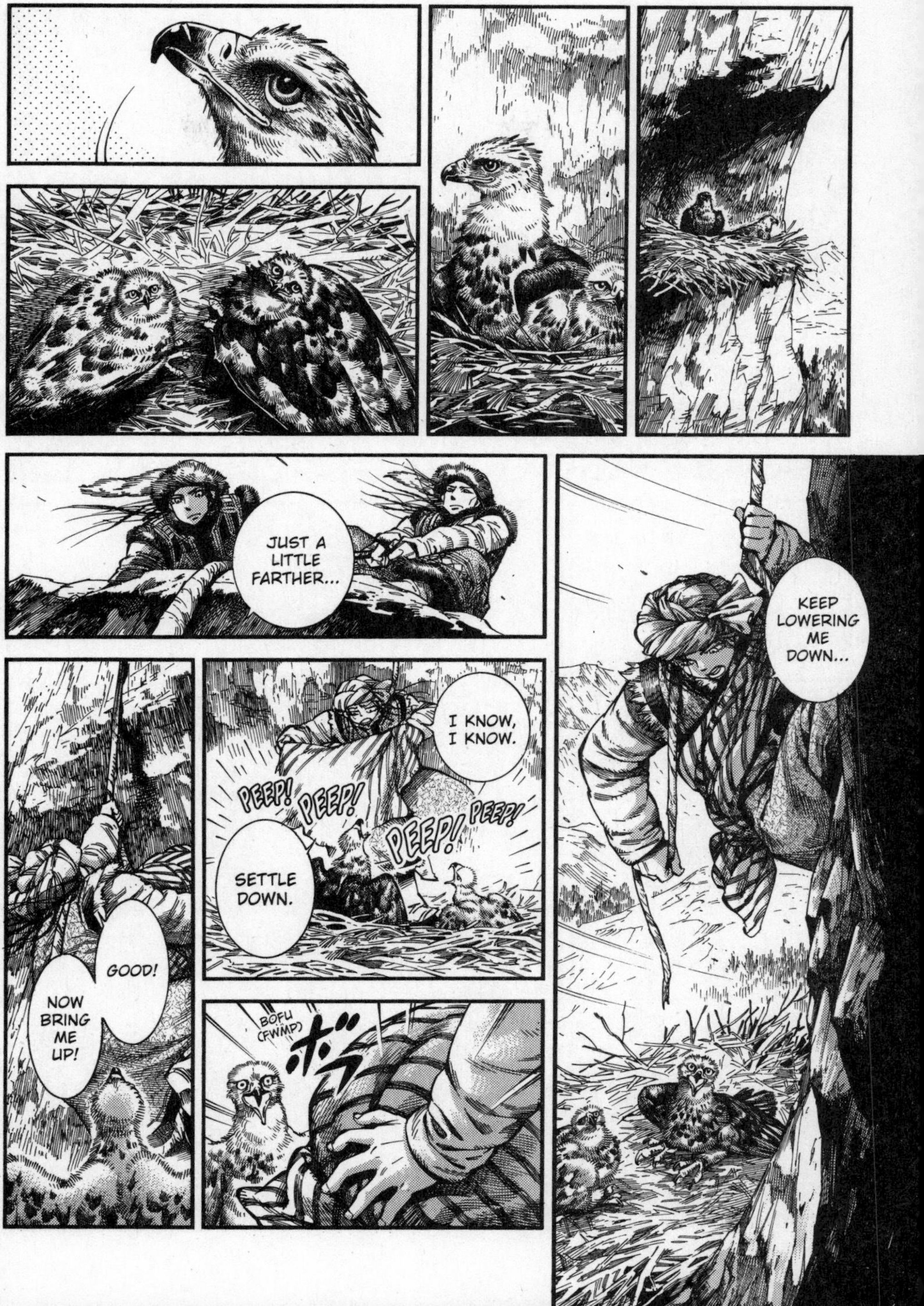
KEEP LOWERING ME DOWN...
JUST A LITTLE FARTHER...
I KNOW, I KNOW.
PEEP! PEEP! PEEP! PEEP!
SETTLE DOWN.
BOFU (FWMP)
GOOD!
NOW BRING ME UP!

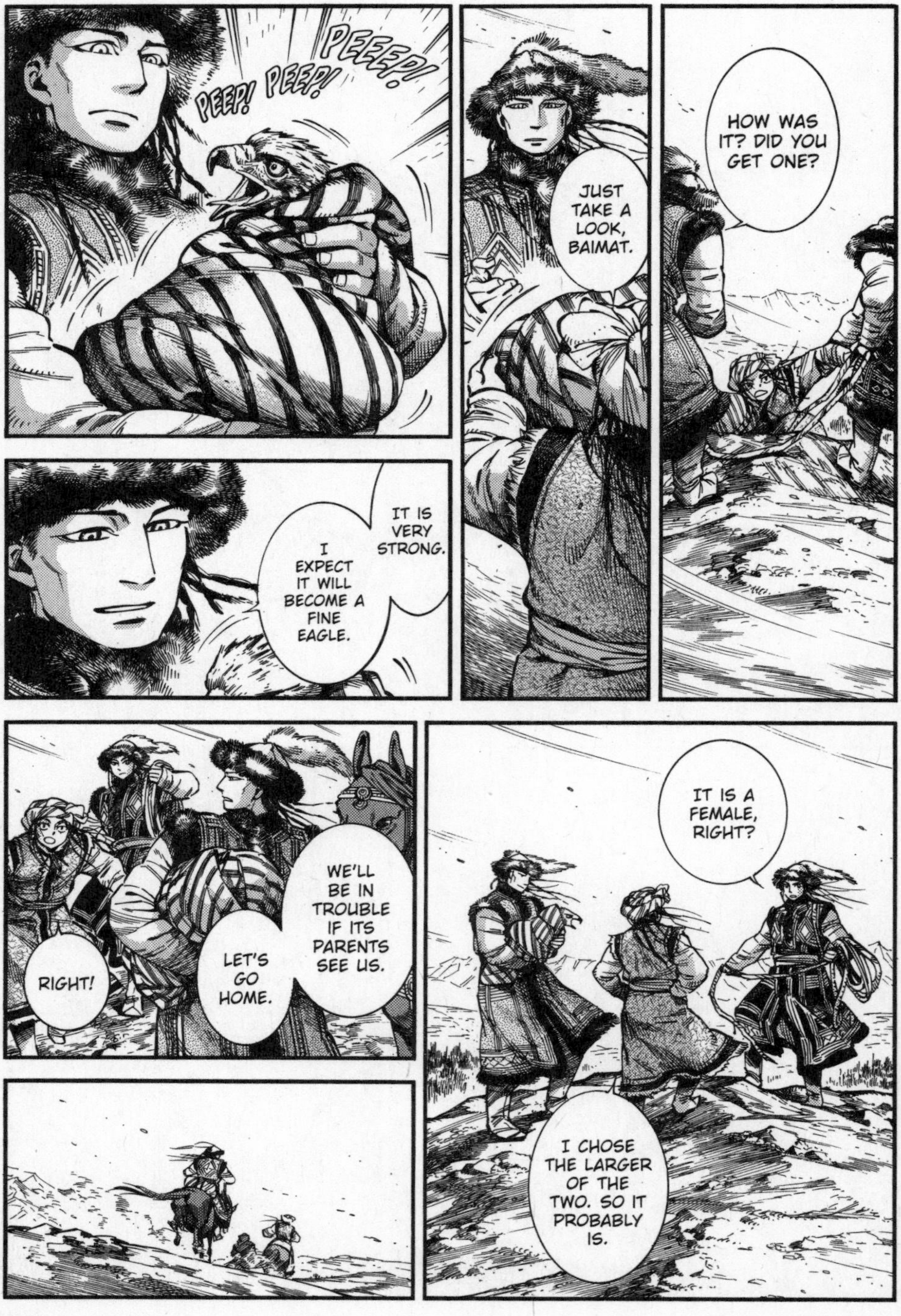
HOW WAS IT? DID YOU GET ONE?
JUST TAKE A LOOK, BAIMAT.
PEEEP!
PEEP! PEEP!
IT IS VERY STRONG.
I EXPECT IT WILL BECOME A FINE EAGLE.
IT IS A FEMALE, RIGHT?
I CHOSE THE LARGER OF THE TWO. SO IT PROBABLY IS.
WE'LL BE IN TROUBLE IF ITS PARENTS SEE US.
LET'S GO HOME.
RIGHT!

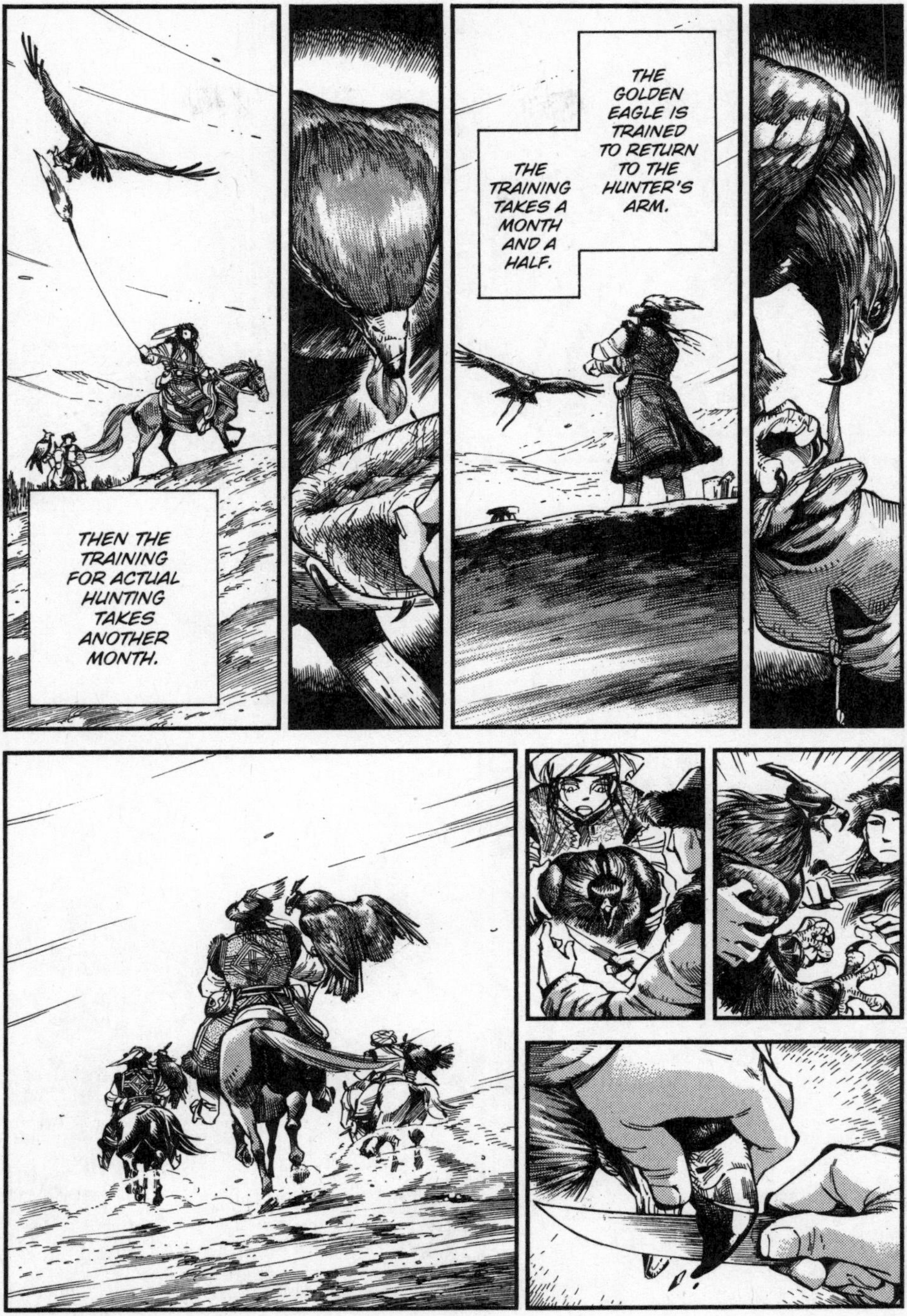
THE GOLDEN EAGLE IS TRAINED TO RETURN TO THE HUNTER'S ARM.
THE TRAINING TAKES A MONTH AND A HALF.
THEN THE TRAINING FOR ACTUAL HUNTING TAKES ANOTHER MONTH.

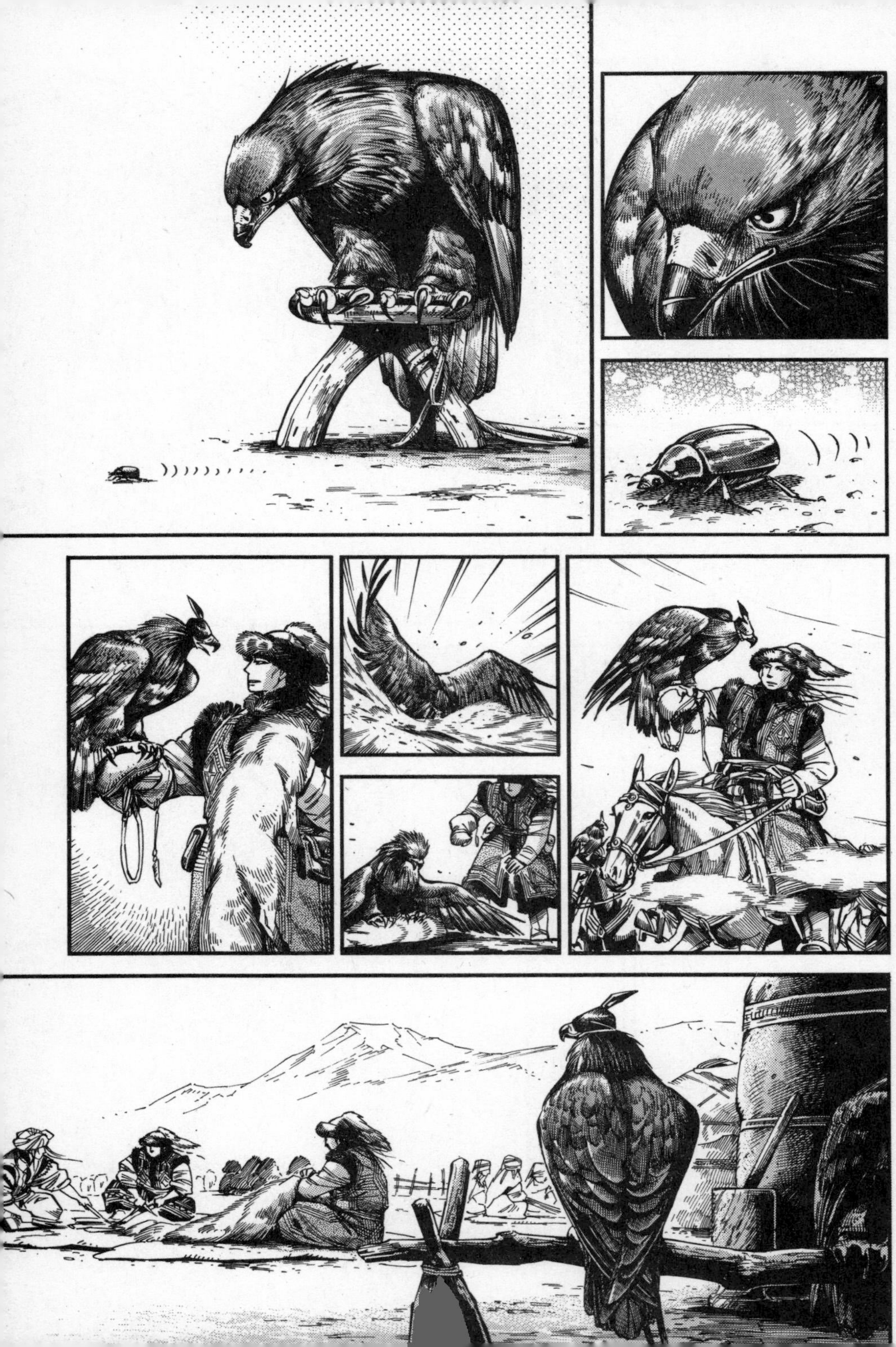

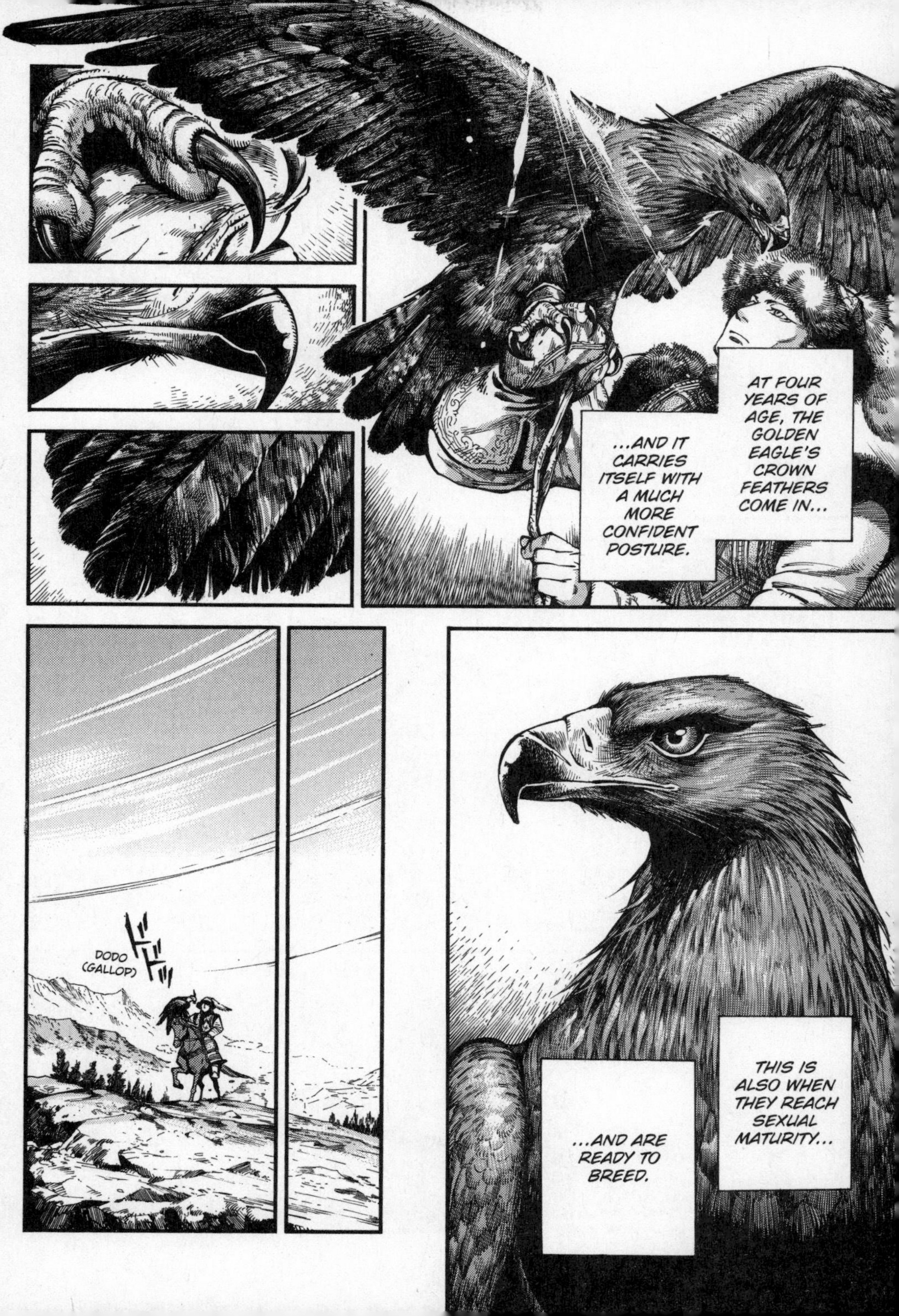
AT FOUR YEARS OF AGE, THE GOLDEN EAGLE'S CROWN FEATHERS COME IN...
...AND IT CARRIES ITSELF WITH A MUCH MORE CONFIDENT POSTURE.
THIS IS ALSO WHEN THEY REACH SEXUAL MATURITY...
...AND ARE READY TO BREED.
DODO (GALLOP)

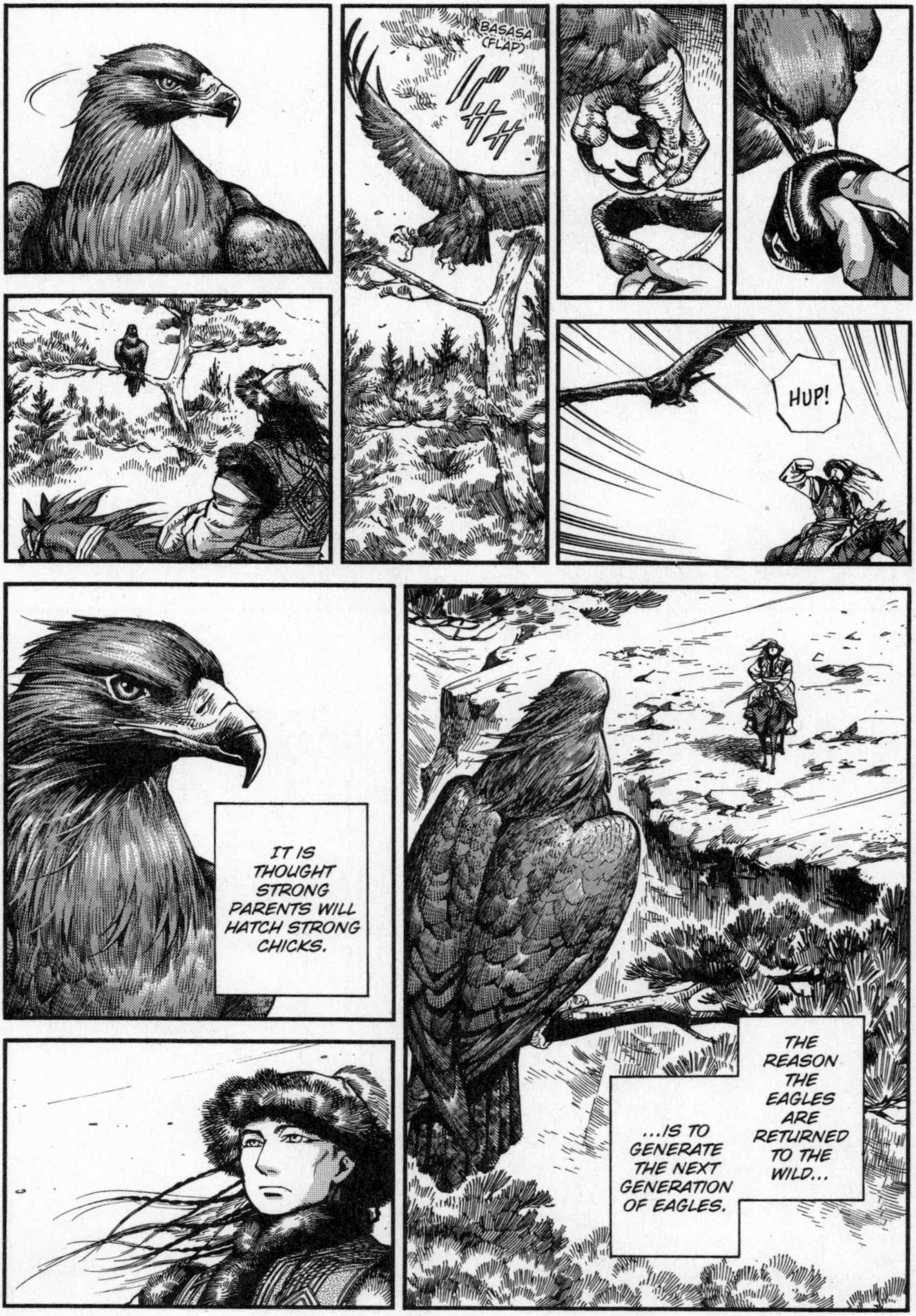
HUP!
BASASA (FLAP)
THE REASON THE EAGLES ARE RETURNED TO THE WILD...
...IS TO GENERATE THE NEXT GENERATION OF EAGLES.
IT IS THOUGHT STRONG PARENTS WILL HATCH STRONG CHICKS.

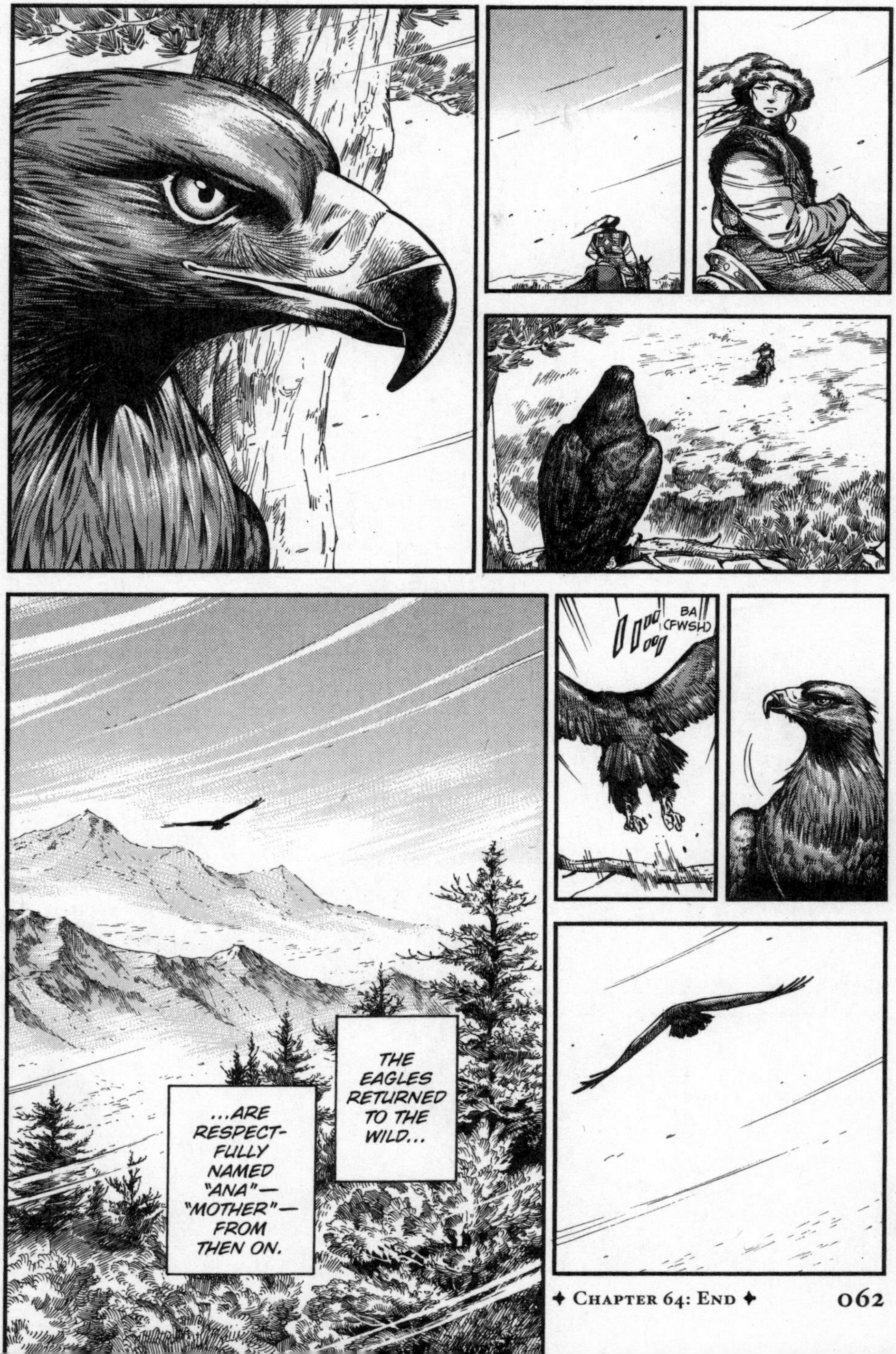
BA (FWSH)
THE EAGLES RETURNED TO THE WILD...
...ARE RESPECT-FULLY NAMED "ANA"—"MOTHER"—FROM THEN ON.

✦ Chapter 64: End ✦

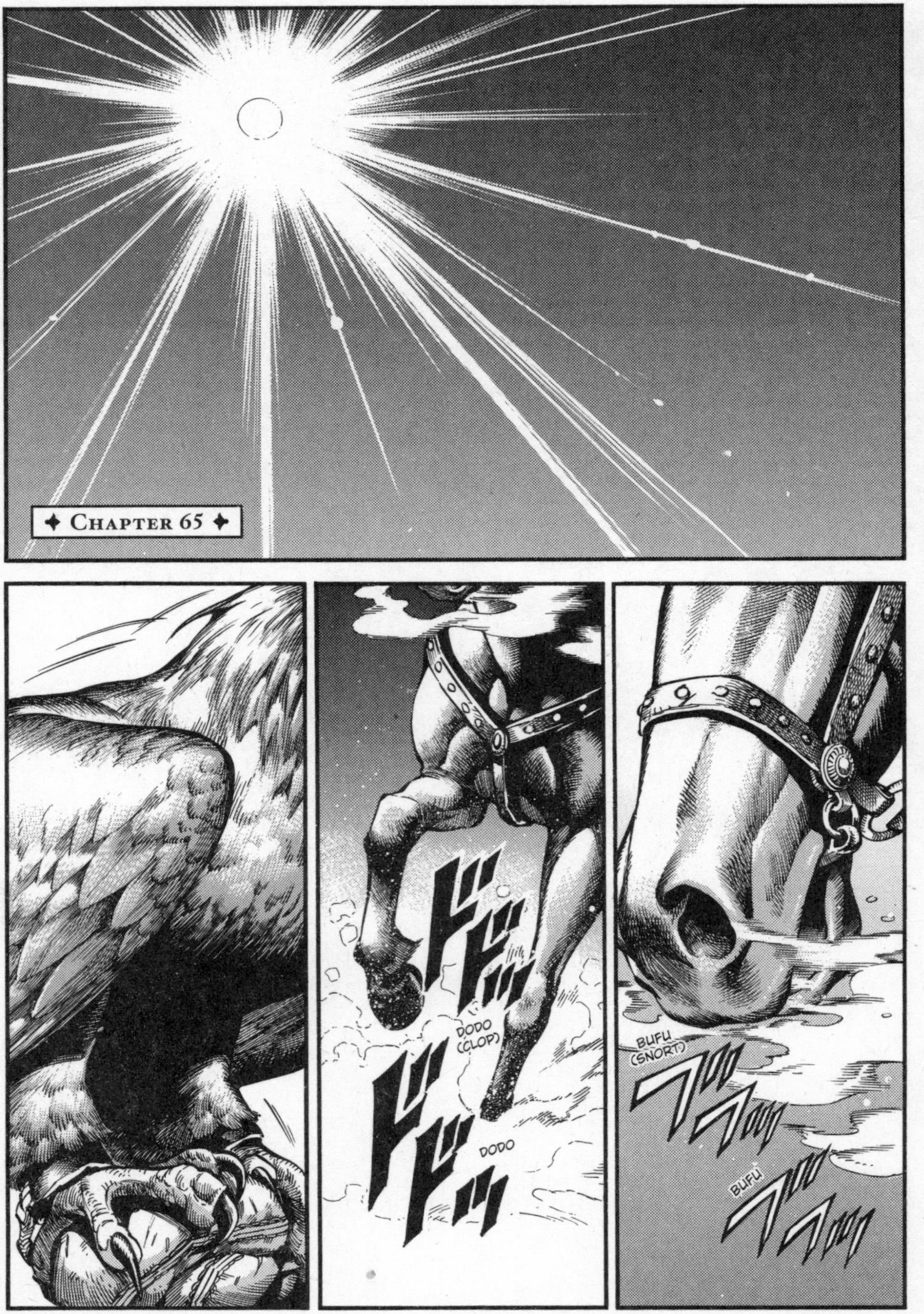
✦ Chapter 65 ✦
BUFU (SNORT)
BUFU
DODO (CLOP)
DODO

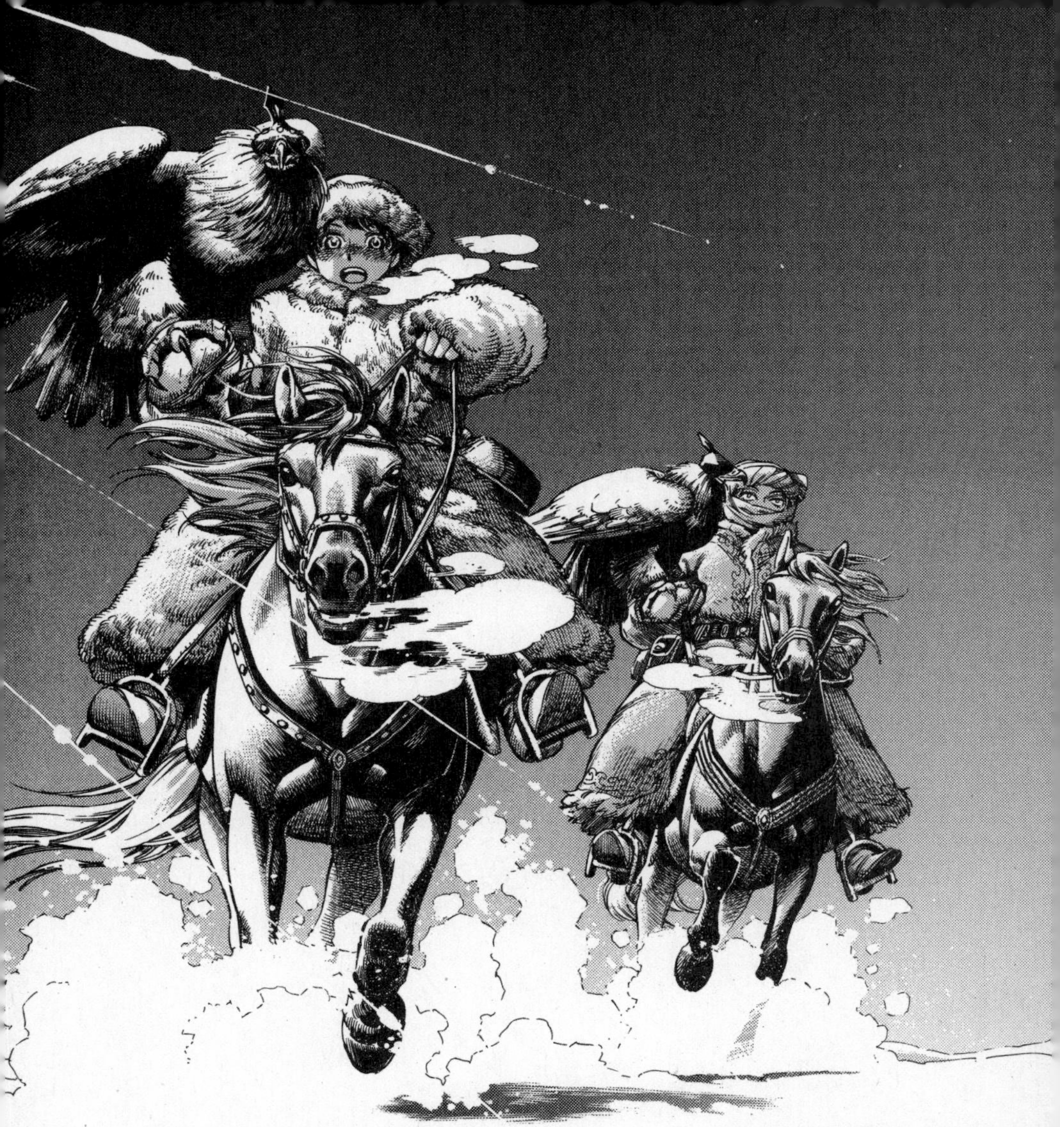

Chapter 65
Mounted Falconry

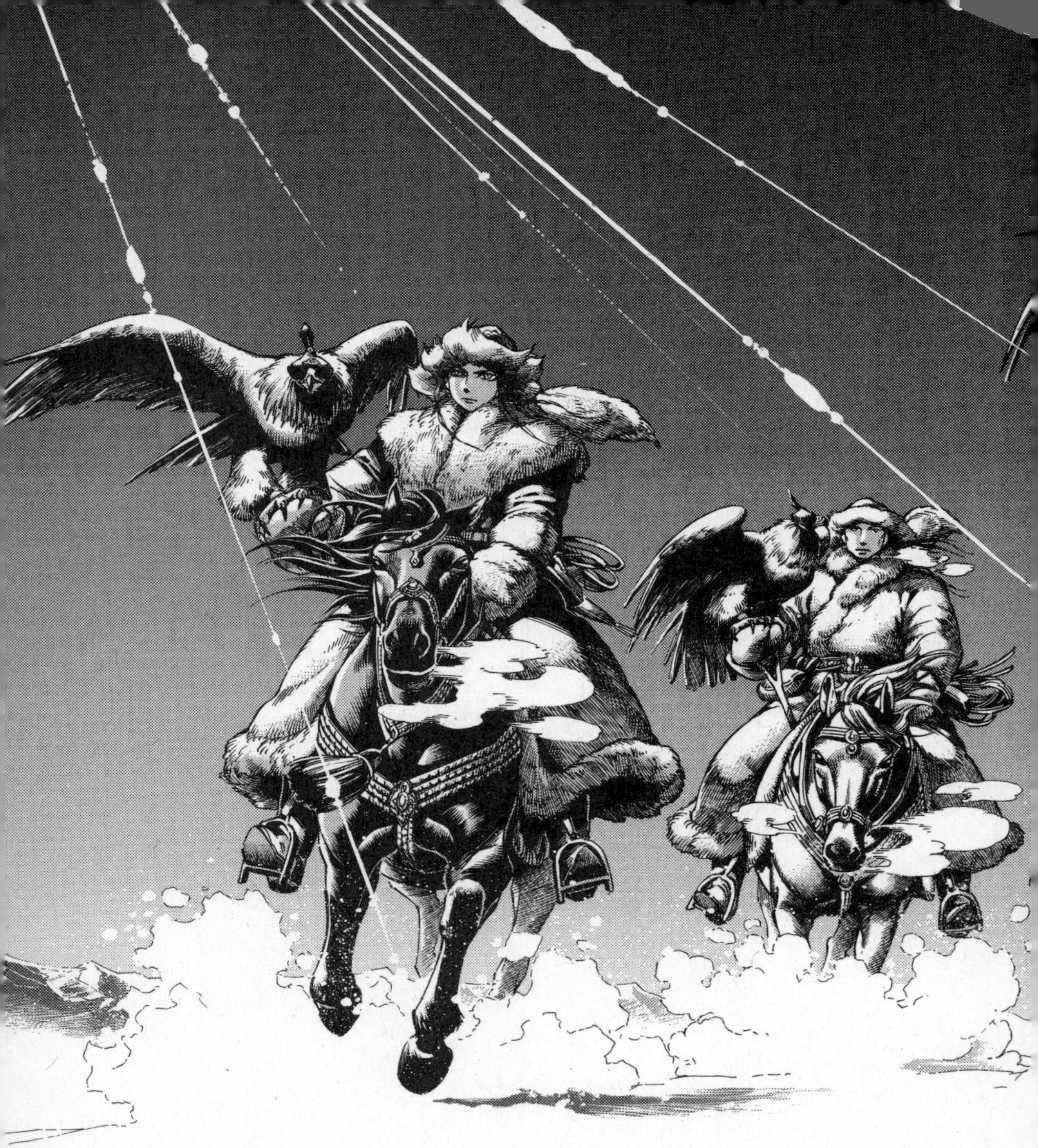

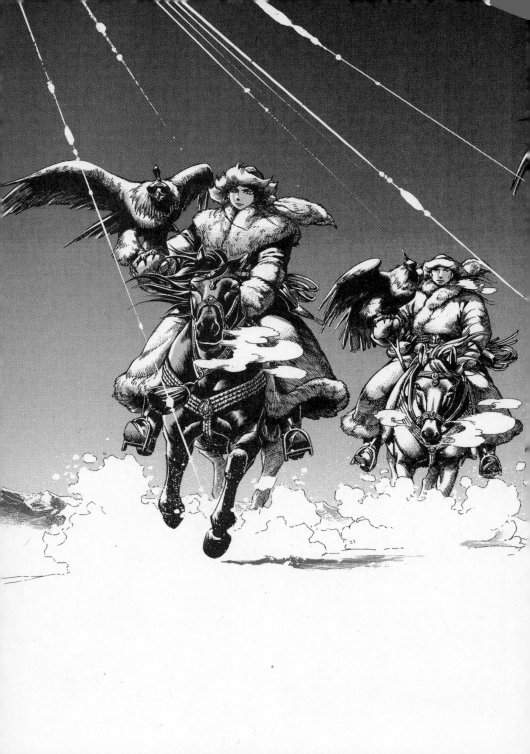

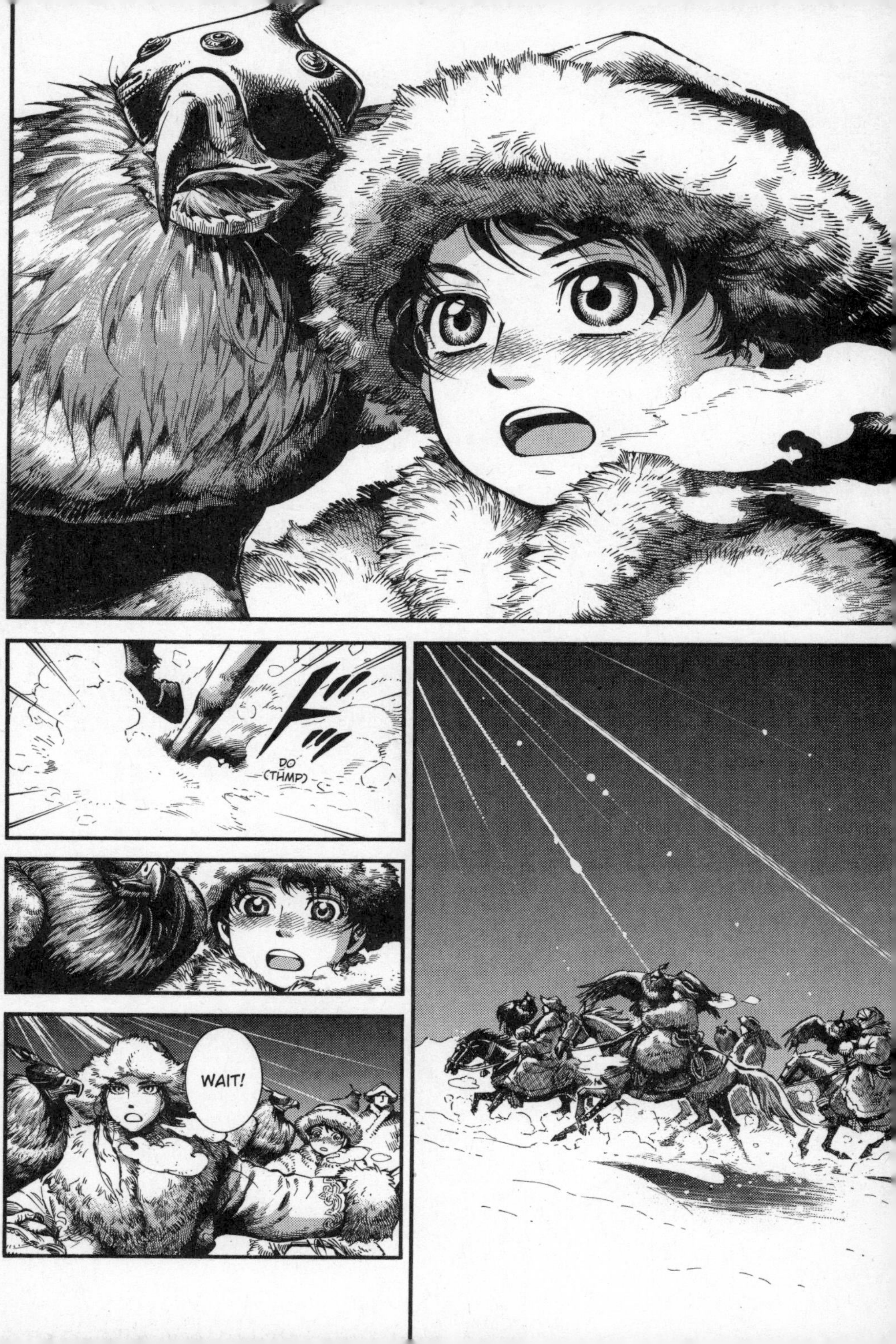
DO
(THMP)
WAIT!

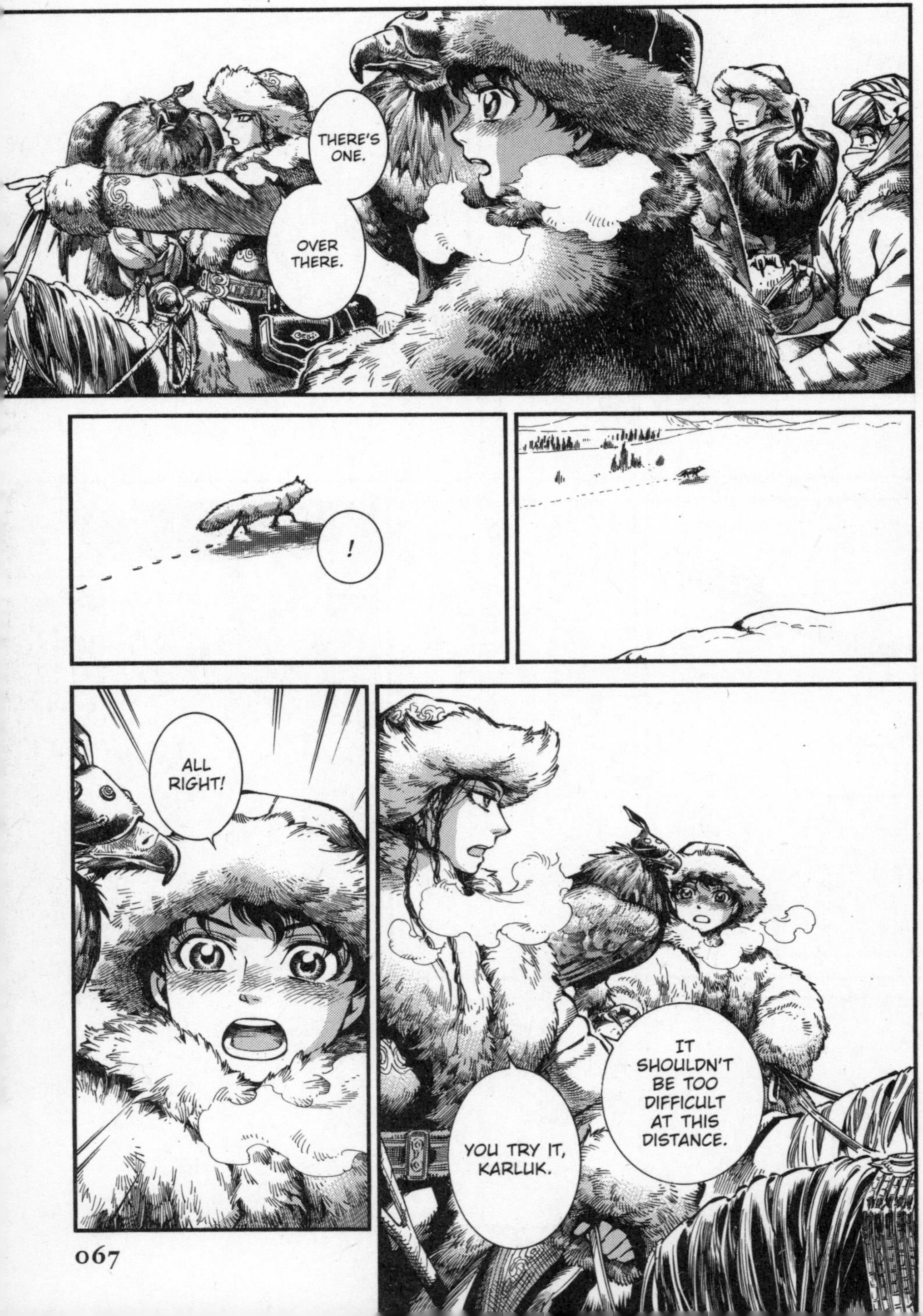
THERE'S ONE.
OVER THERE.
!
IT SHOULDN'T BE TOO DIFFICULT AT THIS DISTANCE.
YOU TRY IT, KARLUK.
ALL RIGHT!

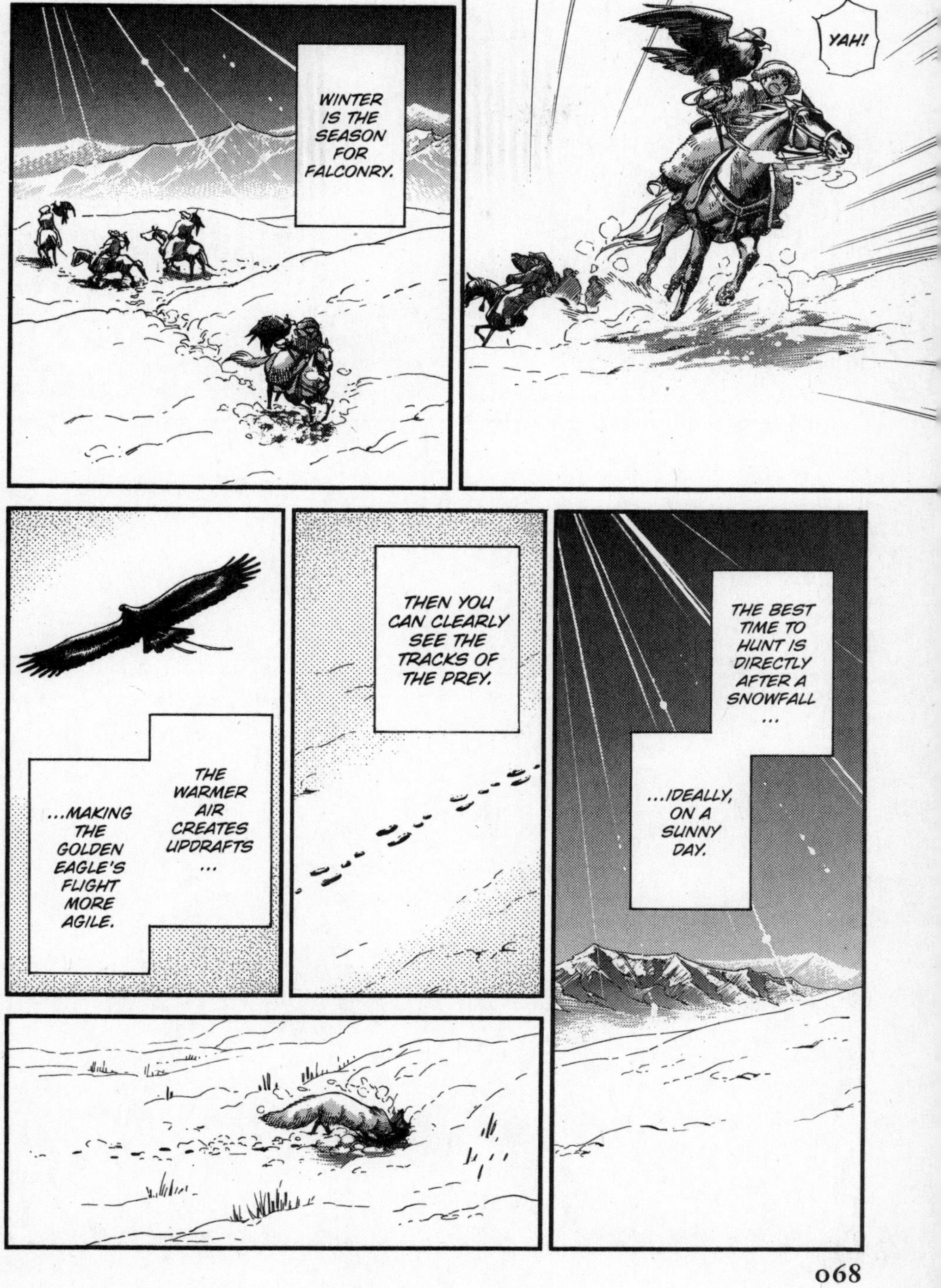
YAH!
WINTER IS THE SEASON FOR FALCONRY.
THE BEST TIME TO HUNT IS DIRECTLY AFTER A SNOWFALL ...
...IDEALLY, ON A SUNNY DAY.
THEN YOU CAN CLEARLY SEE THE TRACKS OF THE PREY.
THE WARMER AIR CREATES UPDRAFTS ...
...MAKING THE GOLDEN EAGLE'S FLIGHT MORE AGILE.

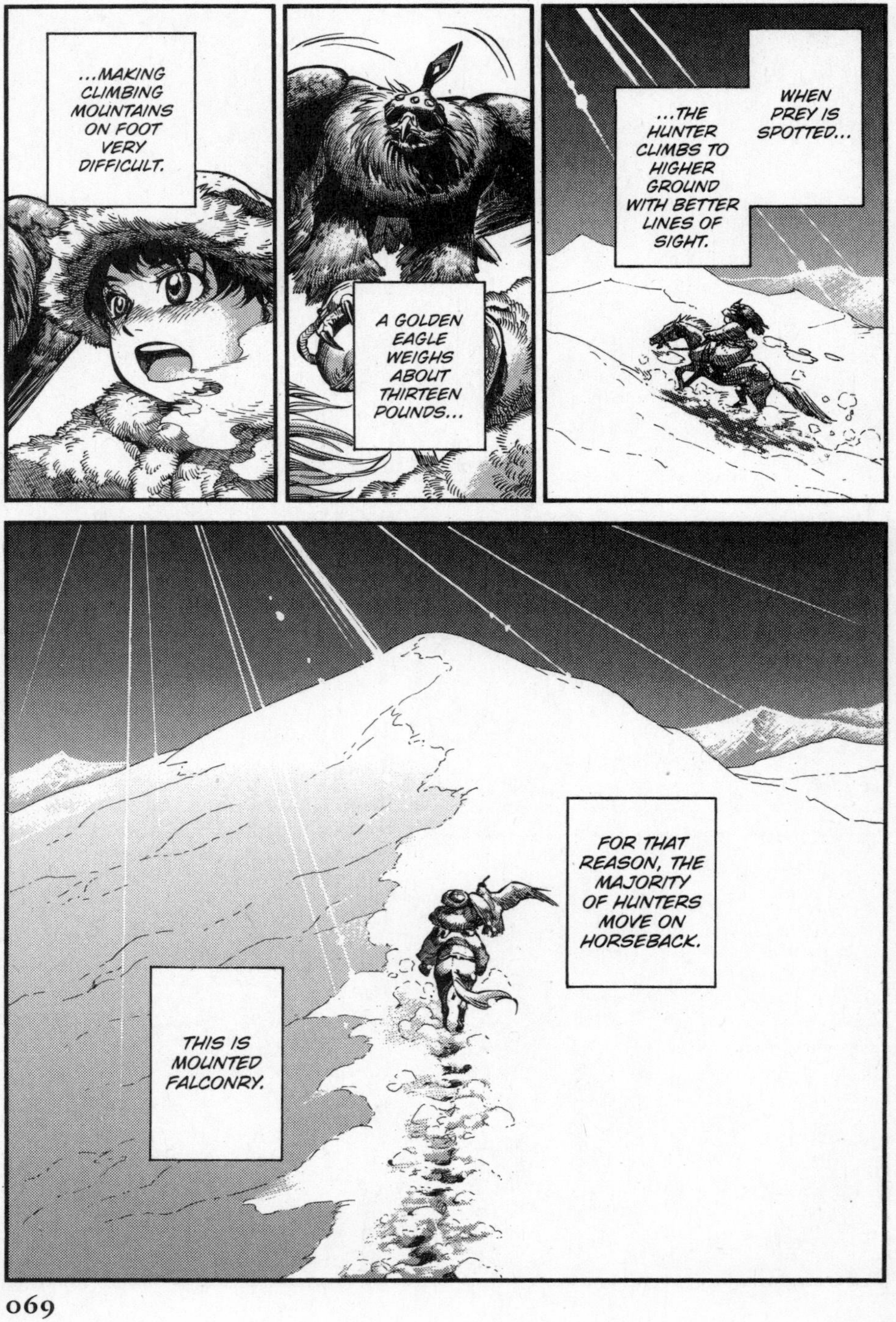
WHEN PREY IS SPOTTED...
...THE HUNTER CLIMBS TO HIGHER GROUND WITH BETTER LINES OF SIGHT.
A GOLDEN EAGLE WEIGHS ABOUT THIRTEEN POUNDS...
...MAKING CLIMBING MOUNTAINS ON FOOT VERY DIFFICULT.
FOR THAT REASON, THE MAJORITY OF HUNTERS MOVE ON HORSEBACK.
THIS IS MOUNTED FALCONRY.

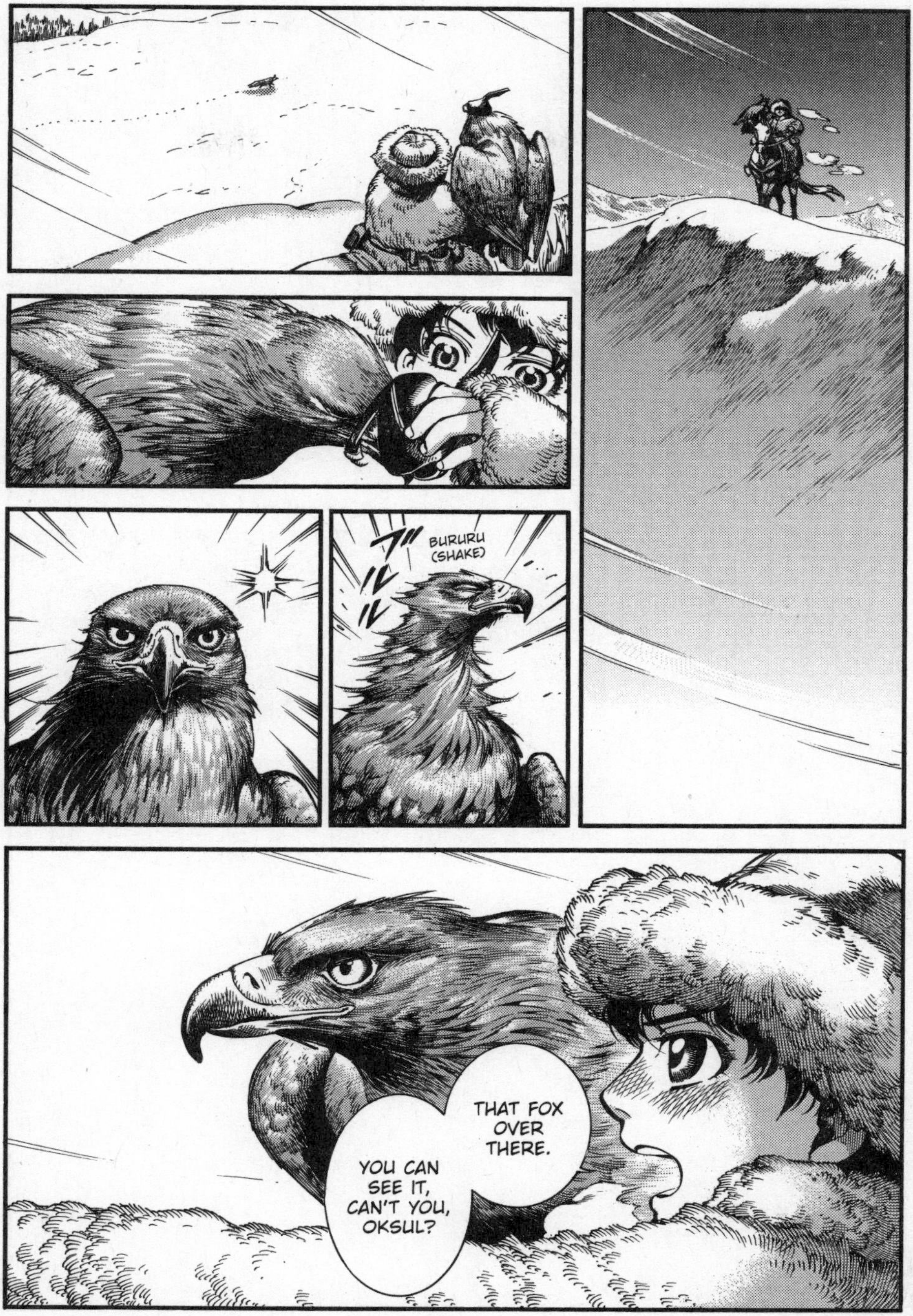
ブルル
BURURU (SHAKE)
THAT FOX OVER THERE.
YOU CAN SEE IT, CAN'T YOU, OKSUL?

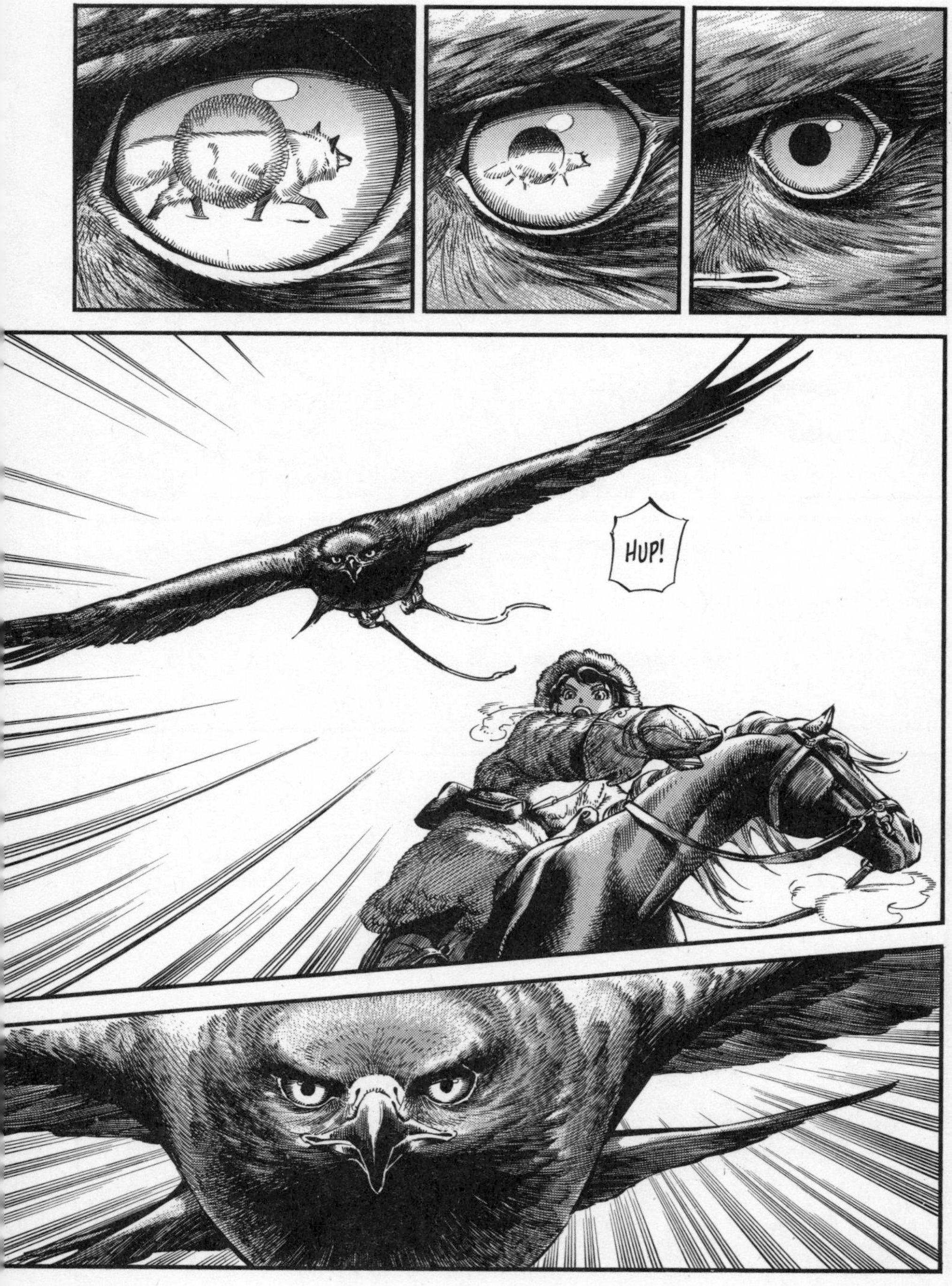
HUP!

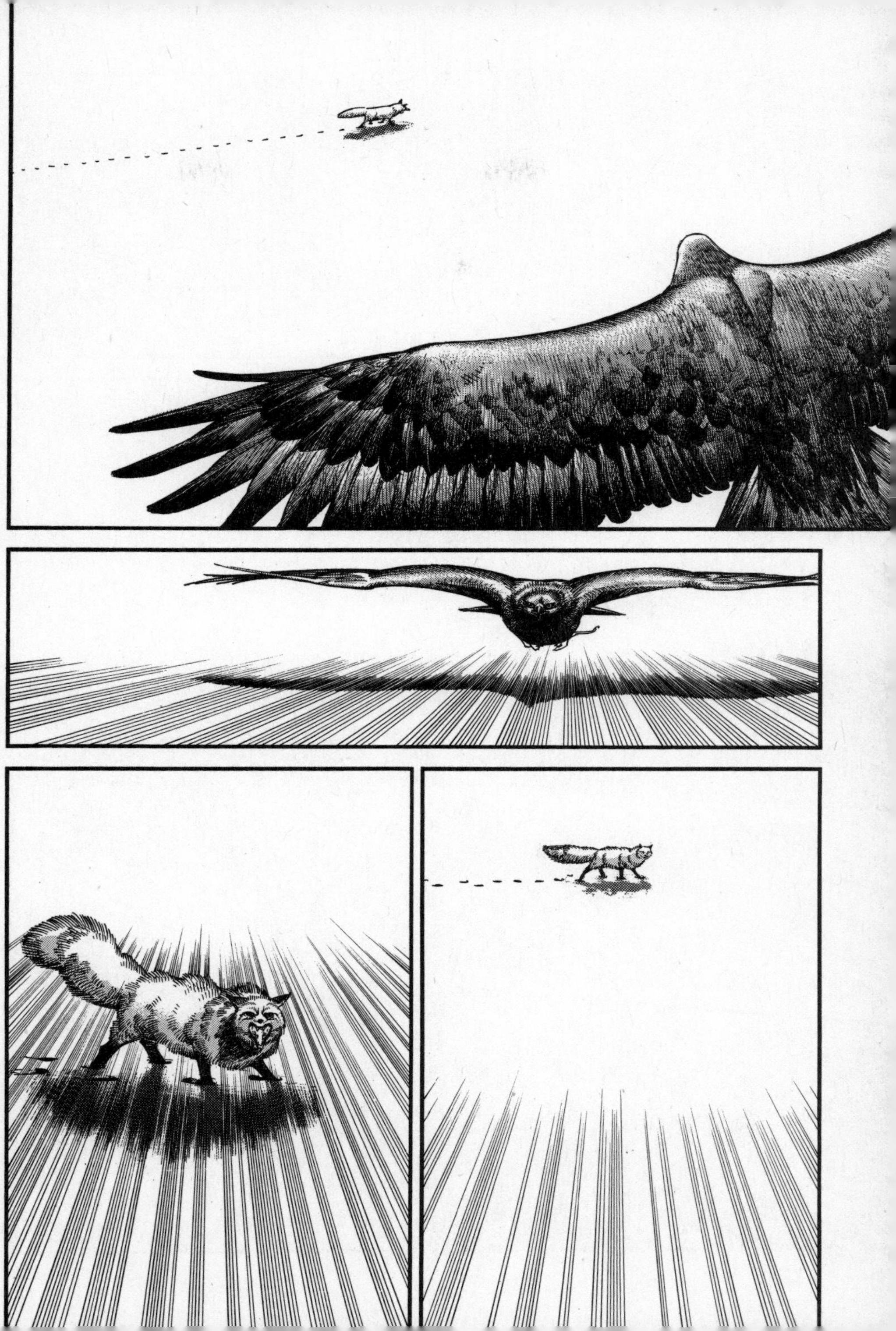

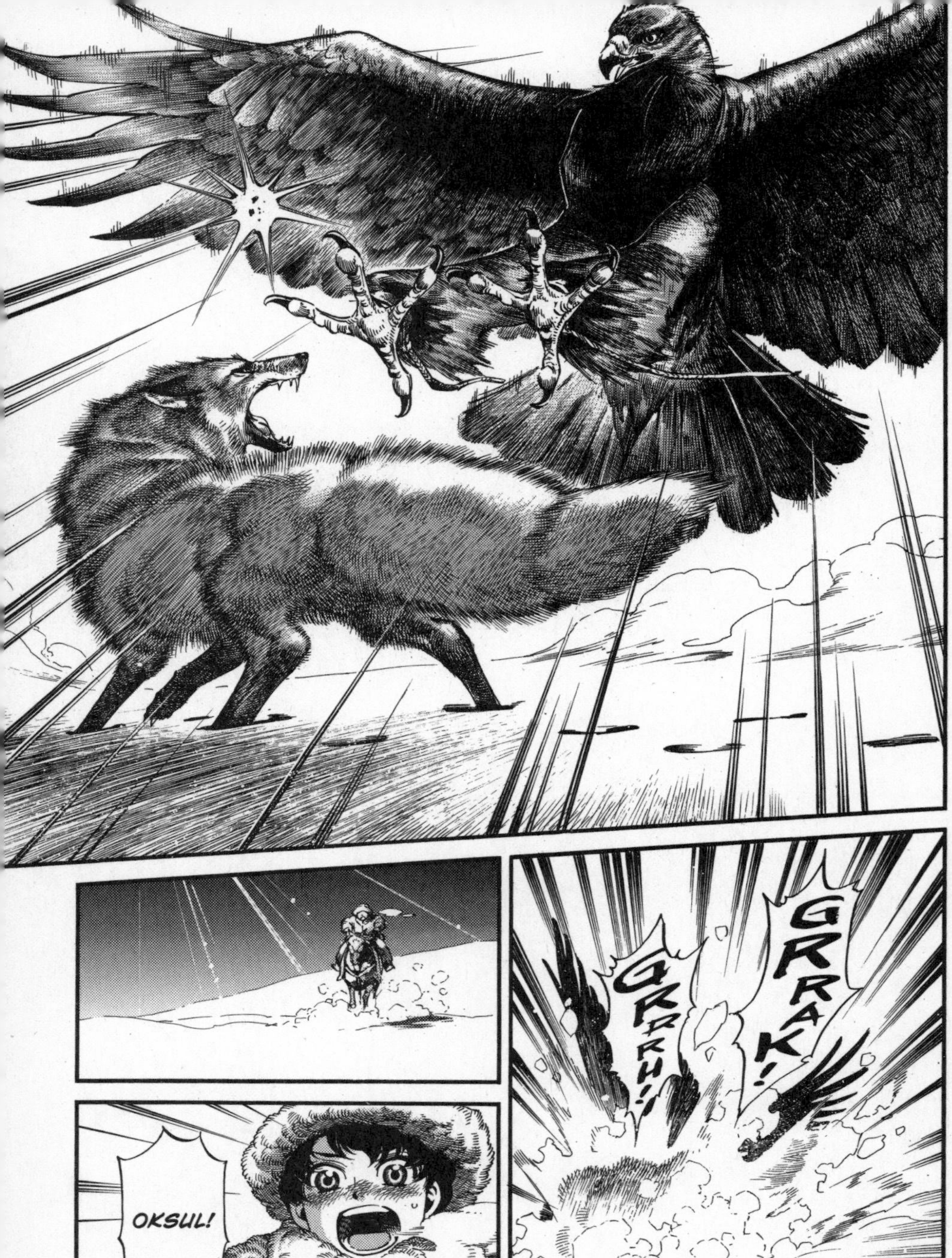
GRRAK!
GRRRUH!!
OKSUL!

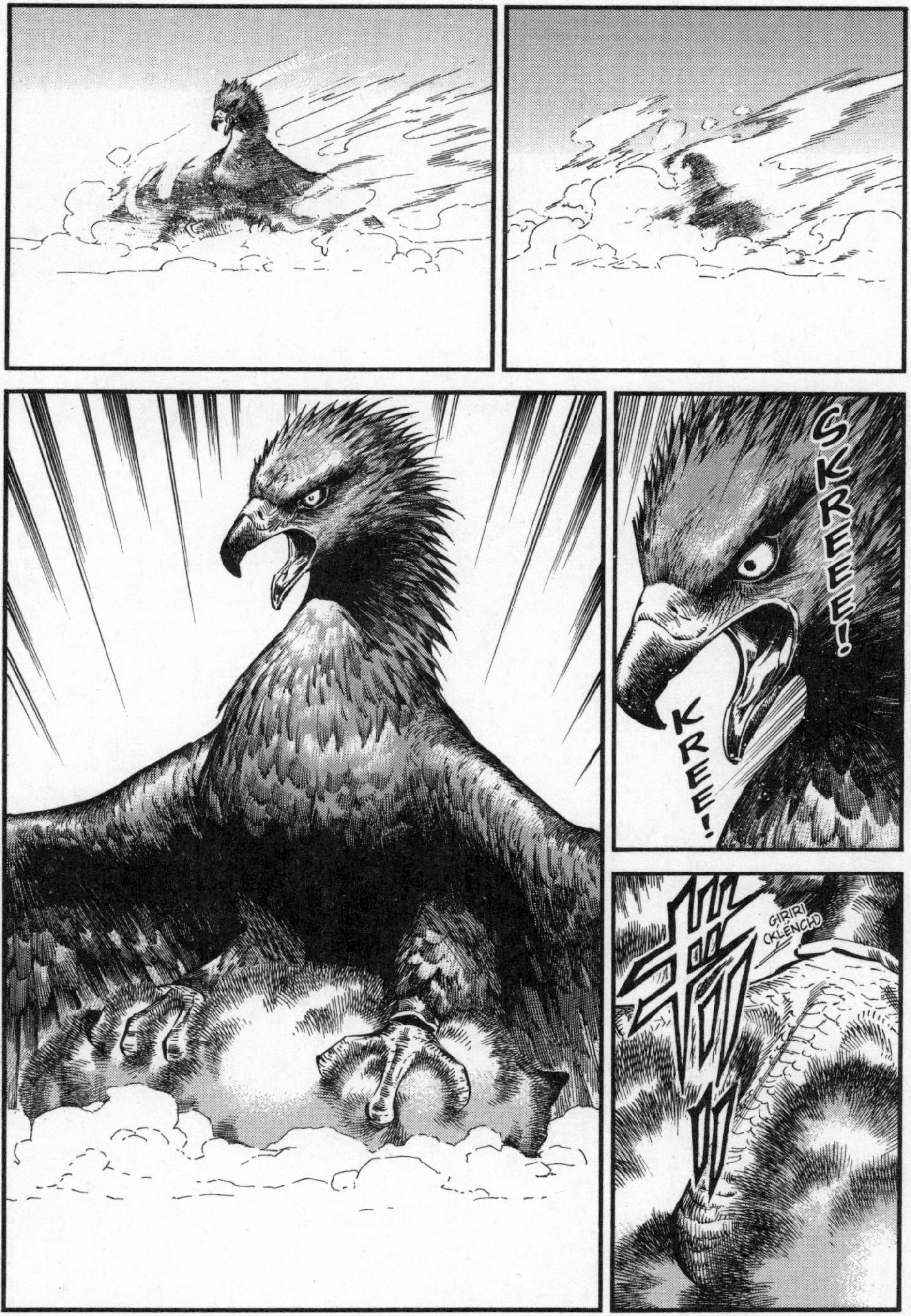
SKREEEE!
KREE!
GIRIRI (KLENCH)

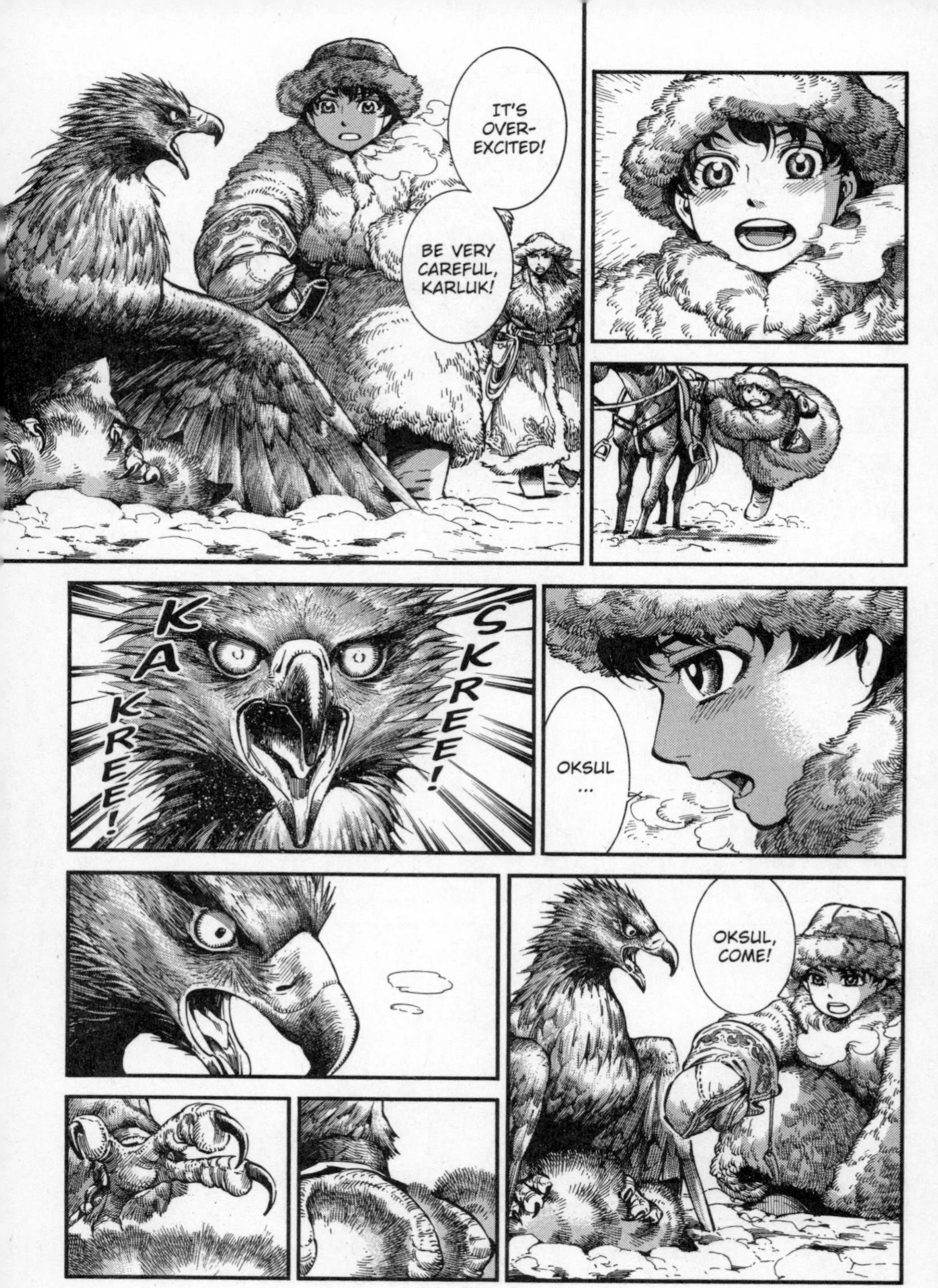
IT'S OVER-EXCITED!
BE VERY CAREFUL, KARLUK!
OKSUL ...
SKREE!
KAKREE!
OKSUL, COME!

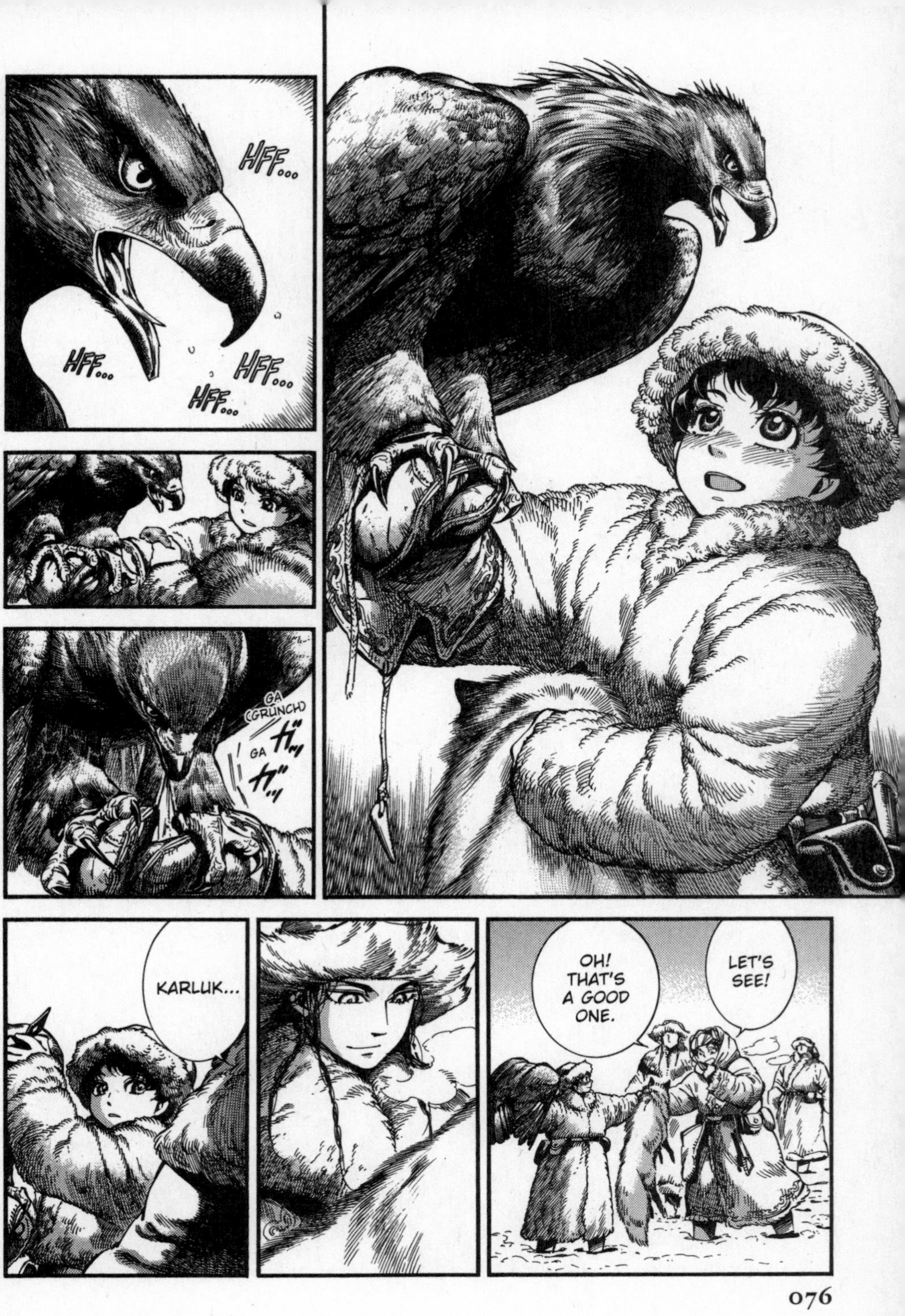
HFF...
HFF...
HFF...
HFF...
GA (GRUNCH)
ガッ
GA
ガッ
LET'S SEE!
OH! THAT'S A GOOD ONE.
KARLUK...

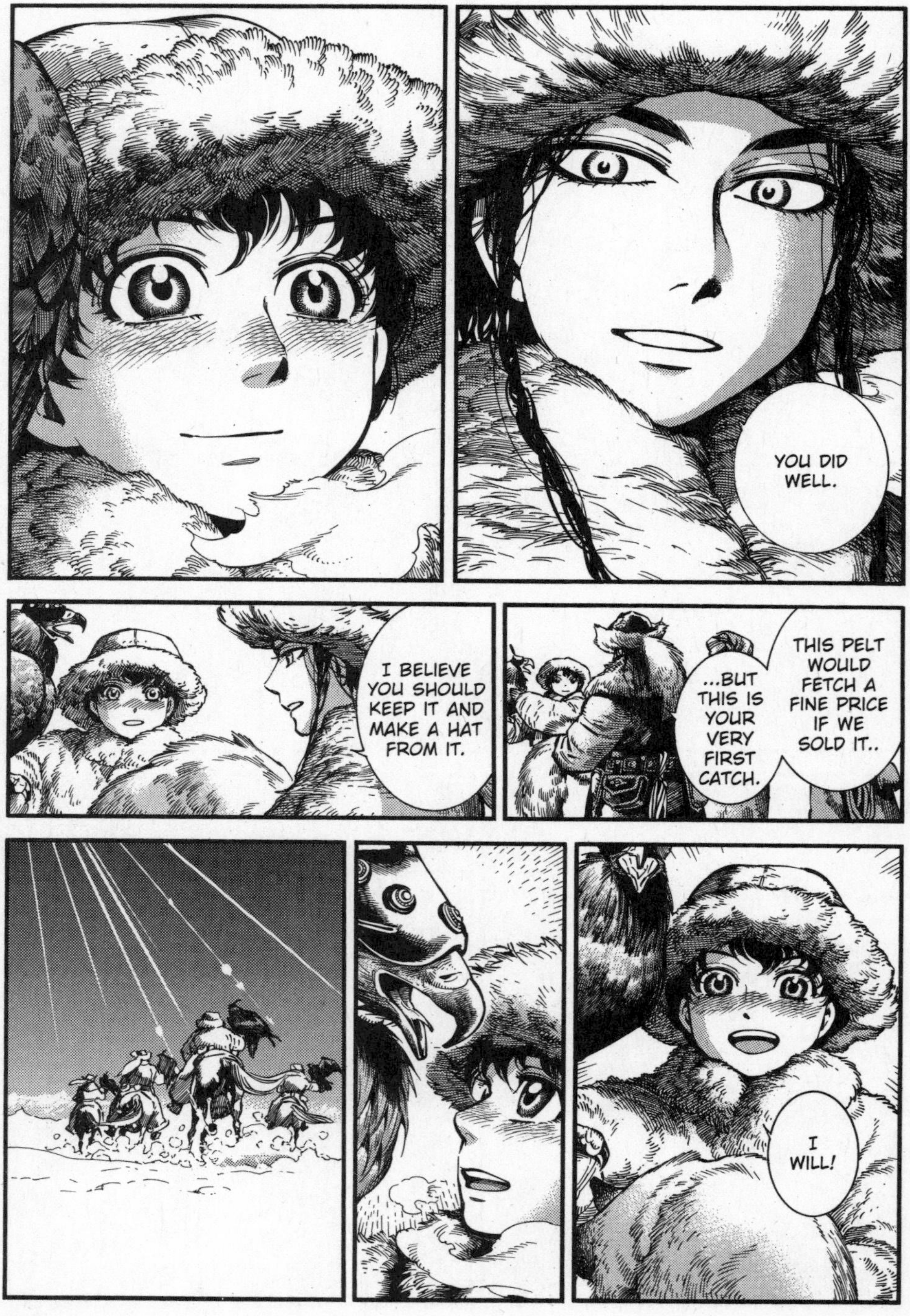
YOU DID WELL.
THIS PELT WOULD FETCH A FINE PRICE IF WE SOLD IT..
...BUT THIS IS YOUR VERY FIRST CATCH.
I BELIEVE YOU SHOULD KEEP IT AND MAKE A HAT FROM IT.
I WILL!

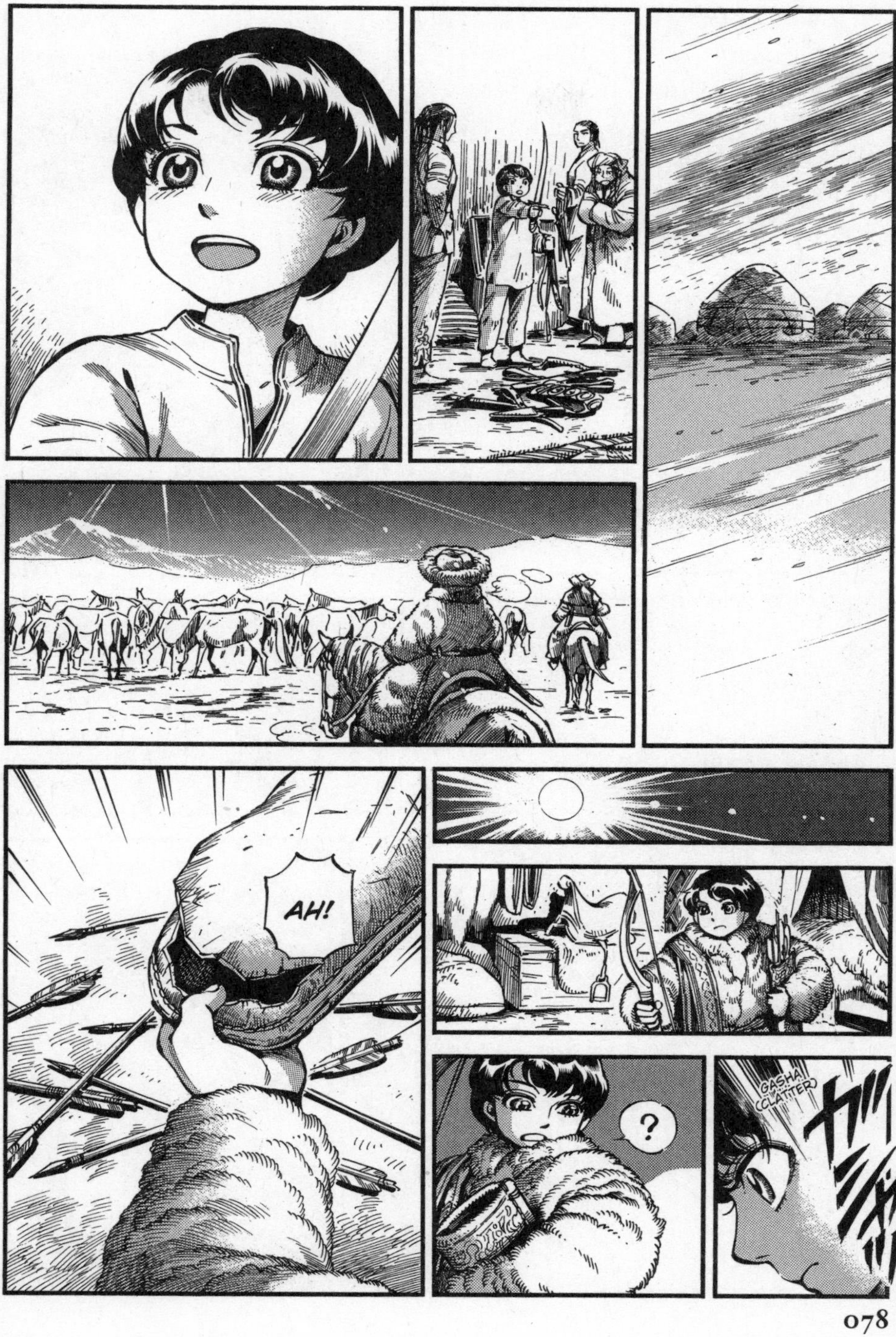
GASHA (CLATTER)
?
AH!

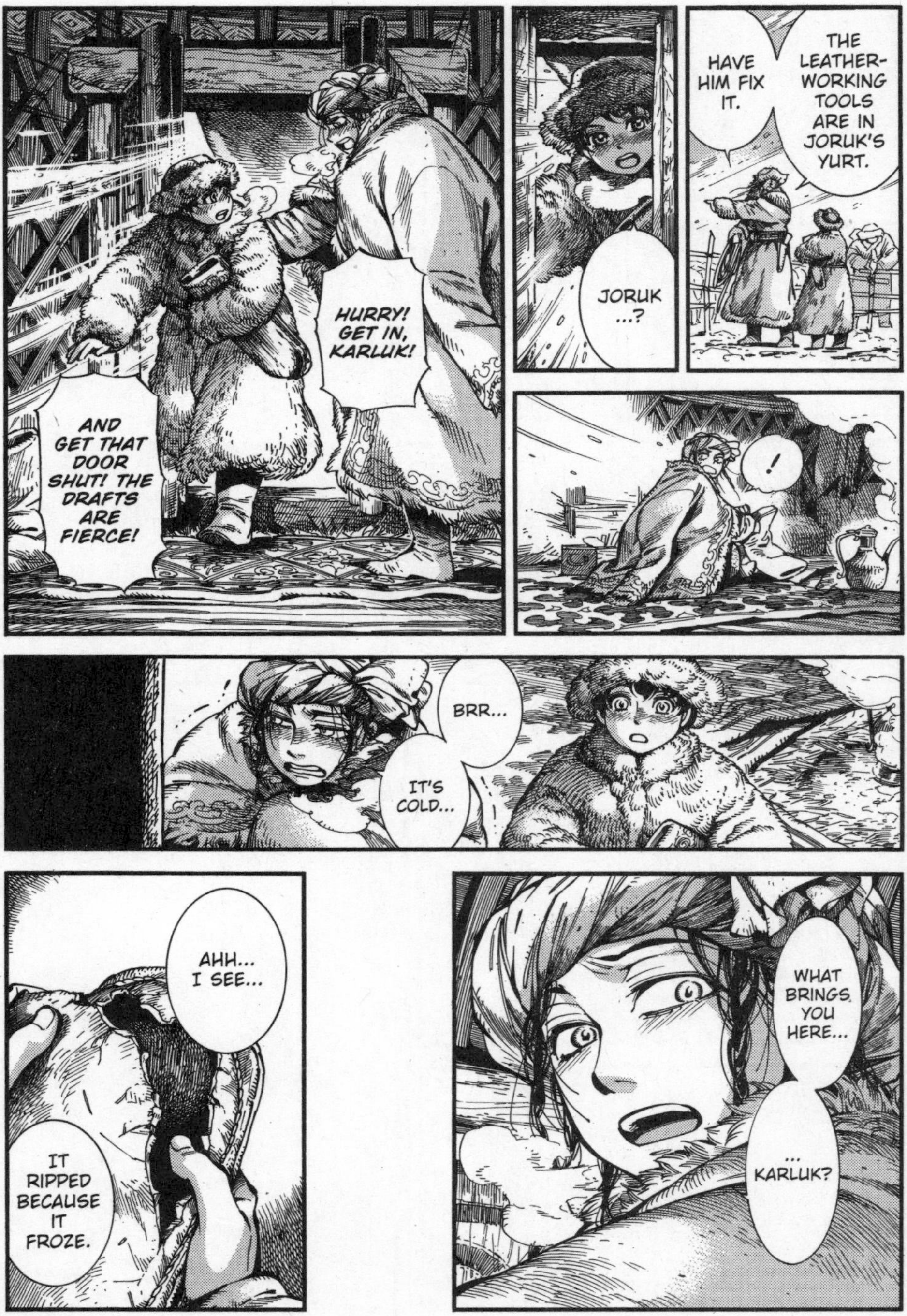

THE LEATHER-WORKING TOOLS ARE IN JORUK'S YURT.
HAVE HIM FIX IT.
JORUK ...?
!
HURRY! GET IN, KARLUK!
AND GET THAT DOOR SHUT! THE DRAFTS ARE FIERCE!
BRR...
IT'S COLD...
WHAT BRINGS YOU HERE...
... KARLUK?
AHH... I SEE...
IT RIPPED BECAUSE IT FROZE.

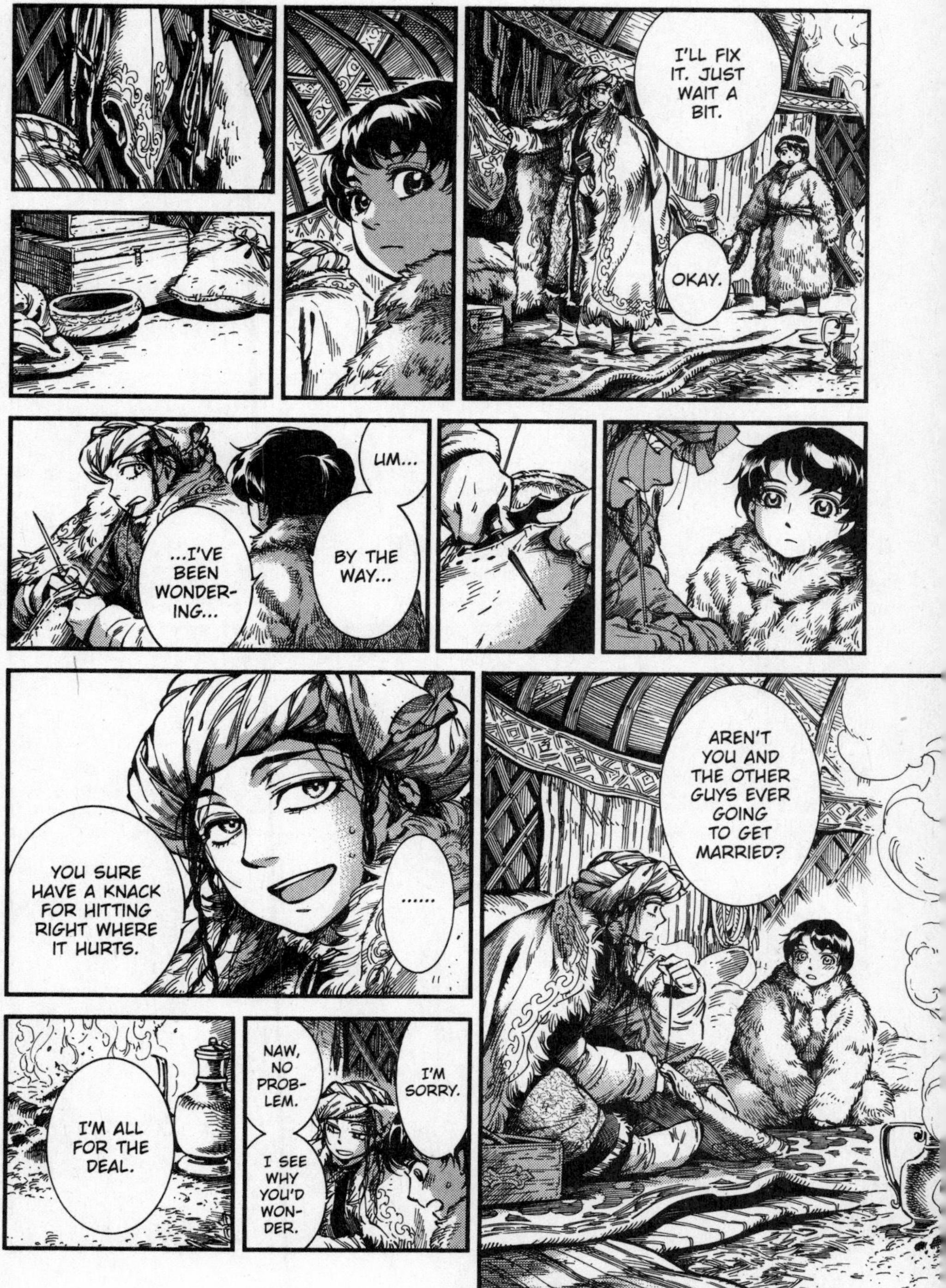
I'LL FIX IT. JUST WAIT A BIT.
OKAY.
UM...
BY THE WAY...
...I'VE BEEN WONDERING...
AREN'T YOU AND THE OTHER GUYS EVER GOING TO GET MARRIED?
......
YOU SURE HAVE A KNACK FOR HITTING RIGHT WHERE IT HURTS.
I'M SORRY.
NAW, NO PROBLEM.
I SEE WHY YOU'D WONDER.
I'M ALL FOR THE DEAL.

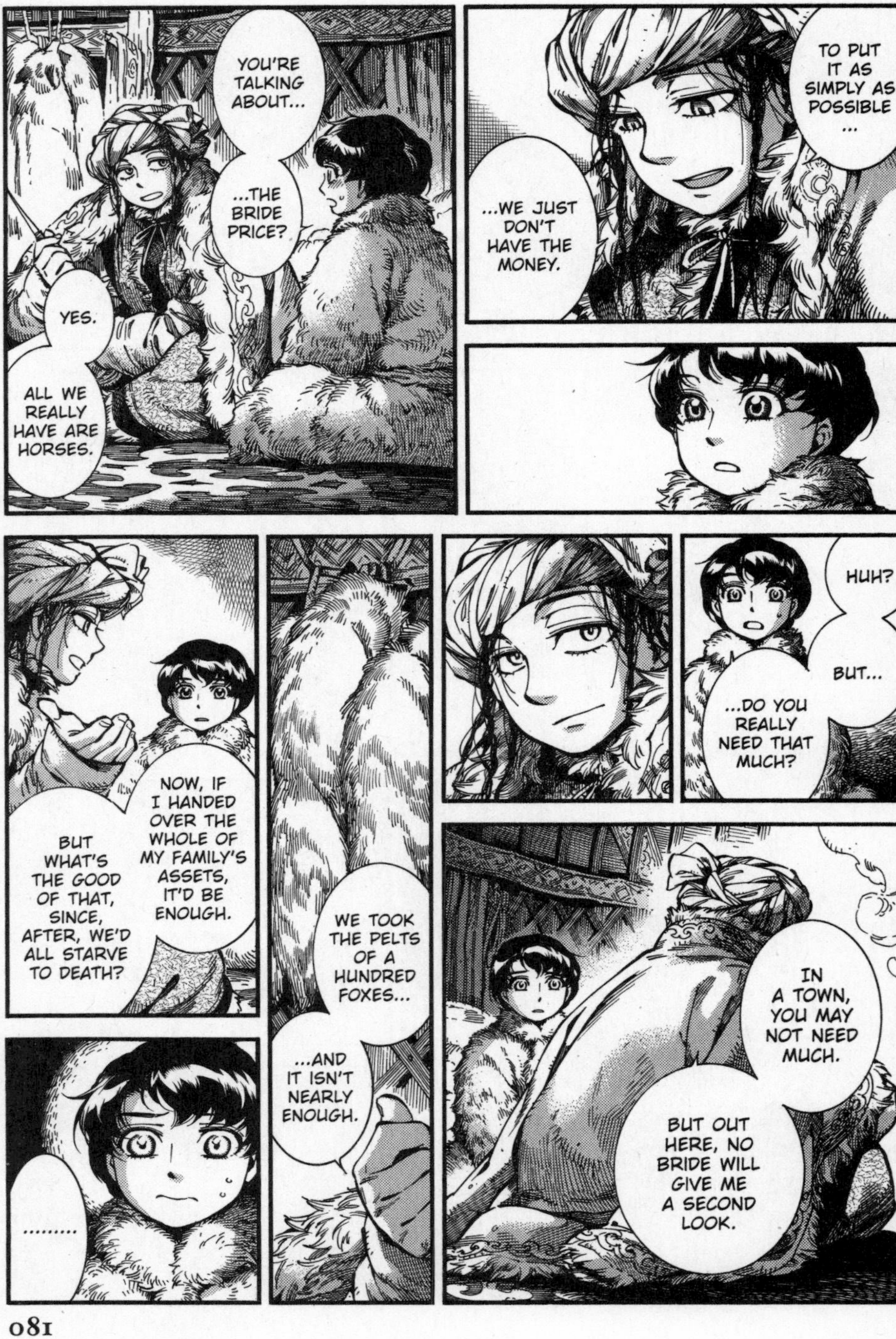
TO PUT IT AS SIMPLY AS POSSIBLE ...
...WE JUST DON'T HAVE THE MONEY.
YOU'RE TALKING ABOUT...
...THE BRIDE PRICE?
YES.
ALL WE REALLY HAVE ARE HORSES.
HUH?
BUT...
...DO YOU REALLY NEED THAT MUCH?
IN A TOWN, YOU MAY NOT NEED MUCH.
BUT OUT HERE, NO BRIDE WILL GIVE ME A SECOND LOOK.
WE TOOK THE PELTS OF A HUNDRED FOXES...
...AND IT ISN'T NEARLY ENOUGH.
NOW, IF I HANDED OVER THE WHOLE OF MY FAMILY'S ASSETS, IT'D BE ENOUGH.
BUT WHAT'S THE GOOD OF THAT, SINCE, AFTER, WE'D ALL STARVE TO DEATH?
....

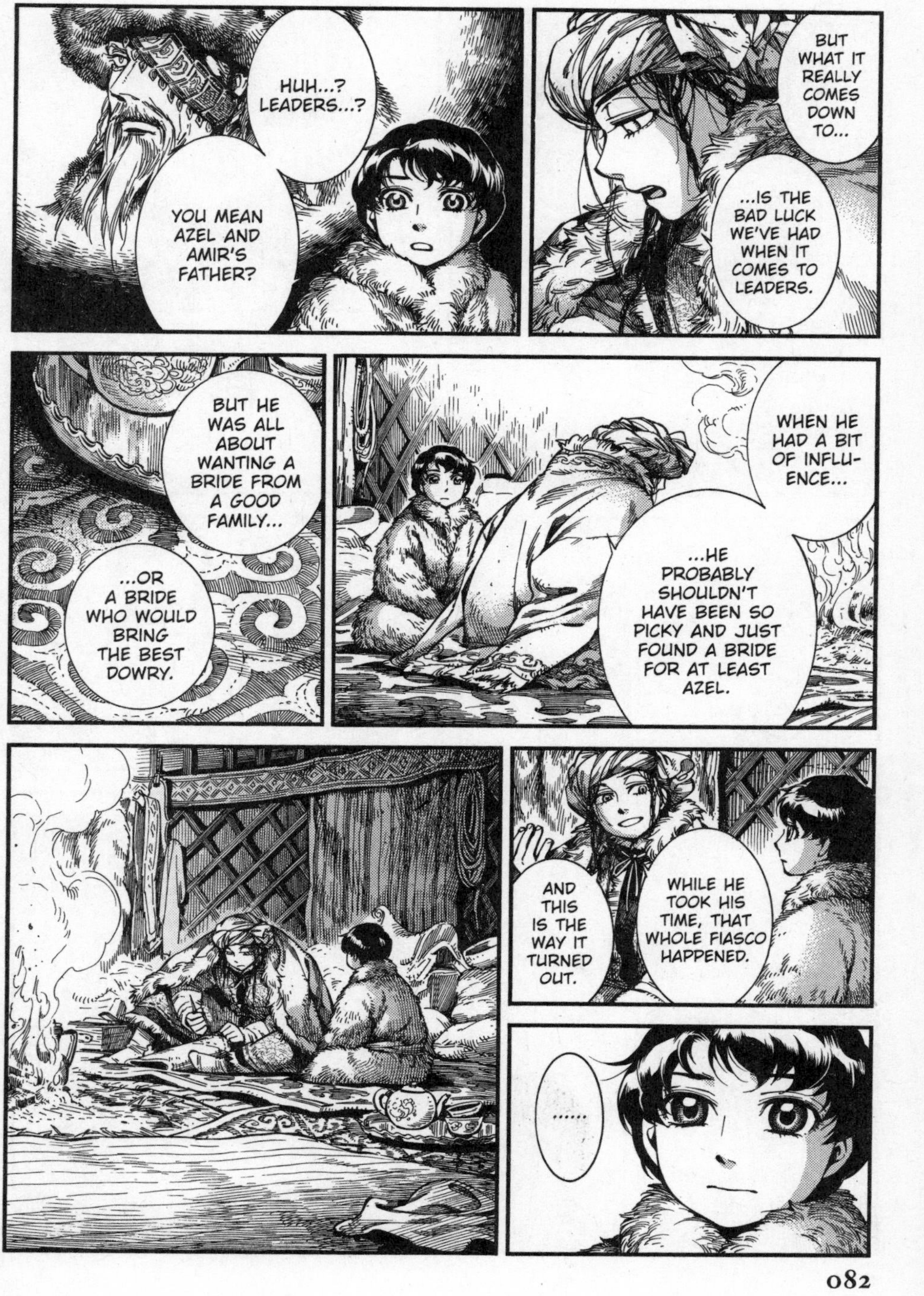
BUT WHAT IT REALLY COMES DOWN TO...
...IS THE BAD LUCK WE'VE HAD WHEN IT COMES TO LEADERS.
HUH...? LEADERS...?
YOU MEAN AZEL AND AMIR'S FATHER?
WHEN HE HAD A BIT OF INFLU-ENCE...
...HE PROBABLY SHOULDN'T HAVE BEEN SO PICKY AND JUST FOUND A BRIDE FOR AT LEAST AZEL.
BUT HE WAS ALL ABOUT WANTING A BRIDE FROM A GOOD FAMILY...
...OR A BRIDE WHO WOULD BRING THE BEST DOWRY.
WHILE HE TOOK HIS TIME, THAT WHOLE FIASCO HAPPENED.
AND THIS IS THE WAY IT TURNED OUT.
......

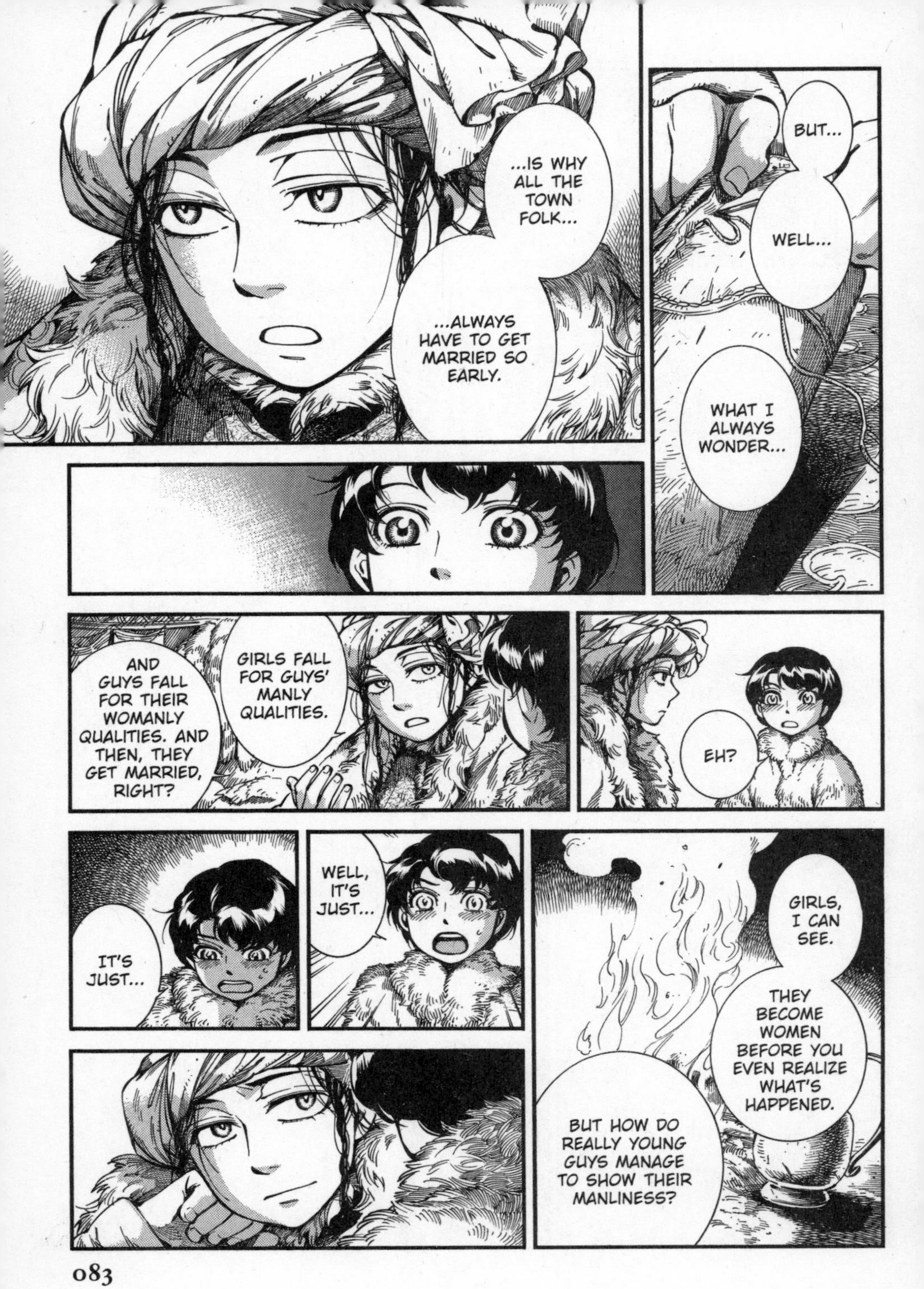
BUT...
WELL...
WHAT I ALWAYS WONDER...
...IS WHY ALL THE TOWN FOLK...
...ALWAYS HAVE TO GET MARRIED SO EARLY.
EH?
GIRLS FALL FOR GUYS' MANLY QUALITIES.
AND GUYS FALL FOR THEIR WOMANLY QUALITIES. AND THEN, THEY GET MARRIED, RIGHT?
GIRLS, I CAN SEE.
THEY BECOME WOMEN BEFORE YOU EVEN REALIZE WHAT'S HAPPENED.
BUT HOW DO REALLY YOUNG GUYS MANAGE TO SHOW THEIR MANLINESS?
WELL, IT'S JUST...
IT'S JUST...

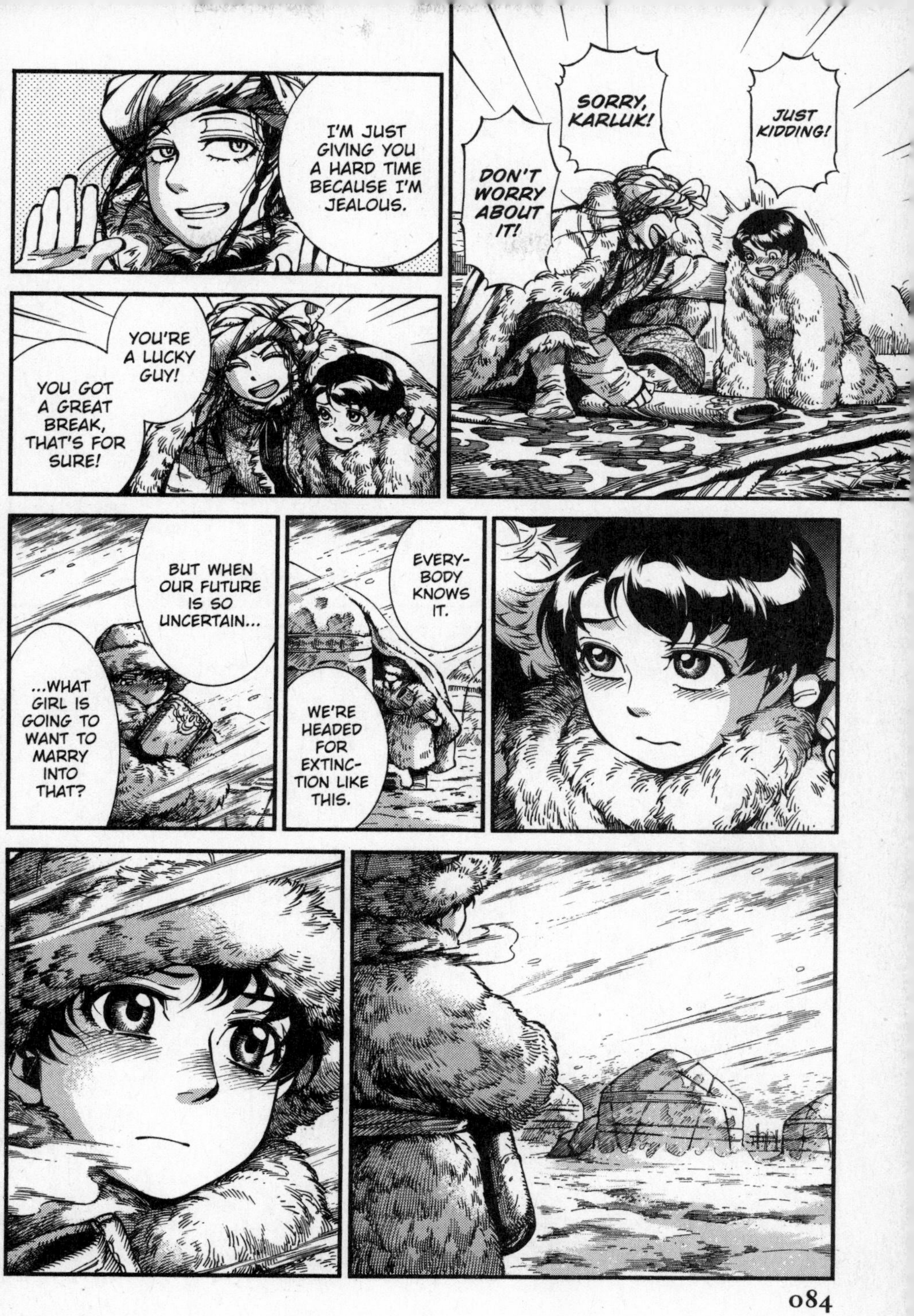
JUST KIDDING!
SORRY, KARLUK!
DON'T WORRY ABOUT IT!
I'M JUST GIVING YOU A HARD TIME BECAUSE I'M JEALOUS.
YOU'RE A LUCKY GUY!
YOU GOT A GREAT BREAK, THAT'S FOR SURE!
EVERY-BODY KNOWS IT.
WE'RE HEADED FOR EXTINC-TION LIKE THIS.
BUT WHEN OUR FUTURE IS SO UNCERTAIN...
...WHAT GIRL IS GOING TO WANT TO MARRY INTO THAT?

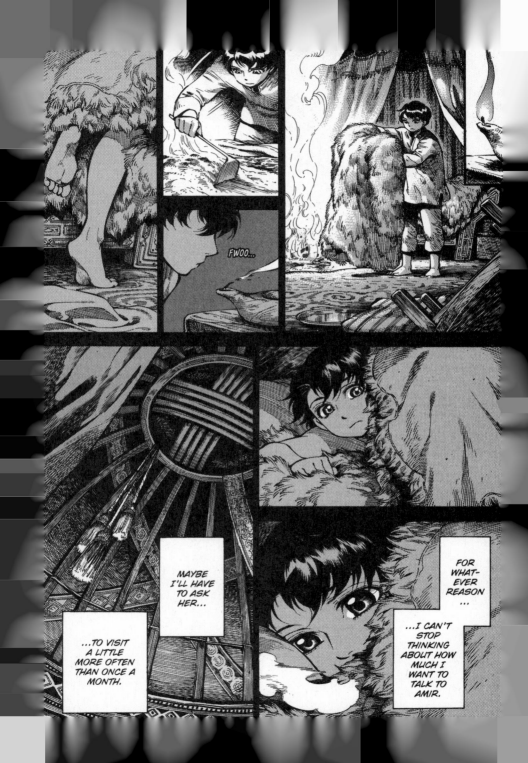

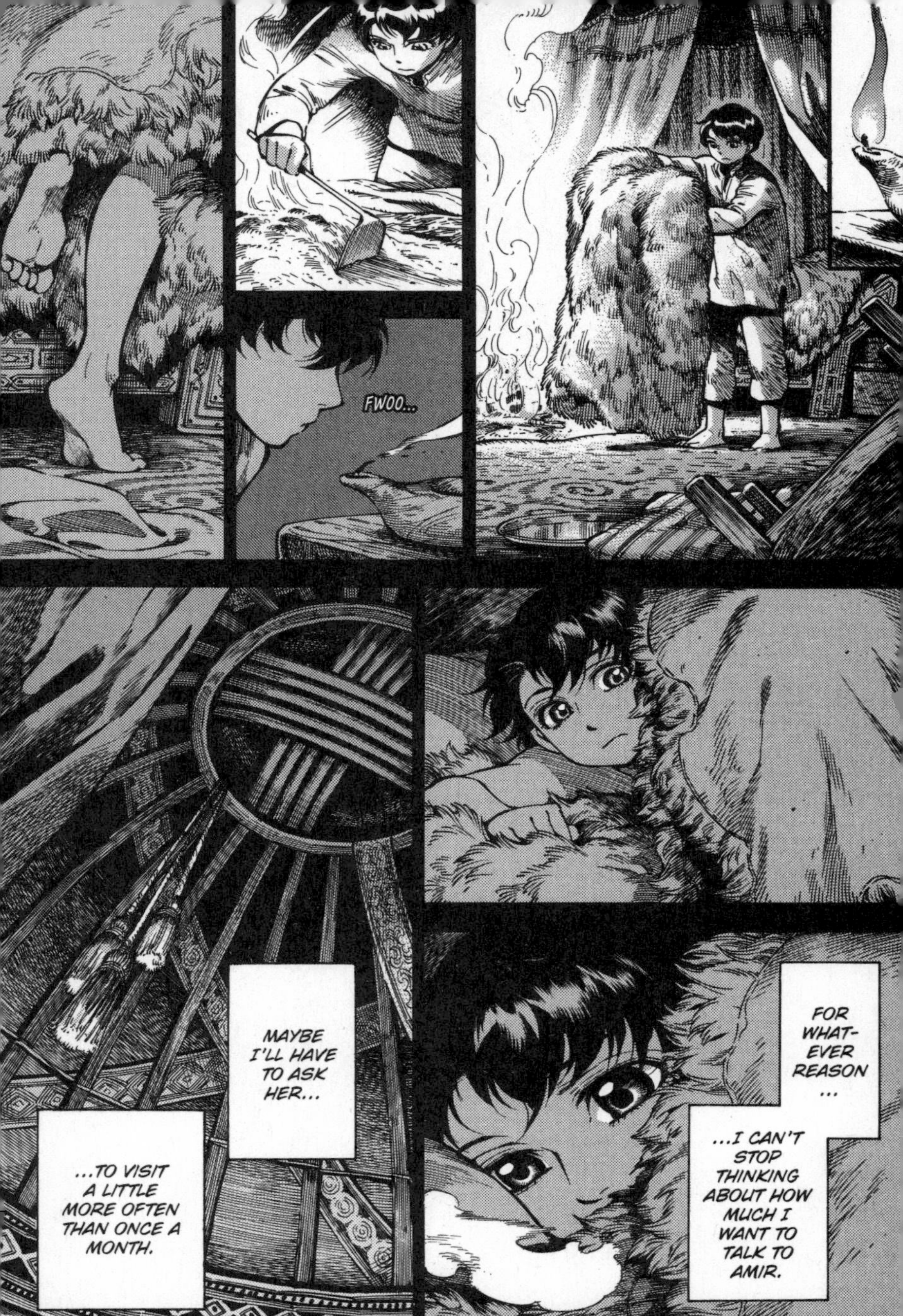
FWOO...
FOR WHATEVER REASON...
...I CAN'T STOP THINKING ABOUT HOW MUCH I WANT TO TALK TO AMIR.
MAYBE I'LL HAVE TO ASK HER...
...TO VISIT A LITTLE MORE OFTEN THAN ONCE A MONTH.

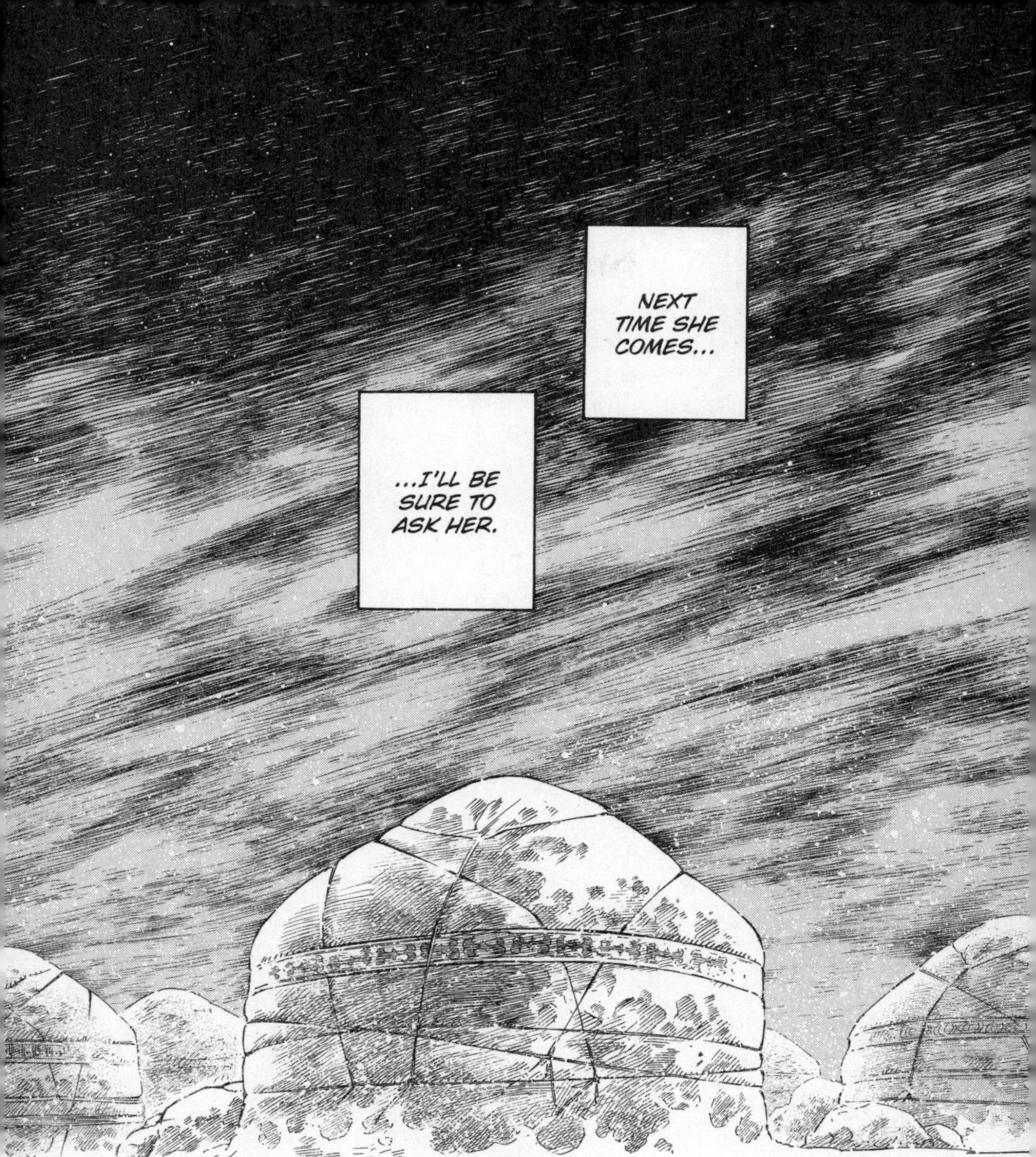
NEXT TIME SHE COMES...
...I'LL BE SURE TO ASK HER.

✦ Chapter 65: End ✦

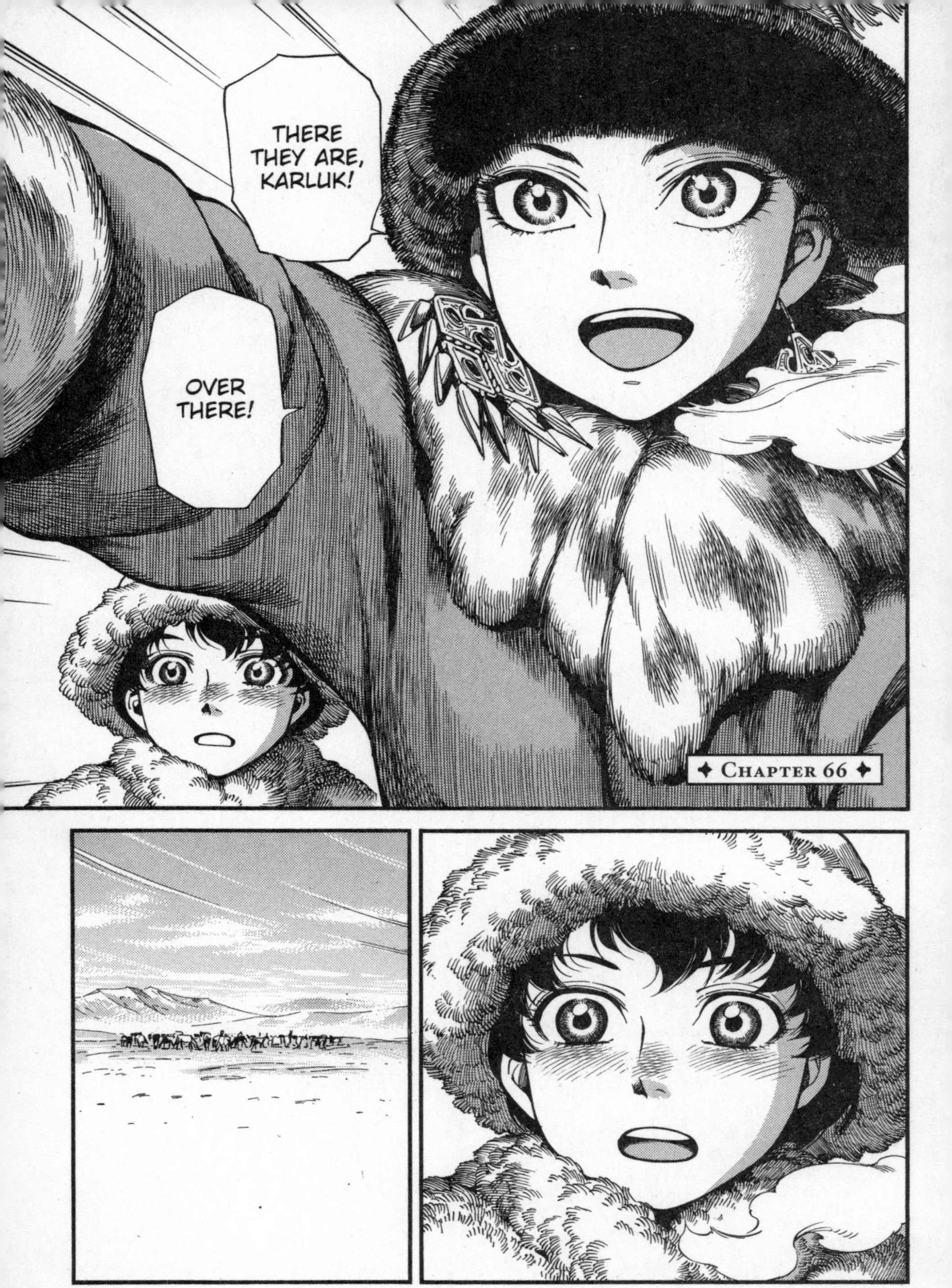
THERE THEY ARE, KARLUK!
OVER THERE!
Chapter 66

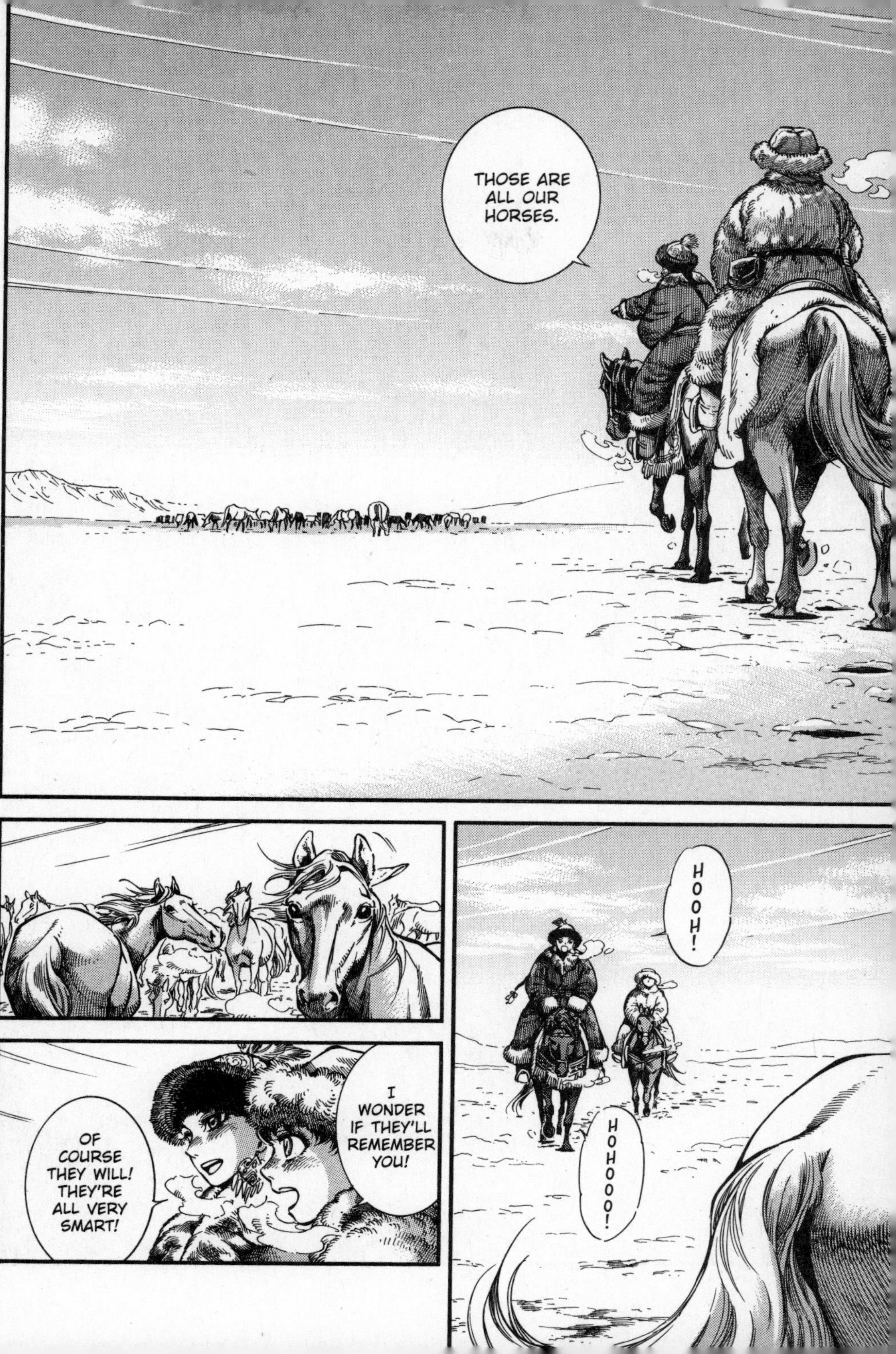
THOSE ARE ALL OUR HORSES.
HOOOH!
HOHOOOO!
I WONDER IF THEY'LL REMEMBER YOU!
OF COURSE THEY WILL! THEY'RE ALL VERY SMART!

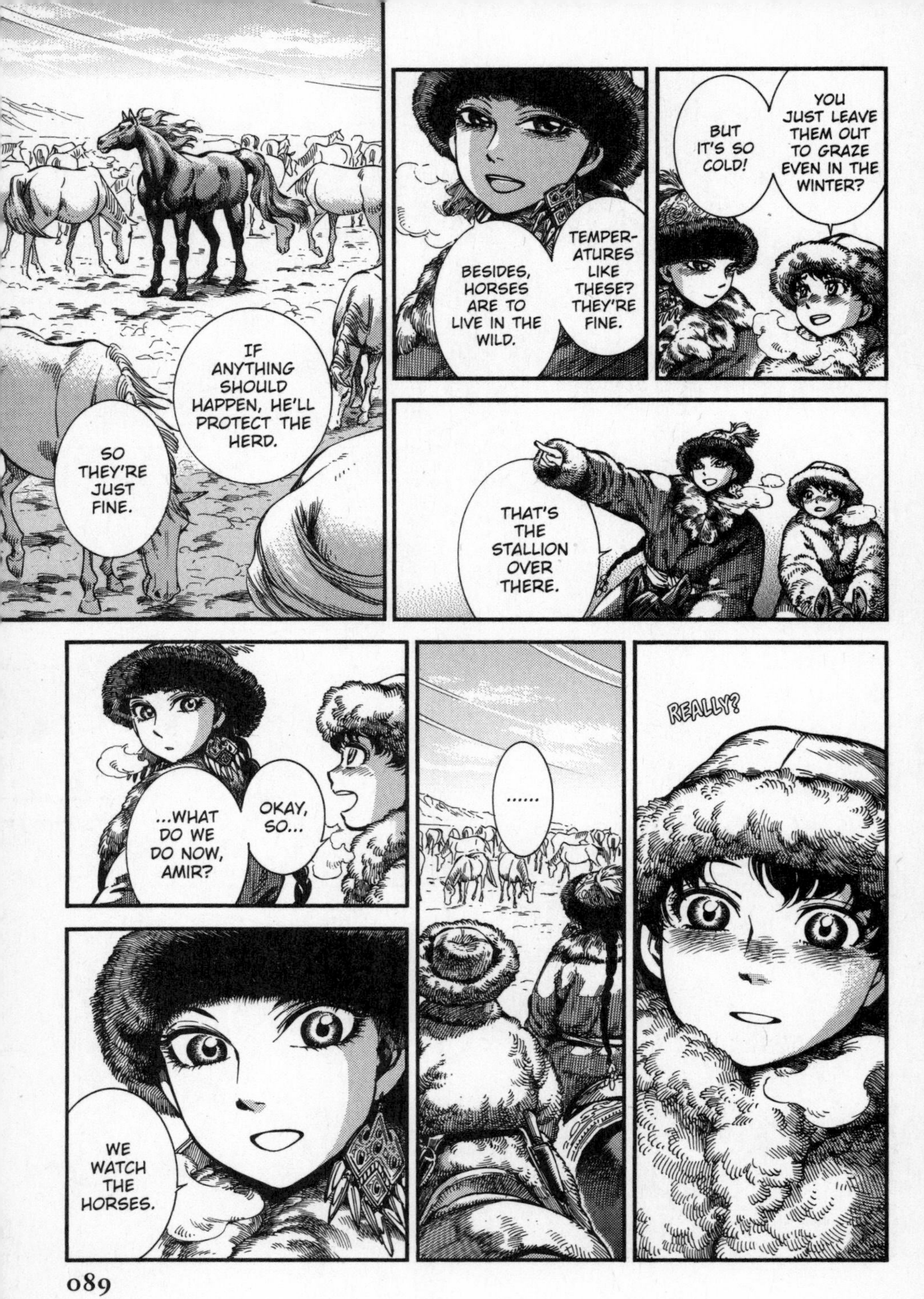
YOU JUST LEAVE THEM OUT TO GRAZE EVEN IN THE WINTER?
BUT IT'S SO COLD!
TEMPER-ATURES LIKE THESE? THEY'RE FINE.
BESIDES, HORSES ARE TO LIVE IN THE WILD.
THAT'S THE STALLION OVER THERE.
IF ANYTHING SHOULD HAPPEN, HE'LL PROTECT THE HERD.
SO THEY'RE JUST FINE.
REALLY?
......
OKAY, SO...
...WHAT DO WE DO NOW, AMIR?
WE WATCH THE HORSES.

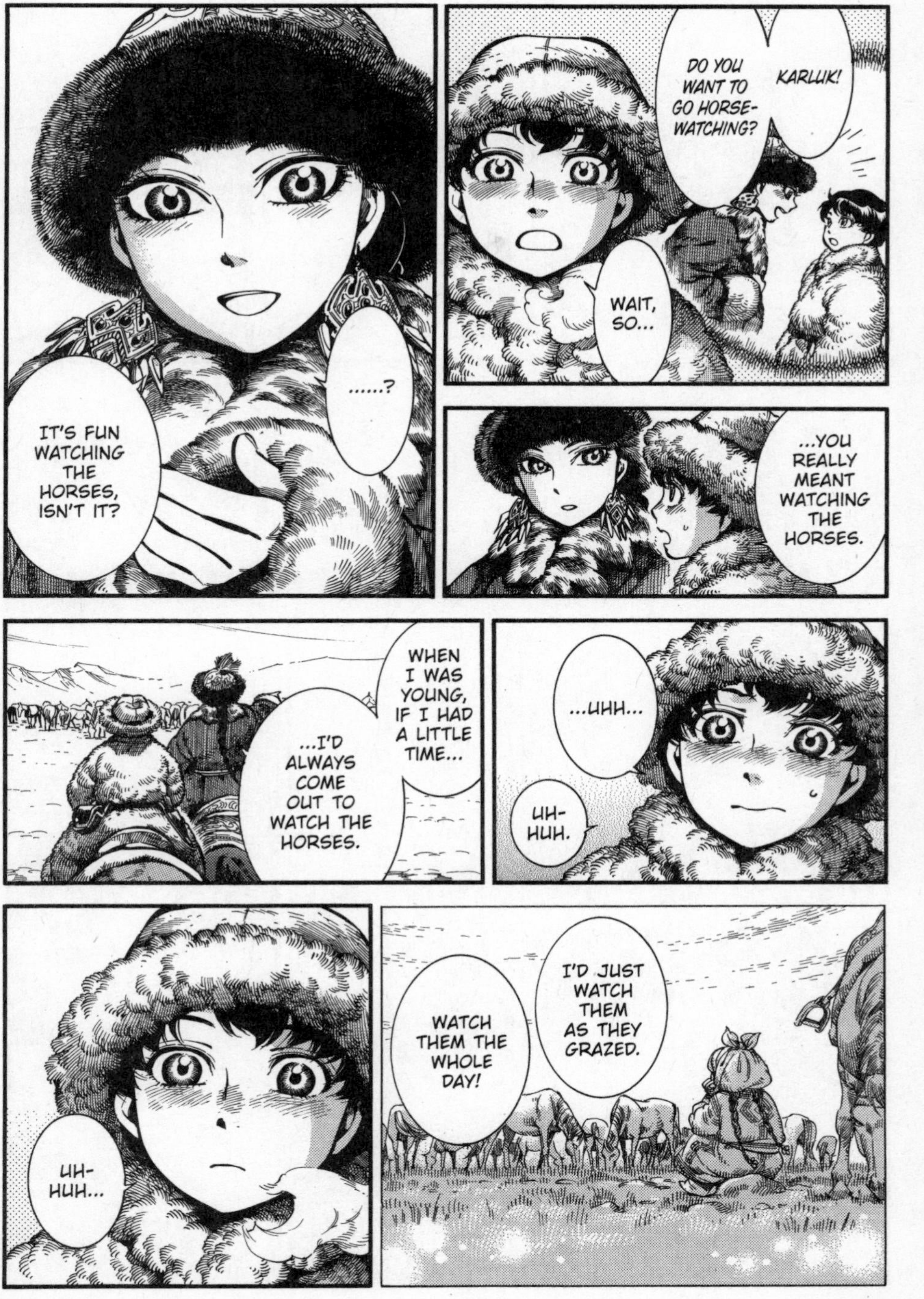
KARLUK!
DO YOU WANT TO GO HORSE-WATCHING?
WAIT, SO...
...YOU REALLY MEANT WATCHING THE HORSES.
......?
IT'S FUN WATCHING THE HORSES, ISN'T IT?
...UHH...
UH-HUH.
WHEN I WAS YOUNG, IF I HAD A LITTLE TIME...
...I'D ALWAYS COME OUT TO WATCH THE HORSES.
I'D JUST WATCH THEM AS THEY GRAZED.
WATCH THEM THE WHOLE DAY!
UH-HUH...

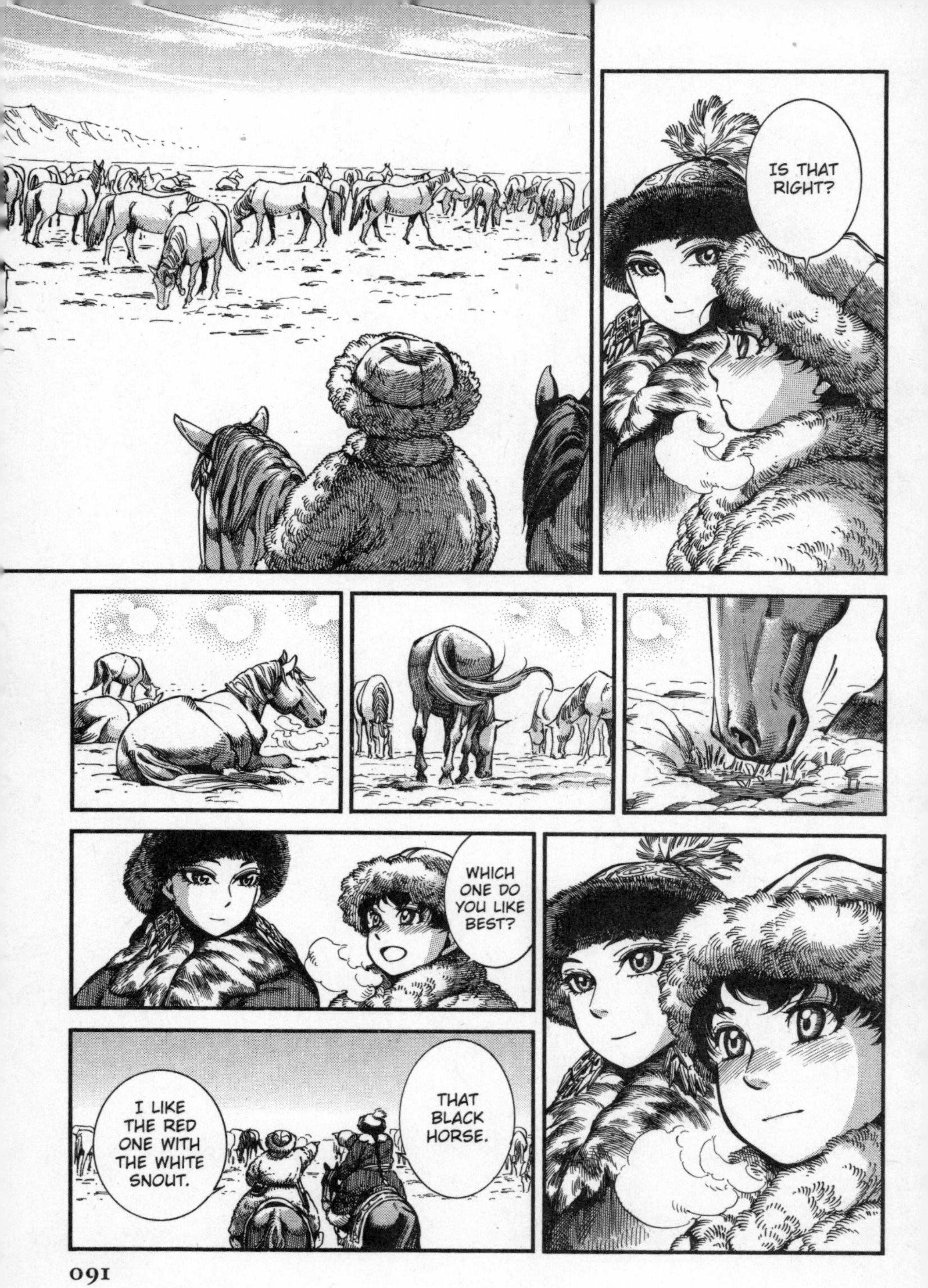
IS THAT RIGHT?
WHICH ONE DO YOU LIKE BEST?
THAT BLACK HORSE.
I LIKE THE RED ONE WITH THE WHITE SNOUT.

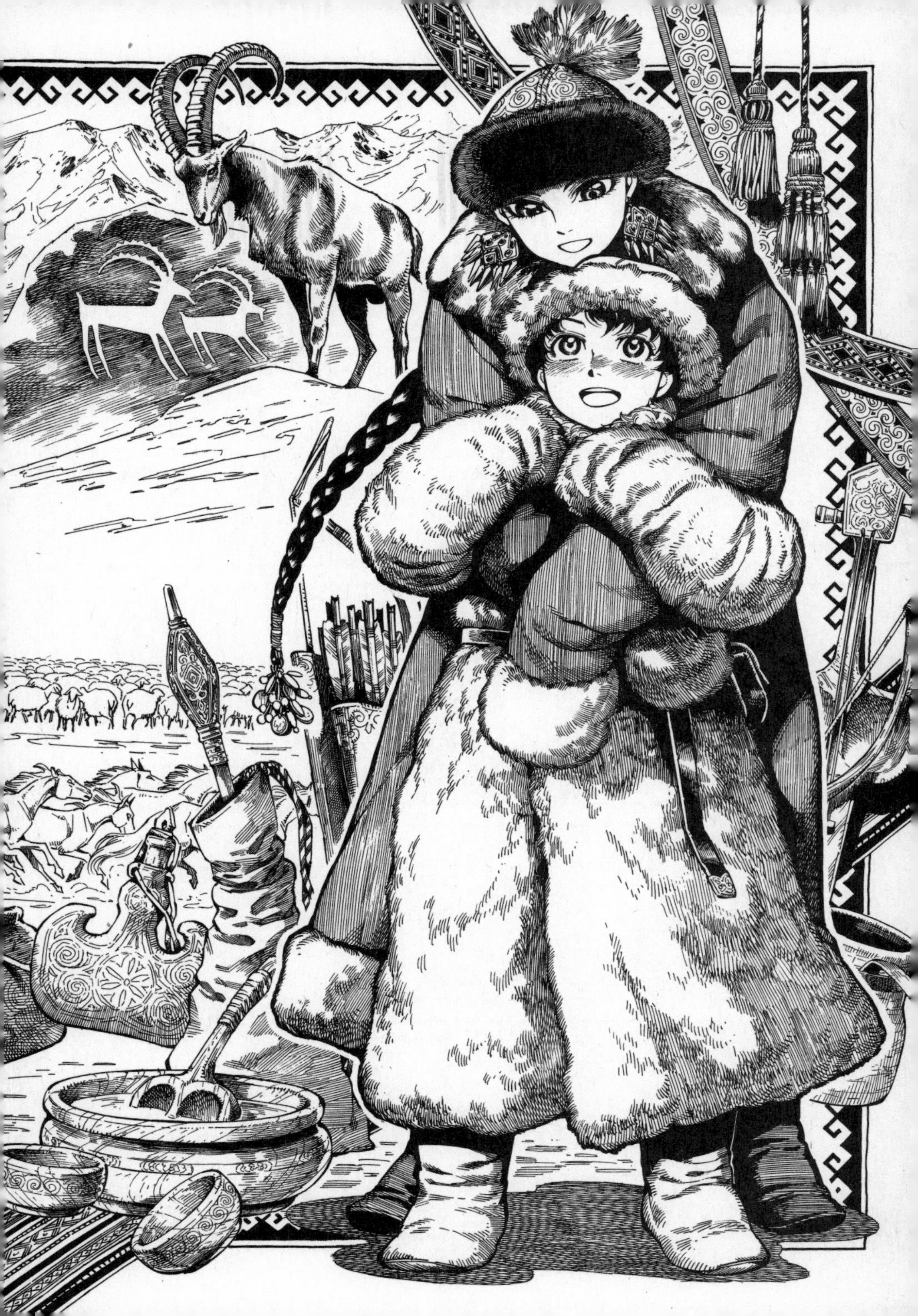

Chapter 66
Going to Watch the Horses

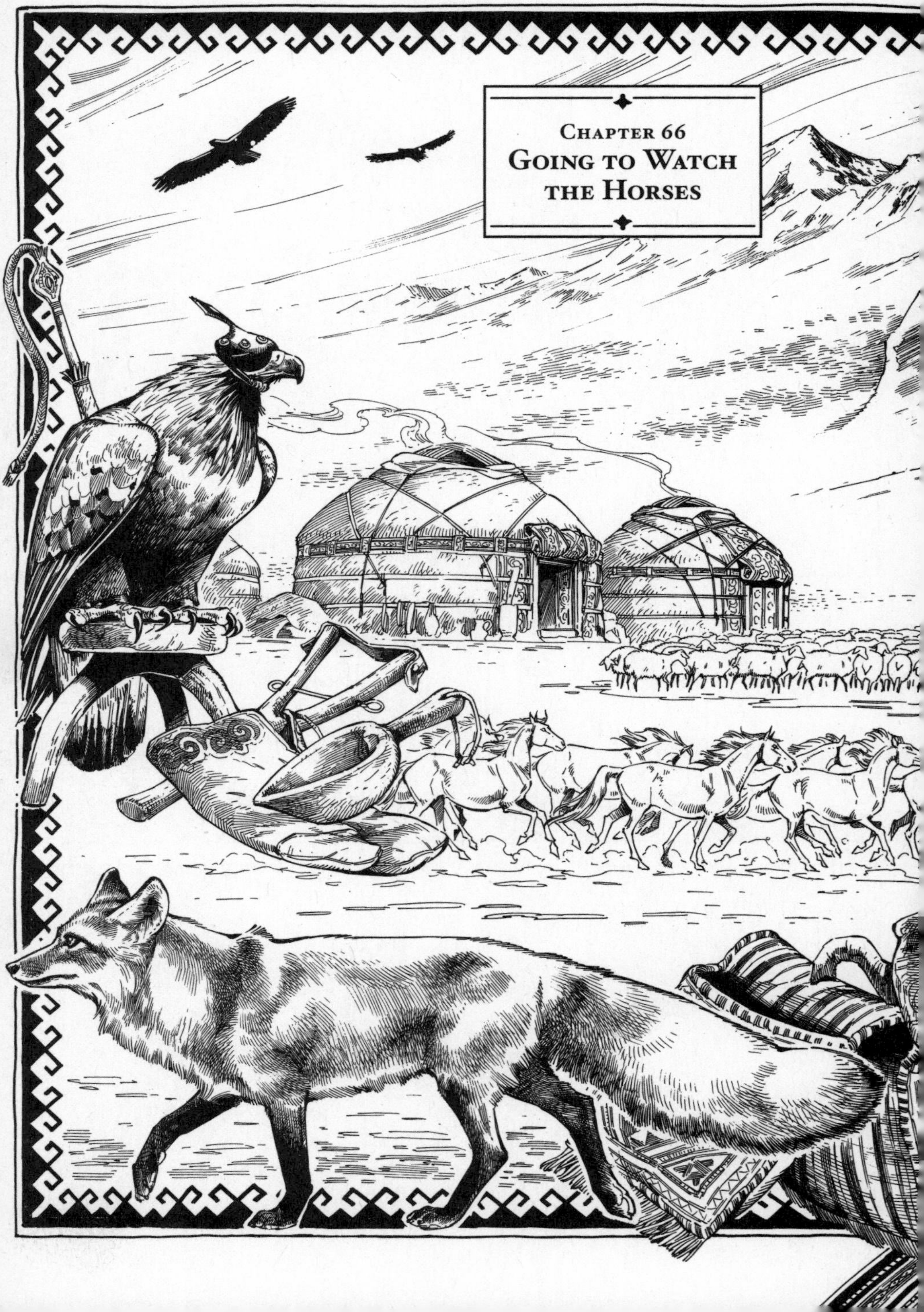

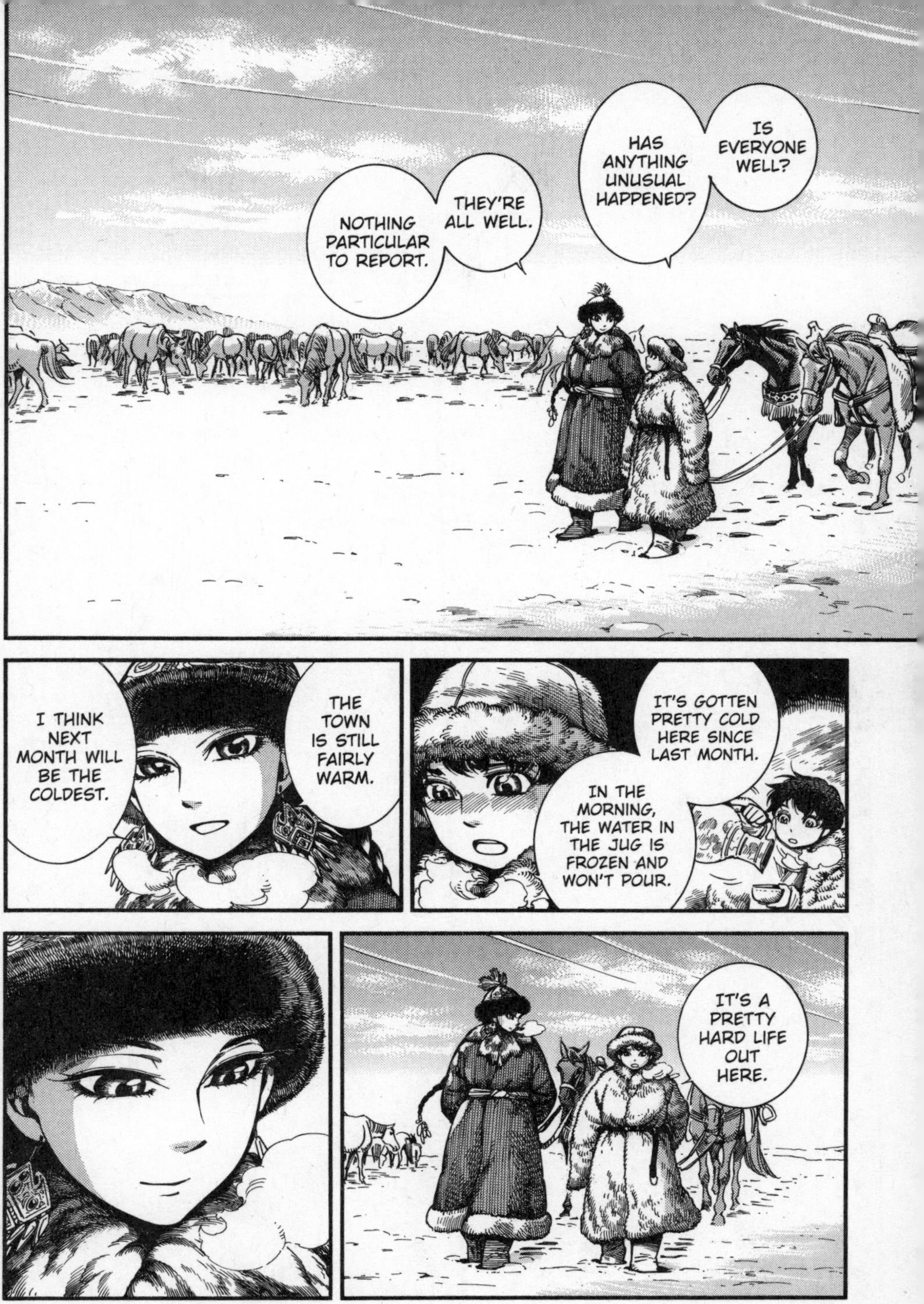
IS EVERYONE WELL?
HAS ANYTHING UNUSUAL HAPPENED?
THEY'RE ALL WELL.
NOTHING PARTICULAR TO REPORT.
IT'S GOTTEN PRETTY COLD HERE SINCE LAST MONTH.
IN THE MORNING, THE WATER IN THE JUG IS FROZEN AND WON'T POUR.
THE TOWN IS STILL FAIRLY WARM.
I THINK NEXT MONTH WILL BE THE COLDEST.
IT'S A PRETTY HARD LIFE OUT HERE.

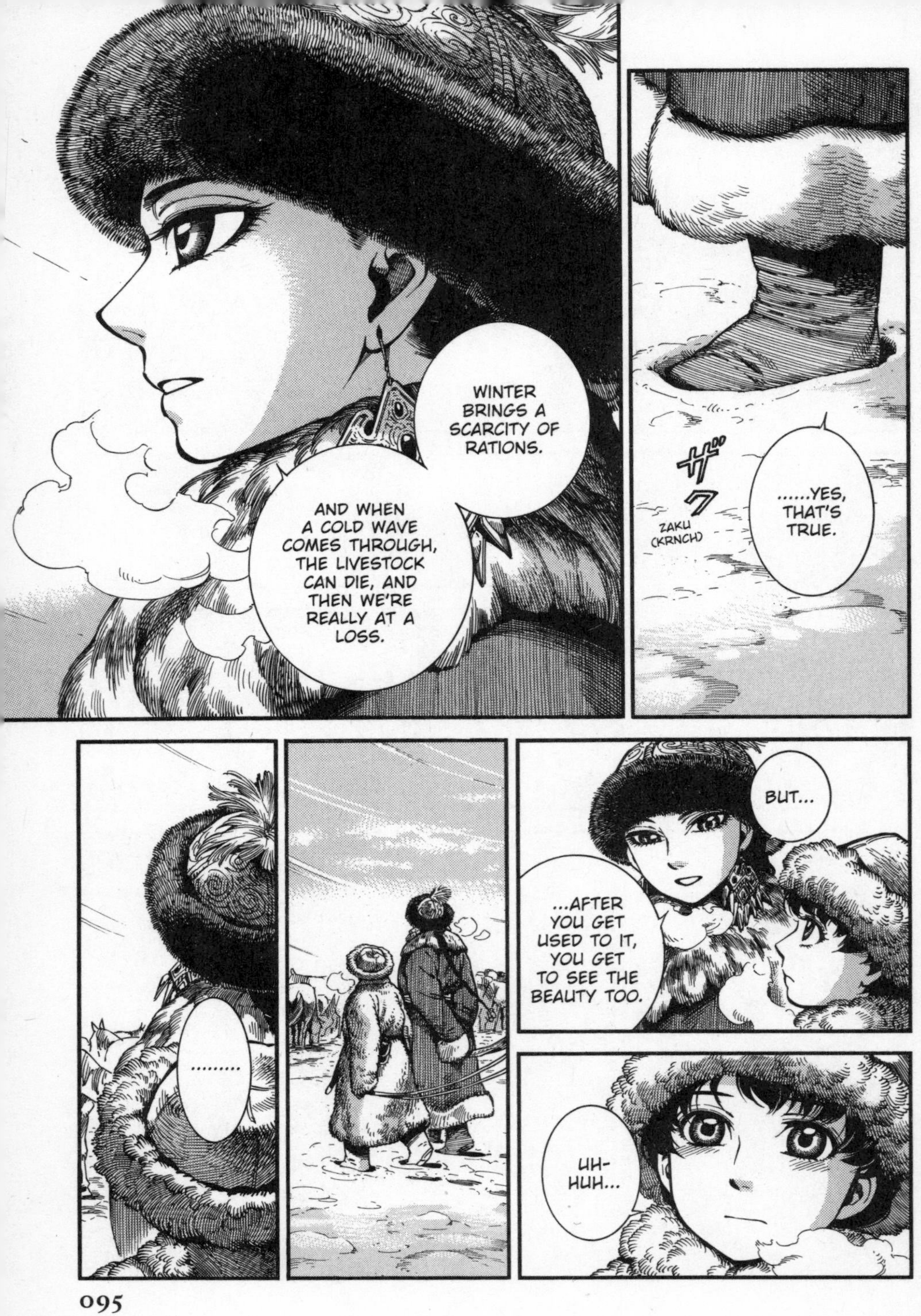
ザク
ZAKU (KRNCH)
......YES, THAT'S TRUE.
WINTER BRINGS A SCARCITY OF RATIONS.
AND WHEN A COLD WAVE COMES THROUGH, THE LIVESTOCK CAN DIE, AND THEN WE'RE REALLY AT A LOSS.
BUT...
...AFTER YOU GET USED TO IT, YOU GET TO SEE THE BEAUTY TOO.
UH-HUH...
....

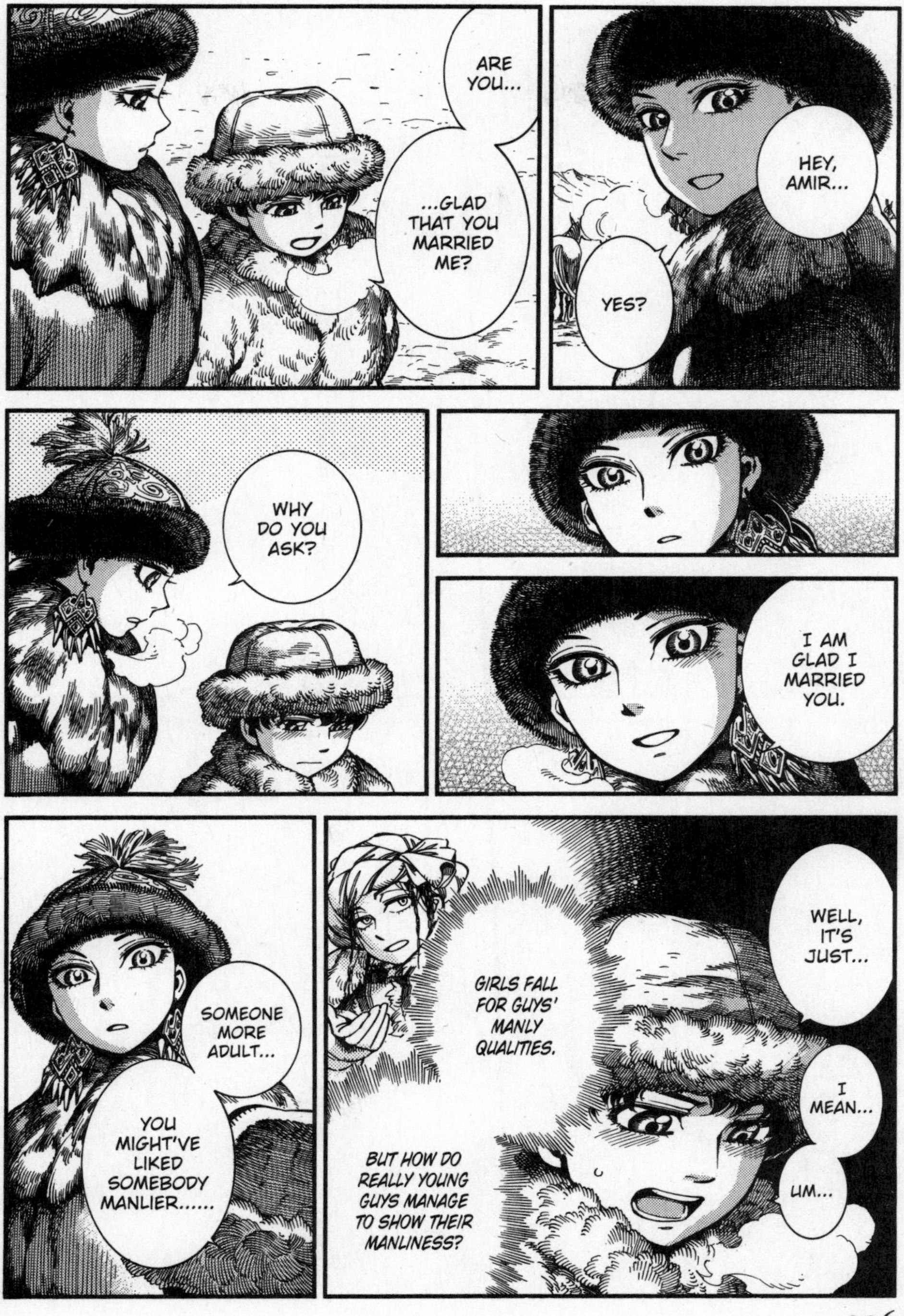
HEY, AMIR...
YES?
ARE YOU...
...GLAD THAT YOU MARRIED ME?
I AM GLAD I MARRIED YOU.
WHY DO YOU ASK?
WELL, IT'S JUST...
I MEAN...
UM...
GIRLS FALL FOR GUYS' MANLY QUALITIES.
BUT HOW DO REALLY YOUNG GUYS MANAGE TO SHOW THEIR MANLINESS?
SOMEONE MORE ADULT...
YOU MIGHT'VE LIKED SOMEBODY MANLIER......

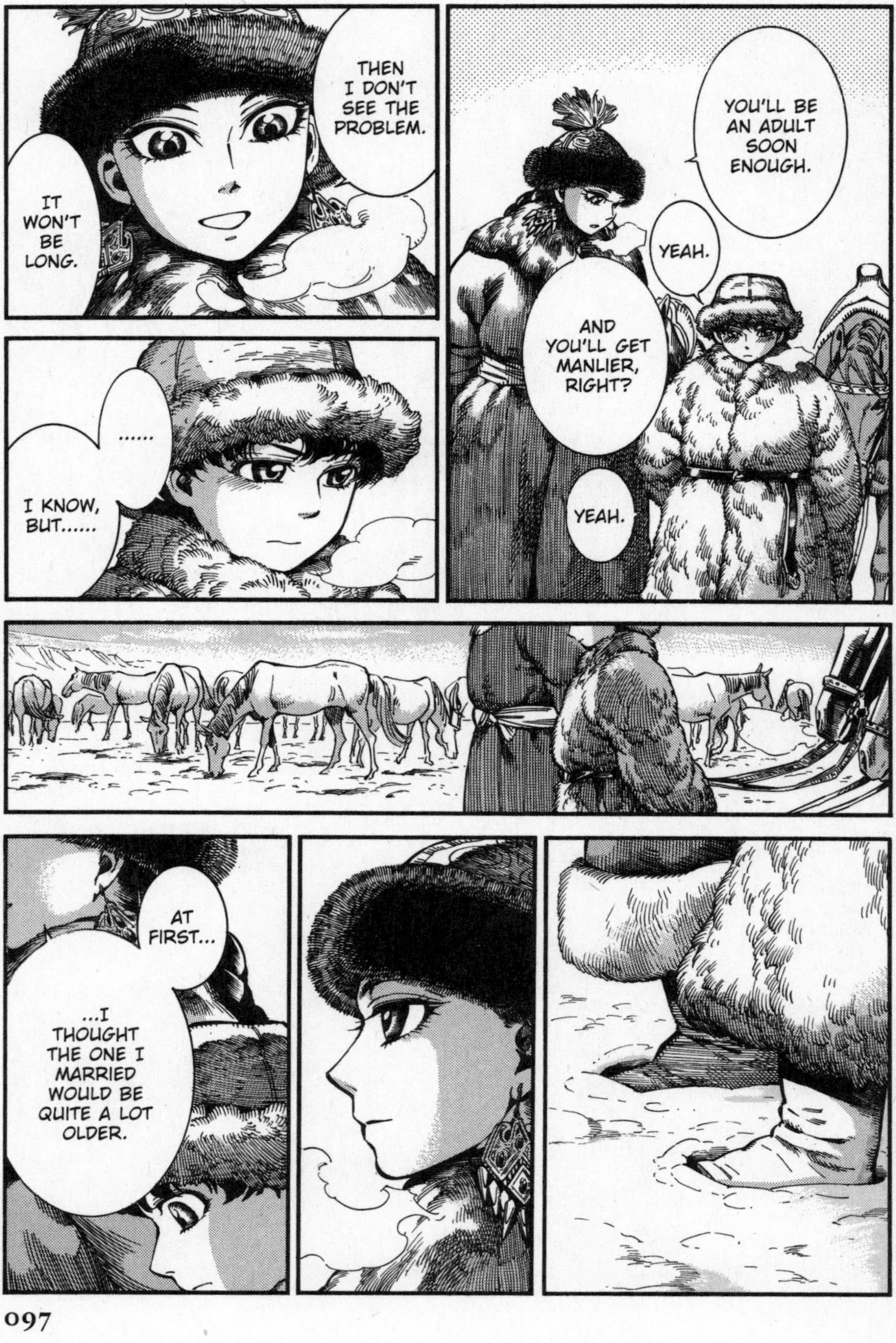
YOU'LL BE AN ADULT SOON ENOUGH.
YEAH.
AND YOU'LL GET MANLIER, RIGHT?
YEAH.
THEN I DON'T SEE THE PROBLEM.
IT WON'T BE LONG.
......
I KNOW, BUT......
AT FIRST...
...I THOUGHT THE ONE I MARRIED WOULD BE QUITE A LOT OLDER.

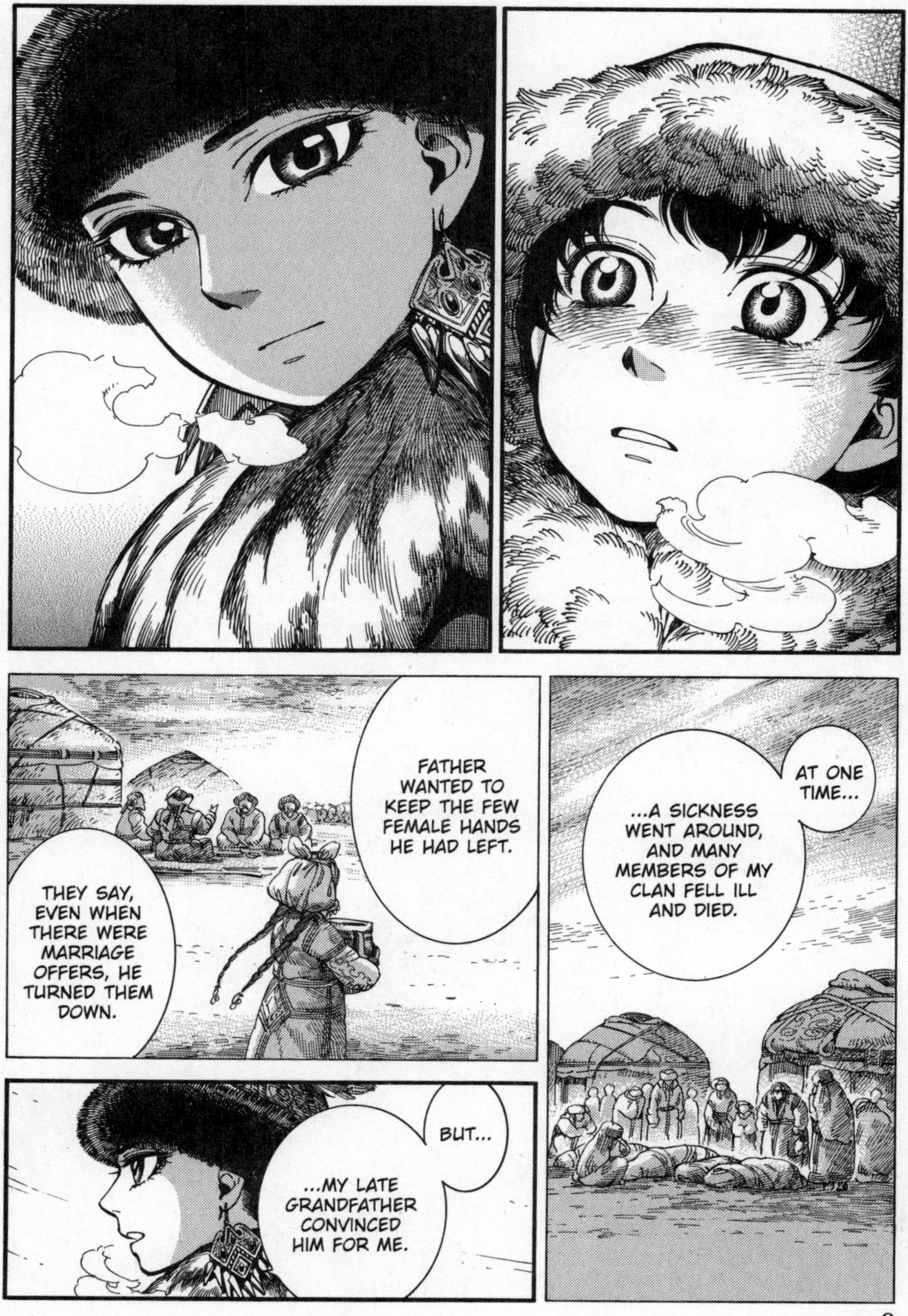
AT ONE TIME...
...A SICKNESS WENT AROUND, AND MANY MEMBERS OF MY CLAN FELL ILL AND DIED.
FATHER WANTED TO KEEP THE FEW FEMALE HANDS HE HAD LEFT.
THEY SAY, EVEN WHEN THERE WERE MARRIAGE OFFERS, HE TURNED THEM DOWN.
BUT...
...MY LATE GRANDFATHER CONVINCED HIM FOR ME.

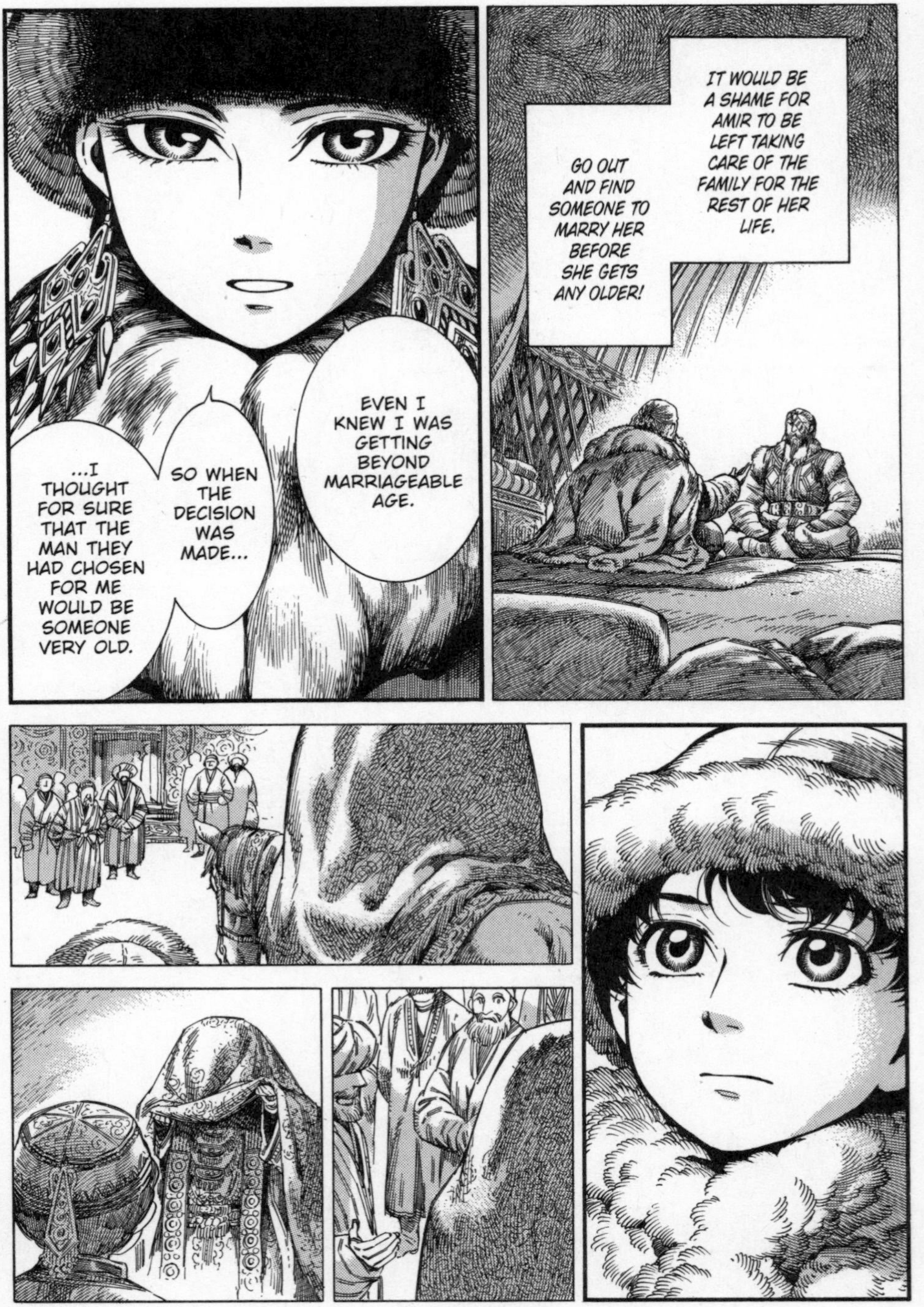
IT WOULD BE A SHAME FOR AMIR TO BE LEFT TAKING CARE OF THE FAMILY FOR THE REST OF HER LIFE.
GO OUT AND FIND SOMEONE TO MARRY HER BEFORE SHE GETS ANY OLDER!
EVEN I KNEW I WAS GETTING BEYOND MARRIAGEABLE AGE.
SO WHEN THE DECISION WAS MADE...
...I THOUGHT FOR SURE THAT THE MAN THEY HAD CHOSEN FOR ME WOULD BE SOMEONE VERY OLD.

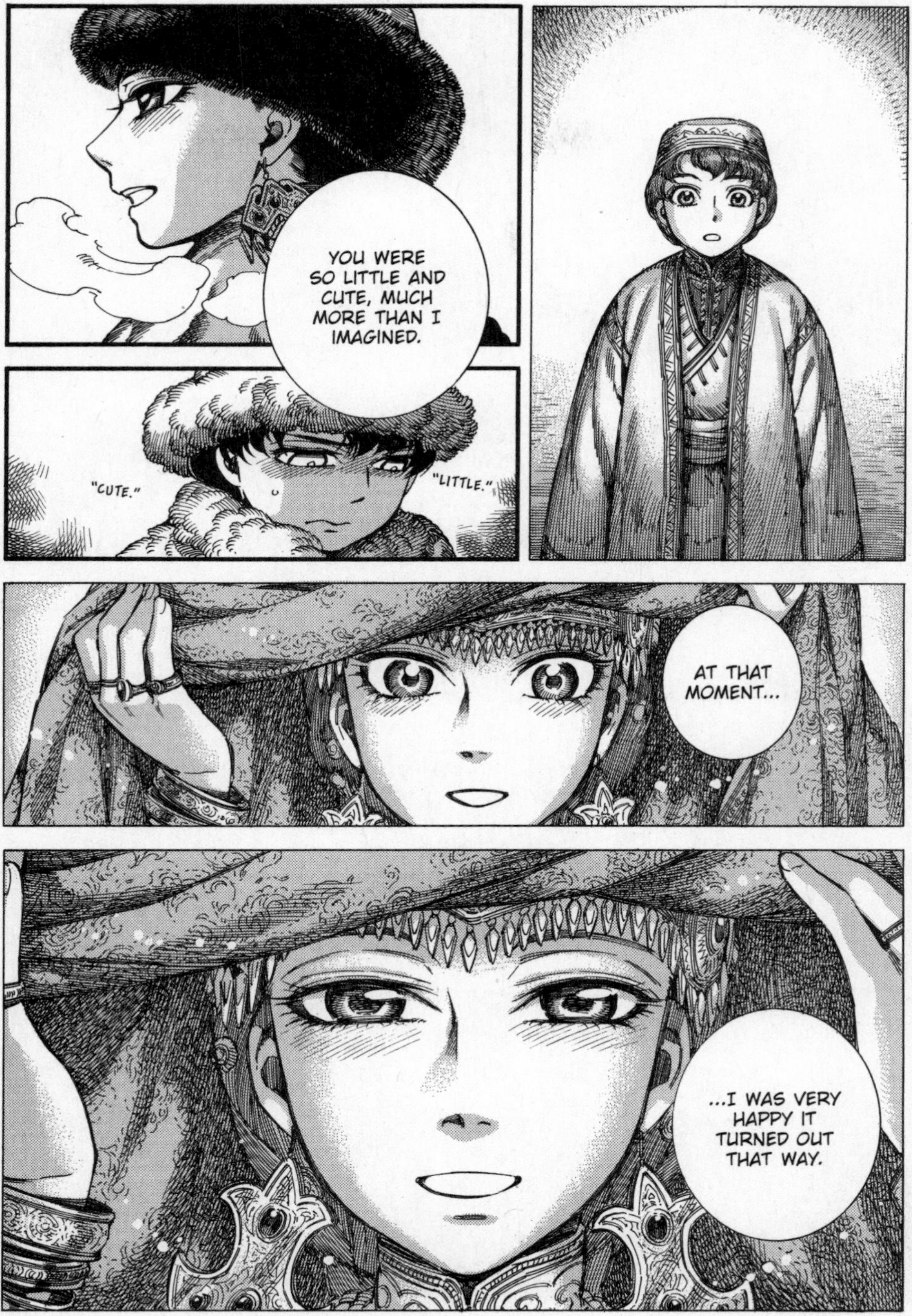
YOU WERE SO LITTLE AND CUTE, MUCH MORE THAN I IMAGINED.
"LITTLE."
"CUTE."
AT THAT MOMENT...
...I WAS VERY HAPPY IT TURNED OUT THAT WAY.

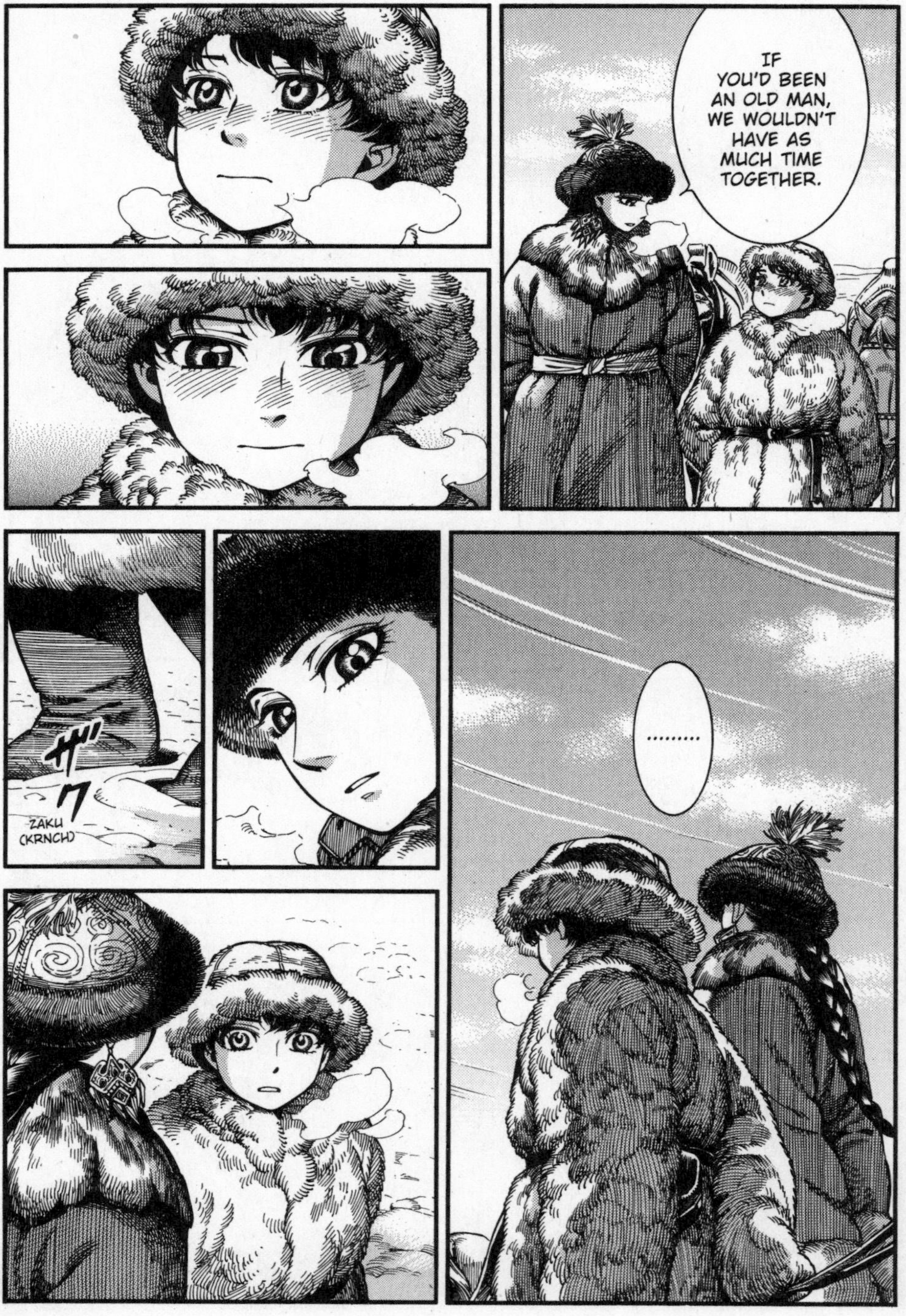
IF YOU'D BEEN AN OLD MAN, WE WOULDN'T HAVE AS MUCH TIME TOGETHER.
....
ザッ
ZAKU (KRNCH)

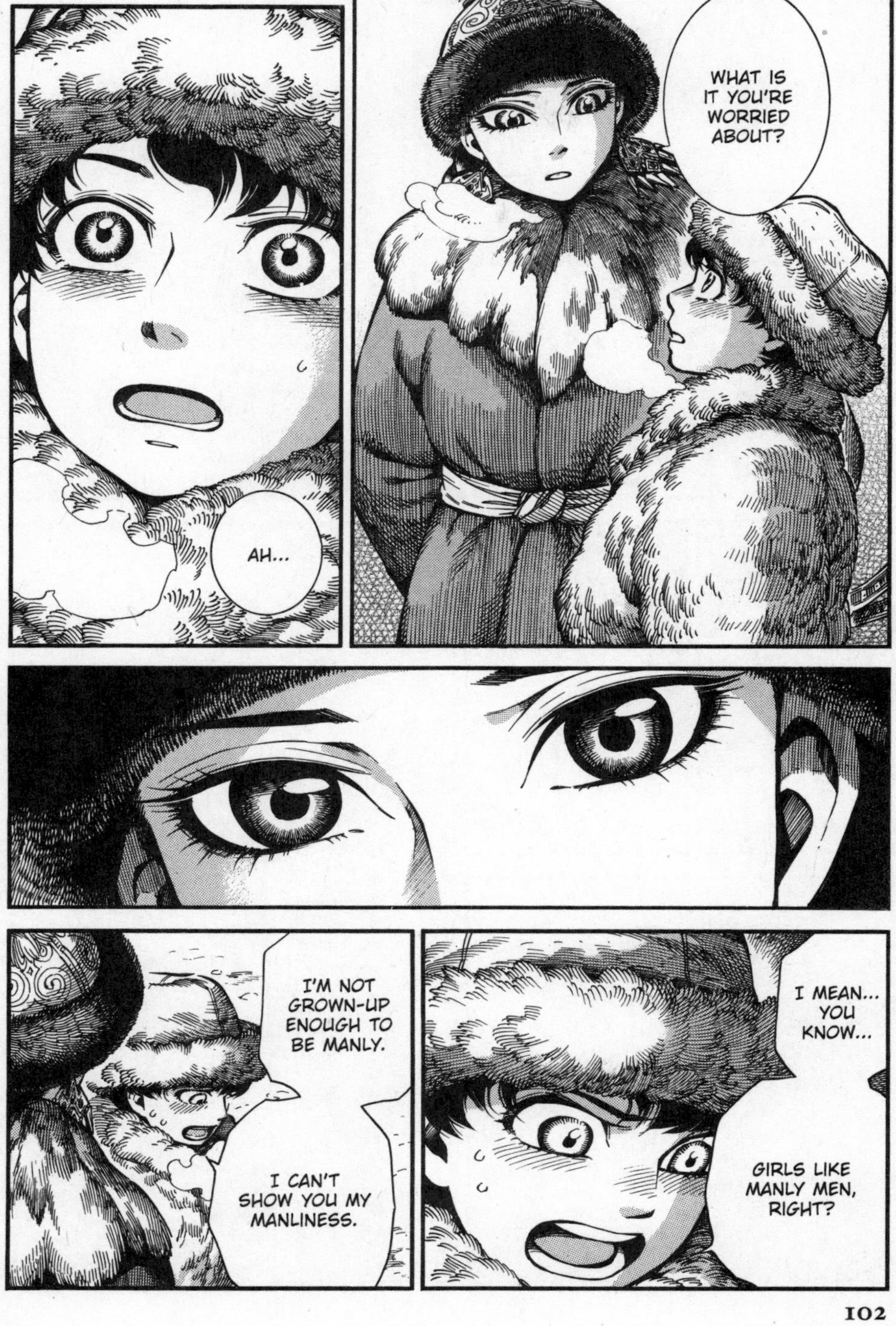
WHAT IS IT YOU'RE WORRIED ABOUT?
AH...
I MEAN... YOU KNOW...
GIRLS LIKE MANLY MEN, RIGHT?
I'M NOT GROWN-UP ENOUGH TO BE MANLY.
I CAN'T SHOW YOU MY MANLINESS.

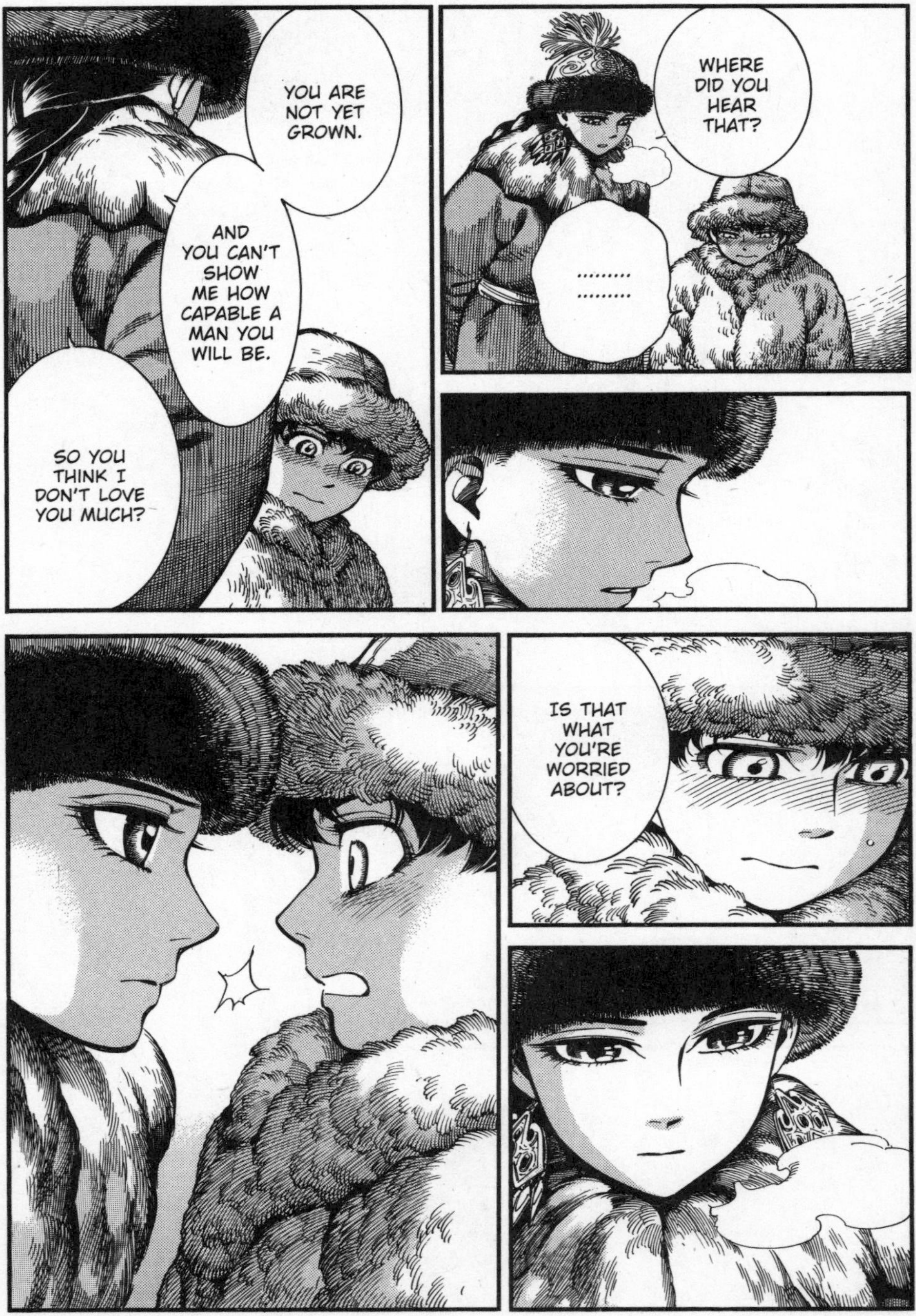
WHERE DID YOU HEAR THAT?
....
....
YOU ARE NOT YET GROWN.
AND YOU CAN'T SHOW ME HOW CAPABLE A MAN YOU WILL BE.
SO YOU THINK I DON'T LOVE YOU MUCH?
IS THAT WHAT YOU'RE WORRIED ABOUT?

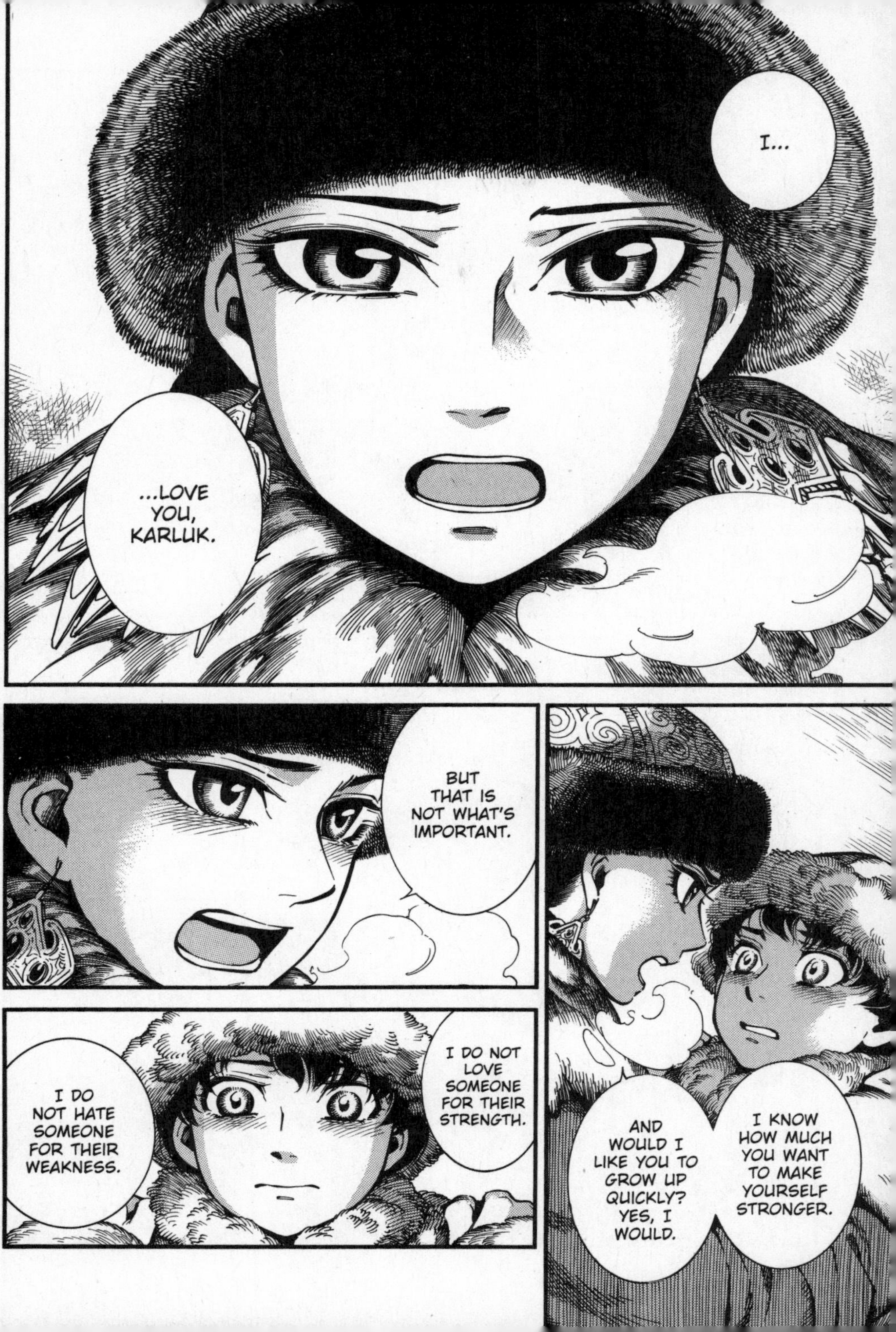
I...
...LOVE YOU, KARLUK.
I KNOW HOW MUCH YOU WANT TO MAKE YOURSELF STRONGER.
AND WOULD I LIKE YOU TO GROW UP QUICKLY? YES, I WOULD.
BUT THAT IS NOT WHAT'S IMPORTANT.
I DO NOT LOVE SOMEONE FOR THEIR STRENGTH.
I DO NOT HATE SOMEONE FOR THEIR WEAKNESS.

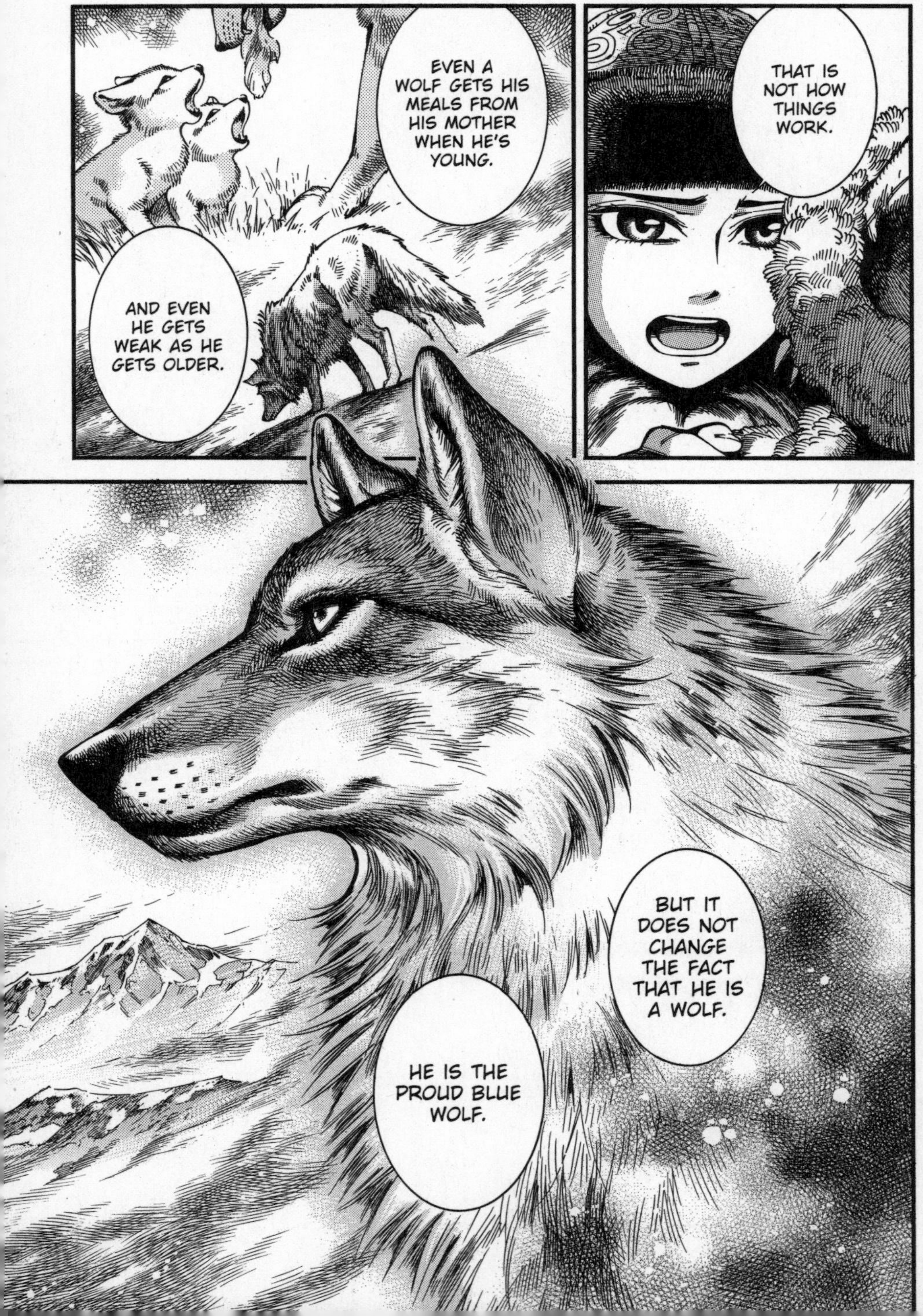
THAT IS NOT HOW THINGS WORK.
EVEN A WOLF GETS HIS MEALS FROM HIS MOTHER WHEN HE'S YOUNG.
AND EVEN HE GETS WEAK AS HE GETS OLDER.
BUT IT DOES NOT CHANGE THE FACT THAT HE IS A WOLF.
HE IS THE PROUD BLUE WOLF.

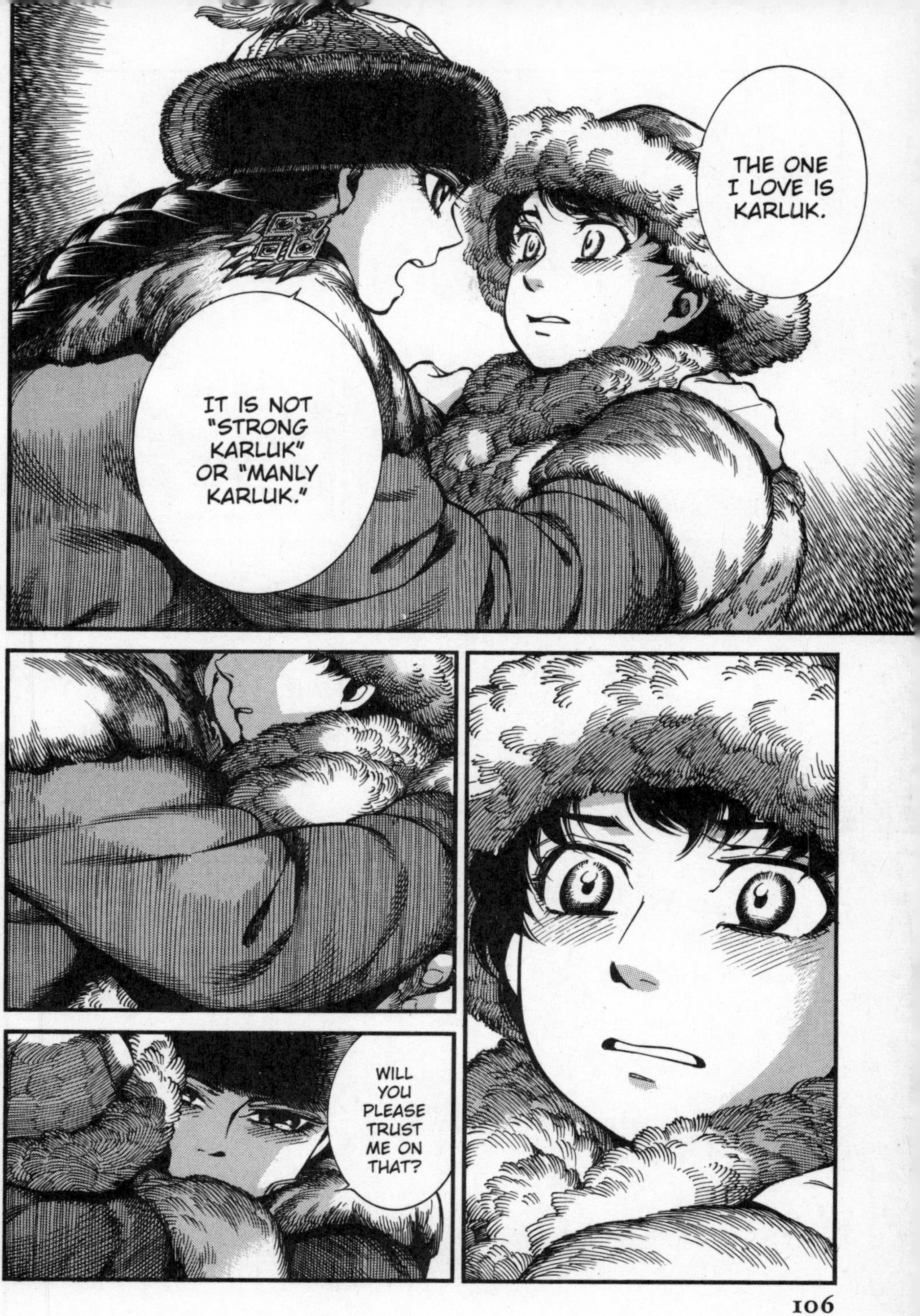
THE ONE I LOVE IS KARLUK.
IT IS NOT "STRONG KARLUK" OR "MANLY KARLUK."
WILL YOU PLEASE TRUST ME ON THAT?

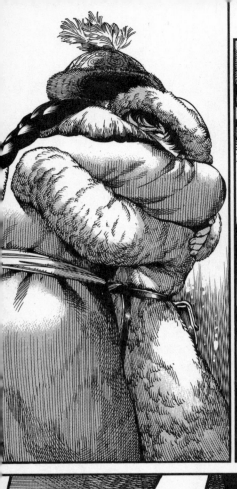
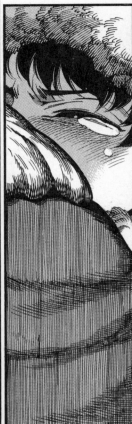
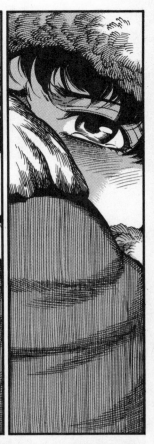
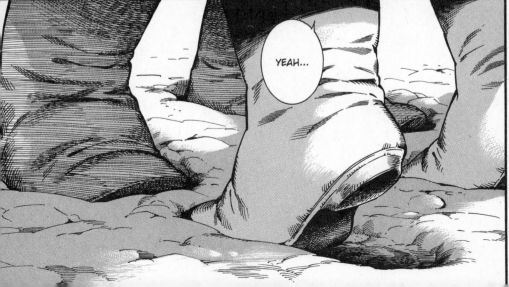

YEAH...

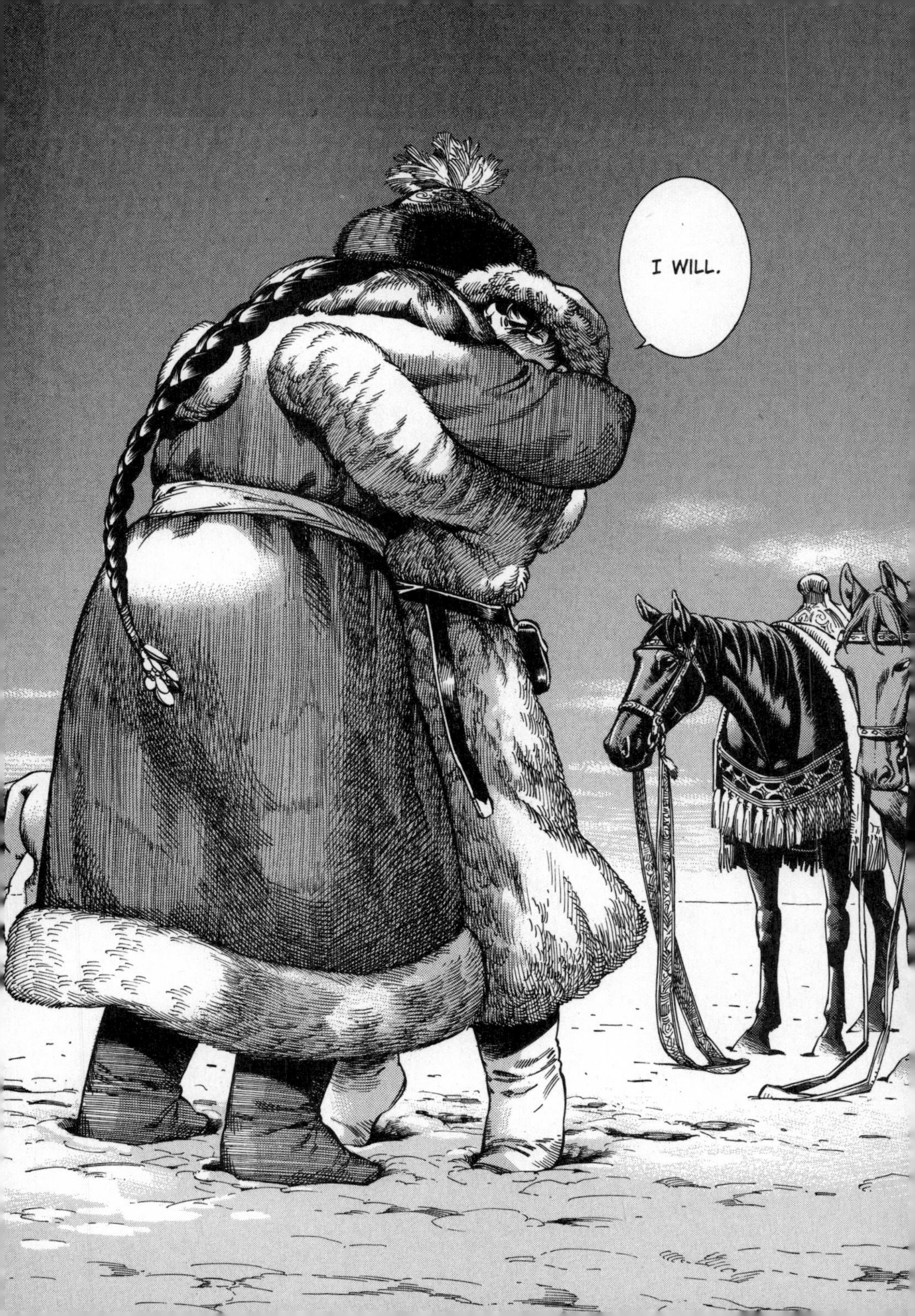
I WILL.

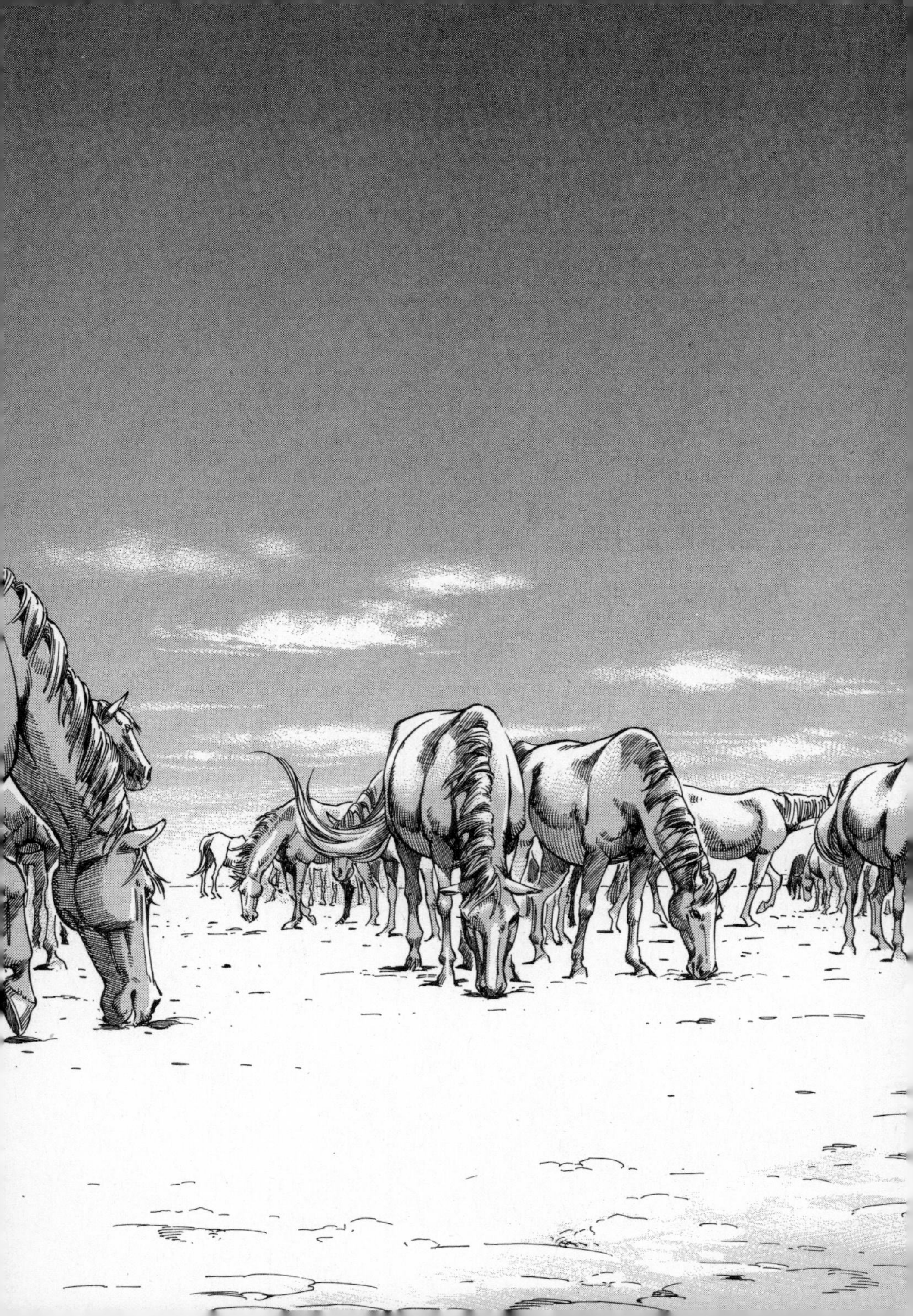

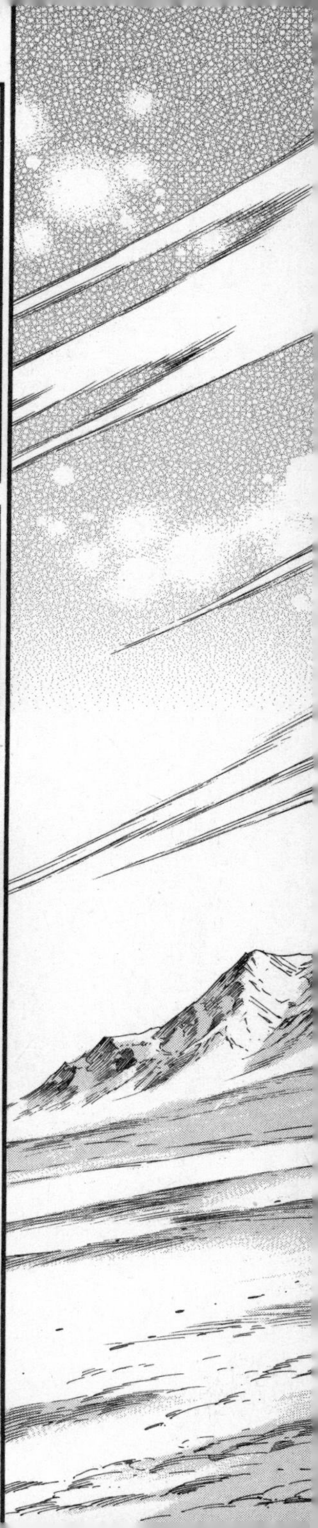

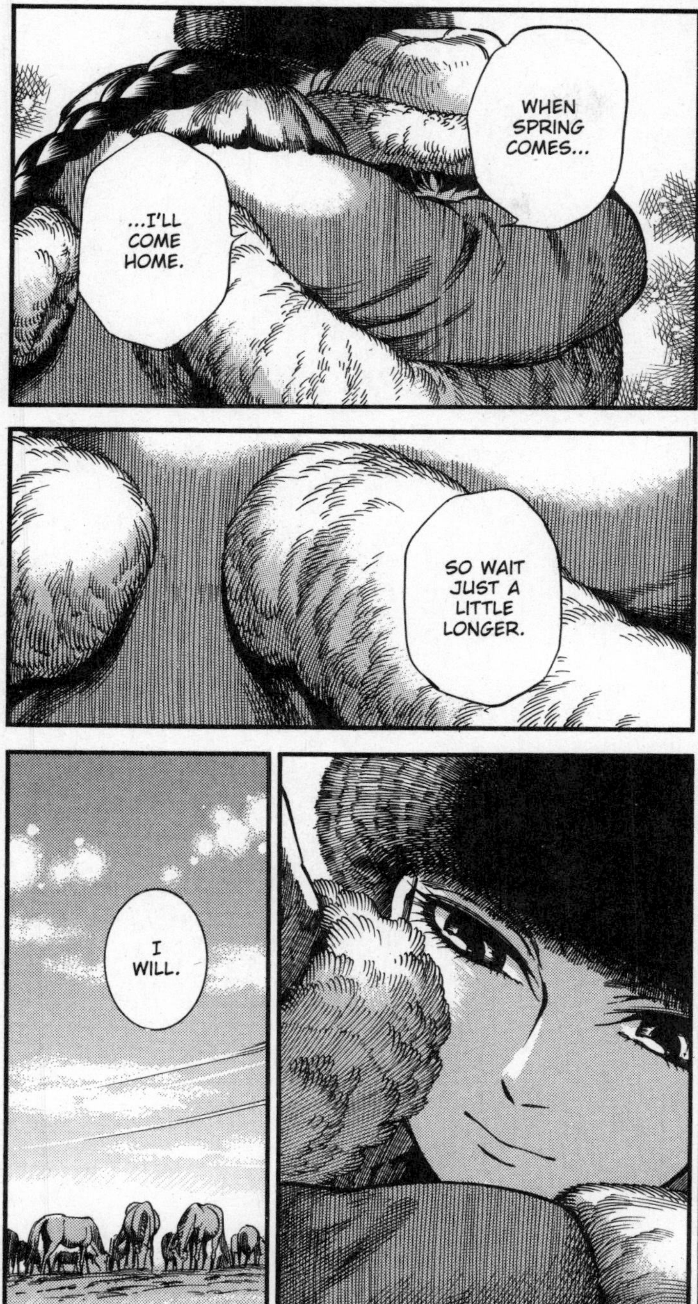
WHEN SPRING COMES...
...I'LL COME HOME.
SO WAIT JUST A LITTLE LONGER.
I WILL.

✦ Chapter 66: End ✦

✦ Chapter 67 ✦

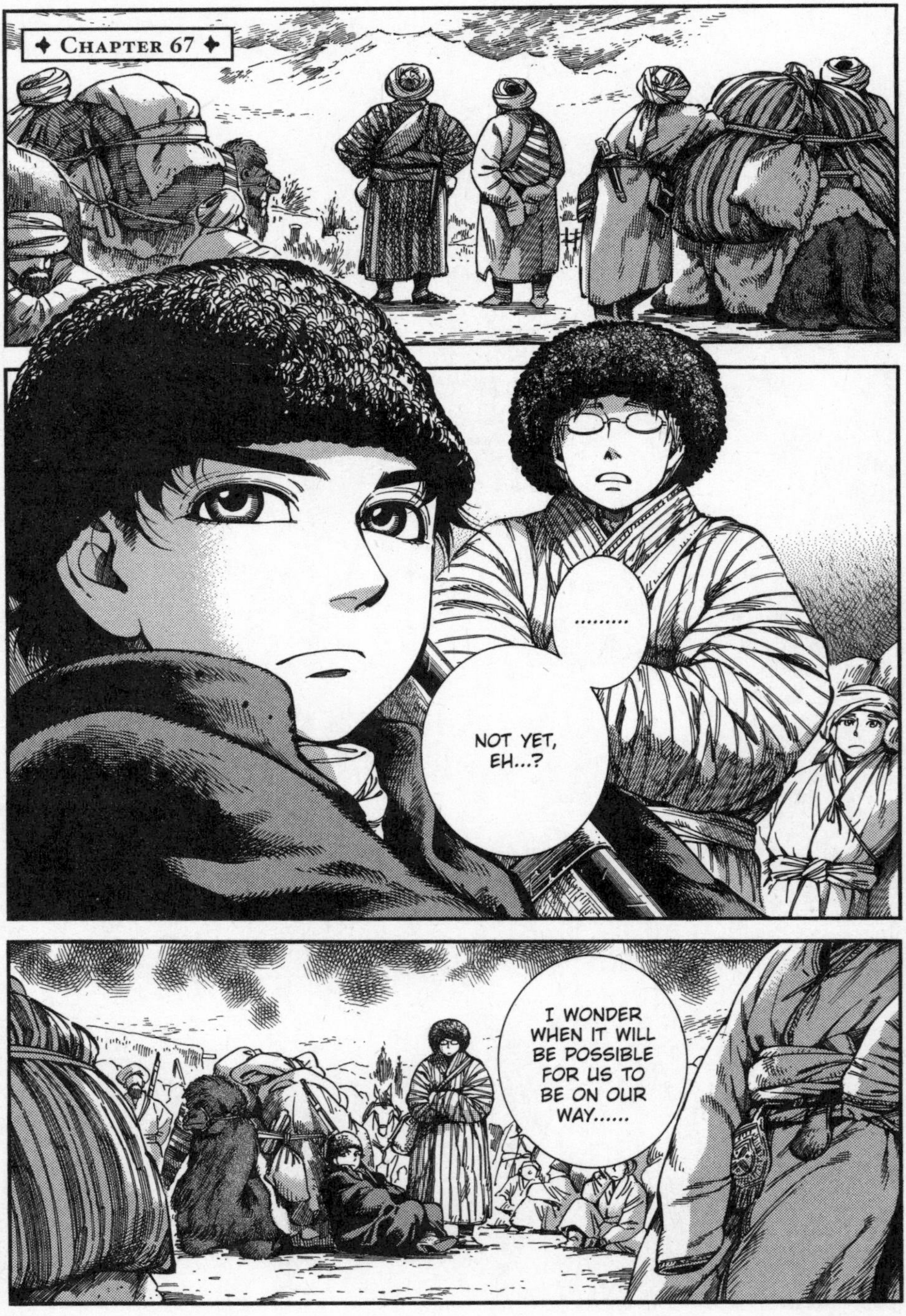

....
NOT YET, EH...?
I WONDER WHEN IT WILL BE POSSIBLE FOR US TO BE ON OUR WAY......

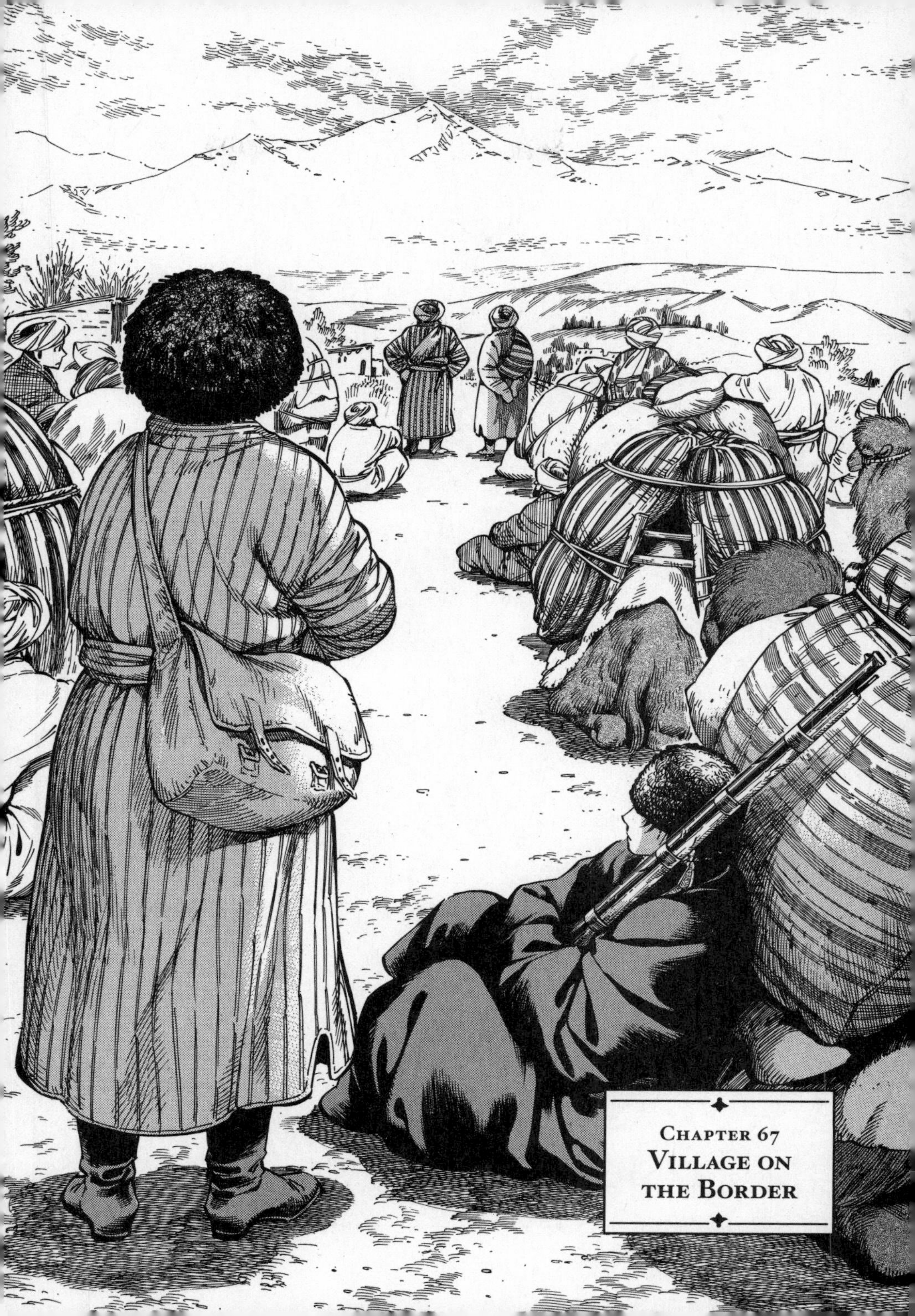

Chapter 67
Village on the Border

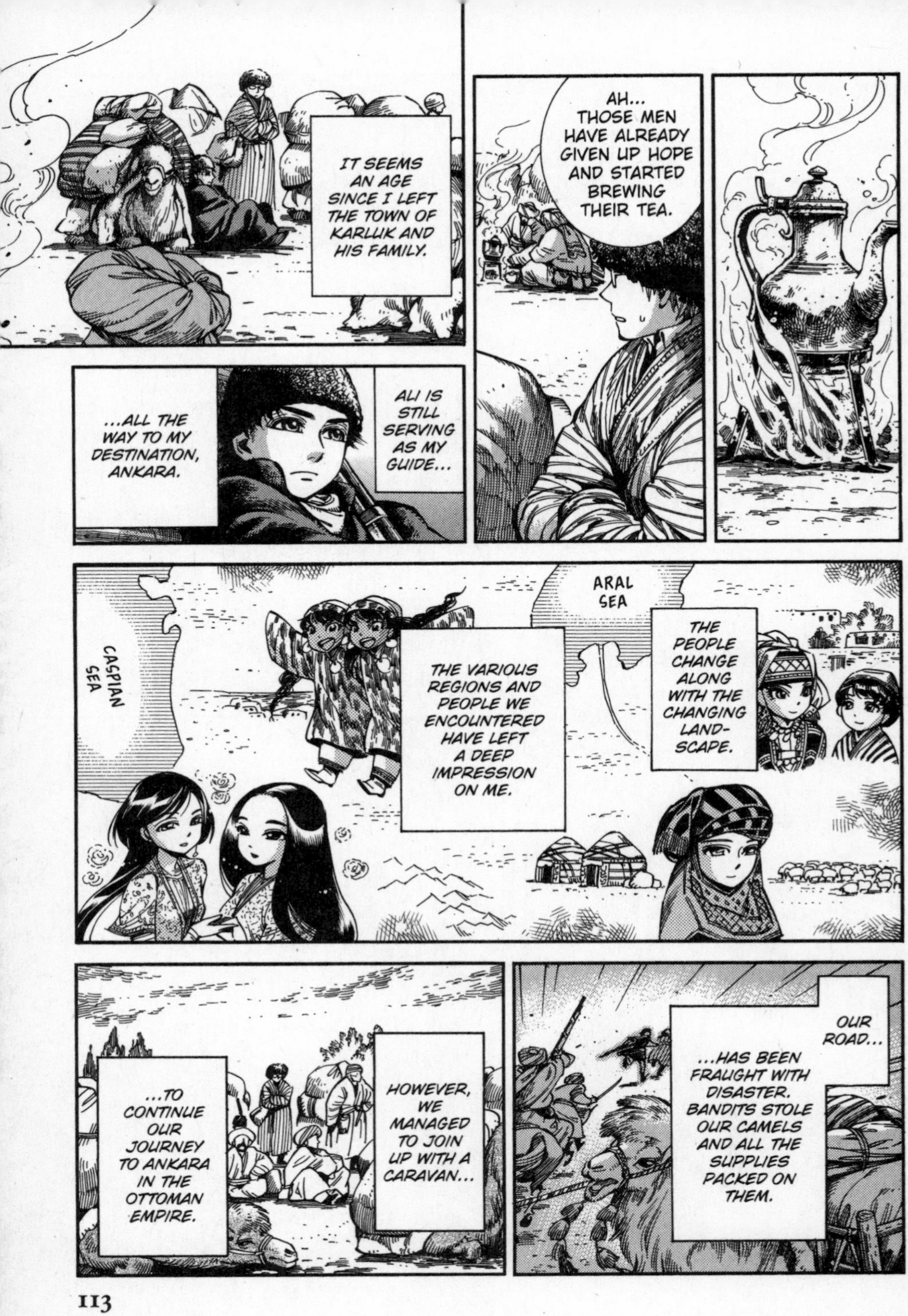
AH... THOSE MEN HAVE ALREADY GIVEN UP HOPE AND STARTED BREWING THEIR TEA.
IT SEEMS AN AGE SINCE I LEFT THE TOWN OF KARLUK AND HIS FAMILY.
ALI IS STILL SERVING AS MY GUIDE...
...ALL THE WAY TO MY DESTINATION, ANKARA.
ARAL SEA
THE PEOPLE CHANGE ALONG WITH THE CHANGING LAND-SCAPE.
THE VARIOUS REGIONS AND PEOPLE WE ENCOUNTERED HAVE LEFT A DEEP IMPRESSION ON ME.
CASPIAN SEA
OUR ROAD...
...HAS BEEN FRAUGHT WITH DISASTER. BANDITS STOLE OUR CAMELS AND ALL THE SUPPLIES PACKED ON THEM.
HOWEVER, WE MANAGED TO JOIN UP WITH A CARAVAN...
...TO CONTINUE OUR JOURNEY TO ANKARA IN THE OTTOMAN EMPIRE.

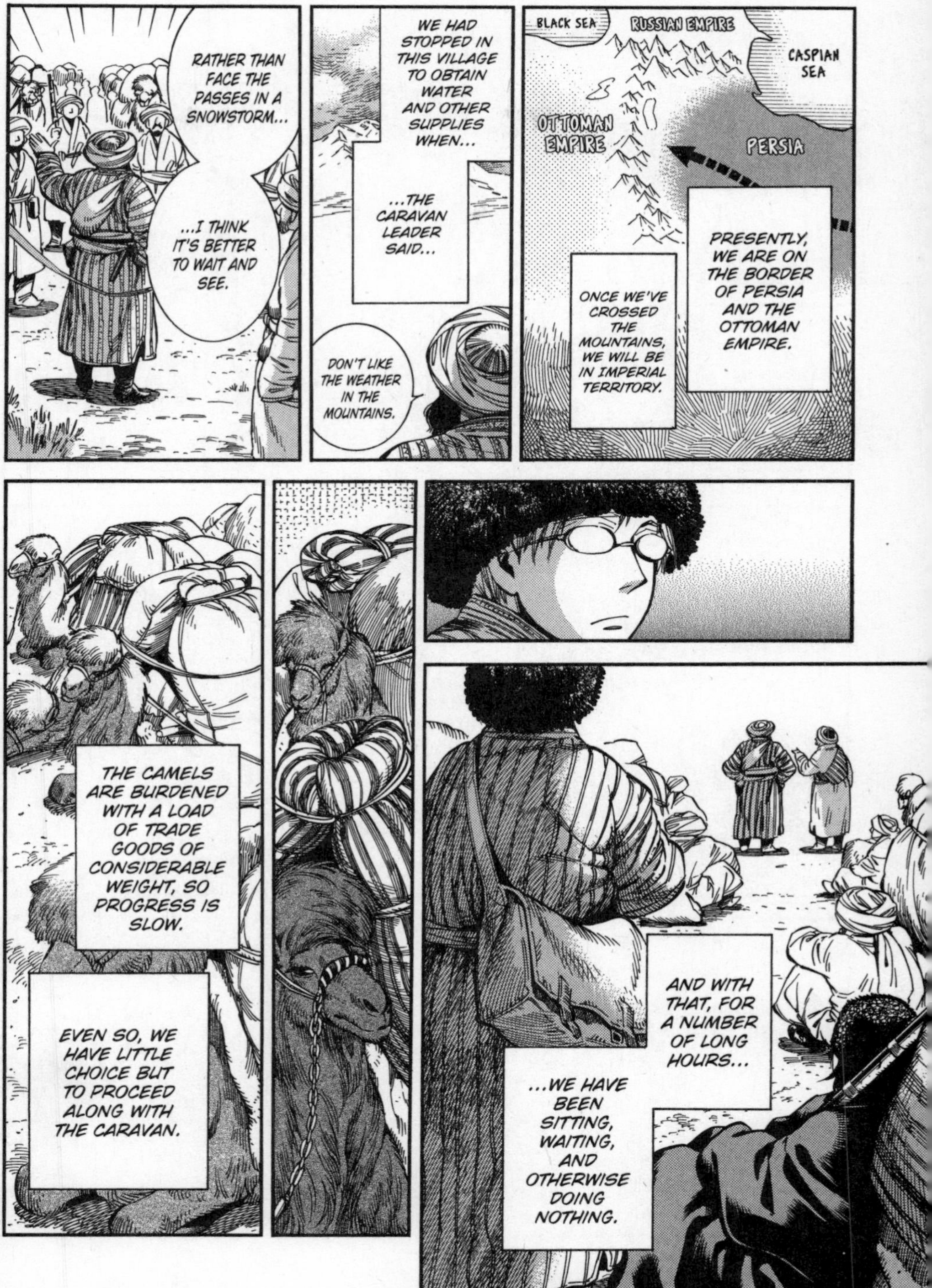
BLACK SEA
RUSSIAN EMPIRE
CASPIAN SEA
OTTOMAN EMPIRE
PERSIA
PRESENTLY, WE ARE ON THE BORDER OF PERSIA AND THE OTTOMAN EMPIRE.
ONCE WE'VE CROSSED THE MOUNTAINS, WE WILL BE IN IMPERIAL TERRITORY.
WE HAD STOPPED IN THIS VILLAGE TO OBTAIN WATER AND OTHER SUPPLIES WHEN...
...THE CARAVAN LEADER SAID...
DON'T LIKE THE WEATHER IN THE MOUNTAINS.
RATHER THAN FACE THE PASSES IN A SNOWSTORM...
...I THINK IT'S BETTER TO WAIT AND SEE.
AND WITH THAT, FOR A NUMBER OF LONG HOURS...
...WE HAVE BEEN SITTING, WAITING, AND OTHERWISE DOING NOTHING.
THE CAMELS ARE BURDENED WITH A LOAD OF TRADE GOODS OF CONSIDERABLE WEIGHT, SO PROGRESS IS SLOW.
EVEN SO, WE HAVE LITTLE CHOICE BUT TO PROCEED ALONG WITH THE CARAVAN.

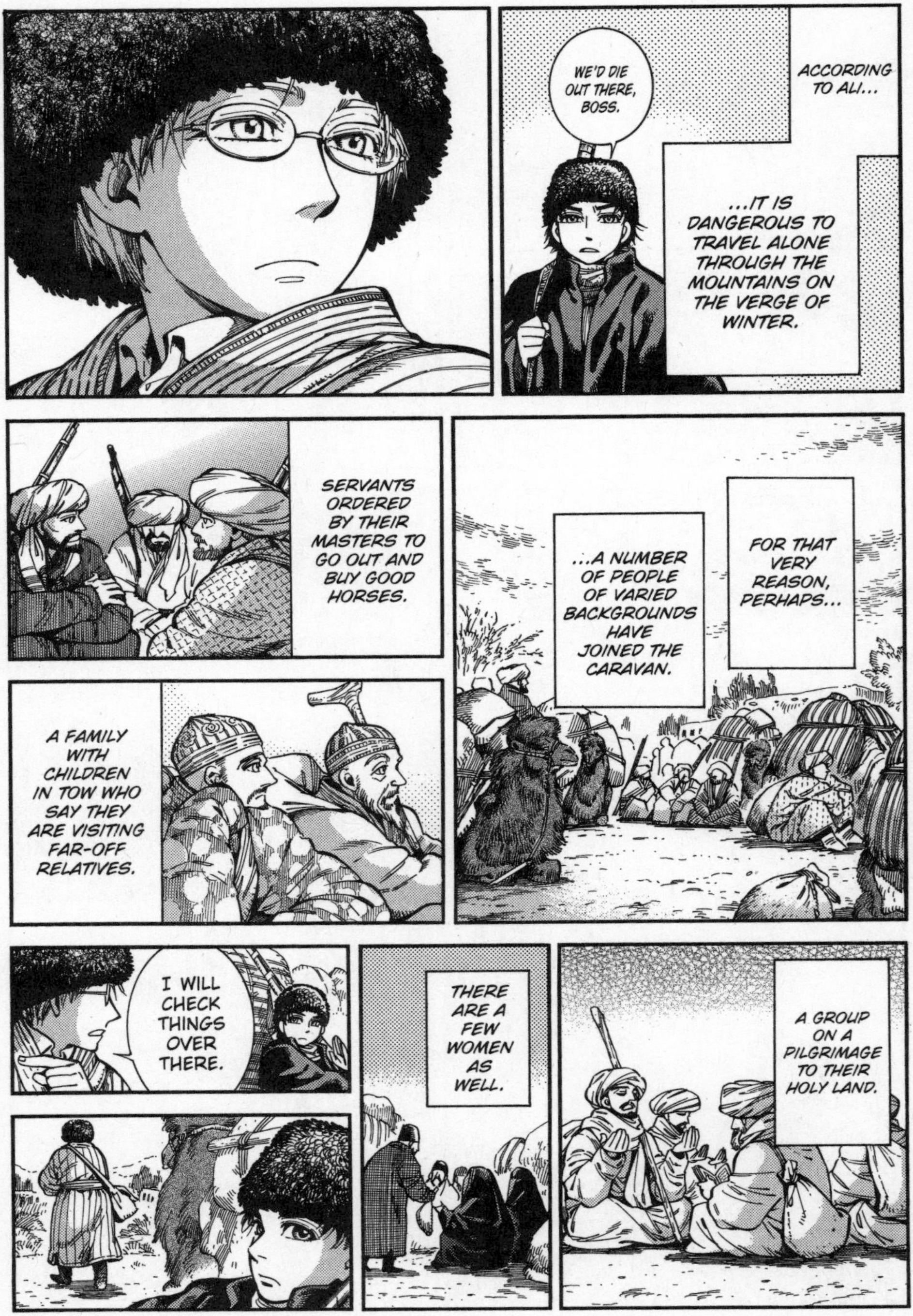
WE'D DIE OUT THERE, BOSS.
ACCORDING TO ALI...
...IT IS DANGEROUS TO TRAVEL ALONE THROUGH THE MOUNTAINS ON THE VERGE OF WINTER.
FOR THAT VERY REASON, PERHAPS...
...A NUMBER OF PEOPLE OF VARIED BACKGROUNDS HAVE JOINED THE CARAVAN.
SERVANTS ORDERED BY THEIR MASTERS TO GO OUT AND BUY GOOD HORSES.
A FAMILY WITH CHILDREN IN TOW WHO SAY THEY ARE VISITING FAR-OFF RELATIVES.
A GROUP ON A PILGRIMAGE TO THEIR HOLY LAND.
THERE ARE A FEW WOMEN AS WELL.
I WILL CHECK THINGS OVER THERE.

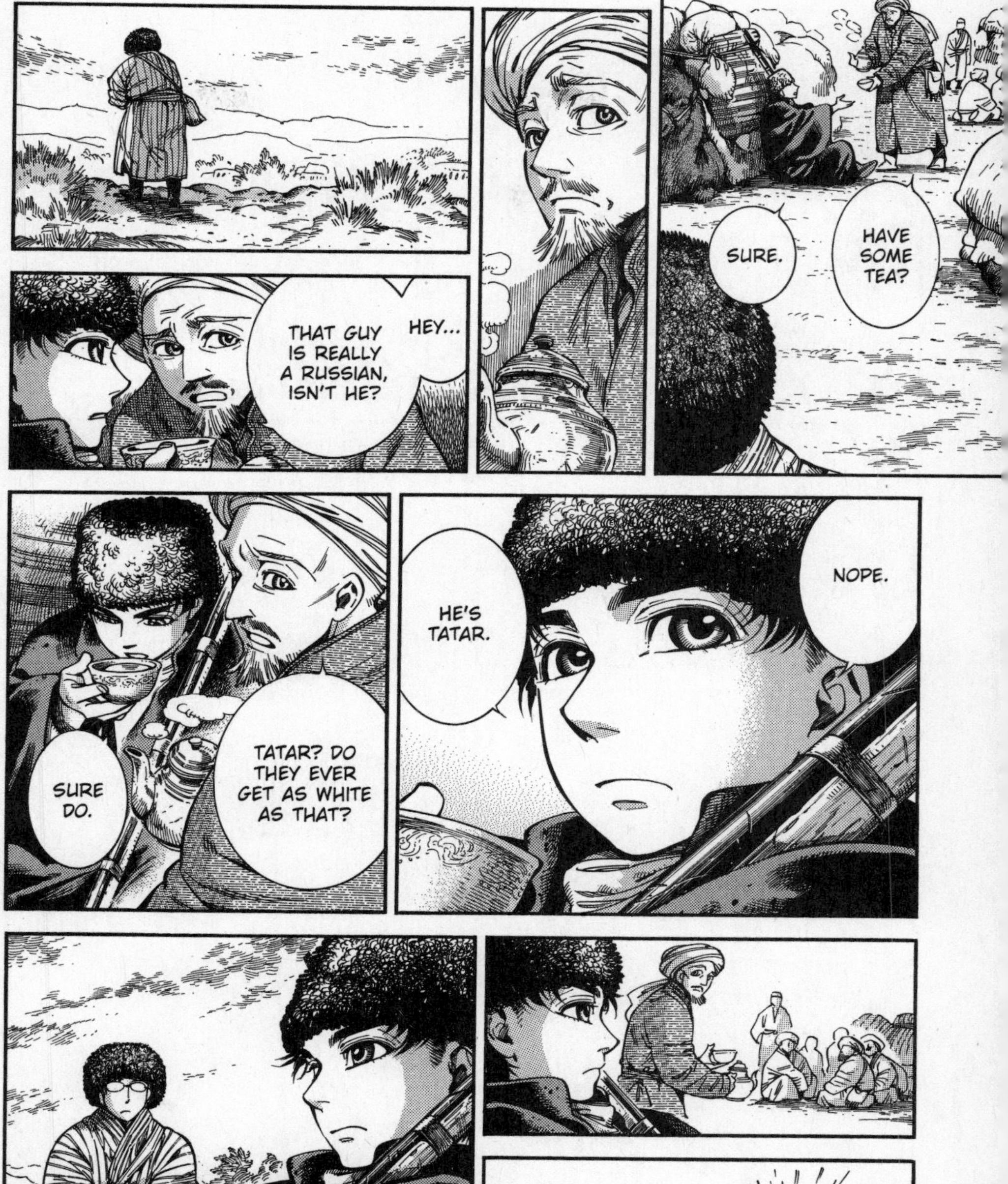
HAVE SOME TEA?
SURE.
HEY...
THAT GUY IS REALLY A RUSSIAN, ISN'T HE?
NOPE.
HE'S TATAR.
TATAR? DO THEY EVER GET AS WHITE AS THAT?
SURE DO.

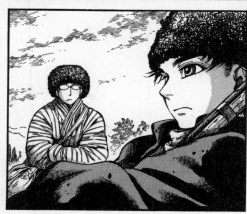

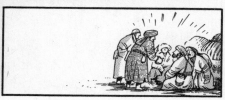

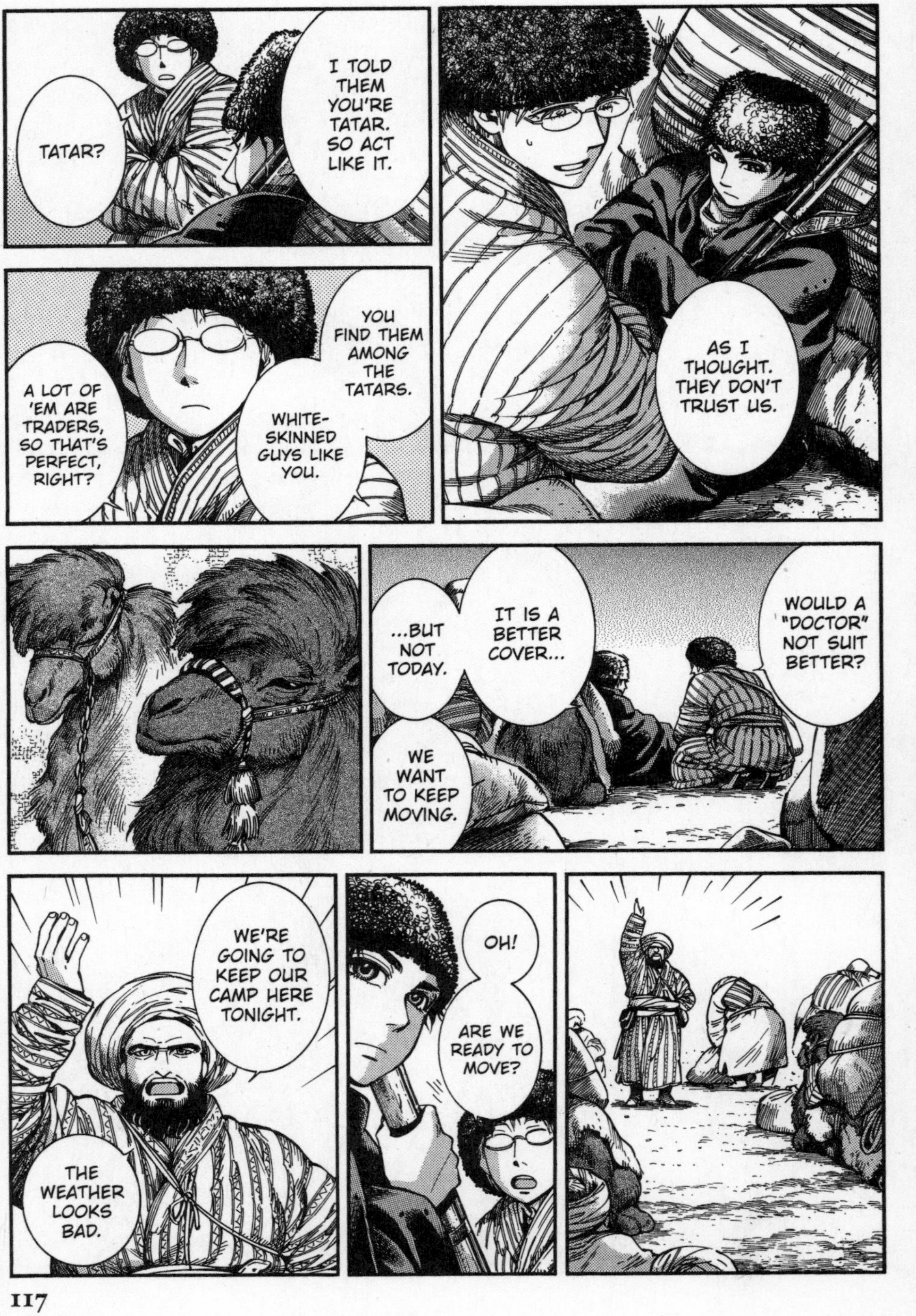
AS I THOUGHT. THEY DON'T TRUST US.
I TOLD THEM YOU'RE TATAR. SO ACT LIKE IT.
TATAR?
YOU FIND THEM AMONG THE TATARS.
WHITE-SKINNED GUYS LIKE YOU.
A LOT OF 'EM ARE TRADERS, SO THAT'S PERFECT, RIGHT?
WOULD A "DOCTOR" NOT SUIT BETTER?
IT IS A BETTER COVER...
...BUT NOT TODAY.
WE WANT TO KEEP MOVING.
OH!
ARE WE READY TO MOVE?
WE'RE GOING TO KEEP OUR CAMP HERE TONIGHT.
THE WEATHER LOOKS BAD.

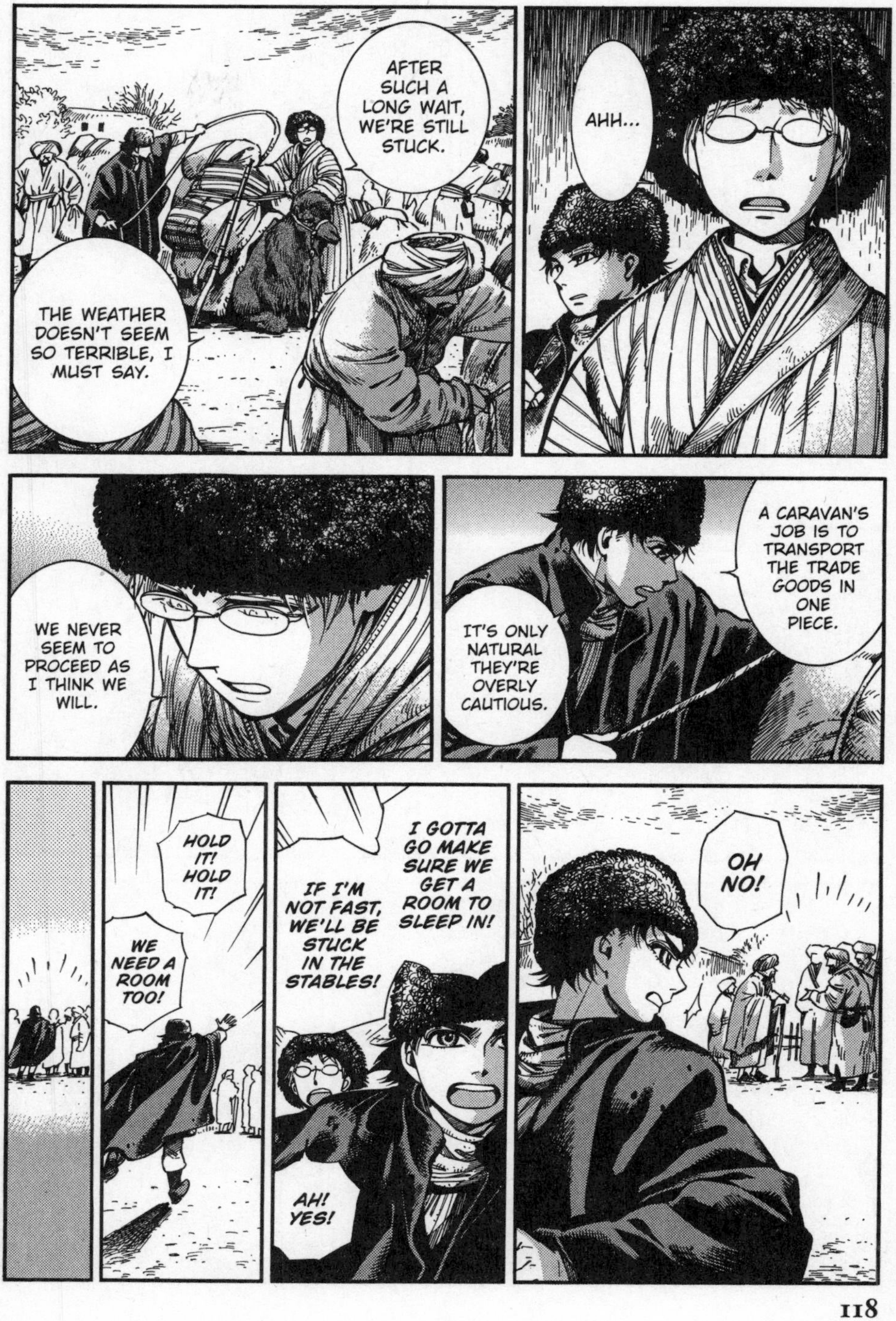
AHH...
AFTER SUCH A LONG WAIT, WE'RE STILL STUCK.
THE WEATHER DOESN'T SEEM SO TERRIBLE, I MUST SAY.
A CARAVAN'S JOB IS TO TRANSPORT THE TRADE GOODS IN ONE PIECE.
IT'S ONLY NATURAL THEY'RE OVERLY CAUTIOUS.
WE NEVER SEEM TO PROCEED AS I THINK WE WILL.
OH NO!
I GOTTA GO MAKE SURE WE GET A ROOM TO SLEEP IN!
IF I'M NOT FAST, WE'LL BE STUCK IN THE STABLES!
AH! YES!
HOLD IT! HOLD IT!
WE NEED A ROOM TOO!

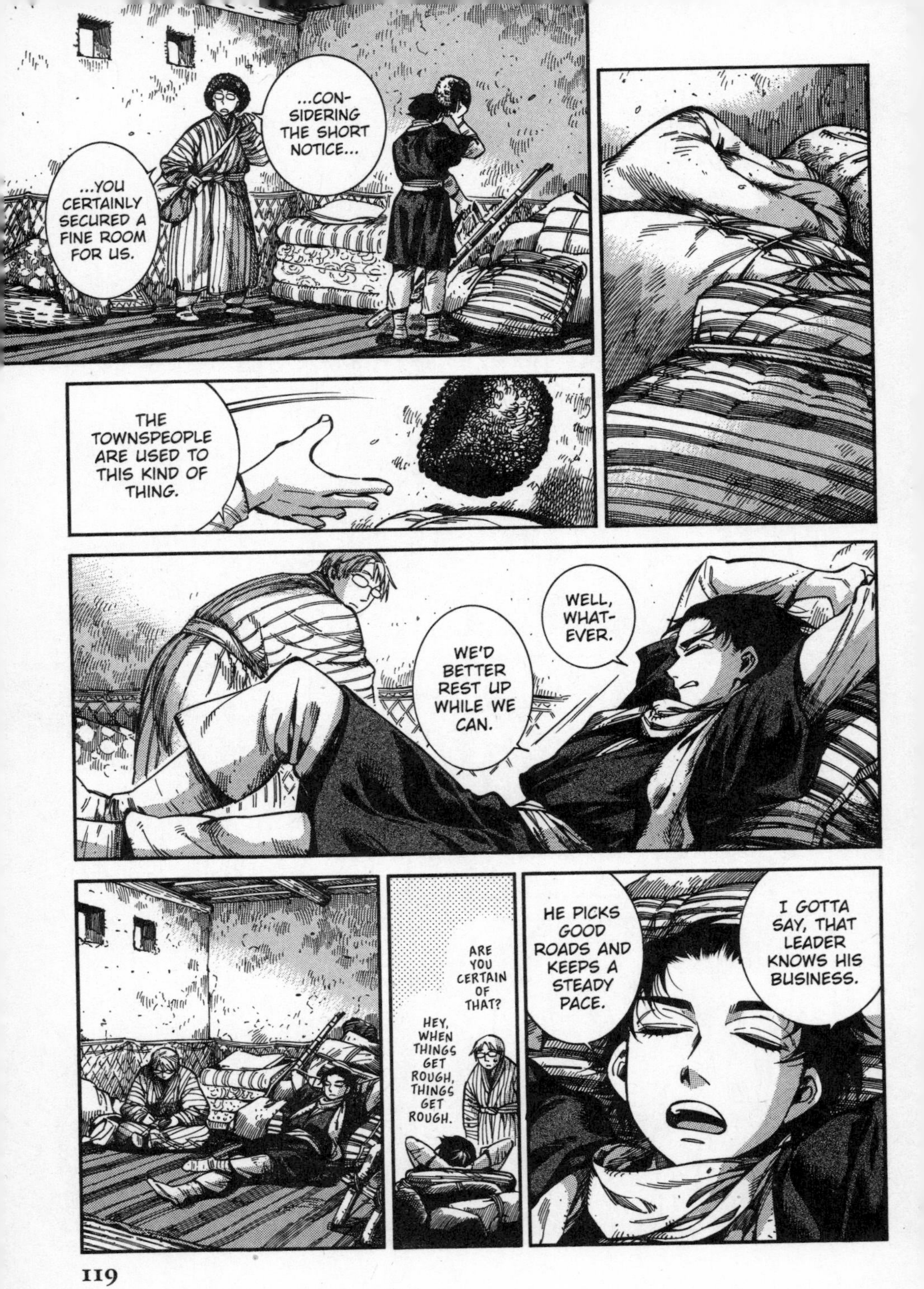
...CON-SIDERING THE SHORT NOTICE...
...YOU CERTAINLY SECURED A FINE ROOM FOR US.
THE TOWNSPEOPLE ARE USED TO THIS KIND OF THING.
WELL, WHAT-EVER.
WE'D BETTER REST UP WHILE WE CAN.
I GOTTA SAY, THAT LEADER KNOWS HIS BUSINESS.
HE PICKS GOOD ROADS AND KEEPS A STEADY PACE.
ARE YOU CERTAIN OF THAT?
HEY, WHEN THINGS GET ROUGH, THINGS GET ROUGH.

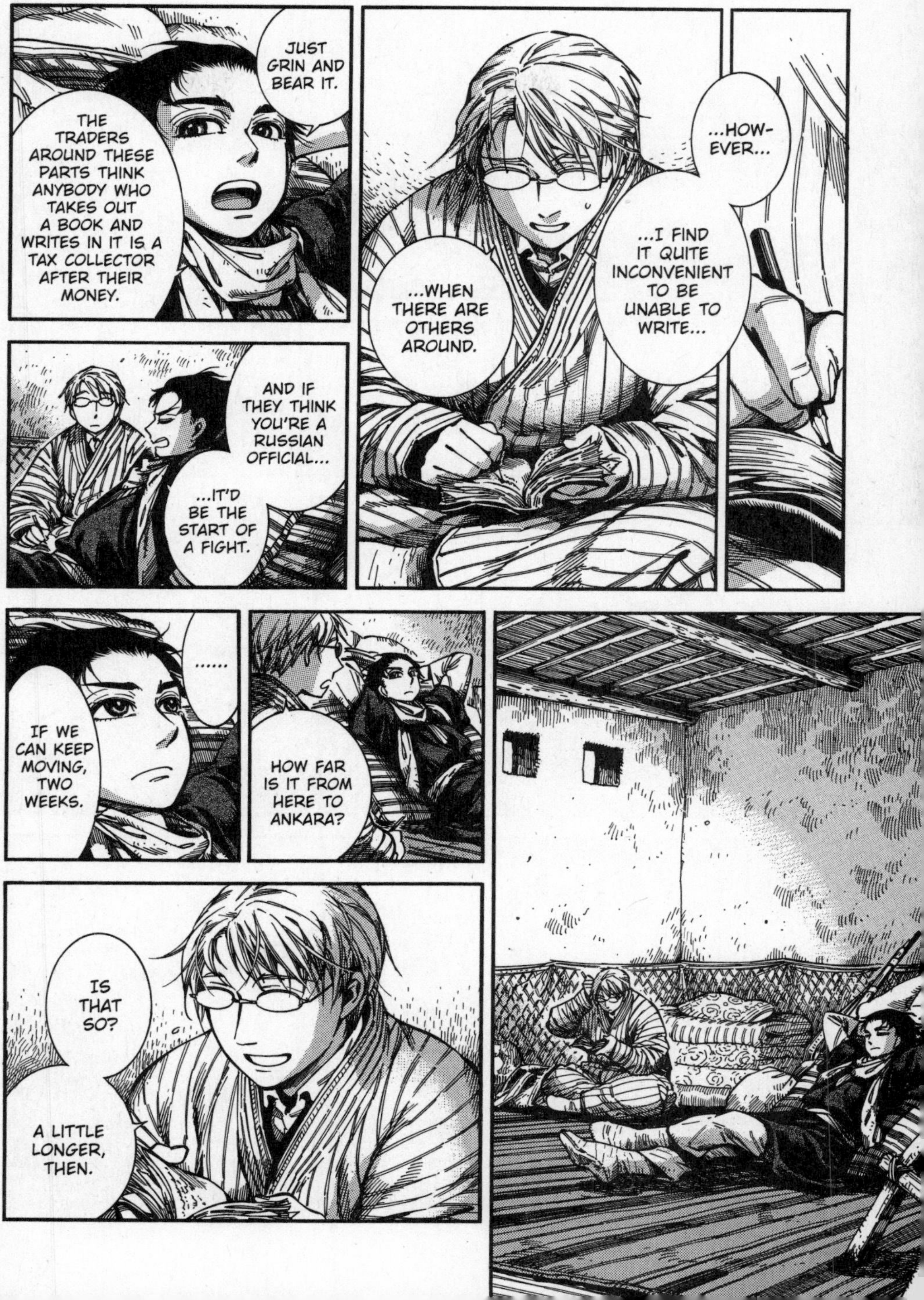
...HOW-EVER...
...I FIND IT QUITE INCONVENIENT TO BE UNABLE TO WRITE...
...WHEN THERE ARE OTHERS AROUND.
JUST GRIN AND BEAR IT.
THE TRADERS AROUND THESE PARTS THINK ANYBODY WHO TAKES OUT A BOOK AND WRITES IN IT IS A TAX COLLECTOR AFTER THEIR MONEY.
AND IF THEY THINK YOU'RE A RUSSIAN OFFICIAL...
...IT'D BE THE START OF A FIGHT.
HOW FAR IS IT FROM HERE TO ANKARA?
......
IF WE CAN KEEP MOVING, TWO WEEKS.
IS THAT SO?
A LITTLE LONGER, THEN.

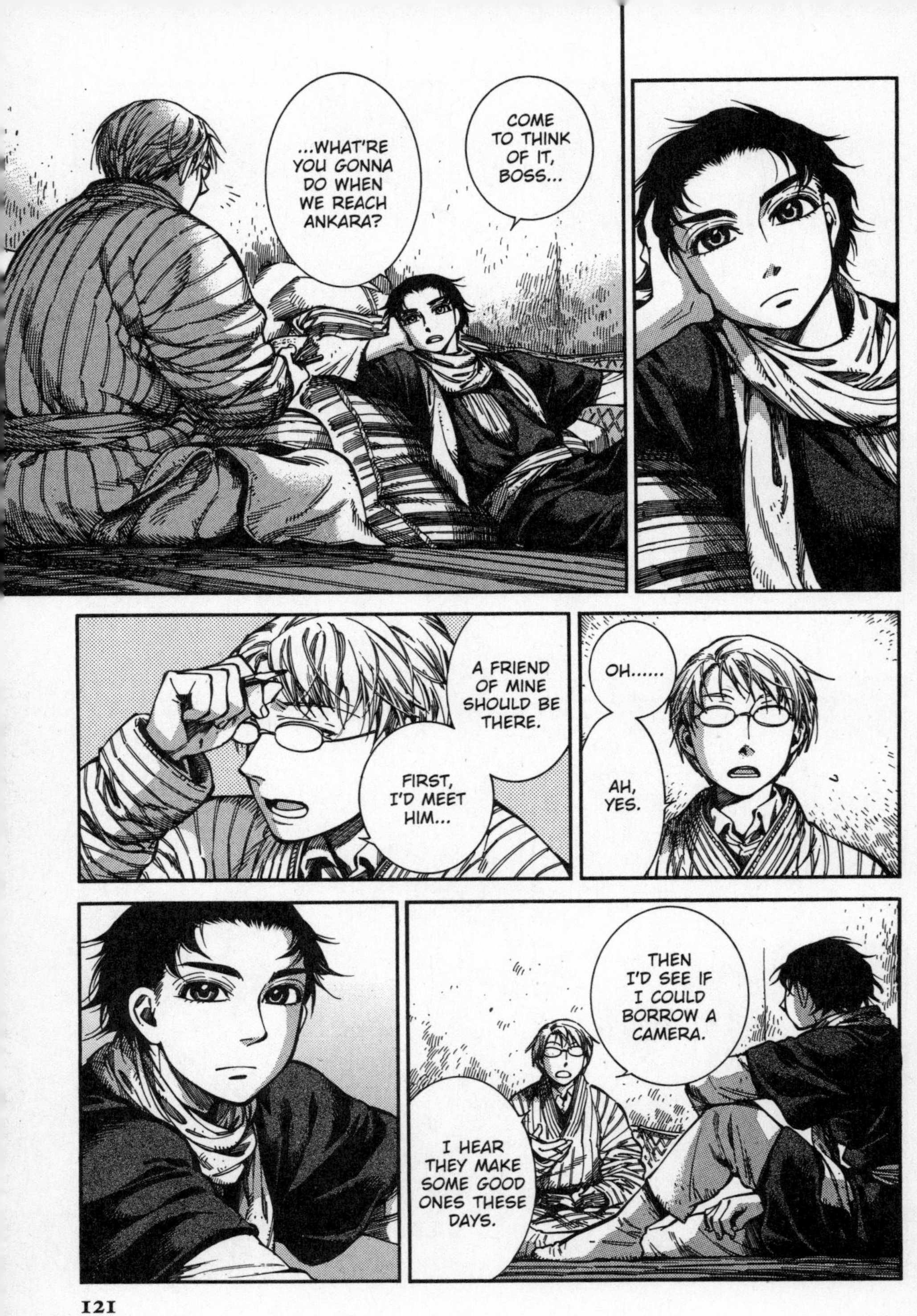
COME TO THINK OF IT, BOSS...
...WHAT'RE YOU GONNA DO WHEN WE REACH ANKARA?
OH......
AH, YES.
A FRIEND OF MINE SHOULD BE THERE.
FIRST, I'D MEET HIM...
THEN I'D SEE IF I COULD BORROW A CAMERA.
I HEAR THEY MAKE SOME GOOD ONES THESE DAYS.

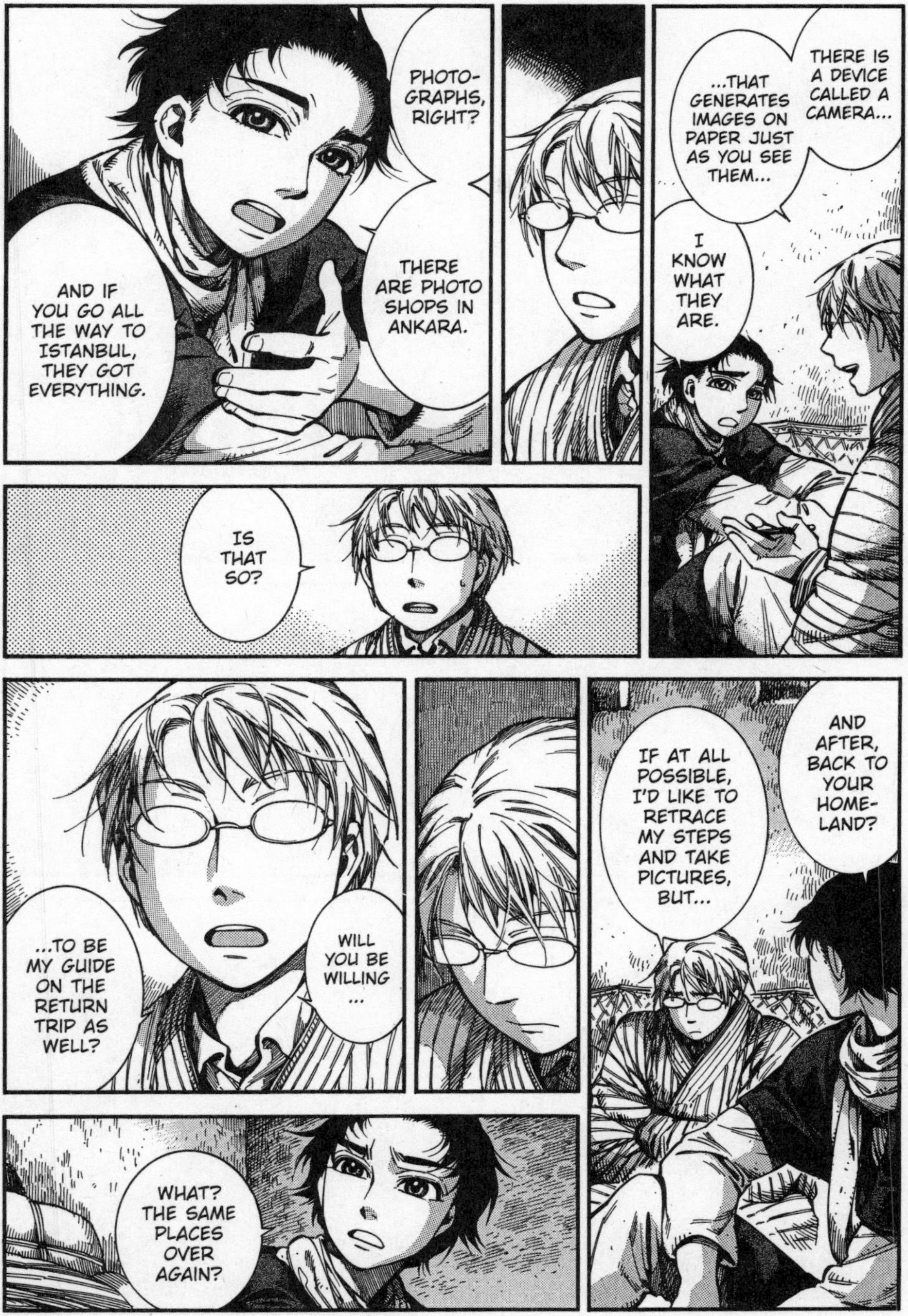
THERE IS A DEVICE CALLED A CAMERA...
...THAT GENERATES IMAGES ON PAPER JUST AS YOU SEE THEM...
I KNOW WHAT THEY ARE.
PHOTO-GRAPHS, RIGHT?
THERE ARE PHOTO SHOPS IN ANKARA.
AND IF YOU GO ALL THE WAY TO ISTANBUL, THEY GOT EVERYTHING.
IS THAT SO?
AND AFTER, BACK TO YOUR HOME-LAND?
IF AT ALL POSSIBLE, I'D LIKE TO RETRACE MY STEPS AND TAKE PICTURES, BUT...
WILL YOU BE WILLING ...
...TO BE MY GUIDE ON THE RETURN TRIP AS WELL?
WHAT? THE SAME PLACES OVER AGAIN?

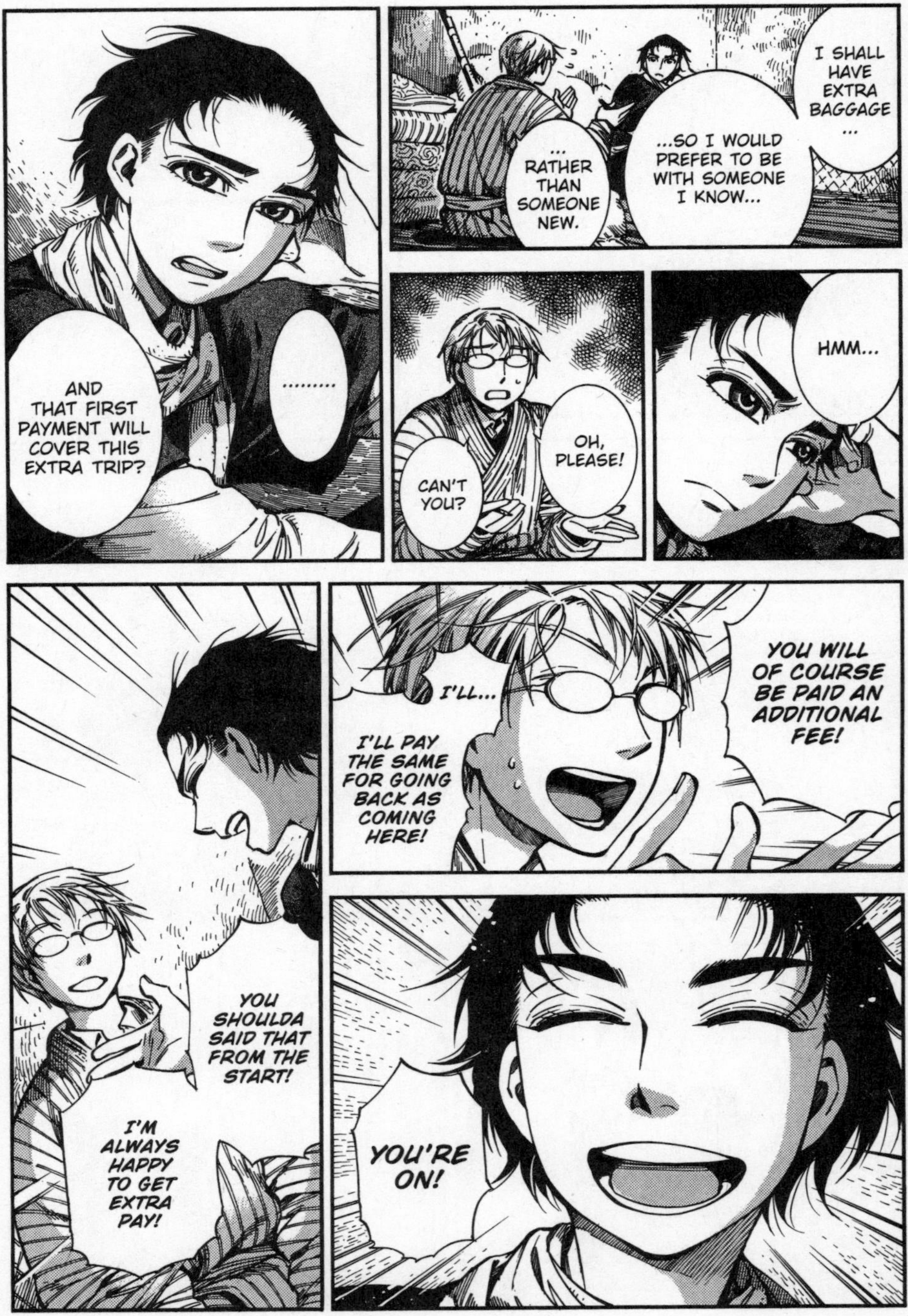
I SHALL HAVE EXTRA BAGGAGE...
...SO I WOULD PREFER TO BE WITH SOMEONE I KNOW...
...RATHER THAN SOMEONE NEW.
HMM...
OH, PLEASE!
CAN'T YOU?
....
AND THAT FIRST PAYMENT WILL COVER THIS EXTRA TRIP?
YOU WILL OF COURSE BE PAID AN ADDITIONAL FEE!
I'LL...
I'LL PAY THE SAME FOR GOING BACK AS COMING HERE!
YOU'RE ON!
YOU SHOULDA SAID THAT FROM THE START!
I'M ALWAYS HAPPY TO GET EXTRA PAY!

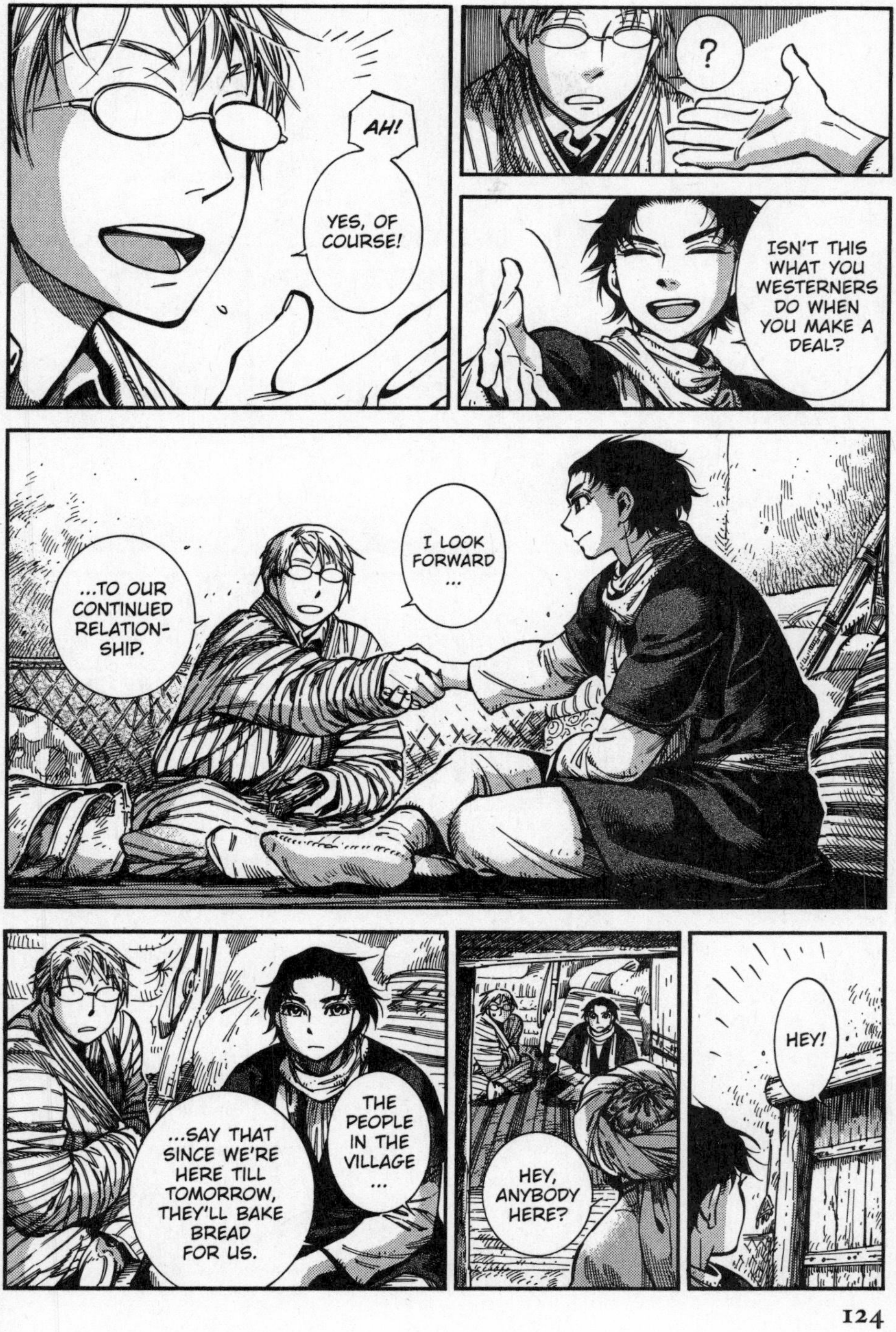
?
ISN'T THIS WHAT YOU WESTERNERS DO WHEN YOU MAKE A DEAL?
AH!
YES, OF COURSE!
I LOOK FORWARD ...
...TO OUR CONTINUED RELATION-SHIP.
HEY!
HEY, ANYBODY HERE?
THE PEOPLE IN THE VILLAGE ...
...SAY THAT SINCE WE'RE HERE TILL TOMORROW, THEY'LL BAKE BREAD FOR US.

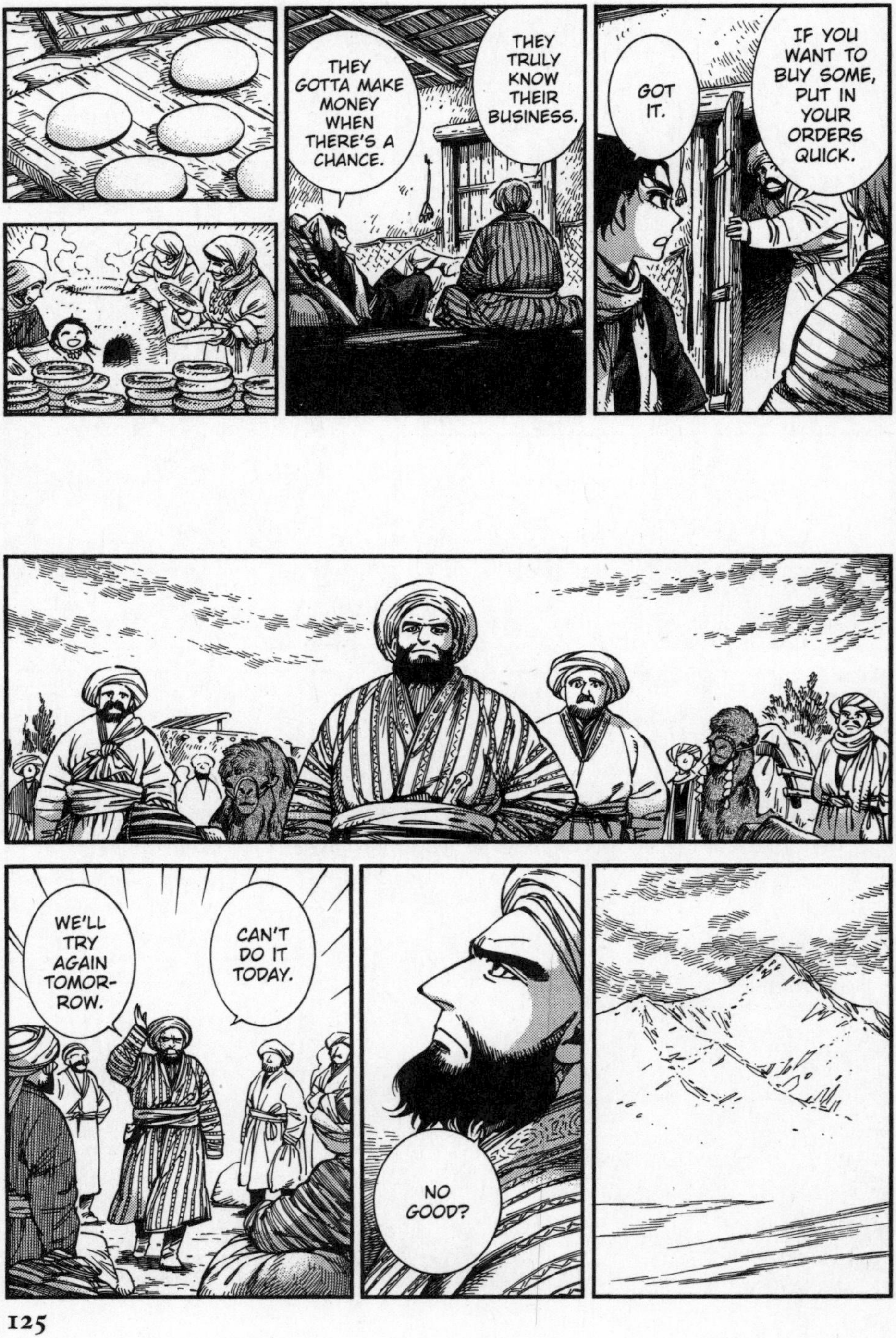
IF YOU WANT TO BUY SOME, PUT IN YOUR ORDERS QUICK.
GOT IT.
THEY TRULY KNOW THEIR BUSINESS.
THEY GOTTA MAKE MONEY WHEN THERE'S A CHANCE.
NO GOOD?
CAN'T DO IT TODAY.
WE'LL TRY AGAIN TOMOR-ROW.

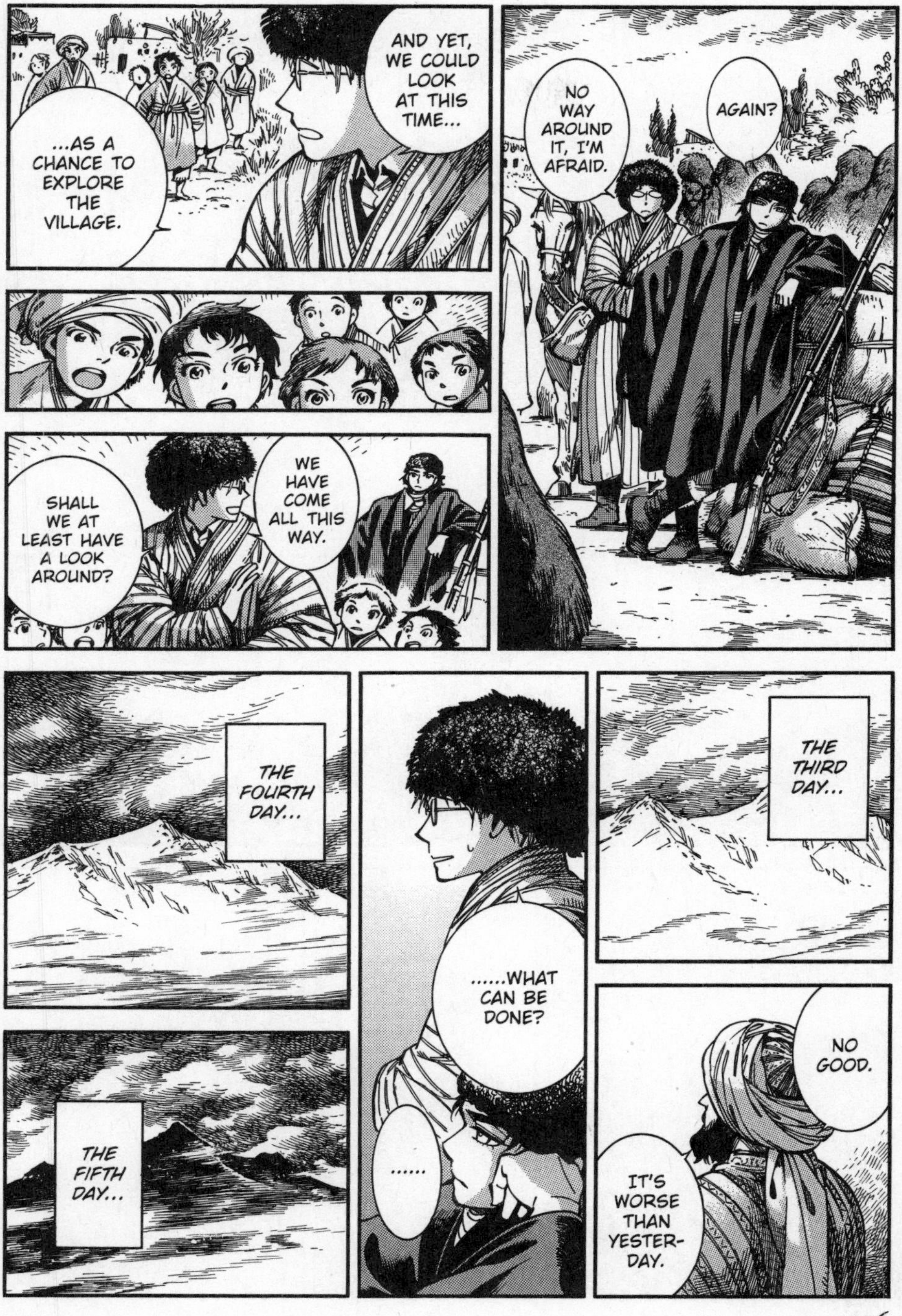
AGAIN?
NO WAY AROUND IT, I'M AFRAID.
AND YET, WE COULD LOOK AT THIS TIME...
...AS A CHANCE TO EXPLORE THE VILLAGE.
WE HAVE COME ALL THIS WAY.
SHALL WE AT LEAST HAVE A LOOK AROUND?
THE THIRD DAY...
NO GOOD.
IT'S WORSE THAN YESTER-DAY.
......WHAT CAN BE DONE?
......
THE FOURTH DAY...
THE FIFTH DAY...

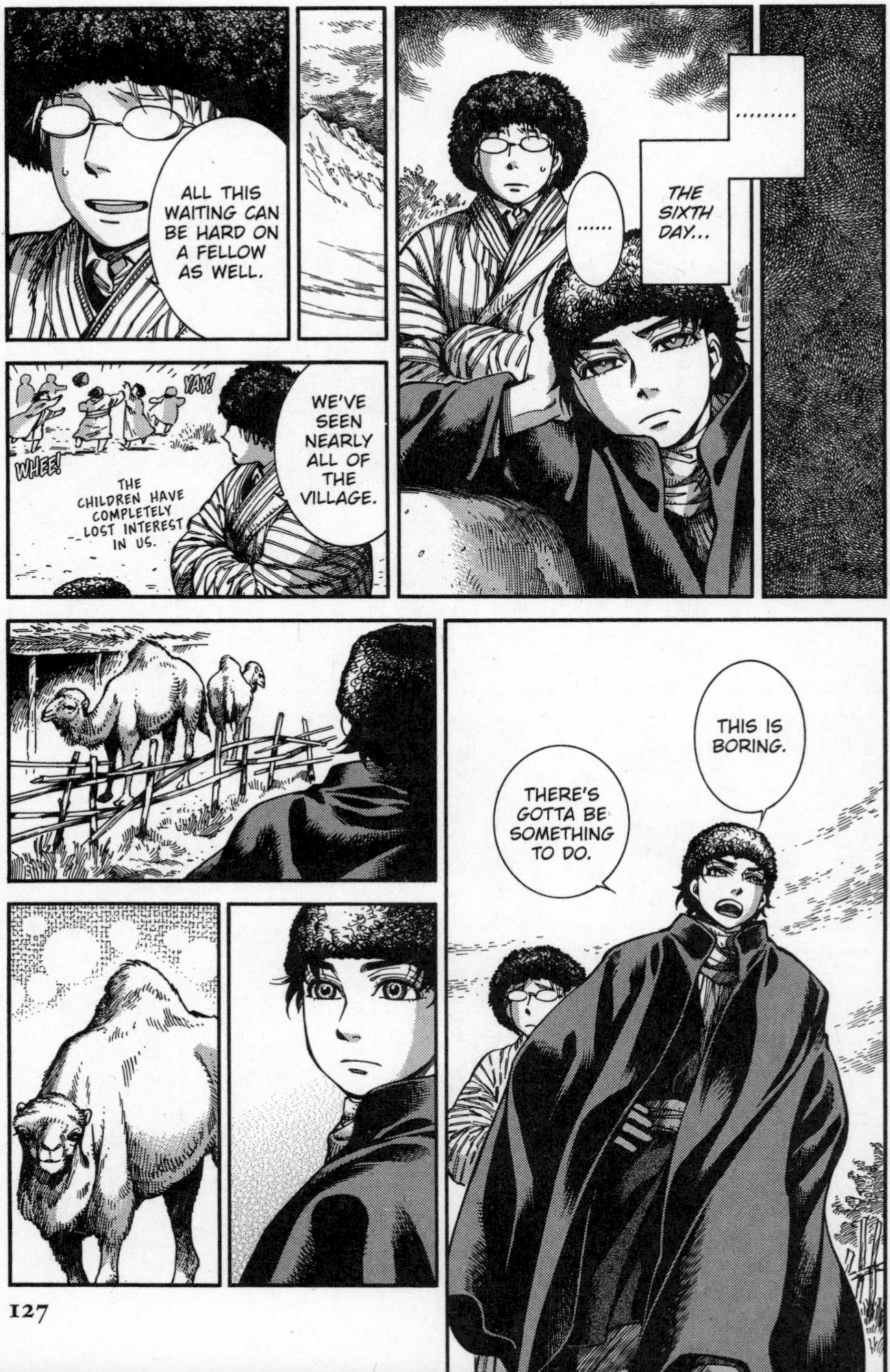
....
THE SIXTH DAY...
......
ALL THIS WAITING CAN BE HARD ON A FELLOW AS WELL.
WE'VE SEEN NEARLY ALL OF THE VILLAGE.
YAY!
WHEE!
THE CHILDREN HAVE COMPLETELY LOST INTEREST IN US.
THIS IS BORING.
THERE'S GOTTA BE SOMETHING TO DO.

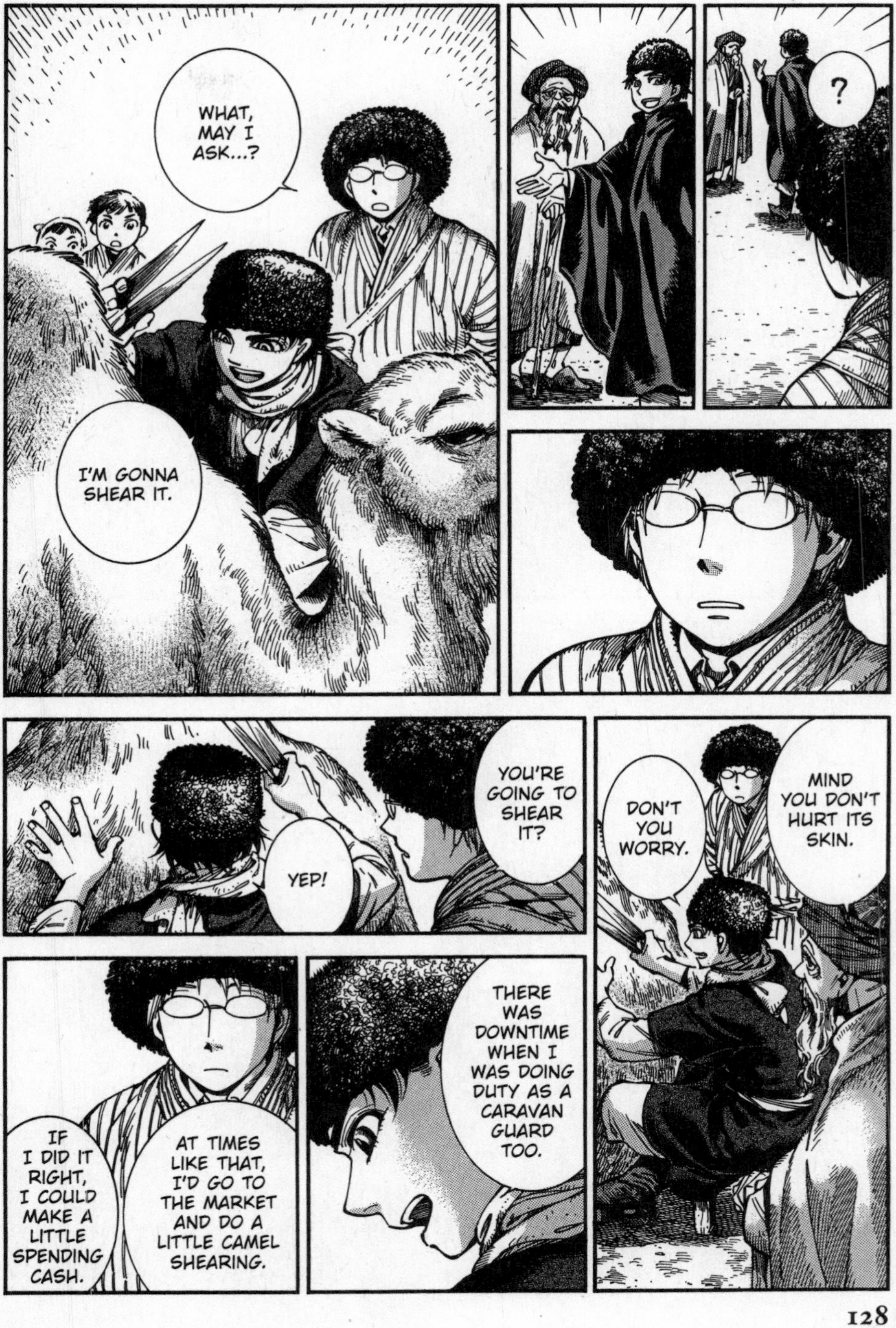
?
WHAT, MAY I ASK...?
I'M GONNA SHEAR IT.
MIND YOU DON'T HURT ITS SKIN.
DON'T YOU WORRY.
YOU'RE GOING TO SHEAR IT?
YEP!
THERE WAS DOWNTIME WHEN I WAS DOING DUTY AS A CARAVAN GUARD TOO.
AT TIMES LIKE THAT, I'D GO TO THE MARKET AND DO A LITTLE CAMEL SHEARING.
IF I DID IT RIGHT, I COULD MAKE A LITTLE SPENDING CASH.

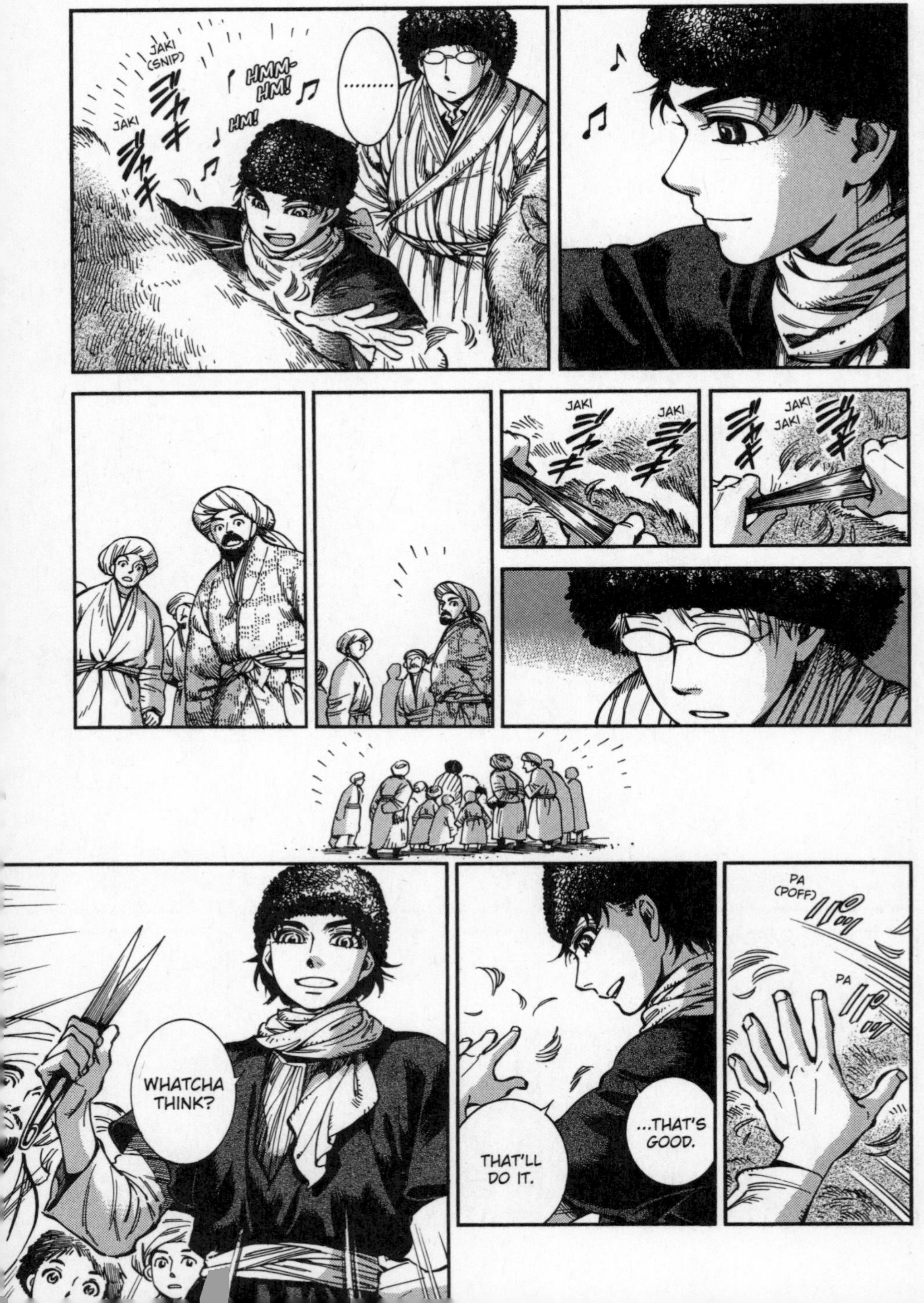
JAKI (SNIP)
ジャキ
HMM-HM!
HM!
....
JAKI
ジャキ
JAKI JAKI
ジャキジャキ
JAKI
ジャキ
JAKI
ジャキ
PA (POFF)
パッ
PA
パッ
...THAT'S GOOD.
THAT'LL DO IT.
WHATCHA THINK?

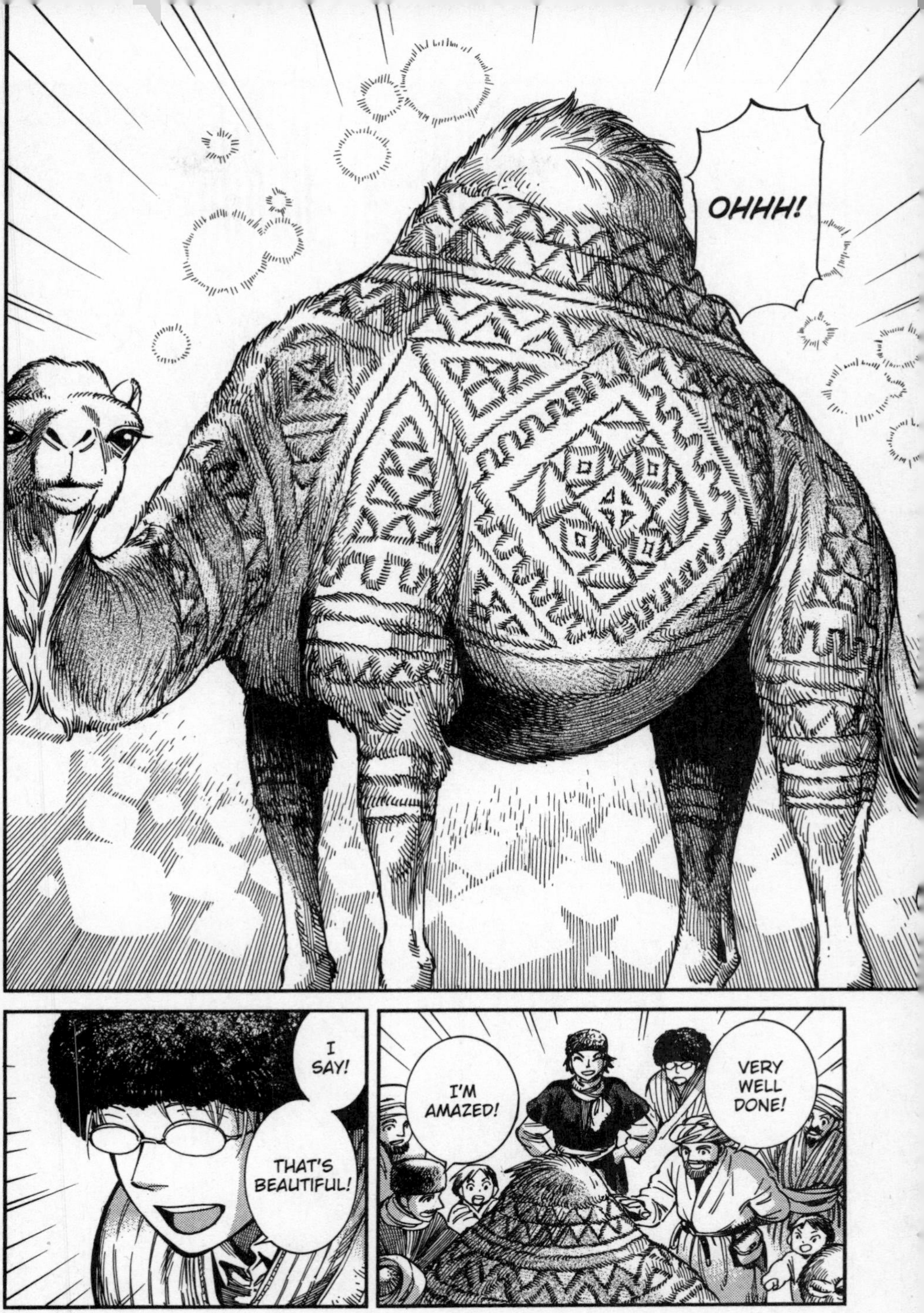
OHHH!
VERY WELL DONE!
I'M AMAZED!
I SAY!
THAT'S BEAUTIFUL!

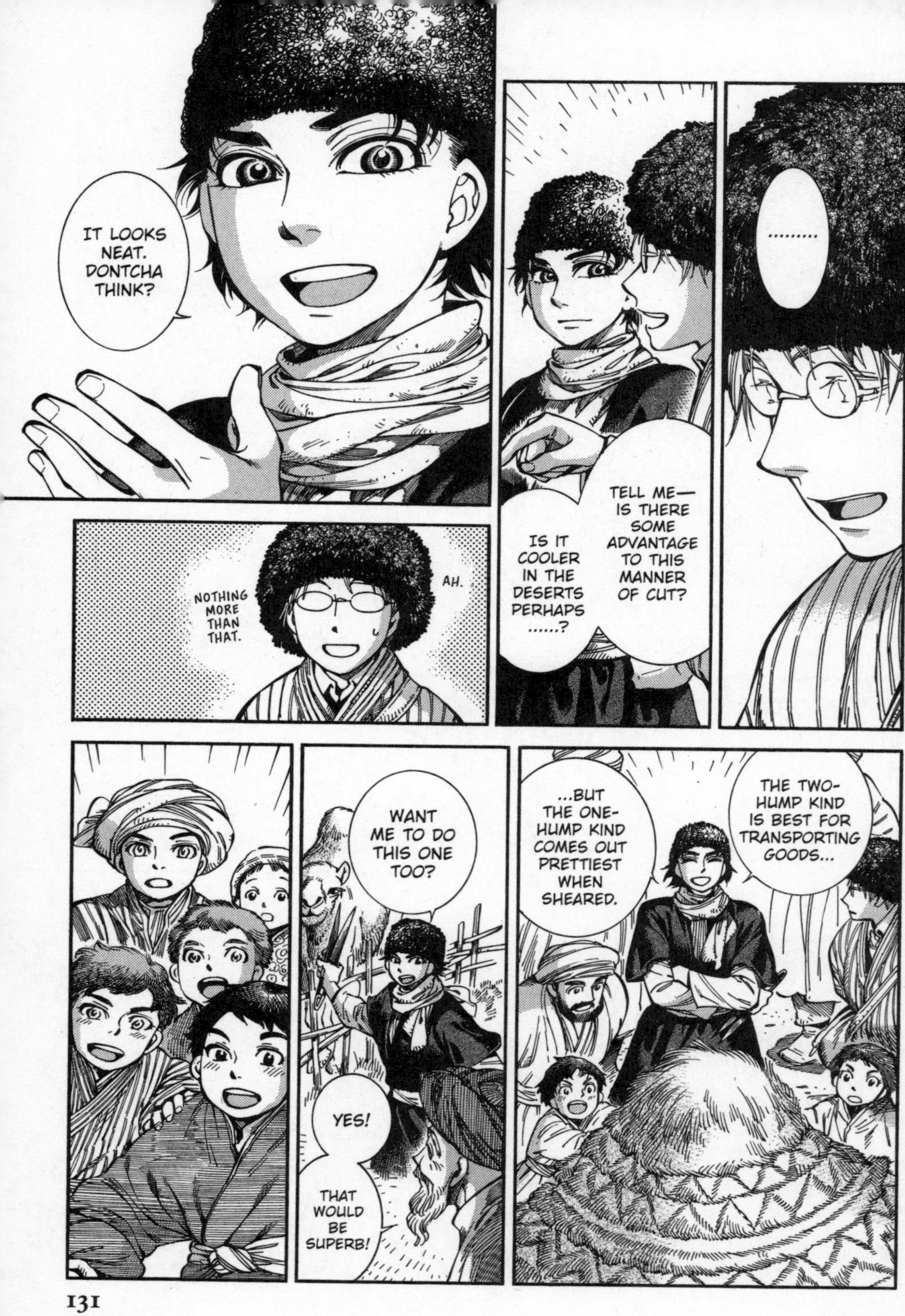
....
TELL ME— IS THERE SOME ADVANTAGE TO THIS MANNER OF CUT?
IS IT COOLER IN THE DESERTS PERHAPS ......?
IT LOOKS NEAT. DONTCHA THINK?
AH.
NOTHING MORE THAN THAT.
THE TWO-HUMP KIND IS BEST FOR TRANSPORTING GOODS...
...BUT THE ONE-HUMP KIND COMES OUT PRETTIEST WHEN SHEARED.
WANT ME TO DO THIS ONE TOO?
YES!
THAT WOULD BE SUPERB!

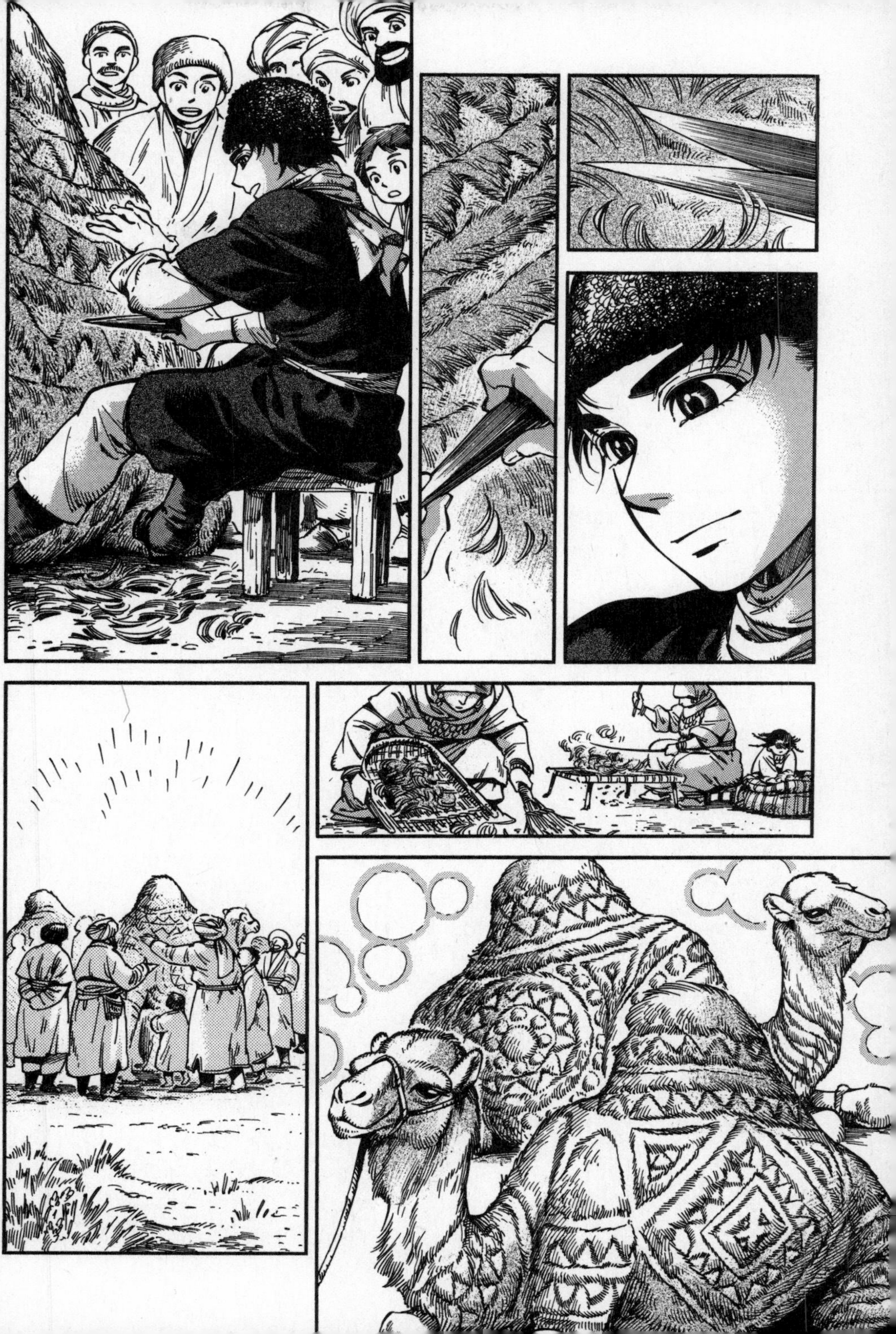

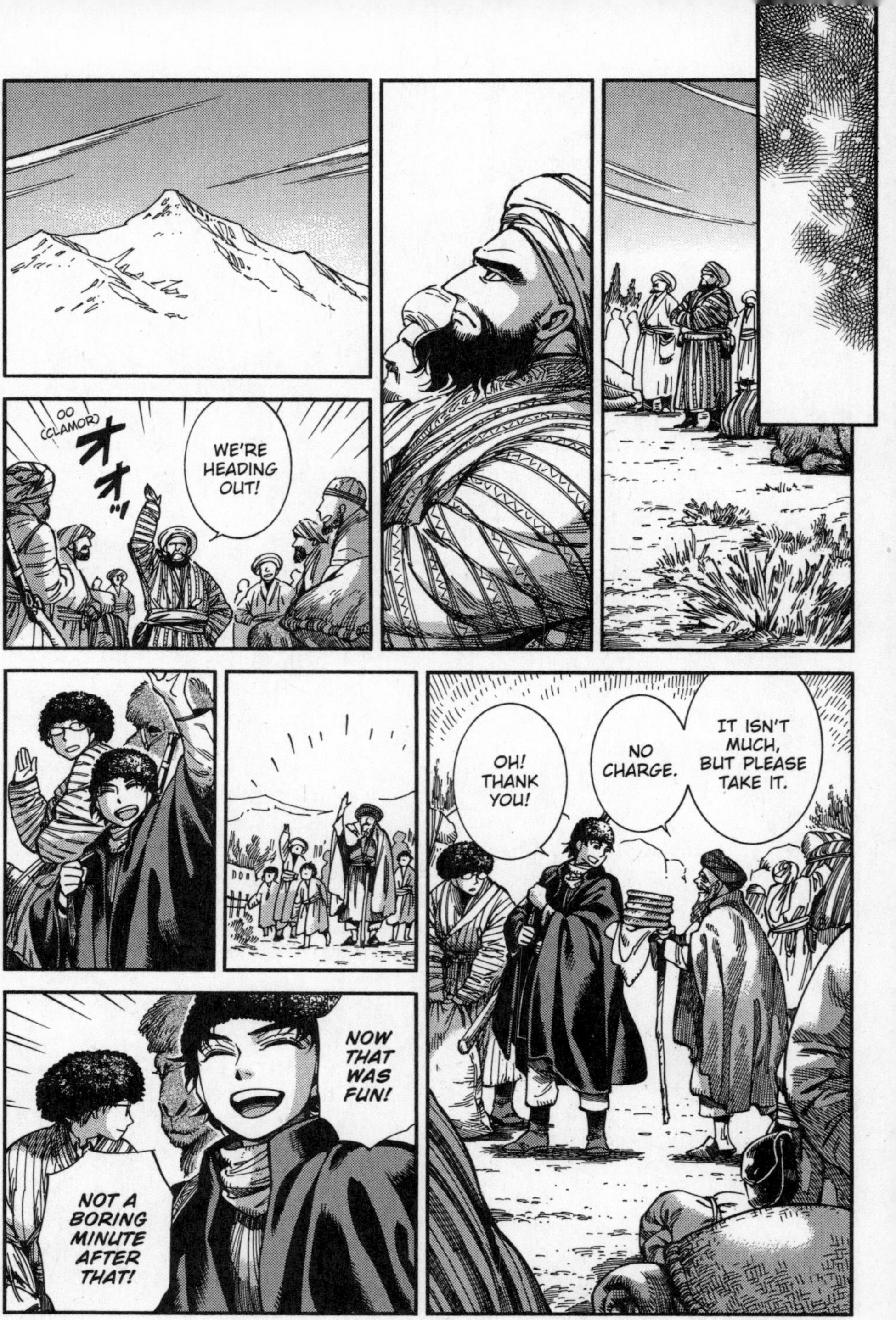
OO (CLAMOR)
オォッ
WE'RE HEADING OUT!
IT ISN'T MUCH, BUT PLEASE TAKE IT.
NO CHARGE.
OH! THANK YOU!
NOW THAT WAS FUN!
NOT A BORING MINUTE AFTER THAT!

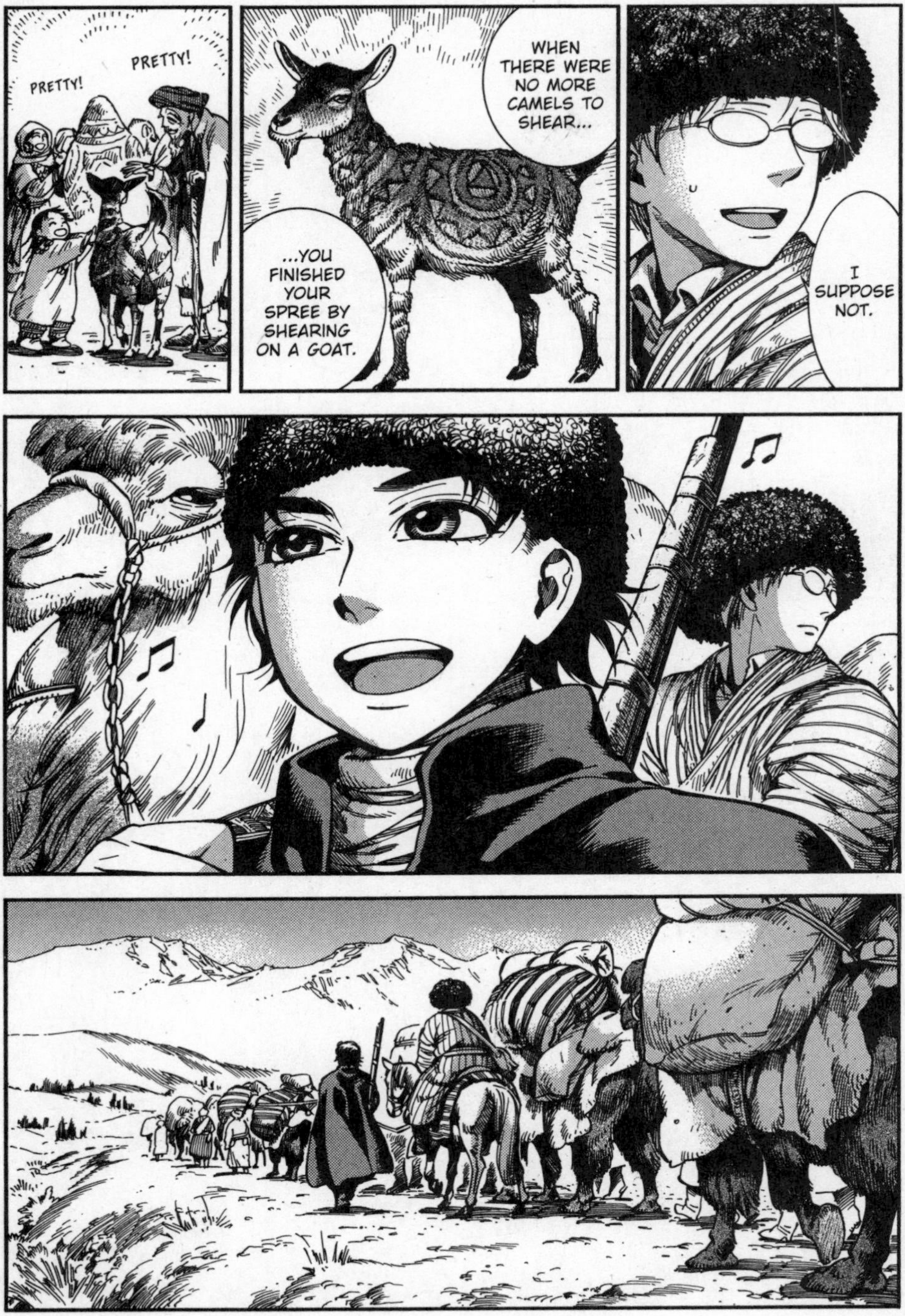
I SUPPOSE NOT.
WHEN THERE WERE NO MORE CAMELS TO SHEAR...
...YOU FINISHED YOUR SPREE BY SHEARING ON A GOAT.
PRETTY!
PRETTY!

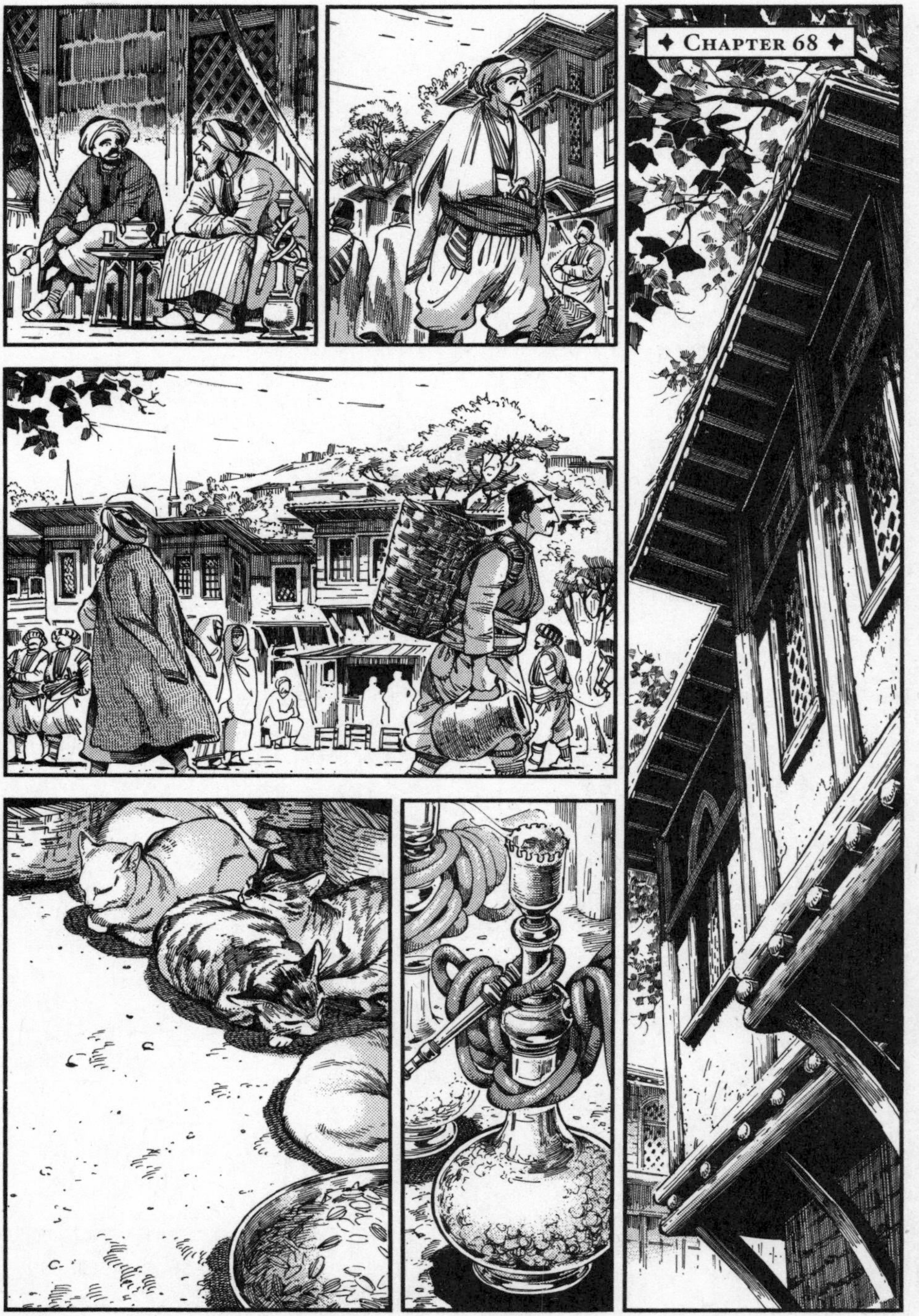
Chapter 68

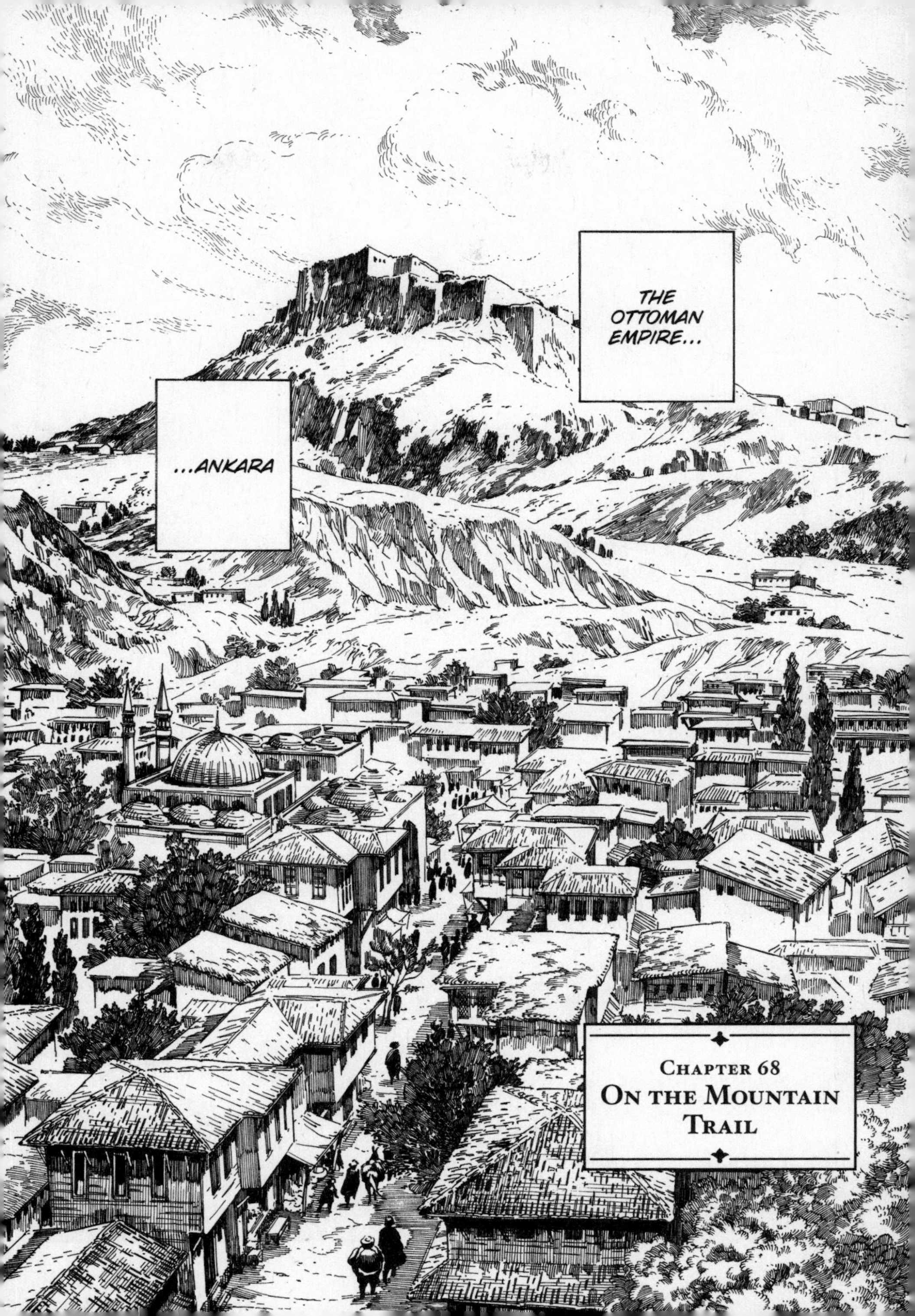
THE OTTOMAN EMPIRE...
...ANKARA
Chapter 68
On the Mountain Trail

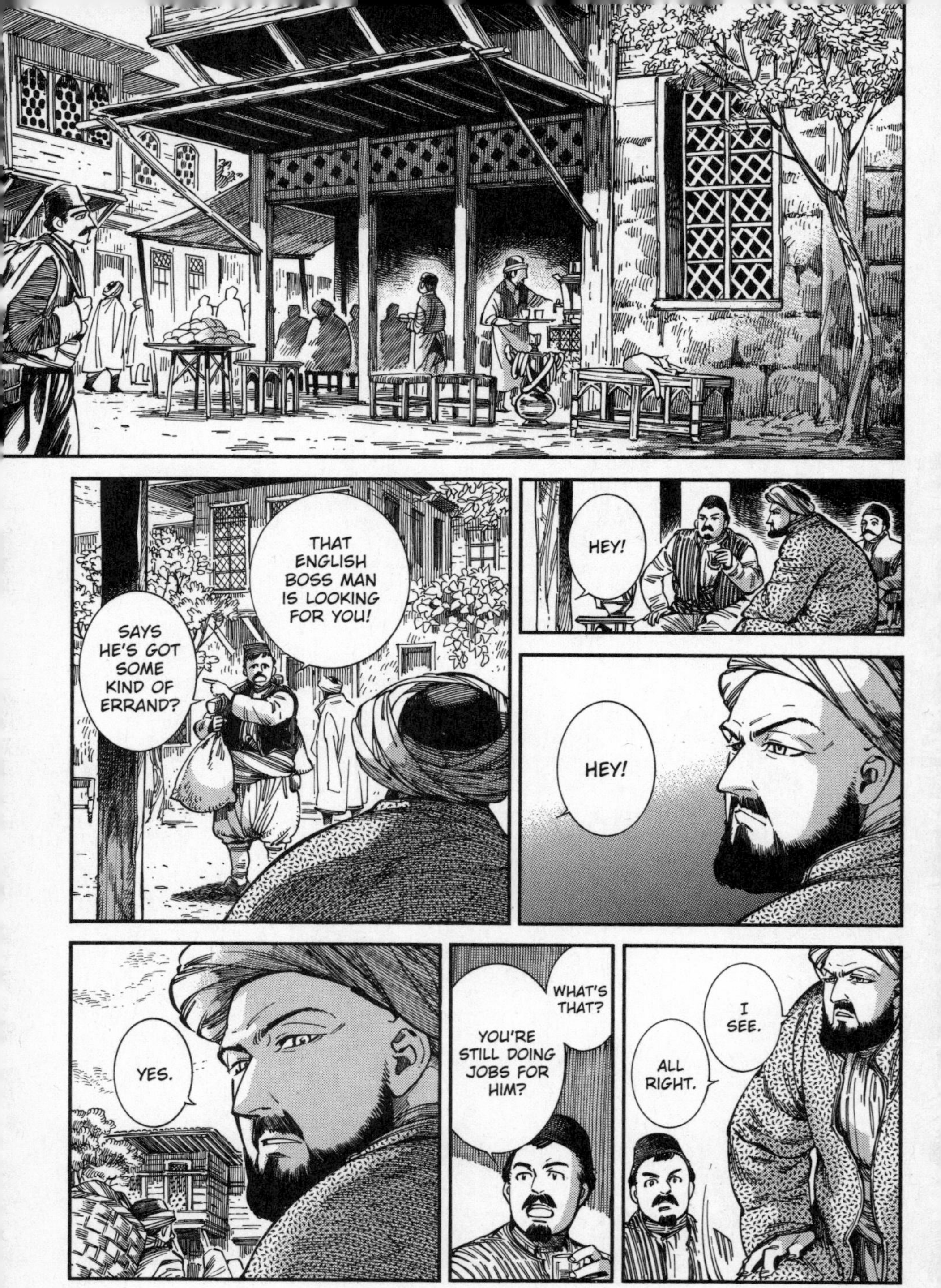
HEY!
HEY!
THAT ENGLISH BOSS MAN IS LOOKING FOR YOU!
SAYS HE'S GOT SOME KIND OF ERRAND?
I SEE.
ALL RIGHT.
WHAT'S THAT?
YOU'RE STILL DOING JOBS FOR HIM?
YES.

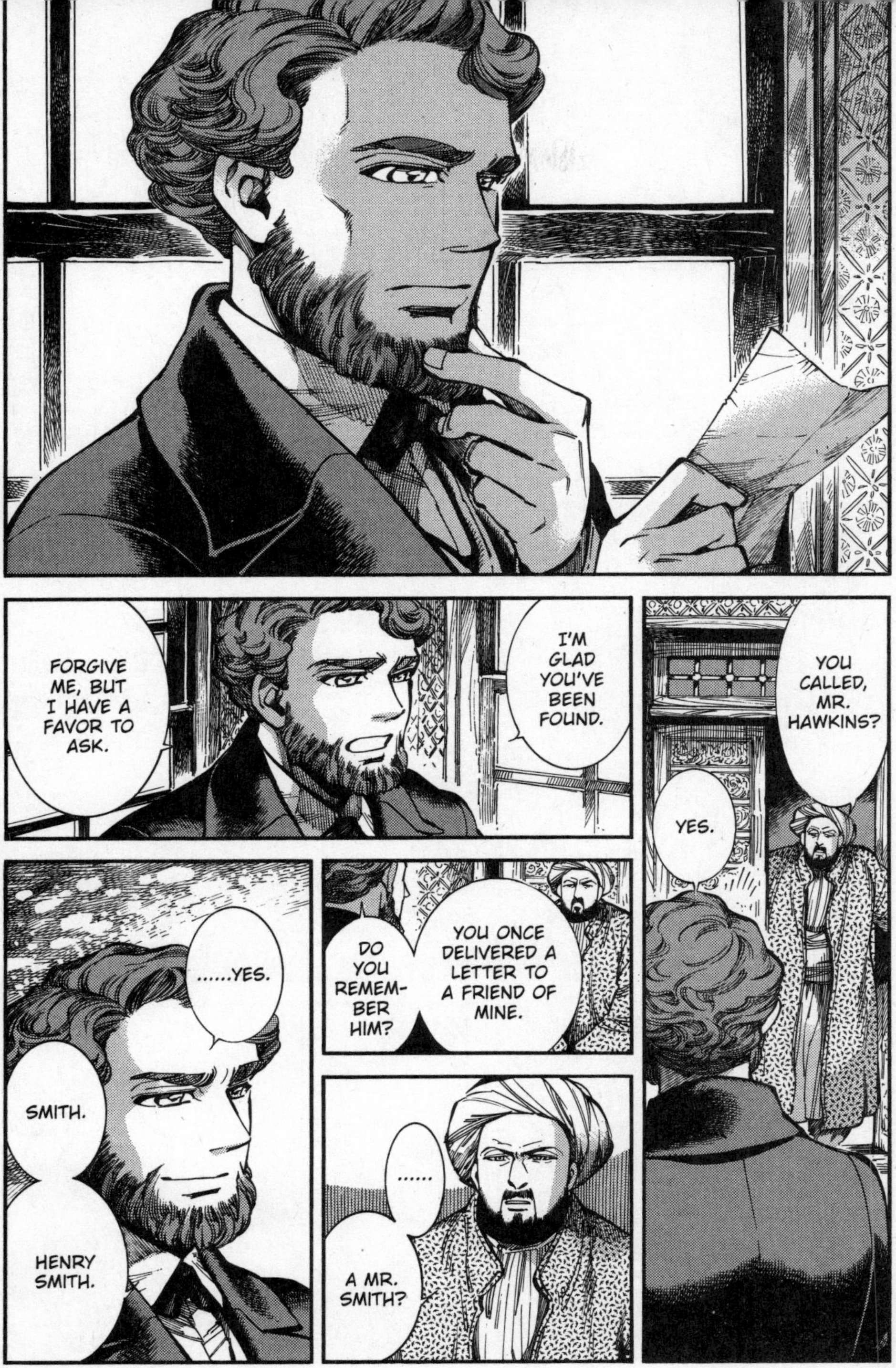
YOU CALLED, MR. HAWKINS?
YES.
I'M GLAD YOU'VE BEEN FOUND.
FORGIVE ME, BUT I HAVE A FAVOR TO ASK.
YOU ONCE DELIVERED A LETTER TO A FRIEND OF MINE.
DO YOU REMEMBER HIM?
......
A MR. SMITH?
......YES.
SMITH.
HENRY SMITH.

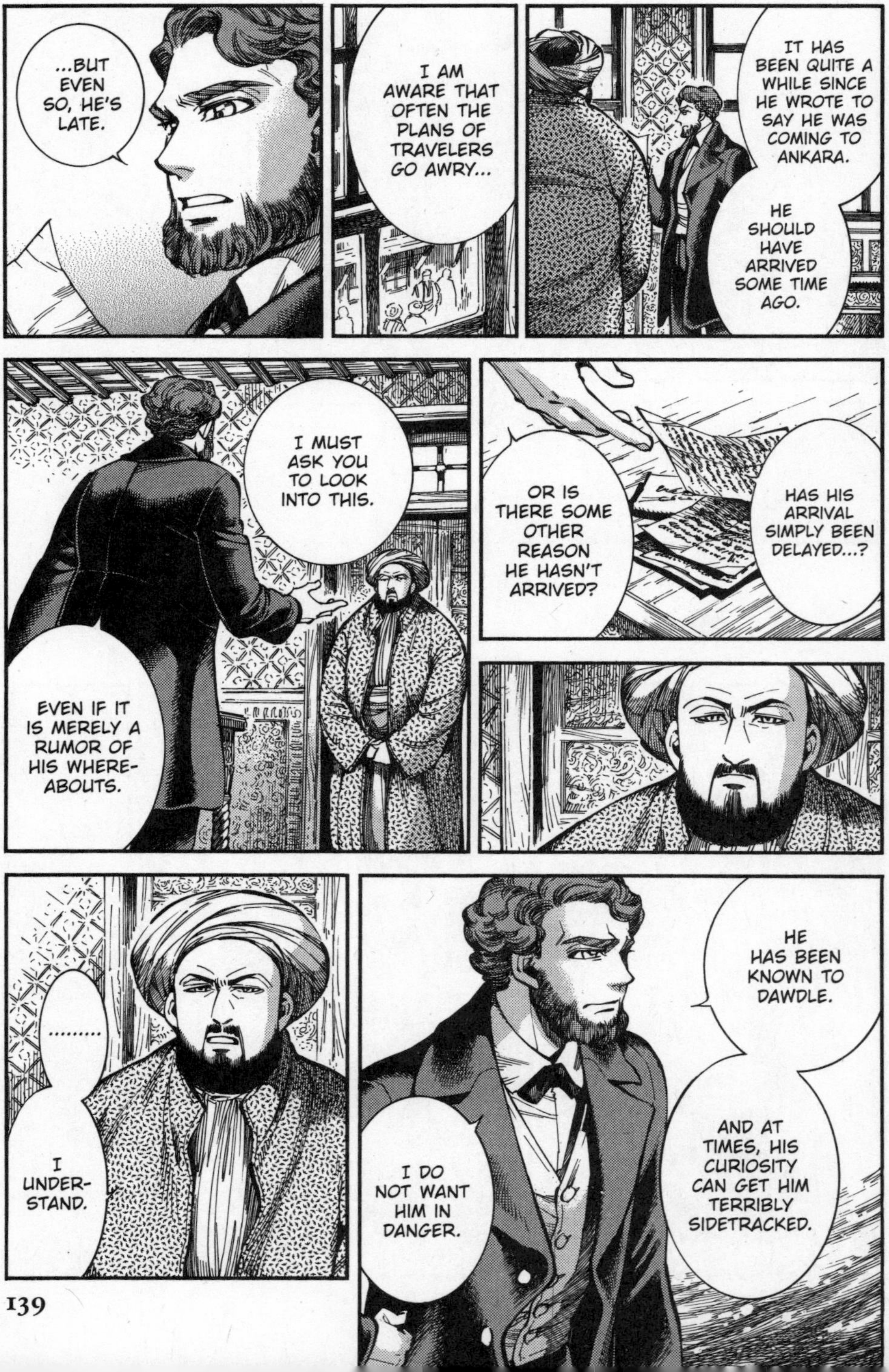
IT HAS BEEN QUITE A WHILE SINCE HE WROTE TO SAY HE WAS COMING TO ANKARA.
HE SHOULD HAVE ARRIVED SOME TIME AGO.
I AM AWARE THAT OFTEN THE PLANS OF TRAVELERS GO AWRY...
...BUT EVEN SO, HE'S LATE.
HAS HIS ARRIVAL SIMPLY BEEN DELAYED...?
OR IS THERE SOME OTHER REASON HE HASN'T ARRIVED?
I MUST ASK YOU TO LOOK INTO THIS.
EVEN IF IT IS MERELY A RUMOR OF HIS WHERE-ABOUTS.
HE HAS BEEN KNOWN TO DAWDLE.
AND AT TIMES, HIS CURIOSITY CAN GET HIM TERRIBLY SIDETRACKED.
I DO NOT WANT HIM IN DANGER.
....
I UNDER-STAND.

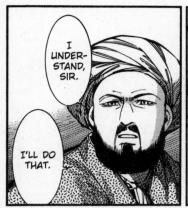

AH! ONE MORE THING.
SHOULD YOU HAPPEN TO HEAR WORD OF RUSSIAN ADVANCEMENT...
...I WOULD APPRECIATE ANY DETAILS.
I UNDERSTAND, SIR.
I'LL DO THAT.

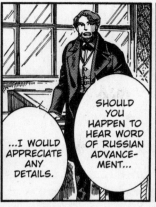

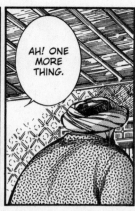

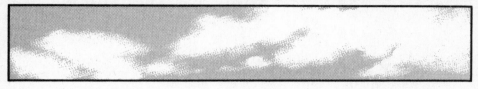

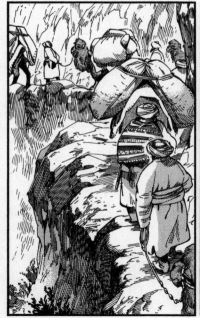

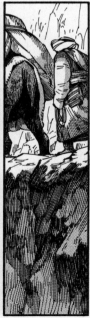

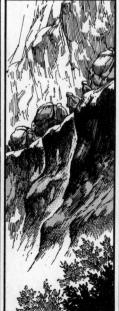

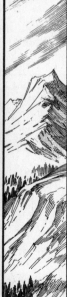

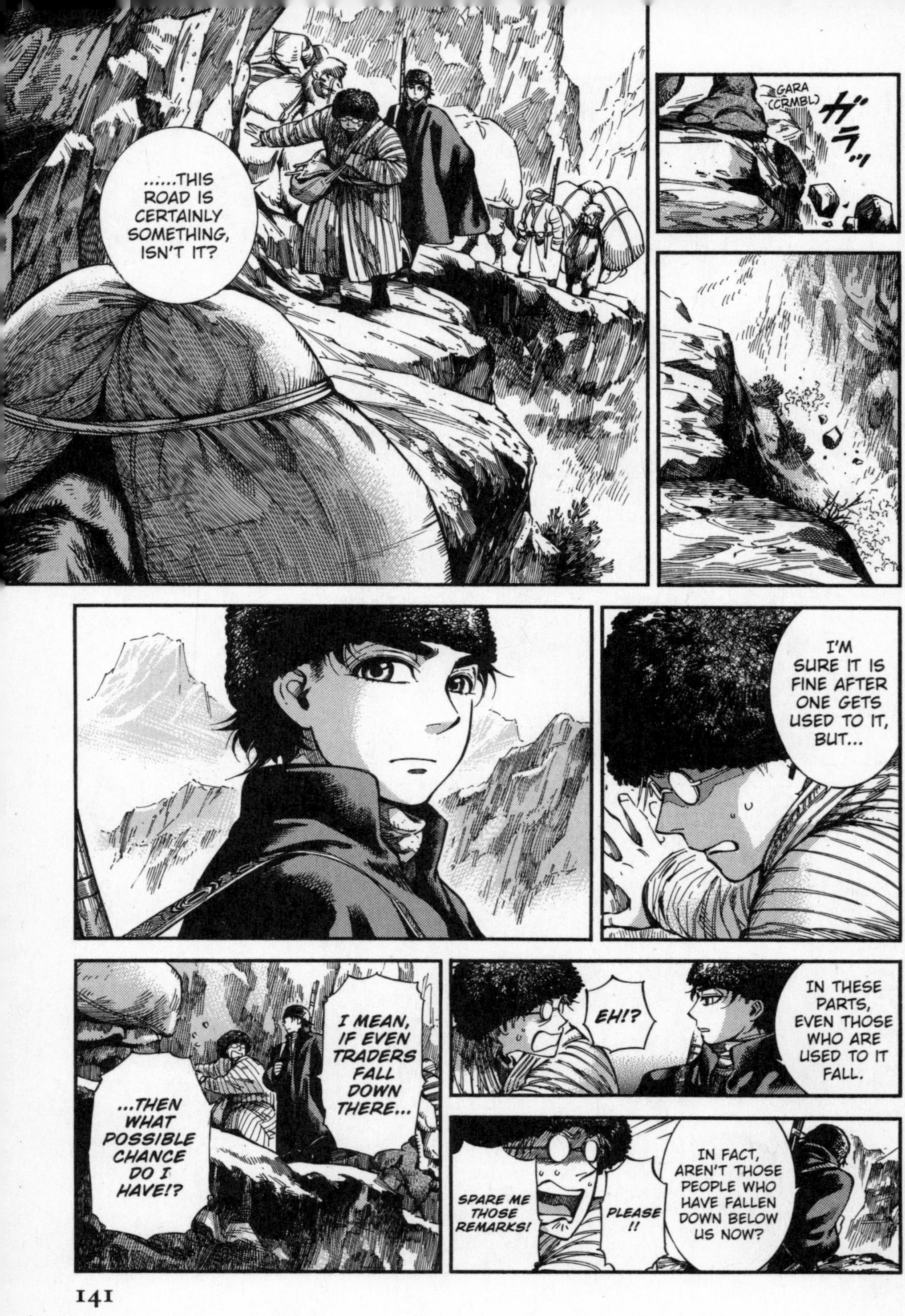
GARA (CRMBL)
ガラッ
......THIS ROAD IS CERTAINLY SOMETHING, ISN'T IT?
I'M SURE IT IS FINE AFTER ONE GETS USED TO IT, BUT...
IN THESE PARTS, EVEN THOSE WHO ARE USED TO IT FALL.
EH!?
IN FACT, AREN'T THOSE PEOPLE WHO HAVE FALLEN DOWN BELOW US NOW?
PLEASE !!
SPARE ME THOSE REMARKS!
I MEAN, IF EVEN TRADERS FALL DOWN THERE...
...THEN WHAT POSSIBLE CHANCE DO I HAVE!?

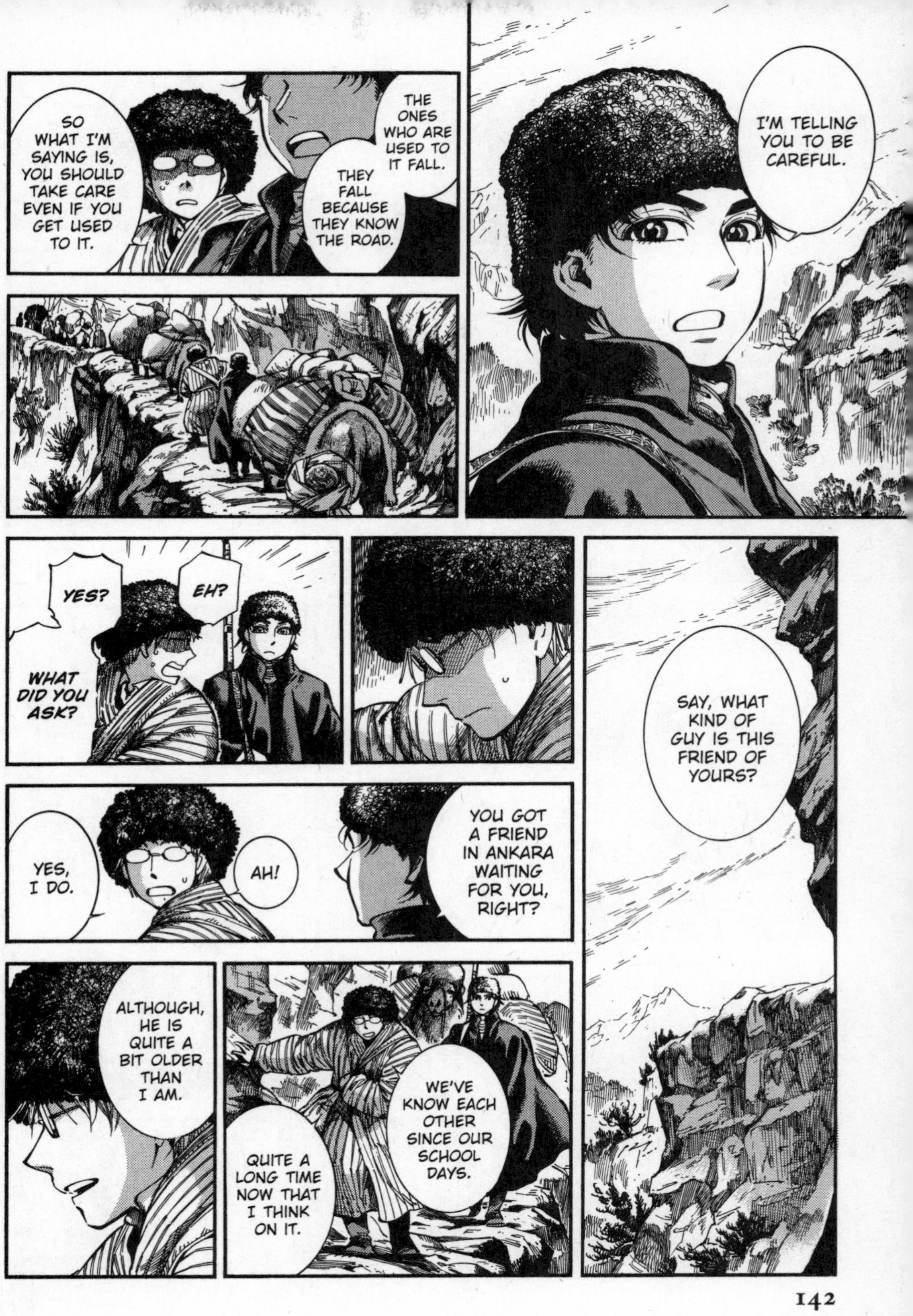
I'M TELLING YOU TO BE CAREFUL.
THE ONES WHO ARE USED TO IT FALL.
THEY FALL BECAUSE THEY KNOW THE ROAD.
SO WHAT I'M SAYING IS, YOU SHOULD TAKE CARE EVEN IF YOU GET USED TO IT.
SAY, WHAT KIND OF GUY IS THIS FRIEND OF YOURS?
EH?
YES?
WHAT DID YOU ASK?
YOU GOT A FRIEND IN ANKARA WAITING FOR YOU, RIGHT?
AH!
YES, I DO.
WE'VE KNOW EACH OTHER SINCE OUR SCHOOL DAYS.
QUITE A LONG TIME NOW THAT I THINK ON IT.
ALTHOUGH, HE IS QUITE A BIT OLDER THAN I AM.

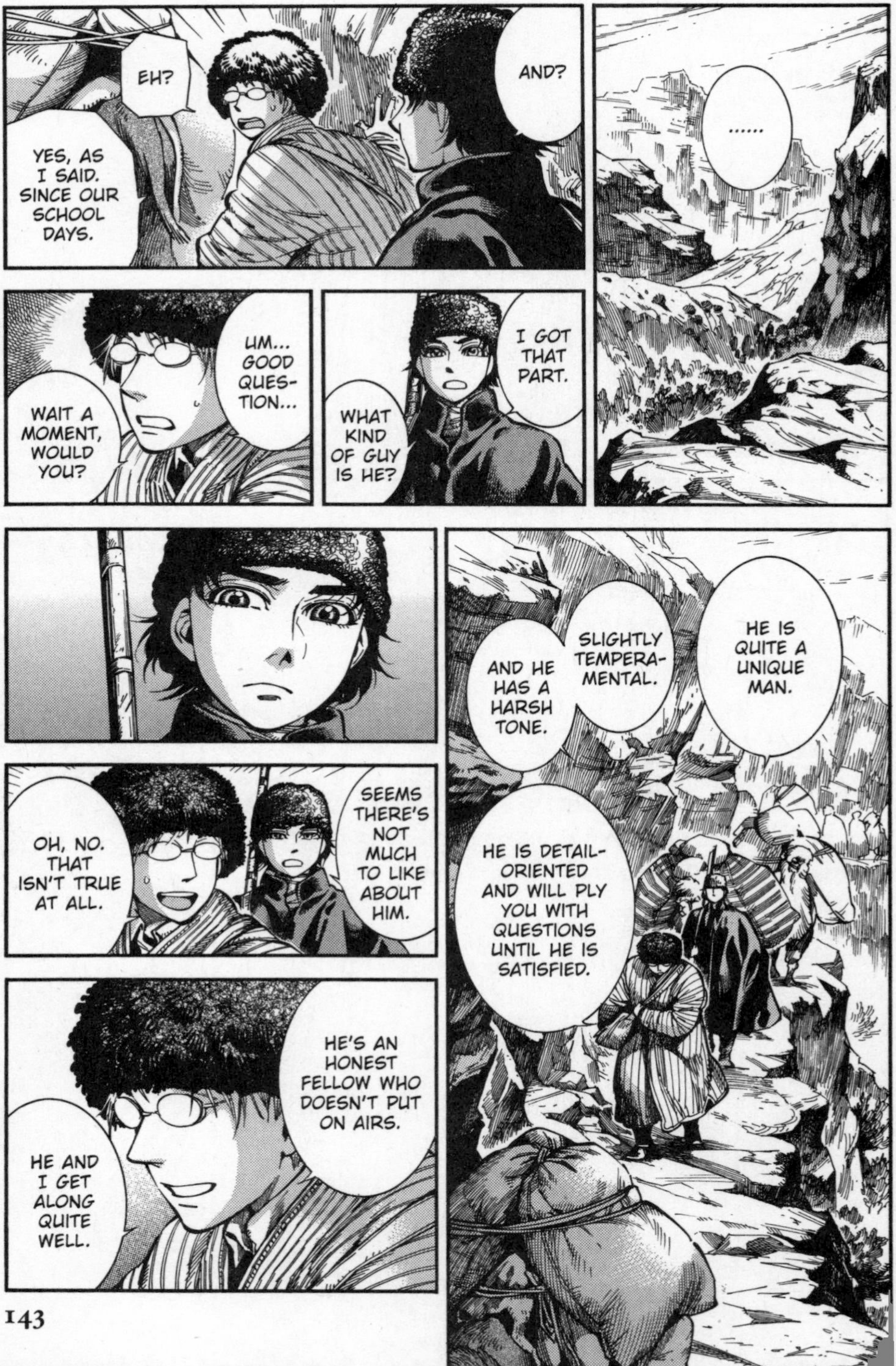
......
AND?
EH?
YES, AS I SAID. SINCE OUR SCHOOL DAYS.
I GOT THAT PART.
WHAT KIND OF GUY IS HE?
UM... GOOD QUESTION...
WAIT A MOMENT, WOULD YOU?
HE IS QUITE A UNIQUE MAN.
SLIGHTLY TEMPERAMENTAL.
AND HE HAS A HARSH TONE.
HE IS DETAIL-ORIENTED AND WILL PLY YOU WITH QUESTIONS UNTIL HE IS SATISFIED.
SEEMS THERE'S NOT MUCH TO LIKE ABOUT HIM.
OH, NO. THAT ISN'T TRUE AT ALL.
HE'S AN HONEST FELLOW WHO DOESN'T PUT ON AIRS.
HE AND I GET ALONG QUITE WELL.

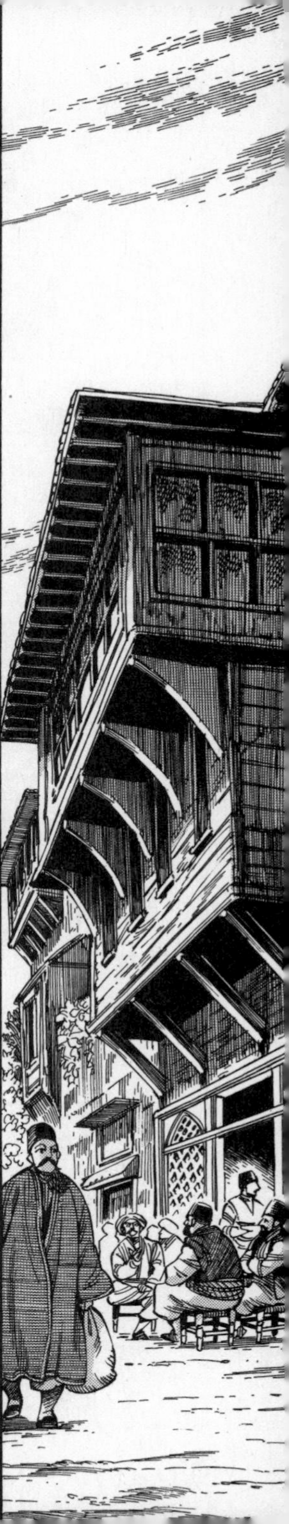
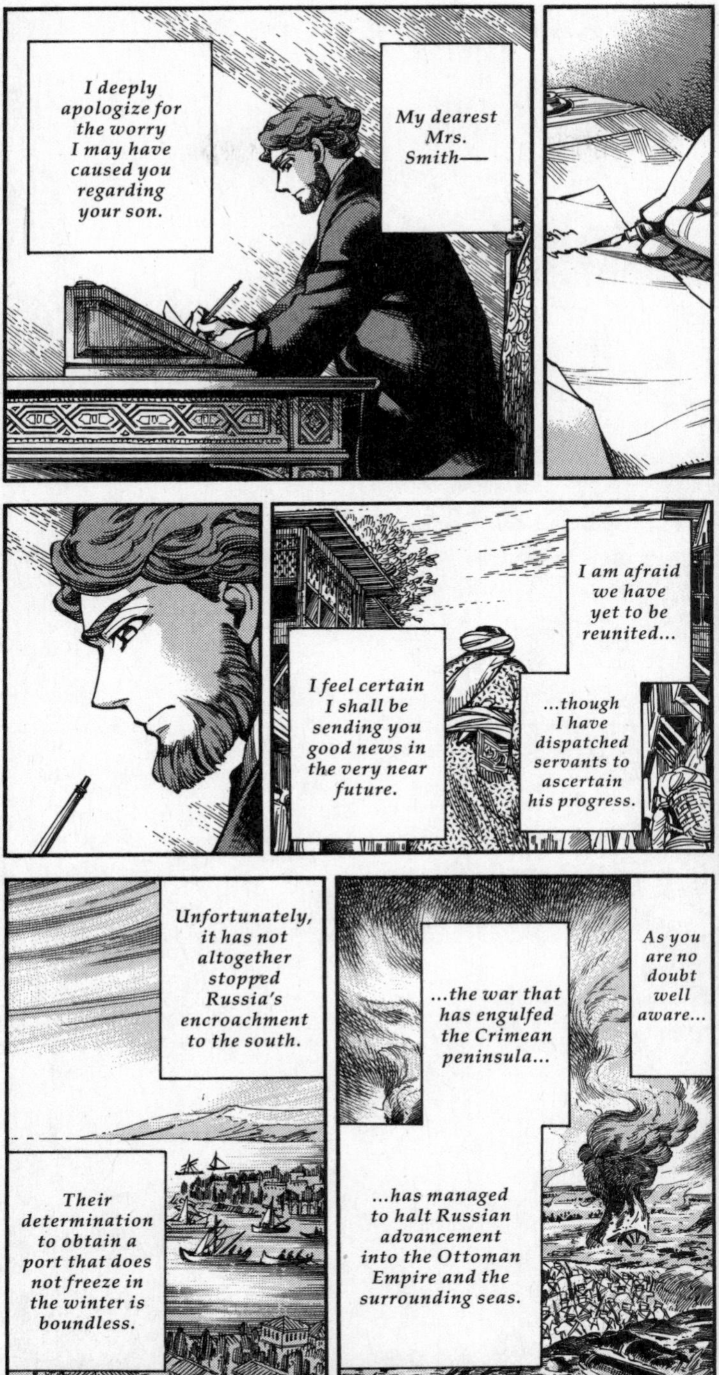
My dearest Mrs. Smith—
I deeply apologize for the worry I may have caused you regarding your son.
I am afraid we have yet to be reunited...
...though I have dispatched servants to ascertain his progress.
I feel certain I shall be sending you good news in the very near future.
As you are no doubt well aware...
...the war that has engulfed the Crimean peninsula...
...has managed to halt Russian advancement into the Ottoman Empire and the surrounding seas.
Unfortunately, it has not altogether stopped Russia's encroachment to the south.
Their determination to obtain a port that does not freeze in the winter is boundless.

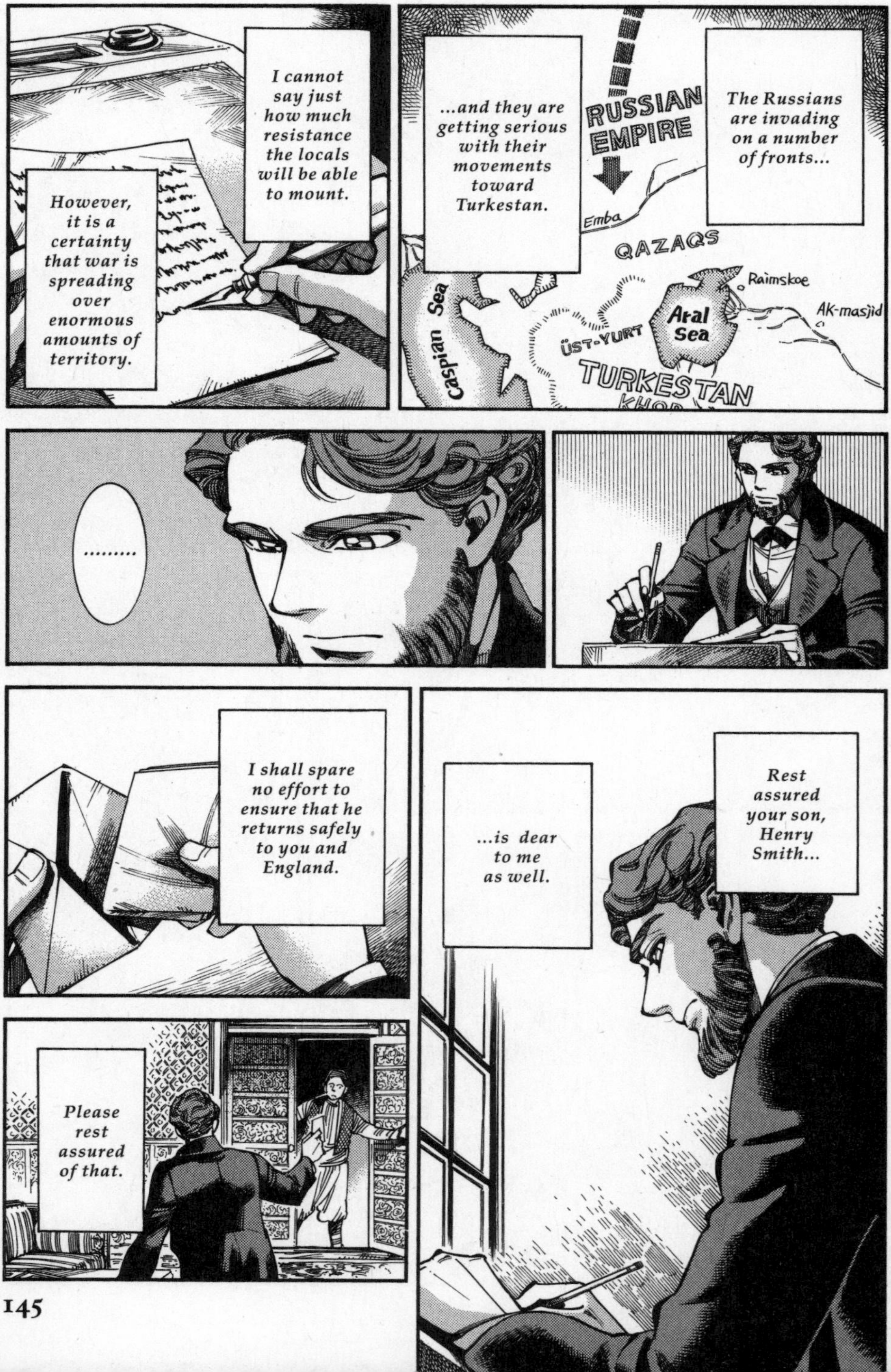
The Russians are invading on a number of fronts...
...and they are getting serious with their movements toward Turkestan.
RUSSIAN EMPIRE
Emba
QAZAQS
Raimskoe
AK-masjid
Aral Sea
ÜST-YURT
Caspian Sea
TURKESTAN
I cannot say just how much resistance the locals will be able to mount.
However, it is a certainty that war is spreading over enormous amounts of territory.
....
Rest assured your son, Henry Smith...
...is dear to me as well.
I shall spare no effort to ensure that he returns safely to you and England.
Please rest assured of that.

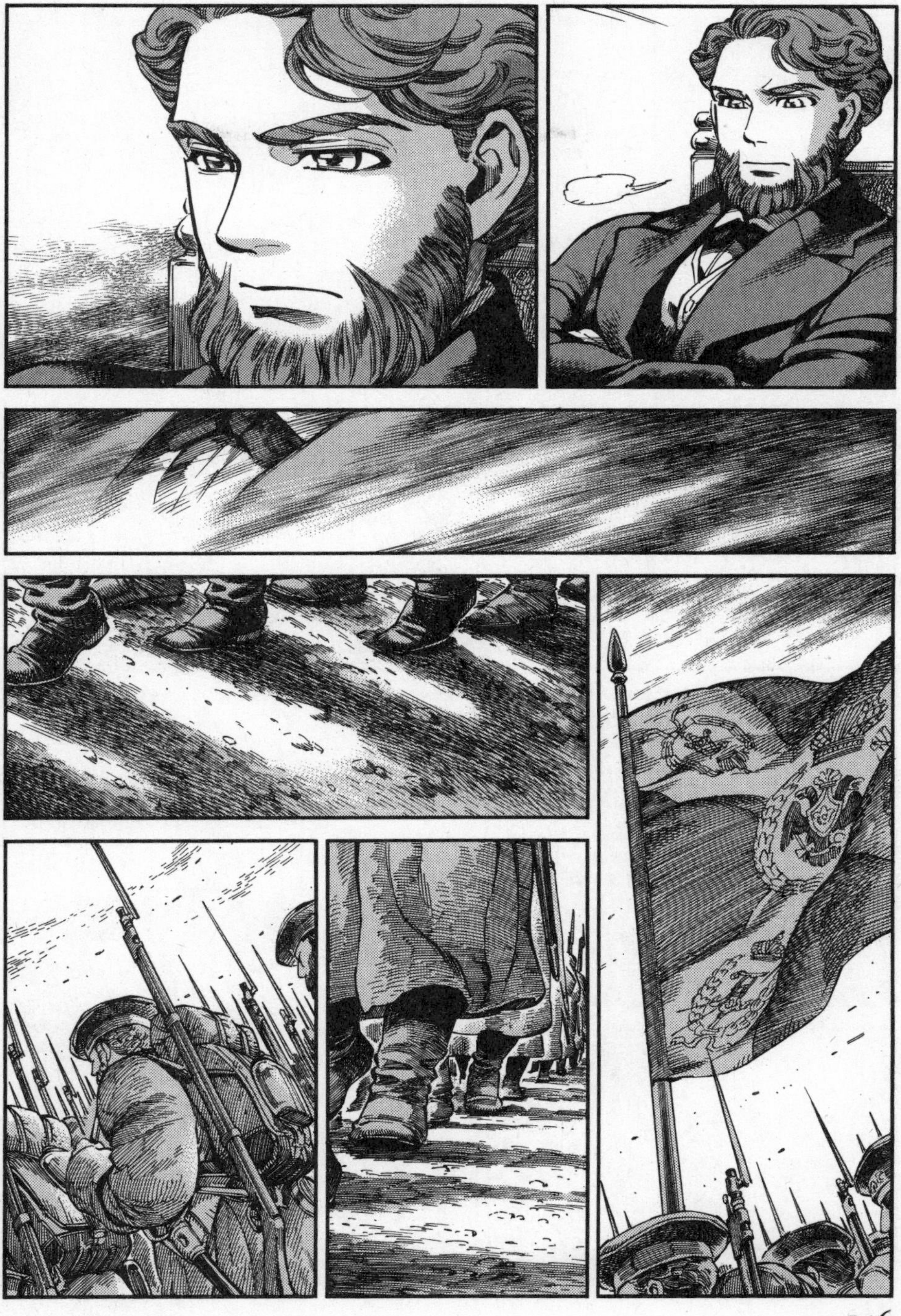

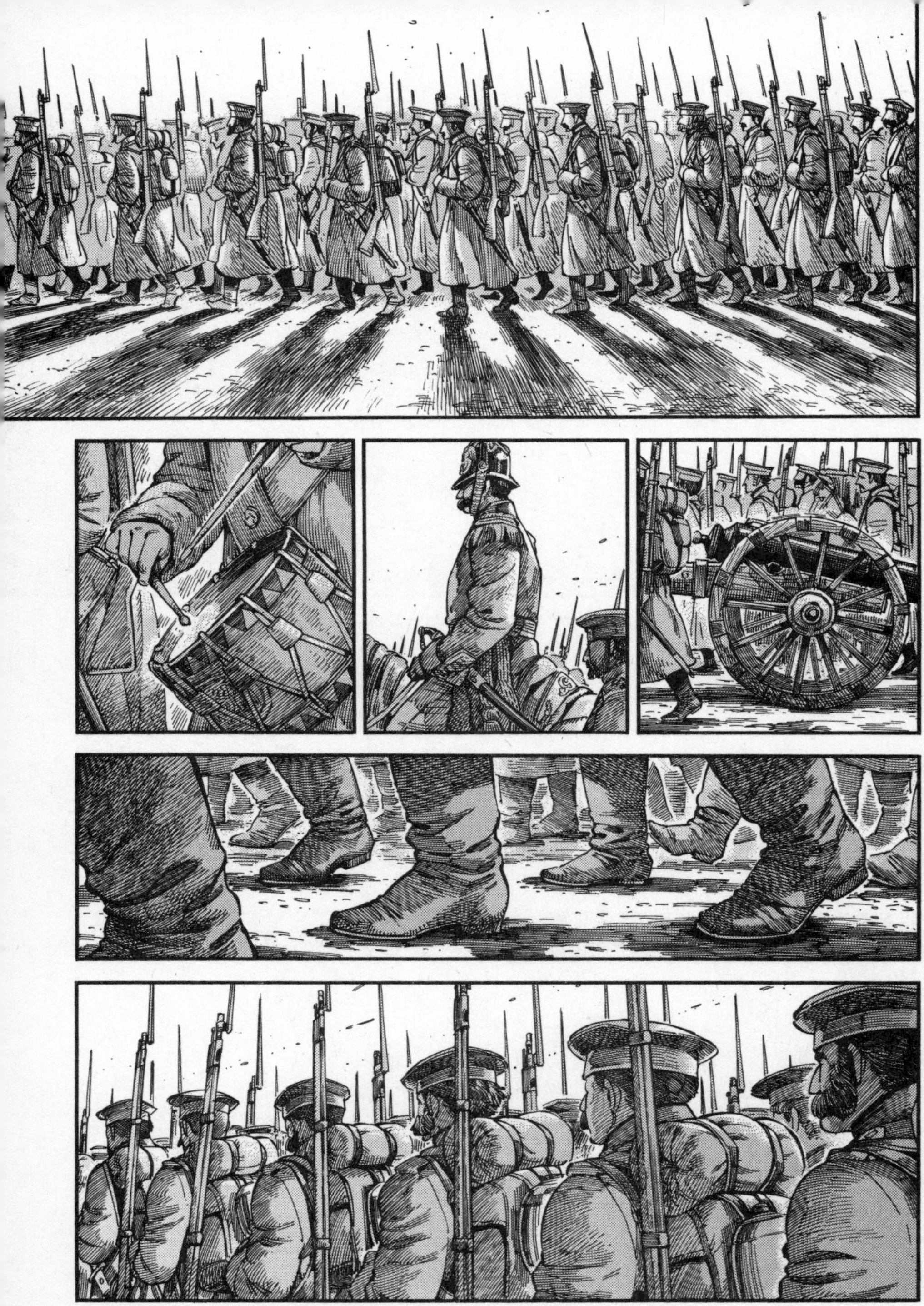

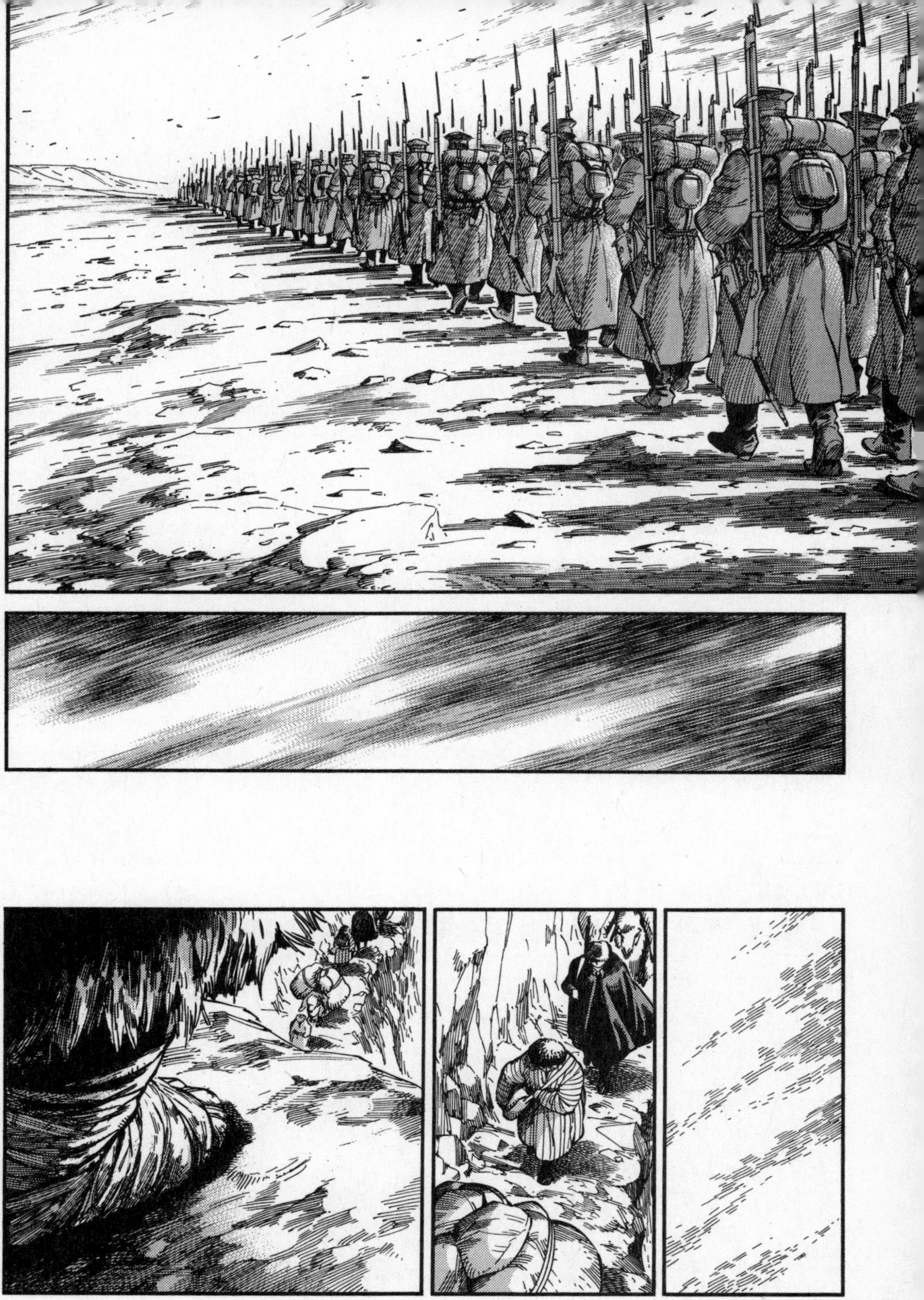

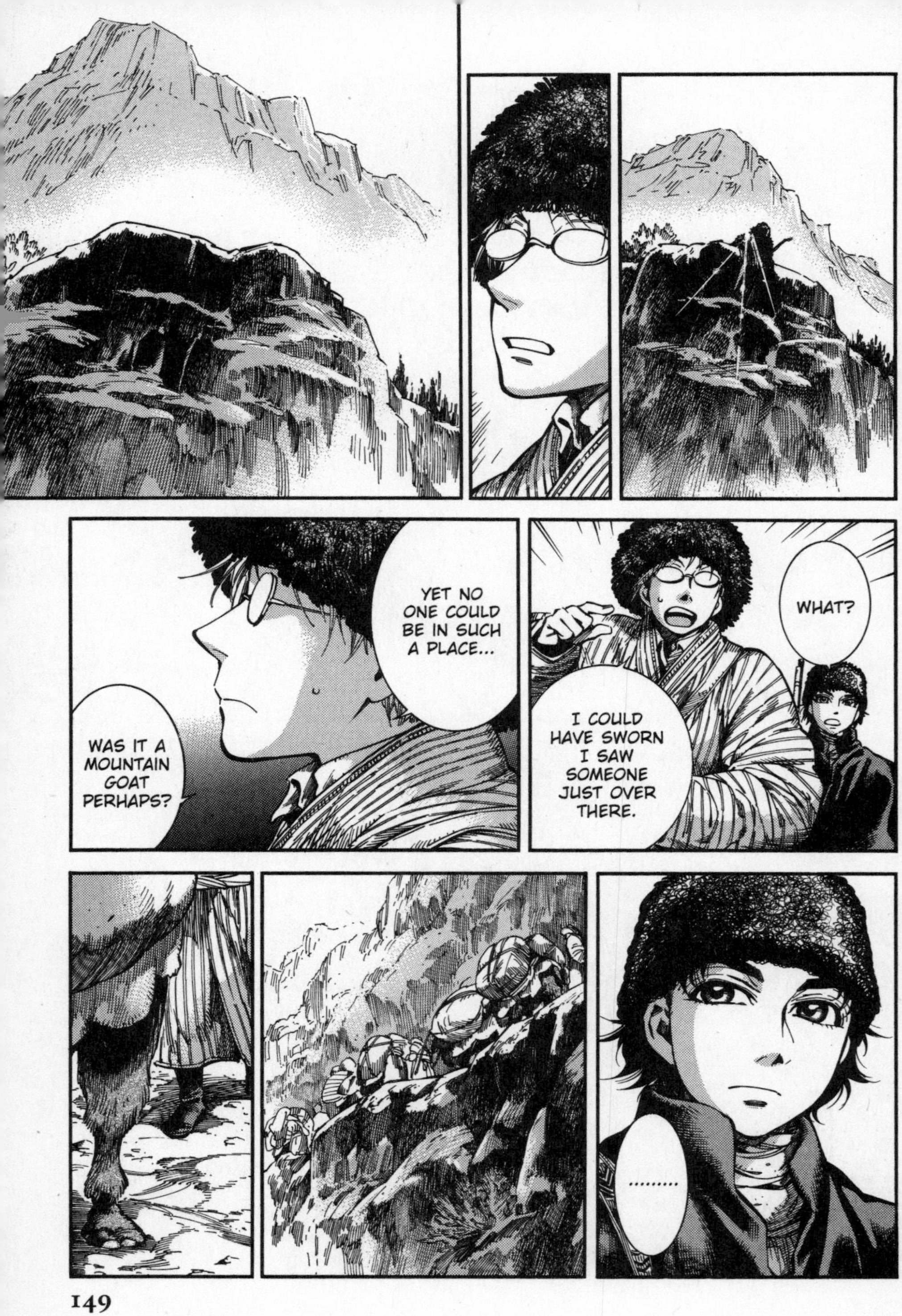
WHAT?
I COULD HAVE SWORN I SAW SOMEONE JUST OVER THERE.
YET NO ONE COULD BE IN SUCH A PLACE...
WAS IT A MOUNTAIN GOAT PERHAPS?
....

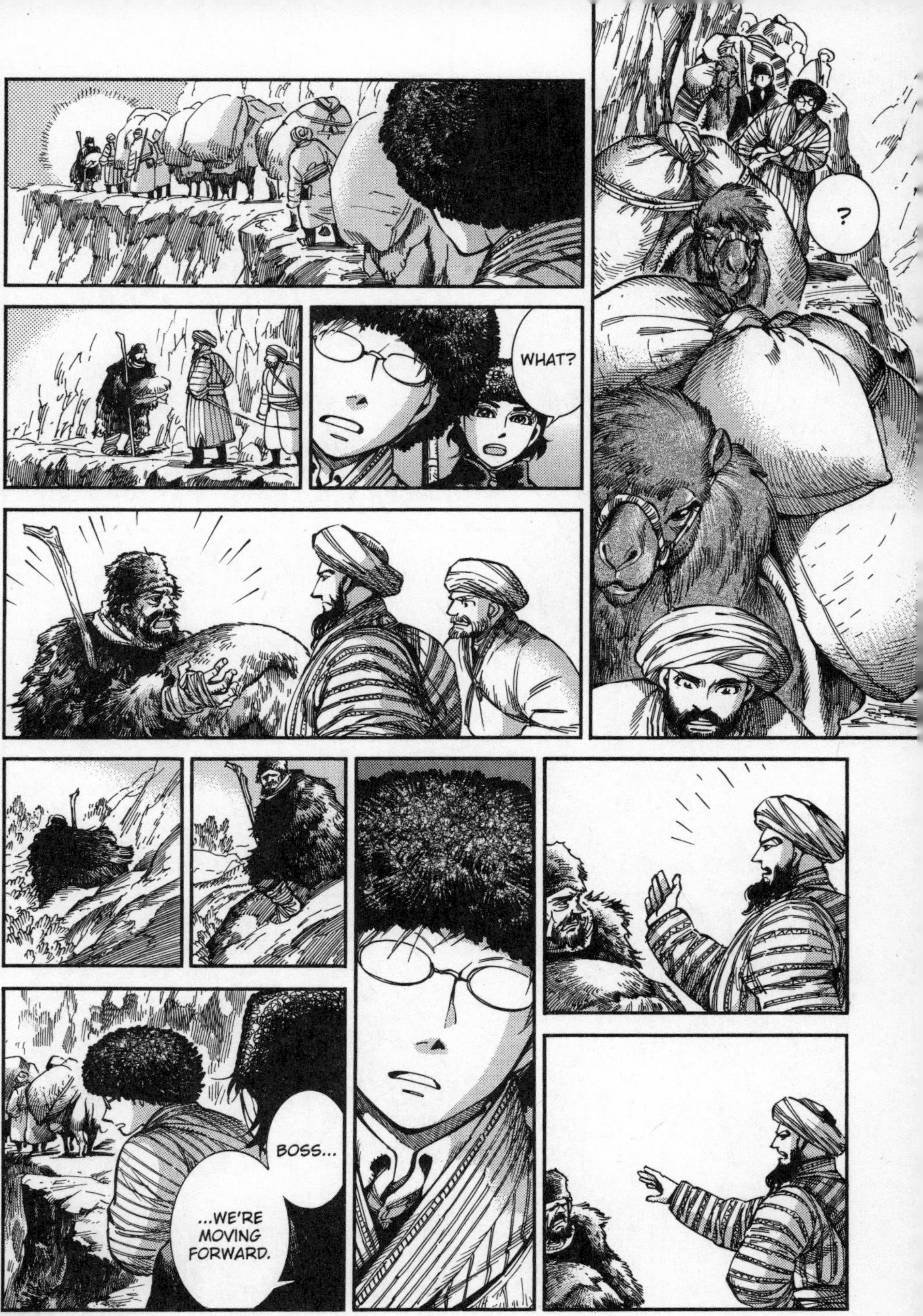
?
WHAT?
BOSS...
...WE'RE MOVING FORWARD.

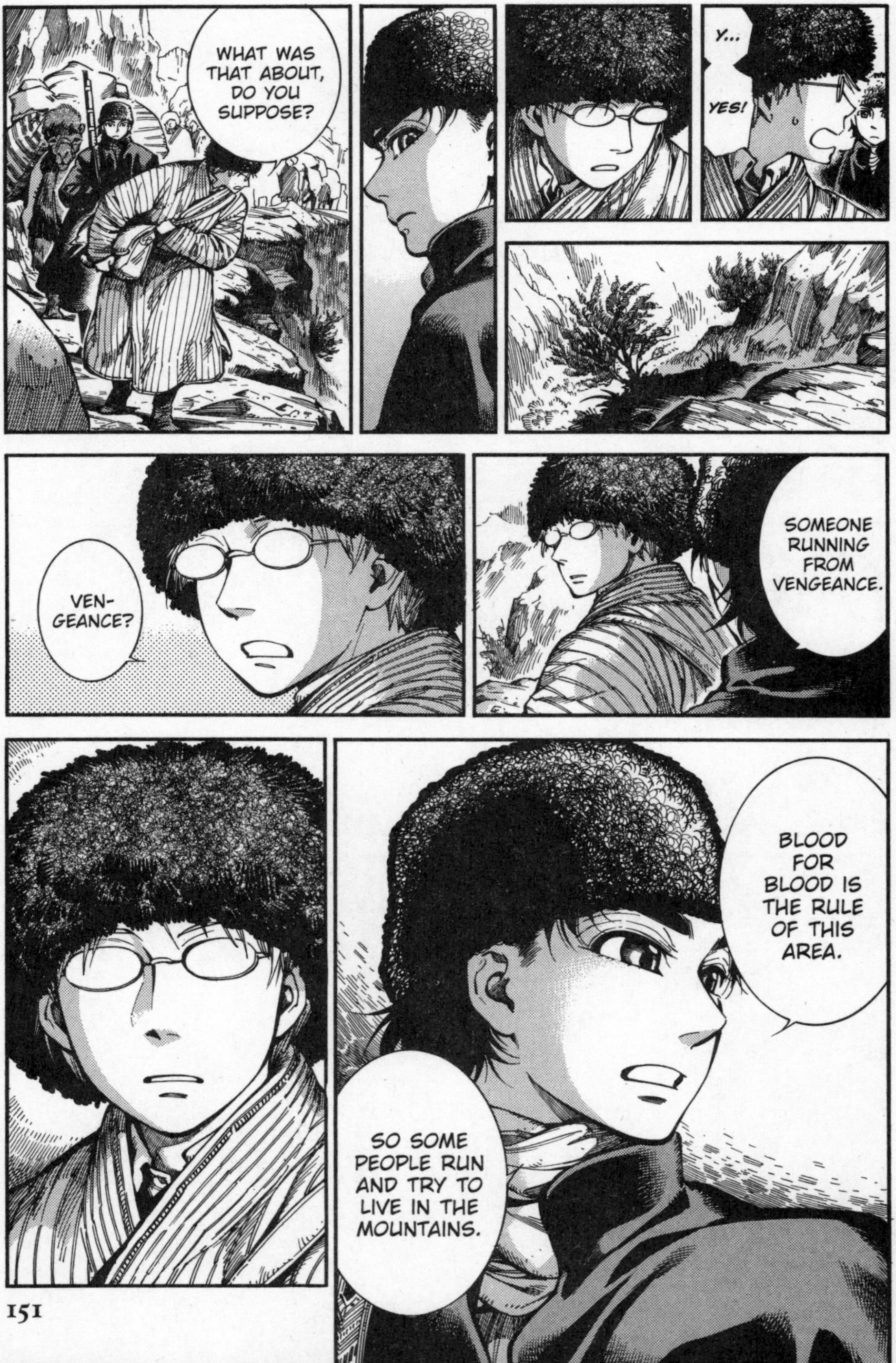
Y...
YES!
WHAT WAS THAT ABOUT, DO YOU SUPPOSE?
SOMEONE RUNNING FROM VENGEANCE.
VEN-GEANCE?
BLOOD FOR BLOOD IS THE RULE OF THIS AREA.
SO SOME PEOPLE RUN AND TRY TO LIVE IN THE MOUNTAINS.

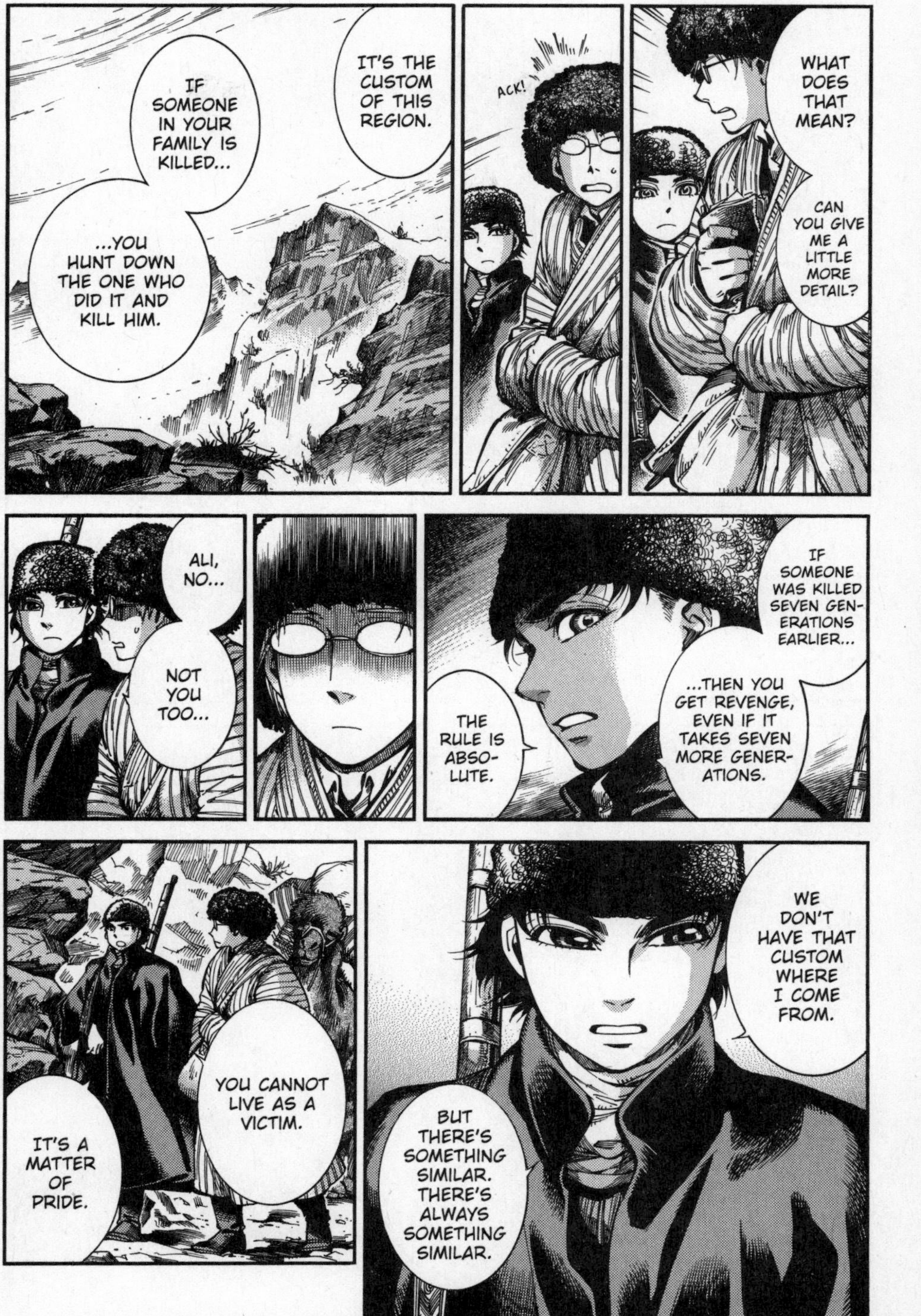
WHAT DOES THAT MEAN?
CAN YOU GIVE ME A LITTLE MORE DETAIL?
ACK!
IT'S THE CUSTOM OF THIS REGION.
IF SOMEONE IN YOUR FAMILY IS KILLED...
...YOU HUNT DOWN THE ONE WHO DID IT AND KILL HIM.
IF SOMEONE WAS KILLED SEVEN GENERATIONS EARLIER...
...THEN YOU GET REVENGE, EVEN IF IT TAKES SEVEN MORE GENERATIONS.
THE RULE IS ABSOLUTE.
ALI, NO...
NOT YOU TOO...
WE DON'T HAVE THAT CUSTOM WHERE I COME FROM.
BUT THERE'S SOMETHING SIMILAR. THERE'S ALWAYS SOMETHING SIMILAR.
YOU CANNOT LIVE AS A VICTIM.
IT'S A MATTER OF PRIDE.

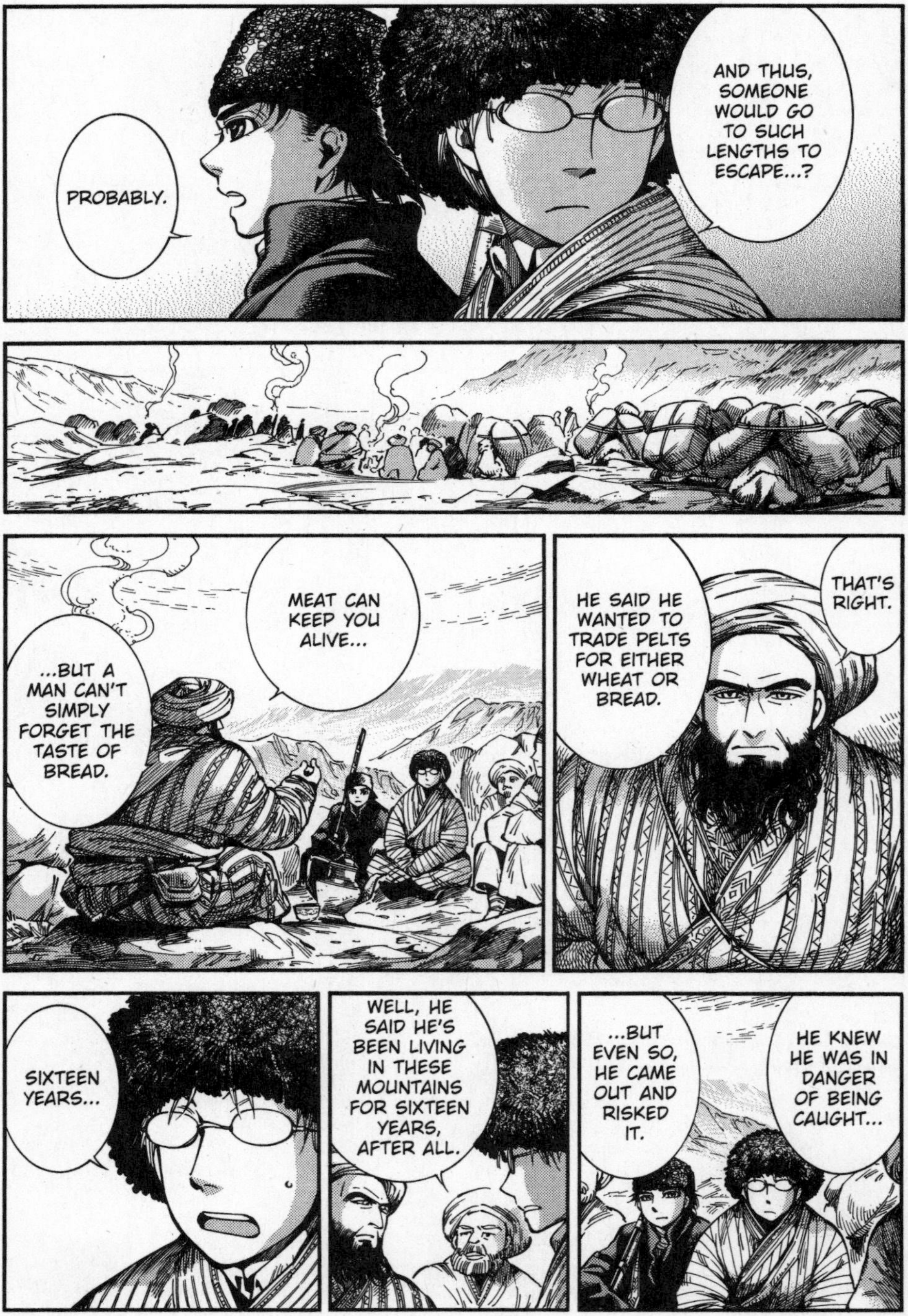
AND THUS, SOMEONE WOULD GO TO SUCH LENGTHS TO ESCAPE...?
PROBABLY.
THAT'S RIGHT.
HE SAID HE WANTED TO TRADE PELTS FOR EITHER WHEAT OR BREAD.
MEAT CAN KEEP YOU ALIVE...
...BUT A MAN CAN'T SIMPLY FORGET THE TASTE OF BREAD.
HE KNEW HE WAS IN DANGER OF BEING CAUGHT...
...BUT EVEN SO, HE CAME OUT AND RISKED IT.
WELL, HE SAID HE'S BEEN LIVING IN THESE MOUNTAINS FOR SIXTEEN YEARS, AFTER ALL.
SIXTEEN YEARS...

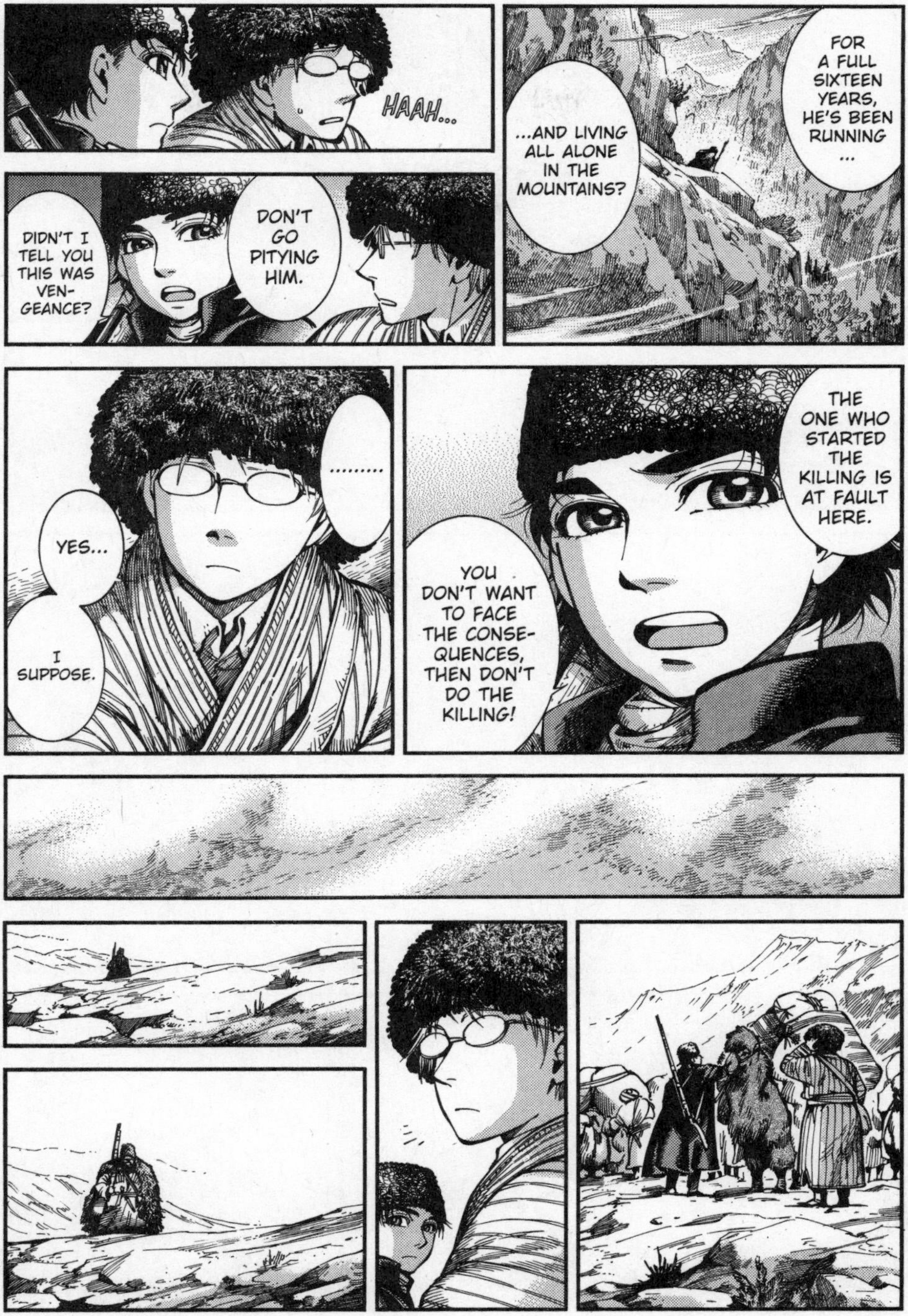
FOR A FULL SIXTEEN YEARS, HE'S BEEN RUNNING ...
...AND LIVING ALL ALONE IN THE MOUNTAINS?
HAAH...
DON'T GO PITYING HIM.
DIDN'T I TELL YOU THIS WAS VEN-GEANCE?
THE ONE WHO STARTED THE KILLING IS AT FAULT HERE.
YOU DON'T WANT TO FACE THE CONSE-QUENCES, THEN DON'T DO THE KILLING!
....
YES...
I SUPPOSE.

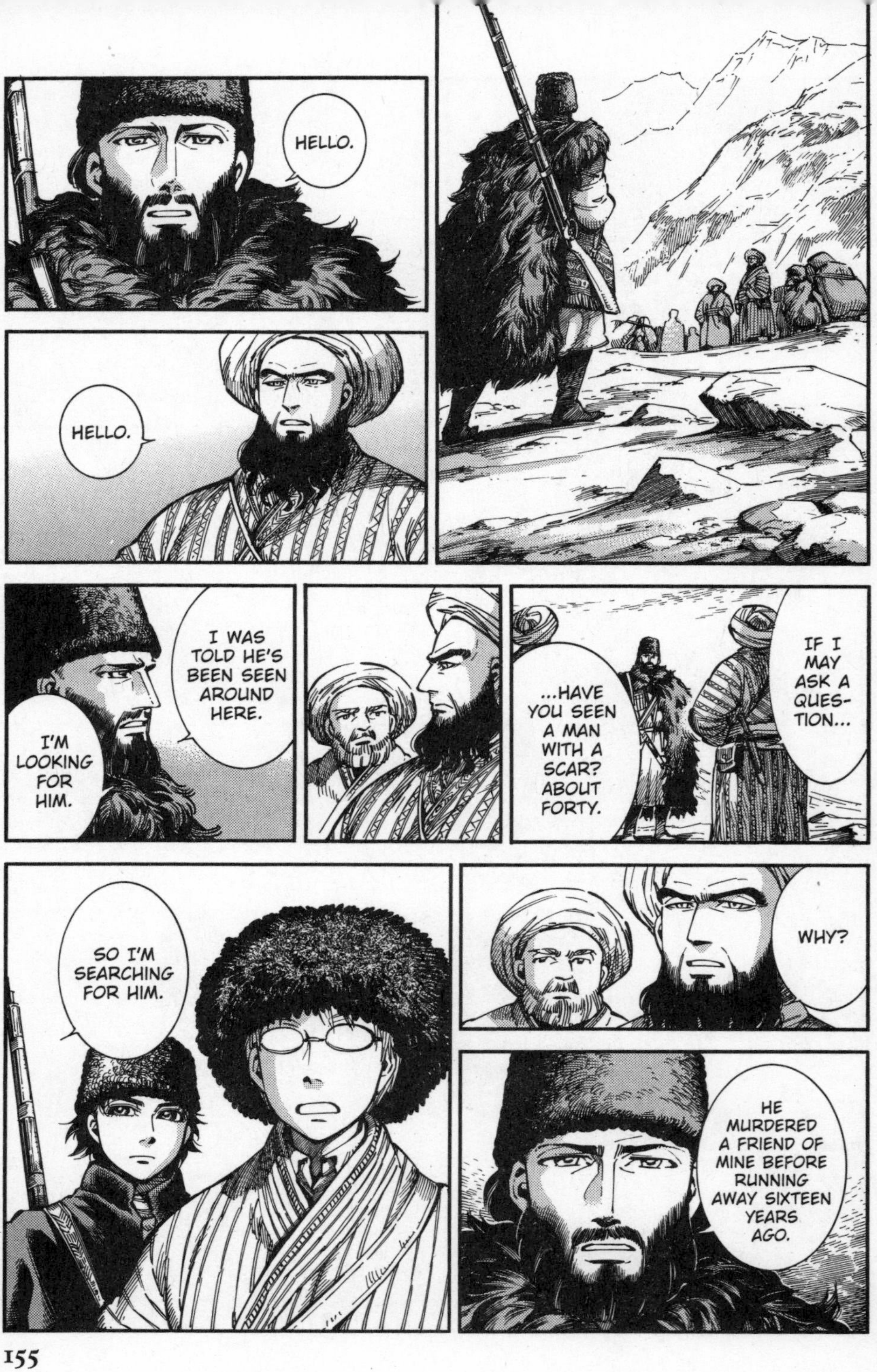
HELLO.
HELLO.
IF I MAY ASK A QUES-TION...
...HAVE YOU SEEN A MAN WITH A SCAR? ABOUT FORTY.
I WAS TOLD HE'S BEEN SEEN AROUND HERE.
I'M LOOKING FOR HIM.
WHY?
HE MURDERED A FRIEND OF MINE BEFORE RUNNING AWAY SIXTEEN YEARS AGO.
SO I'M SEARCHING FOR HIM.

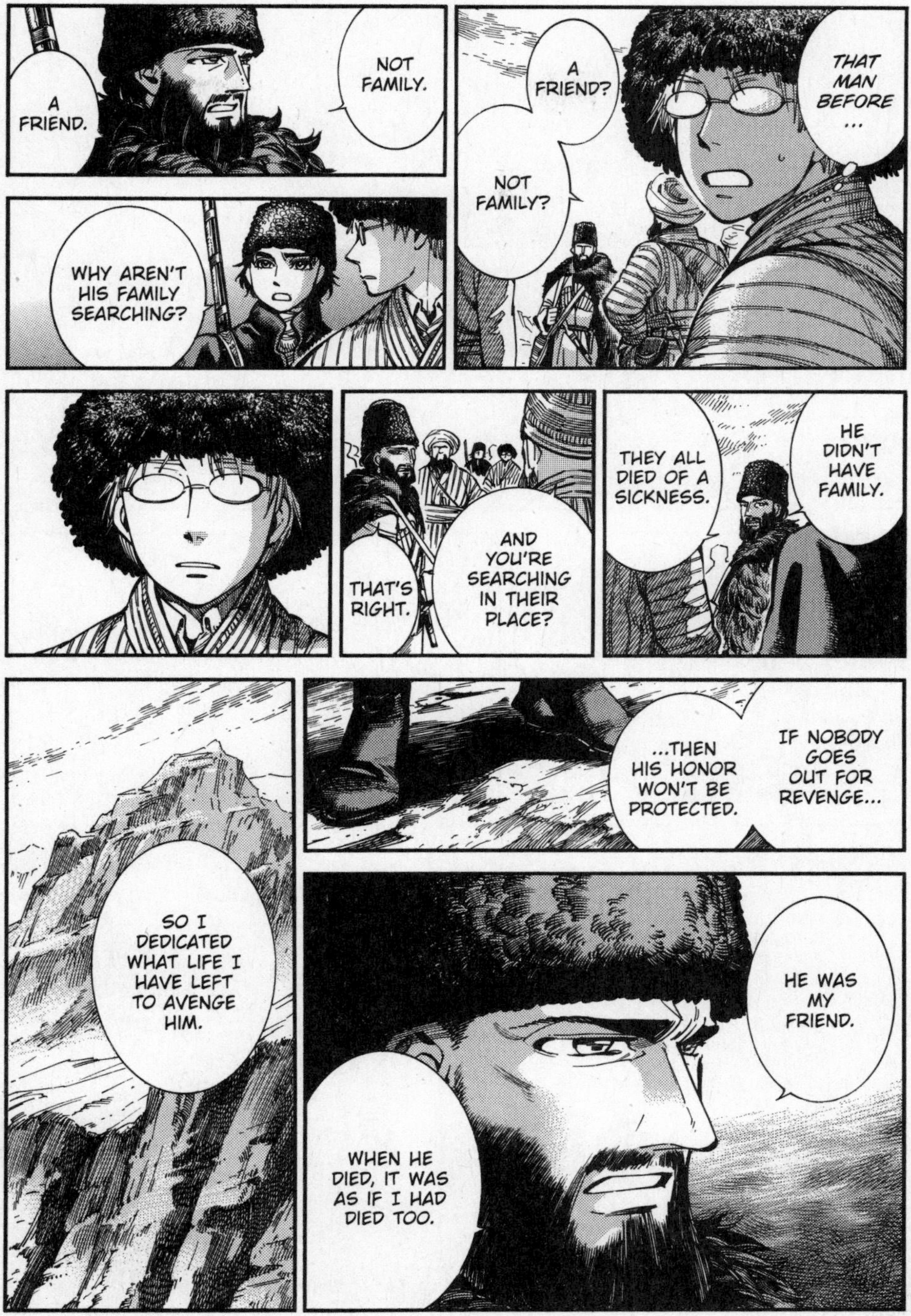
THAT MAN BEFORE ...
A FRIEND?
NOT FAMILY?
NOT FAMILY.
A FRIEND.
WHY AREN'T HIS FAMILY SEARCHING?
HE DIDN'T HAVE FAMILY.
THEY ALL DIED OF A SICKNESS.
AND YOU'RE SEARCHING IN THEIR PLACE?
THAT'S RIGHT.
IF NOBODY GOES OUT FOR REVENGE...
...THEN HIS HONOR WON'T BE PROTECTED.
HE WAS MY FRIEND.
WHEN HE DIED, IT WAS AS IF I HAD DIED TOO.
SO I DEDICATED WHAT LIFE I HAVE LEFT TO AVENGE HIM.

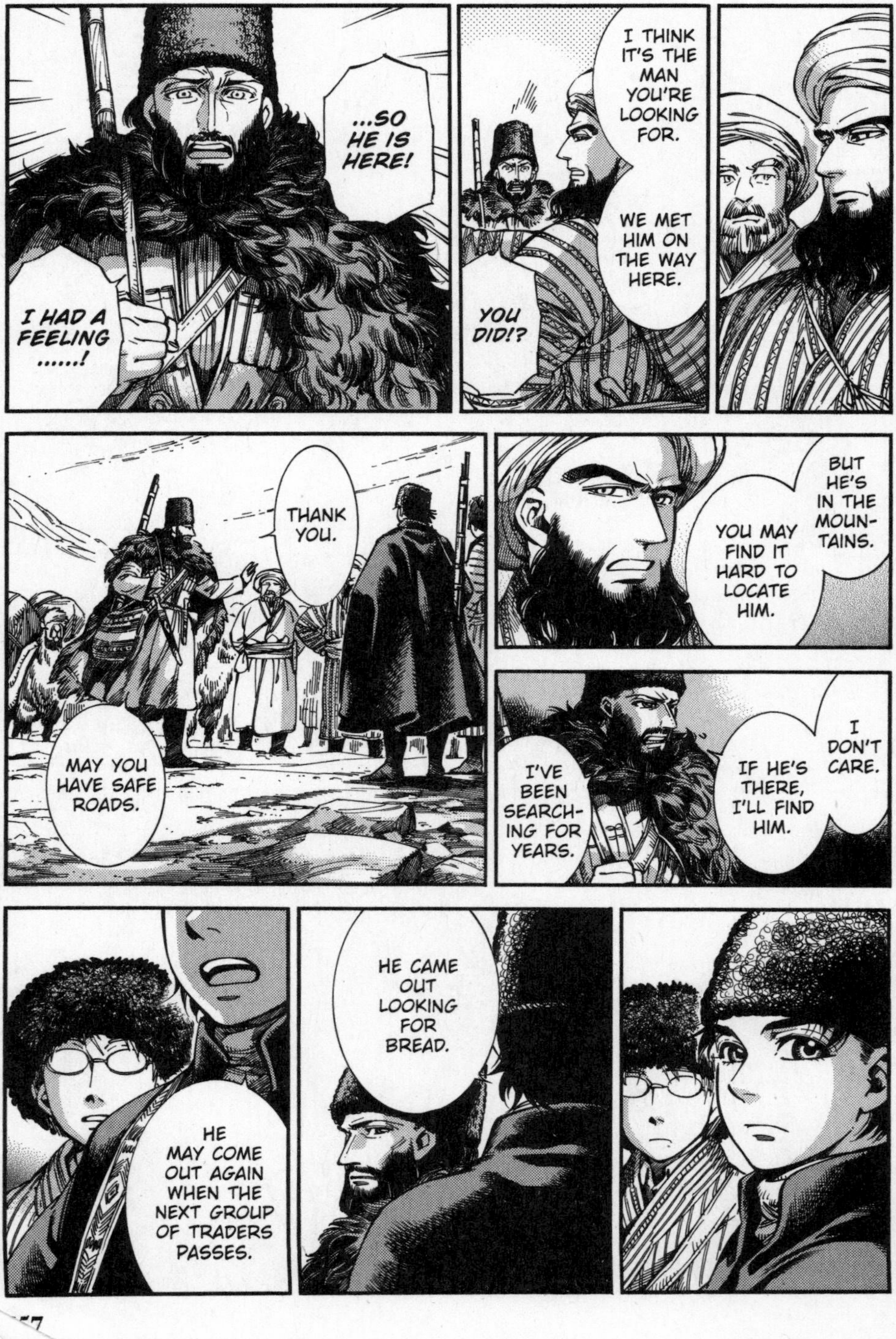
I THINK IT'S THE MAN YOU'RE LOOKING FOR.
WE MET HIM ON THE WAY HERE.
YOU DID!?
...SO HE IS HERE!
I HAD A FEELING ......!
BUT HE'S IN THE MOUNTAINS.
YOU MAY FIND IT HARD TO LOCATE HIM.
I DON'T CARE.
IF HE'S THERE, I'LL FIND HIM.
I'VE BEEN SEARCHING FOR YEARS.
THANK YOU.
MAY YOU HAVE SAFE ROADS.
HE CAME OUT LOOKING FOR BREAD.
HE MAY COME OUT AGAIN WHEN THE NEXT GROUP OF TRADERS PASSES.

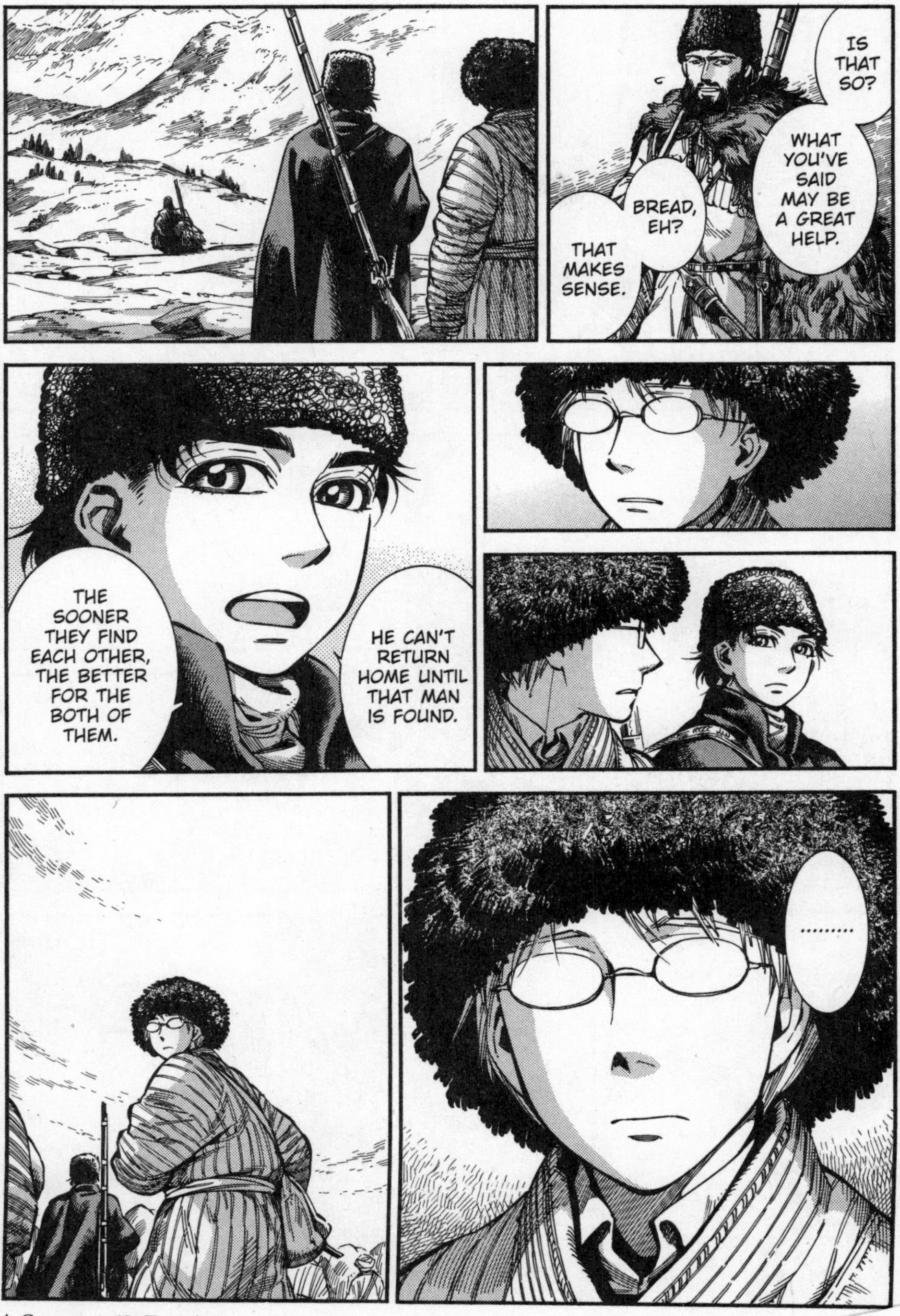
IS THAT SO?
WHAT YOU'VE SAID MAY BE A GREAT HELP.
BREAD, EH?
THAT MAKES SENSE.
HE CAN'T RETURN HOME UNTIL THAT MAN IS FOUND.
THE SOONER THEY FIND EACH OTHER, THE BETTER FOR THE BOTH OF THEM.
....

✦ Chapter 68: End ✦

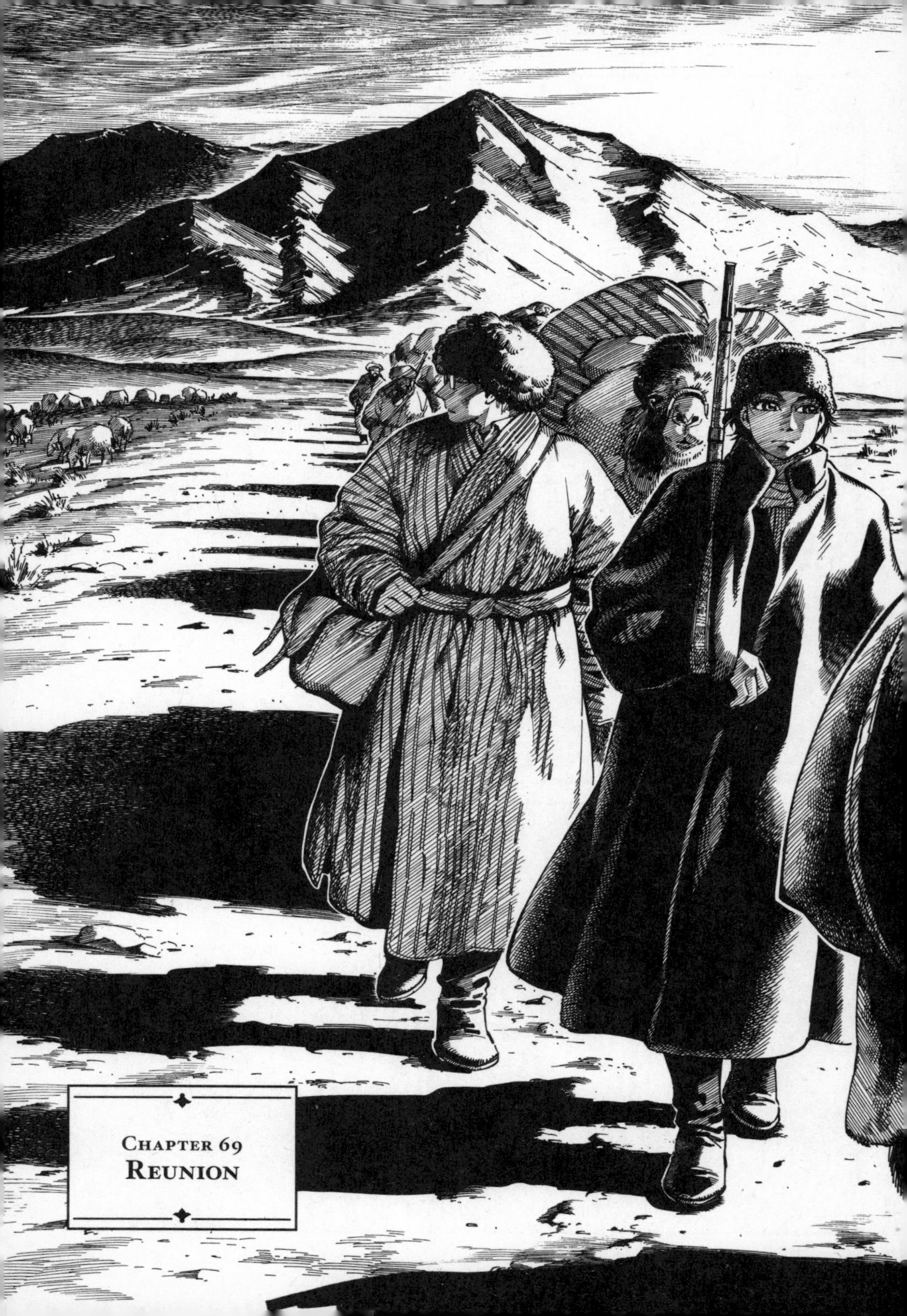
Chapter 69
Reunion

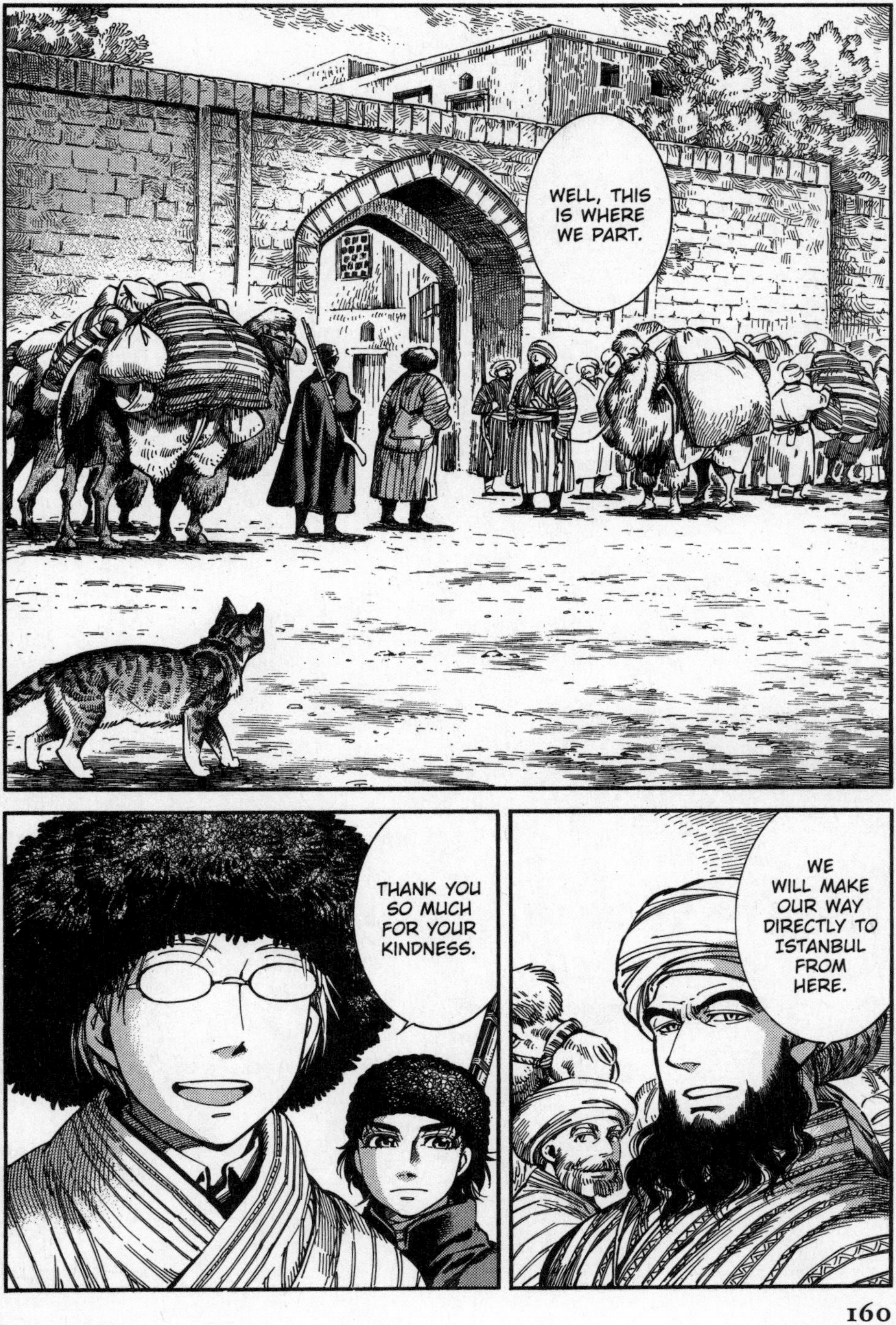
WELL, THIS IS WHERE WE PART.
WE WILL MAKE OUR WAY DIRECTLY TO ISTANBUL FROM HERE.
THANK YOU SO MUCH FOR YOUR KINDNESS.

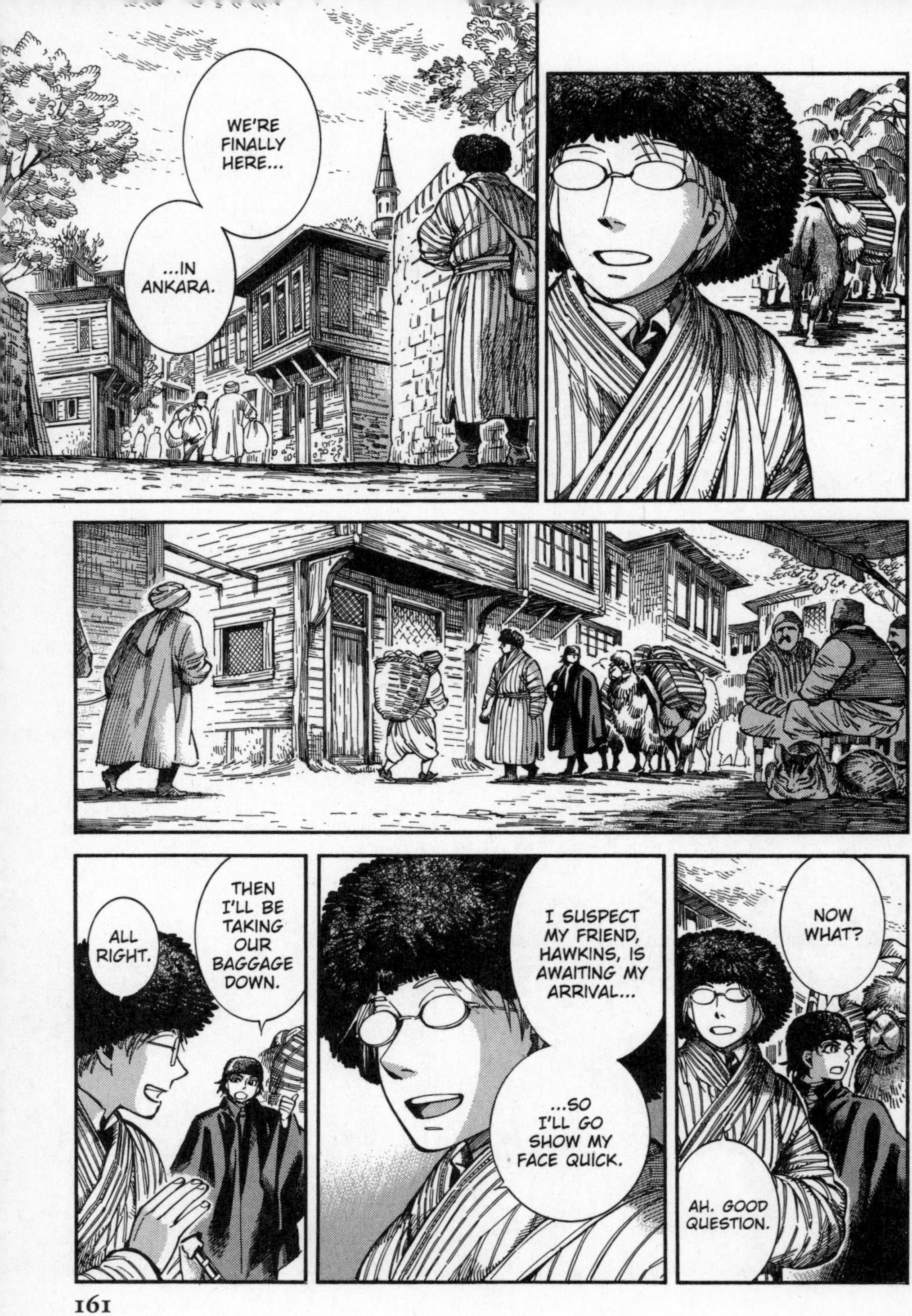
WE'RE FINALLY HERE...
...IN ANKARA.
NOW WHAT?
AH. GOOD QUESTION.
I SUSPECT MY FRIEND, HAWKINS, IS AWAITING MY ARRIVAL...
...SO I'LL GO SHOW MY FACE QUICK.
THEN I'LL BE TAKING OUR BAGGAGE DOWN.
ALL RIGHT.

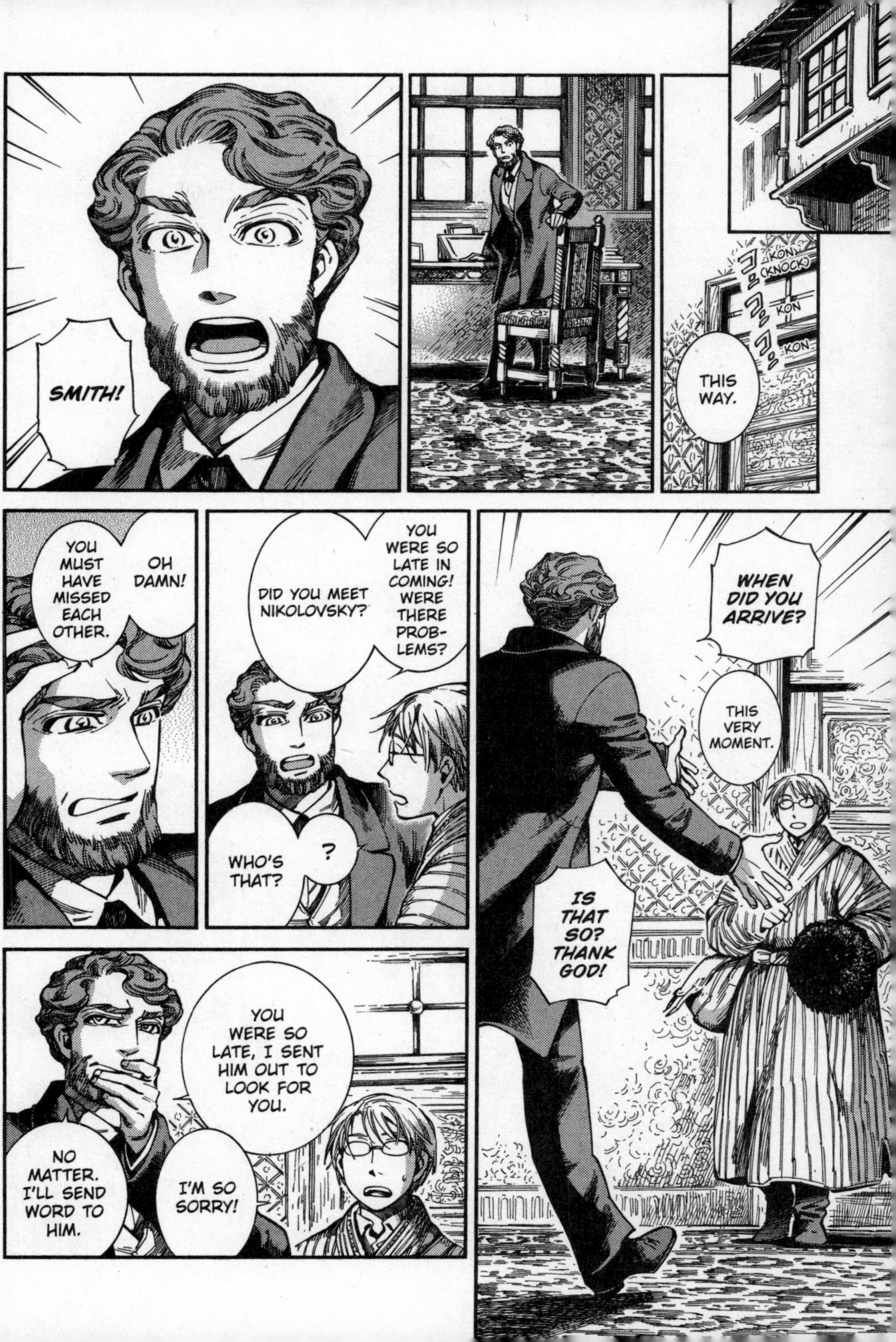
KON (KNOCK)
KON
KON
THIS WAY.
SMITH!
WHEN DID YOU ARRIVE?
THIS VERY MOMENT.
IS THAT SO? THANK GOD!
YOU WERE SO LATE IN COMING! WERE THERE PROBLEMS?
DID YOU MEET NIKOLOVSKY?
?
WHO'S THAT?
OH DAMN!
YOU MUST HAVE MISSED EACH OTHER.
YOU WERE SO LATE, I SENT HIM OUT TO LOOK FOR YOU.
I'M SO SORRY!
NO MATTER. I'LL SEND WORD TO HIM.

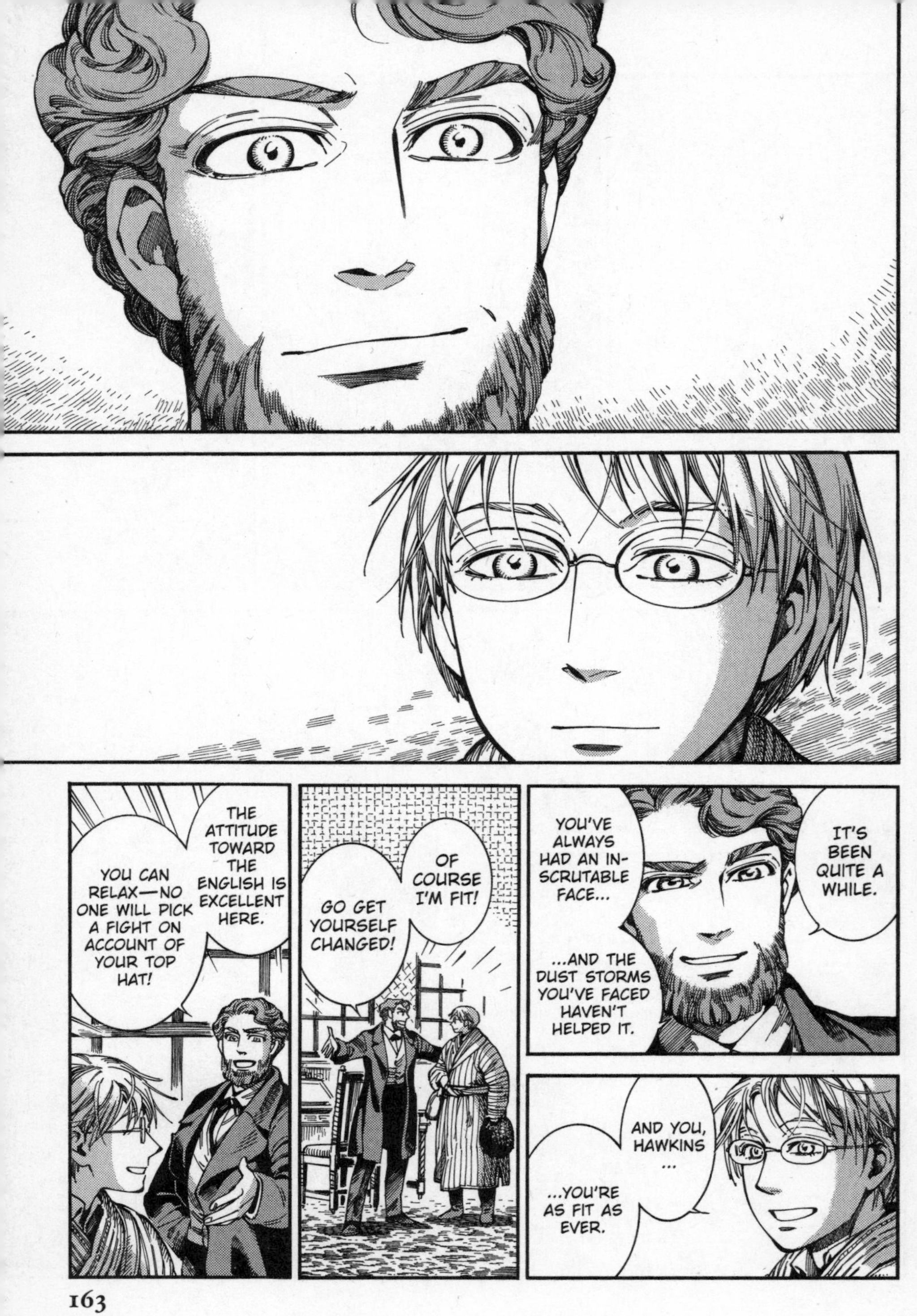
IT'S BEEN QUITE A WHILE.
YOU'VE ALWAYS HAD AN IN-SCRUTABLE FACE...
...AND THE DUST STORMS YOU'VE FACED HAVEN'T HELPED IT.
AND YOU, HAWKINS...
...YOU'RE AS FIT AS EVER.
OF COURSE I'M FIT!
GO GET YOURSELF CHANGED!
THE ATTITUDE TOWARD THE ENGLISH IS EXCELLENT HERE.
YOU CAN RELAX—NO ONE WILL PICK A FIGHT ON ACCOUNT OF YOUR TOP HAT!

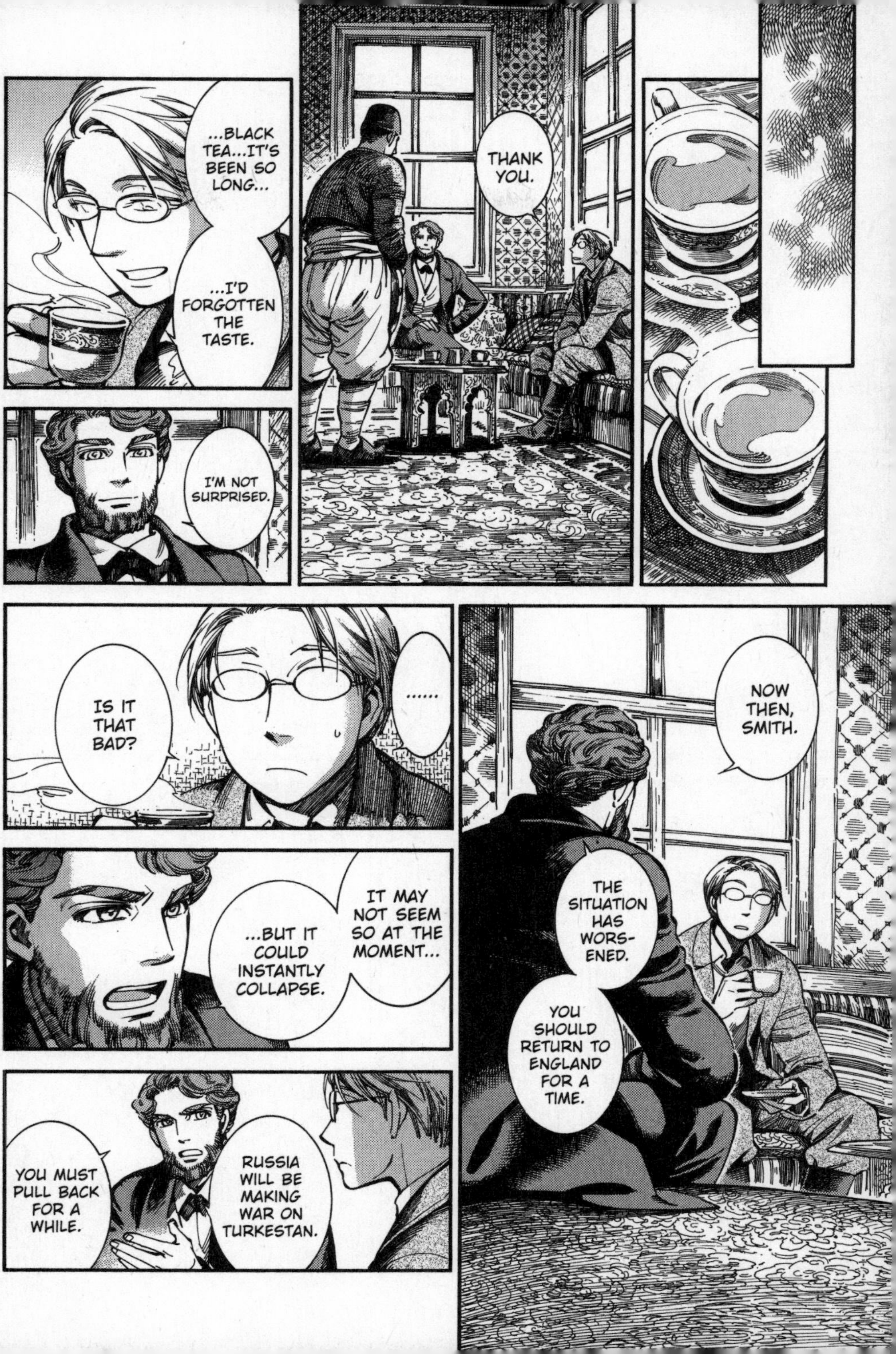
THANK YOU.
...BLACK TEA...IT'S BEEN SO LONG...
...I'D FORGOTTEN THE TASTE.
I'M NOT SURPRISED.
NOW THEN, SMITH.
THE SITUATION HAS WORSENED.
YOU SHOULD RETURN TO ENGLAND FOR A TIME.
......
IS IT THAT BAD?
IT MAY NOT SEEM SO AT THE MOMENT...
...BUT IT COULD INSTANTLY COLLAPSE.
RUSSIA WILL BE MAKING WAR ON TURKESTAN.
YOU MUST PULL BACK FOR A WHILE.

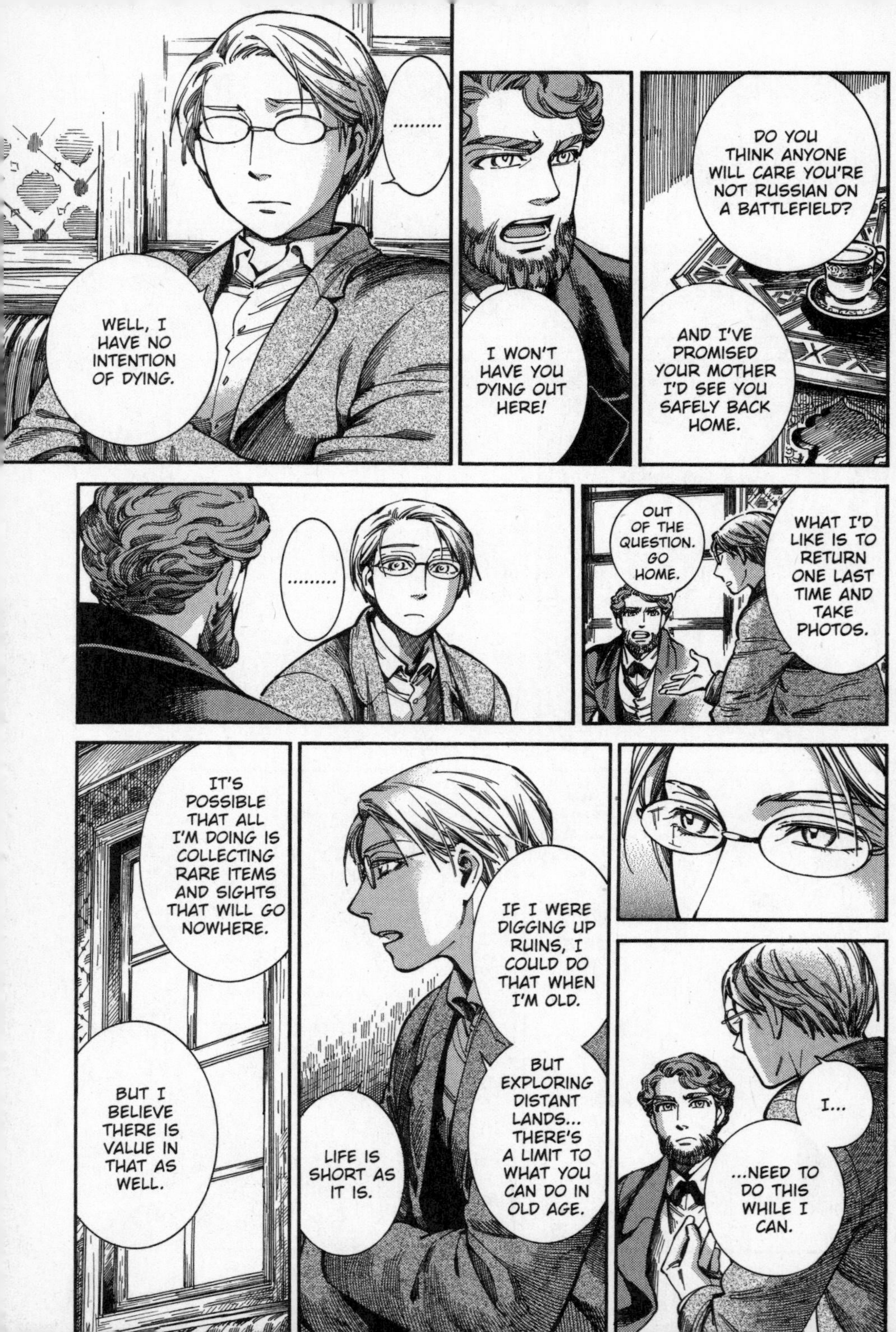
DO YOU THINK ANYONE WILL CARE YOU'RE NOT RUSSIAN ON A BATTLEFIELD?
AND I'VE PROMISED YOUR MOTHER I'D SEE YOU SAFELY BACK HOME.
I WON'T HAVE YOU DYING OUT HERE!
....
WELL, I HAVE NO INTENTION OF DYING.
WHAT I'D LIKE IS TO RETURN ONE LAST TIME AND TAKE PHOTOS.
OUT OF THE QUESTION. GO HOME.
....
I...
...NEED TO DO THIS WHILE I CAN.
IF I WERE DIGGING UP RUINS, I COULD DO THAT WHEN I'M OLD.
BUT EXPLORING DISTANT LANDS... THERE'S A LIMIT TO WHAT YOU CAN DO IN OLD AGE.
LIFE IS SHORT AS IT IS.
IT'S POSSIBLE THAT ALL I'M DOING IS COLLECTING RARE ITEMS AND SIGHTS THAT WILL GO NOWHERE.
BUT I BELIEVE THERE IS VALUE IN THAT AS WELL.

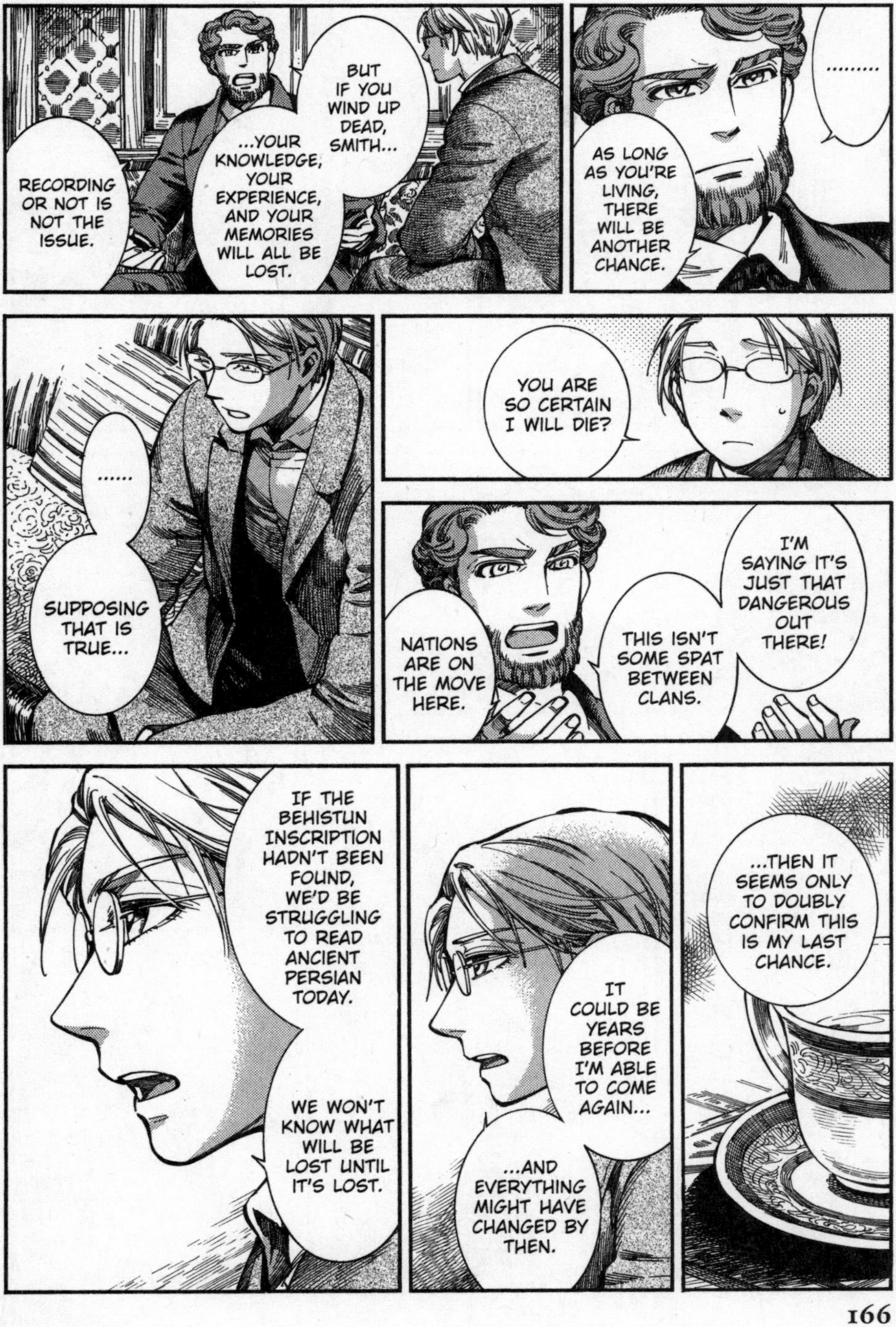
....
AS LONG AS YOU'RE LIVING, THERE WILL BE ANOTHER CHANCE.
BUT IF YOU WIND UP DEAD, SMITH...
...YOUR KNOWLEDGE, YOUR EXPERIENCE, AND YOUR MEMORIES WILL ALL BE LOST.
RECORDING OR NOT IS NOT THE ISSUE.
YOU ARE SO CERTAIN I WILL DIE?
I'M SAYING IT'S JUST THAT DANGEROUS OUT THERE!
THIS ISN'T SOME SPAT BETWEEN CLANS.
NATIONS ARE ON THE MOVE HERE.
......
SUPPOSING THAT IS TRUE...
...THEN IT SEEMS ONLY TO DOUBLY CONFIRM THIS IS MY LAST CHANCE.
IT COULD BE YEARS BEFORE I'M ABLE TO COME AGAIN...
...AND EVERYTHING MIGHT HAVE CHANGED BY THEN.
IF THE BEHISTUN INSCRIPTION HADN'T BEEN FOUND, WE'D BE STRUGGLING TO READ ANCIENT PERSIAN TODAY.
WE WON'T KNOW WHAT WILL BE LOST UNTIL IT'S LOST.

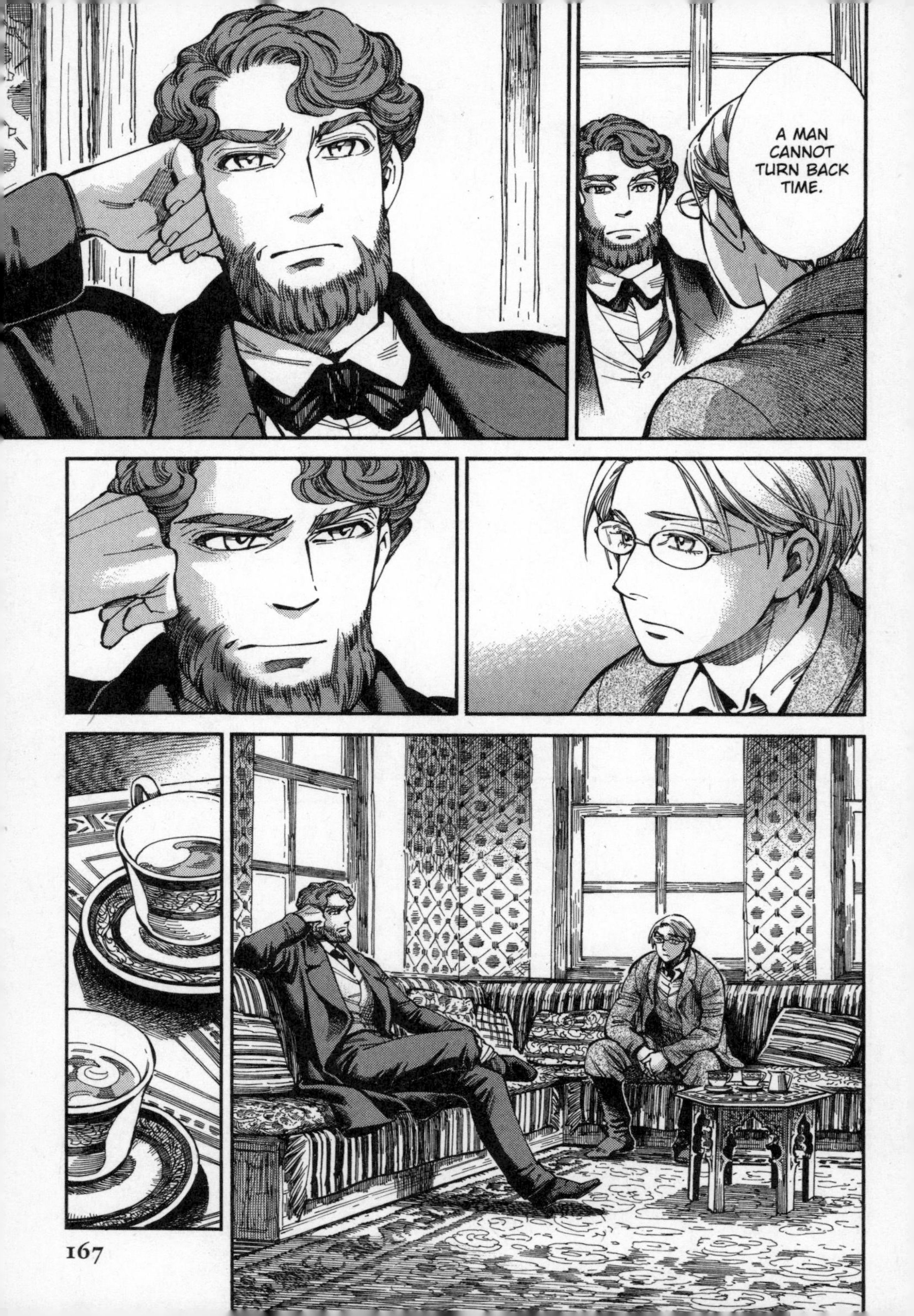
A MAN CANNOT TURN BACK TIME.

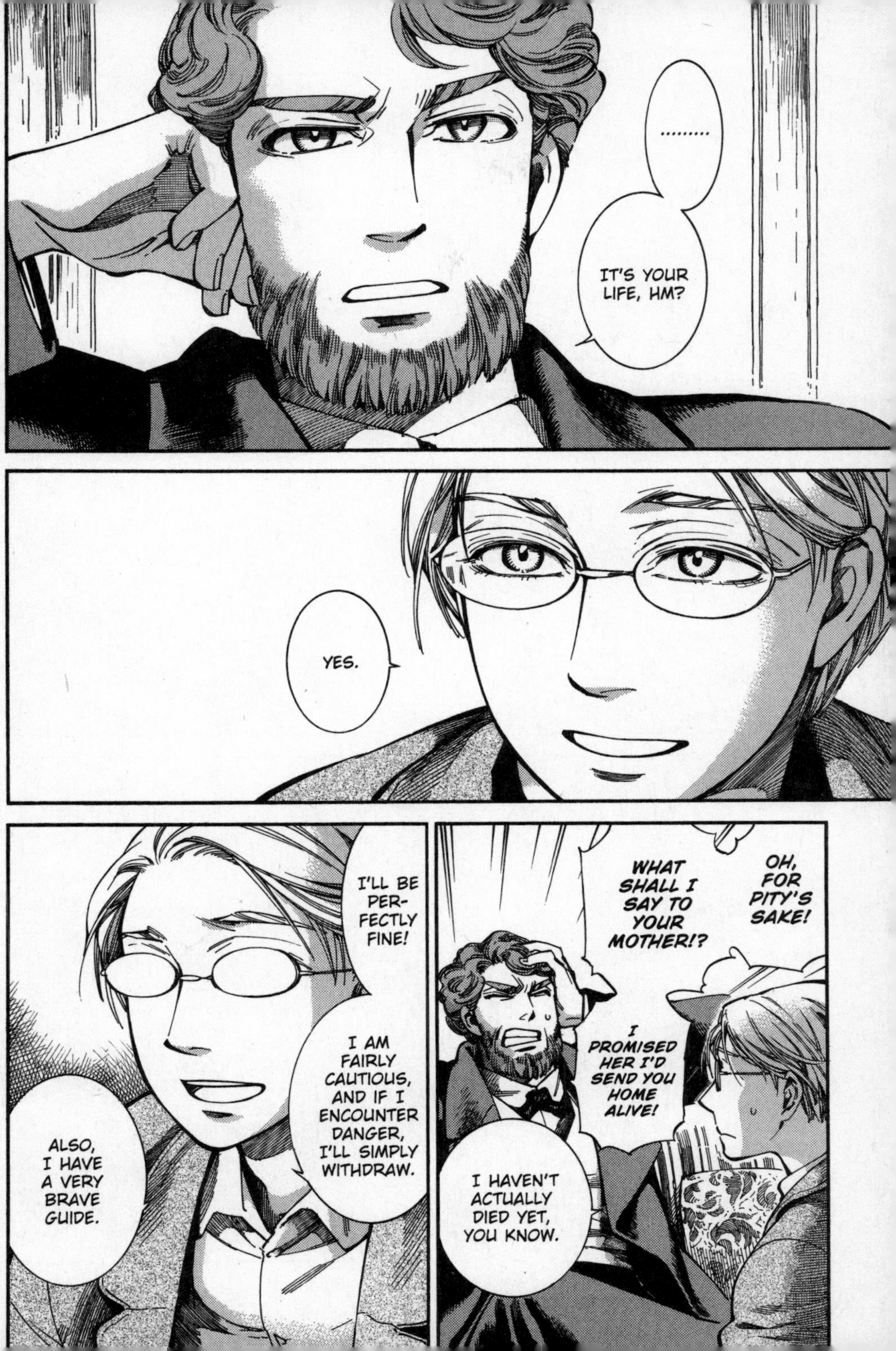
....
IT'S YOUR LIFE, HM?
YES.
OH, FOR PITY'S SAKE!
WHAT SHALL I SAY TO YOUR MOTHER!?
I PROMISED HER I'D SEND YOU HOME ALIVE!
I HAVEN'T ACTUALLY DIED YET, YOU KNOW.
I'LL BE PER-FECTLY FINE!
I AM FAIRLY CAUTIOUS, AND IF I ENCOUNTER DANGER, I'LL SIMPLY WITHDRAW.
ALSO, I HAVE A VERY BRAVE GUIDE.

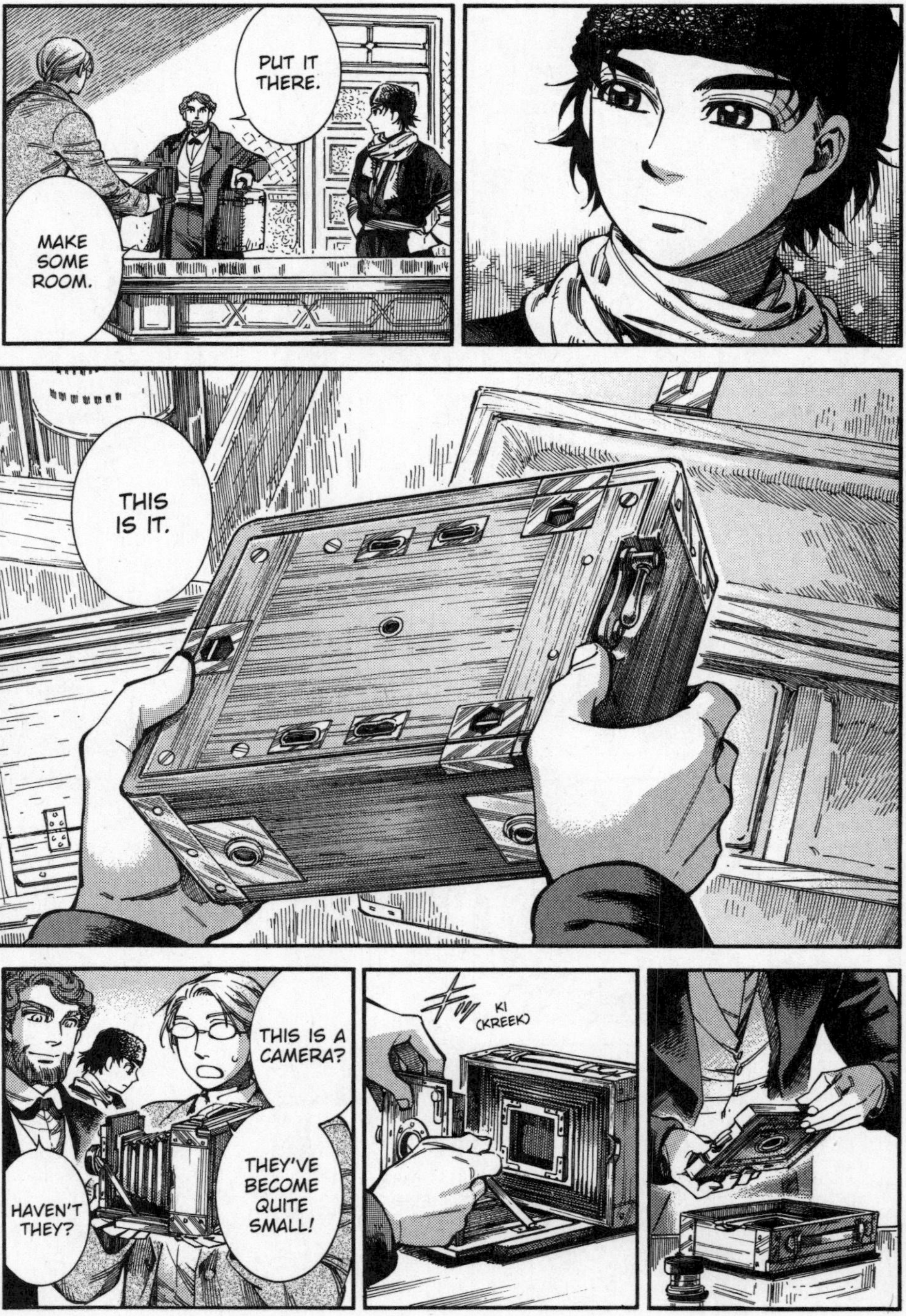
PUT IT THERE.
MAKE SOME ROOM.
THIS IS IT.
KI (KREEK)
THIS IS A CAMERA?
THEY'VE BECOME QUITE SMALL!
HAVEN'T THEY?

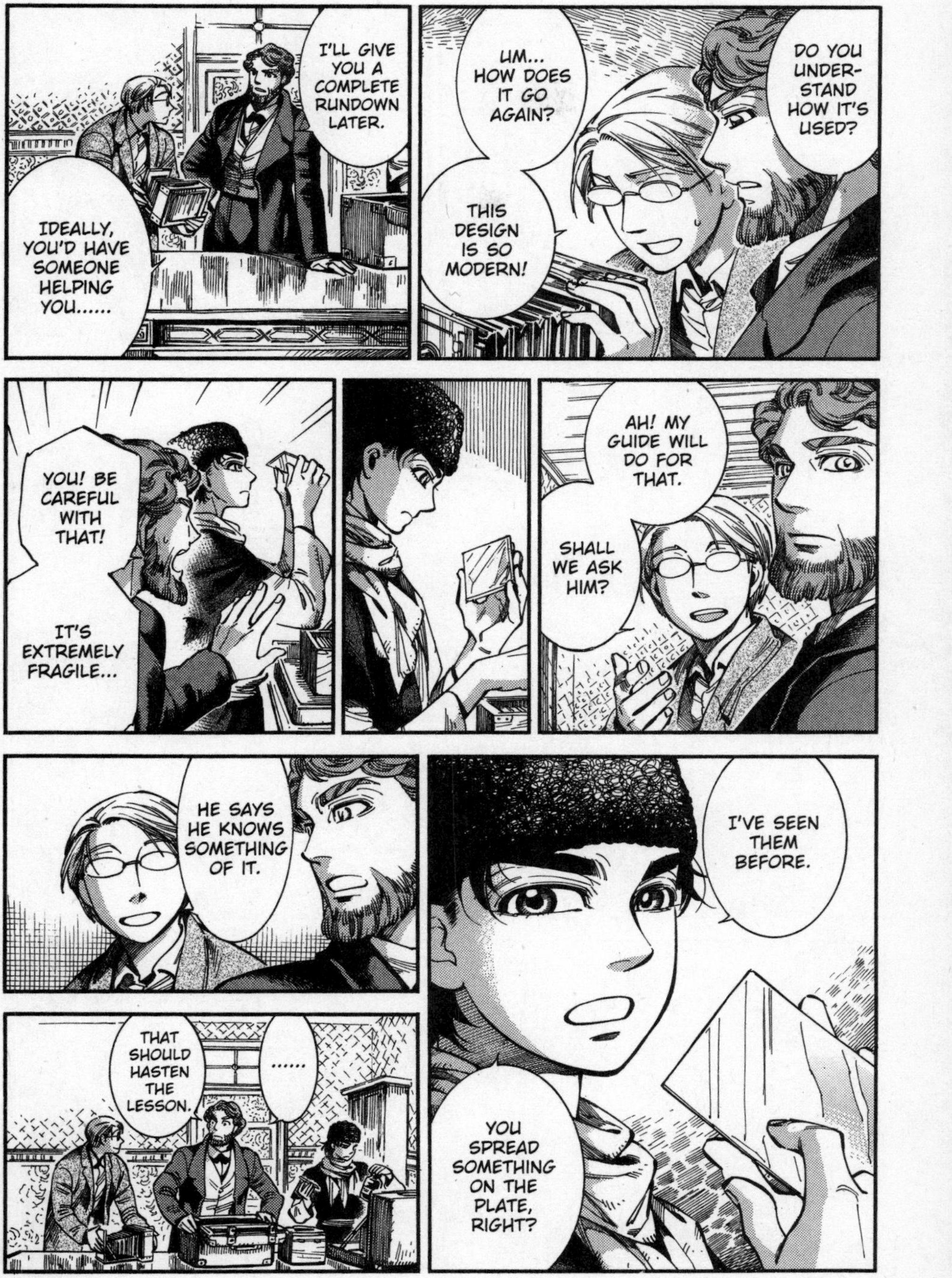
DO YOU UNDER-STAND HOW IT'S USED?
UM... HOW DOES IT GO AGAIN?
THIS DESIGN IS SO MODERN!
I'LL GIVE YOU A COMPLETE RUNDOWN LATER.
IDEALLY, YOU'D HAVE SOMEONE HELPING YOU......
AH! MY GUIDE WILL DO FOR THAT.
SHALL WE ASK HIM?
YOU! BE CAREFUL WITH THAT!
IT'S EXTREMELY FRAGILE...
I'VE SEEN THEM BEFORE.
YOU SPREAD SOMETHING ON THE PLATE, RIGHT?
HE SAYS HE KNOWS SOMETHING OF IT.
......
THAT SHOULD HASTEN THE LESSON.

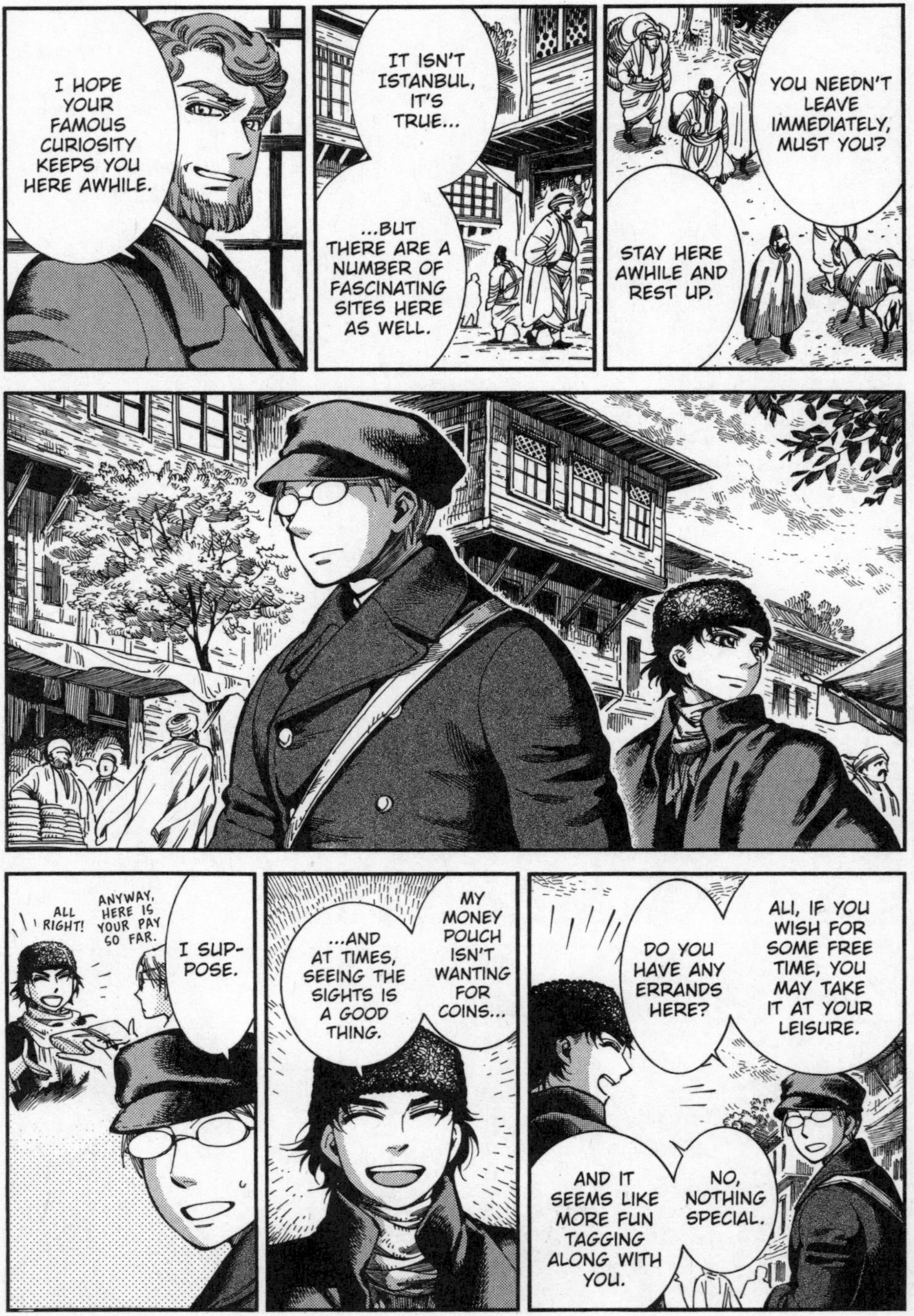
YOU NEEDN'T LEAVE IMMEDIATELY, MUST YOU?
STAY HERE AWHILE AND REST UP.
IT ISN'T ISTANBUL, IT'S TRUE...
...BUT THERE ARE A NUMBER OF FASCINATING SITES HERE AS WELL.
I HOPE YOUR FAMOUS CURIOSITY KEEPS YOU HERE AWHILE.
ALI, IF YOU WISH FOR SOME FREE TIME, YOU MAY TAKE IT AT YOUR LEISURE.
DO YOU HAVE ANY ERRANDS HERE?
NO, NOTHING SPECIAL.
AND IT SEEMS LIKE MORE FUN TAGGING ALONG WITH YOU.
MY MONEY POUCH ISN'T WANTING FOR COINS...
...AND AT TIMES, SEEING THE SIGHTS IS A GOOD THING.
I SUPPOSE.
ANYWAY, HERE IS YOUR PAY SO FAR.
ALL RIGHT!

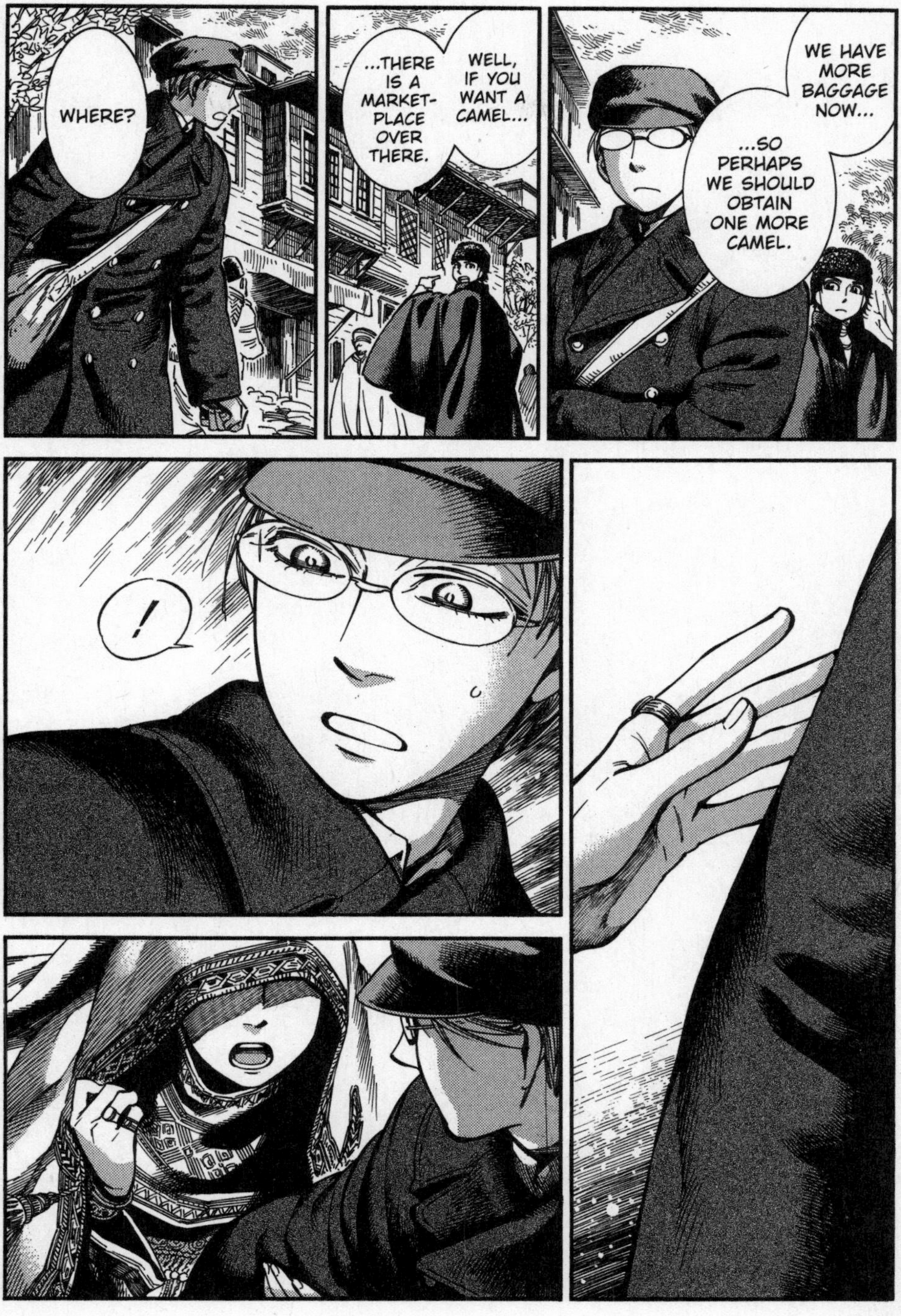
WE HAVE MORE BAGGAGE NOW...
...SO PERHAPS WE SHOULD OBTAIN ONE MORE CAMEL.
WELL, IF YOU WANT A CAMEL...
...THERE IS A MARKET-PLACE OVER THERE.
WHERE?
!

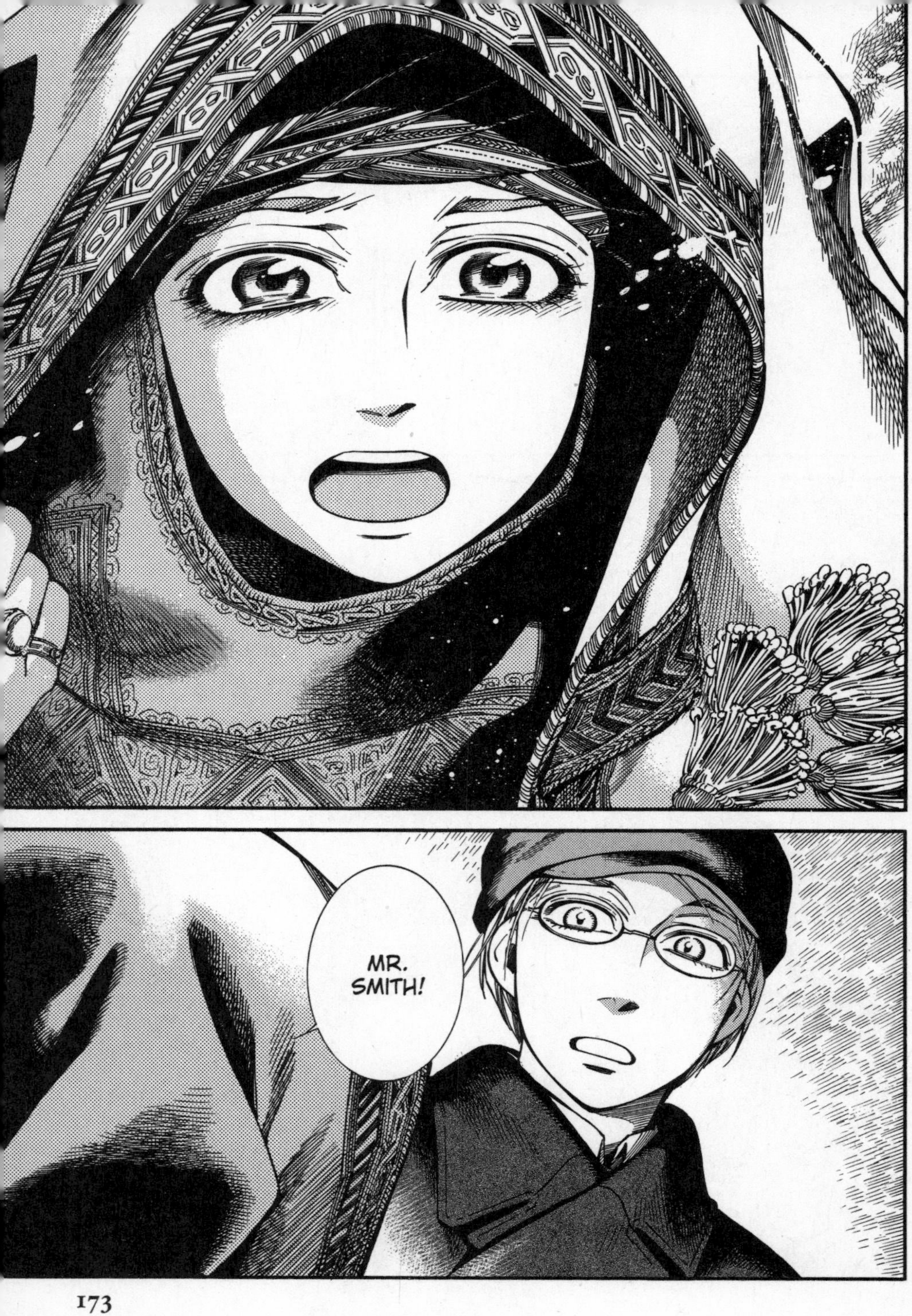
MR. SMITH!

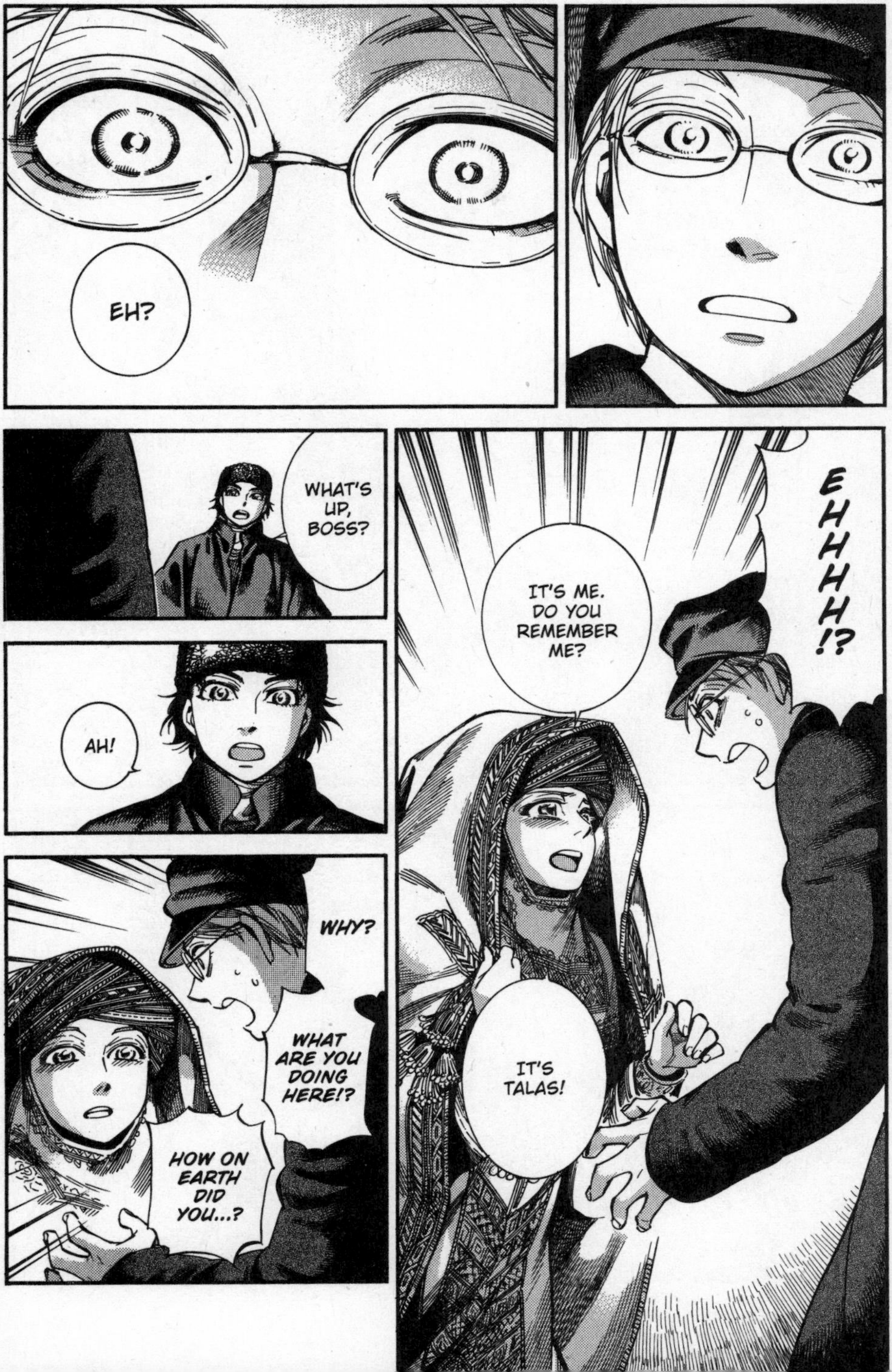
EH?
EHHHHH!?
IT'S ME. DO YOU REMEMBER ME?
IT'S TALAS!
WHAT'S UP, BOSS?
AH!
WHY?
WHAT ARE YOU DOING HERE!?
HOW ON EARTH DID YOU...?

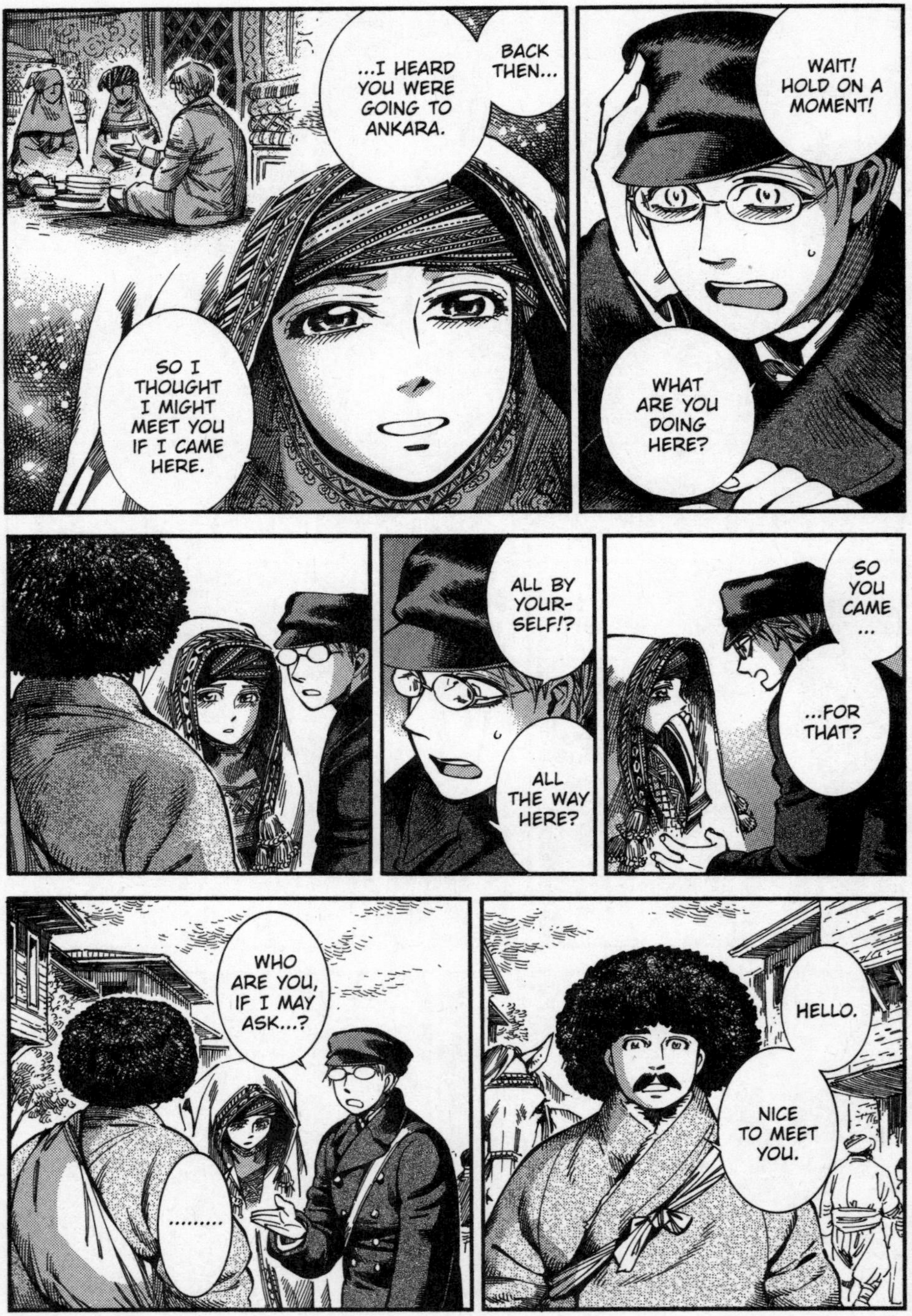
WAIT! HOLD ON A MOMENT!
WHAT ARE YOU DOING HERE?
BACK THEN...
...I HEARD YOU WERE GOING TO ANKARA.
SO I THOUGHT I MIGHT MEET YOU IF I CAME HERE.
SO YOU CAME ...
...FOR THAT?
ALL BY YOUR-SELF!?
ALL THE WAY HERE?
HELLO.
NICE TO MEET YOU.
WHO ARE YOU, IF I MAY ASK...?
....

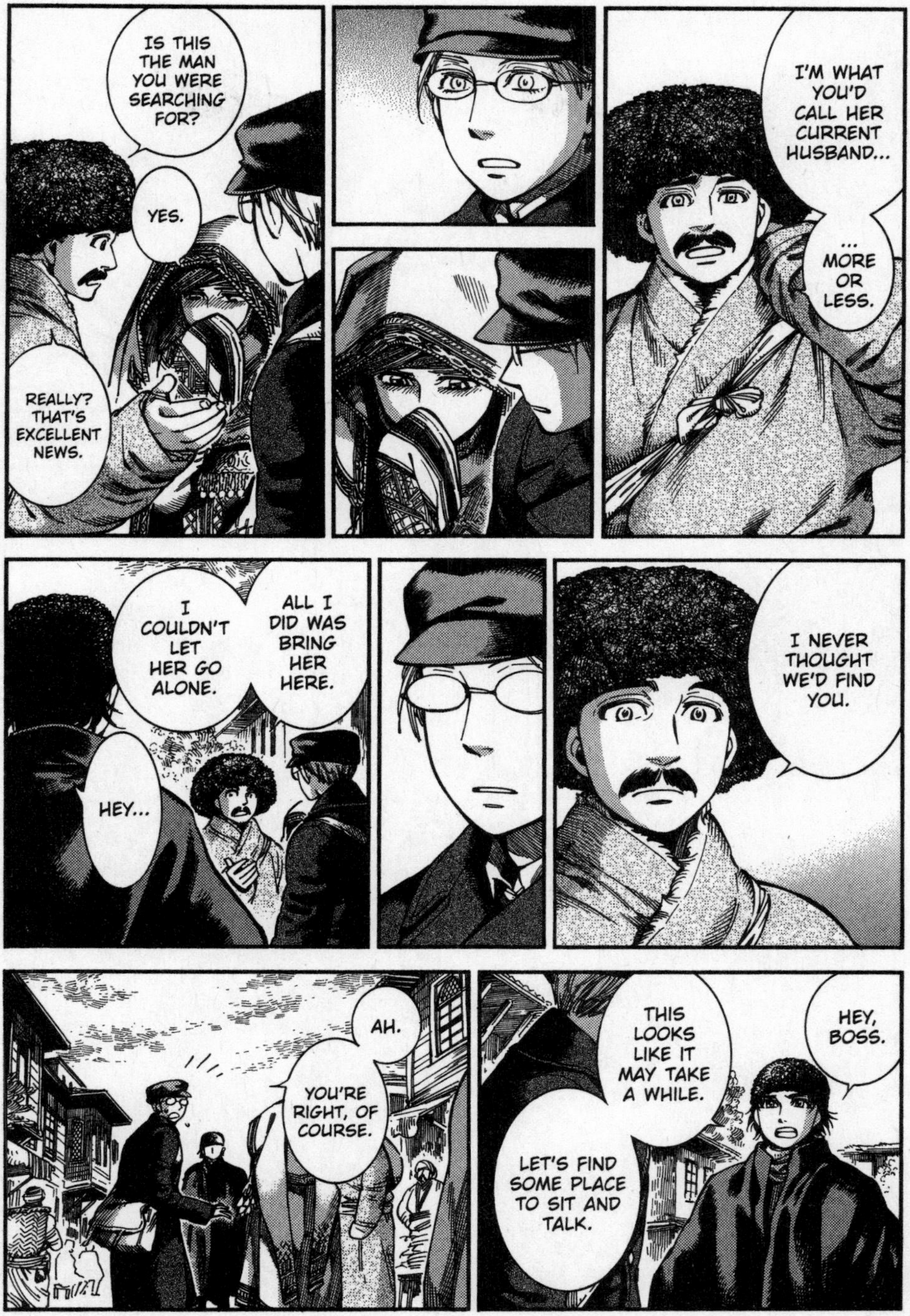
I'M WHAT YOU'D CALL HER CURRENT HUSBAND...
... MORE OR LESS.
IS THIS THE MAN YOU WERE SEARCHING FOR?
YES.
REALLY? THAT'S EXCELLENT NEWS.
I NEVER THOUGHT WE'D FIND YOU.
ALL I DID WAS BRING HER HERE.
I COULDN'T LET HER GO ALONE.
HEY...
HEY, BOSS.
THIS LOOKS LIKE IT MAY TAKE A WHILE.
LET'S FIND SOME PLACE TO SIT AND TALK.
AH.
YOU'RE RIGHT, OF COURSE.

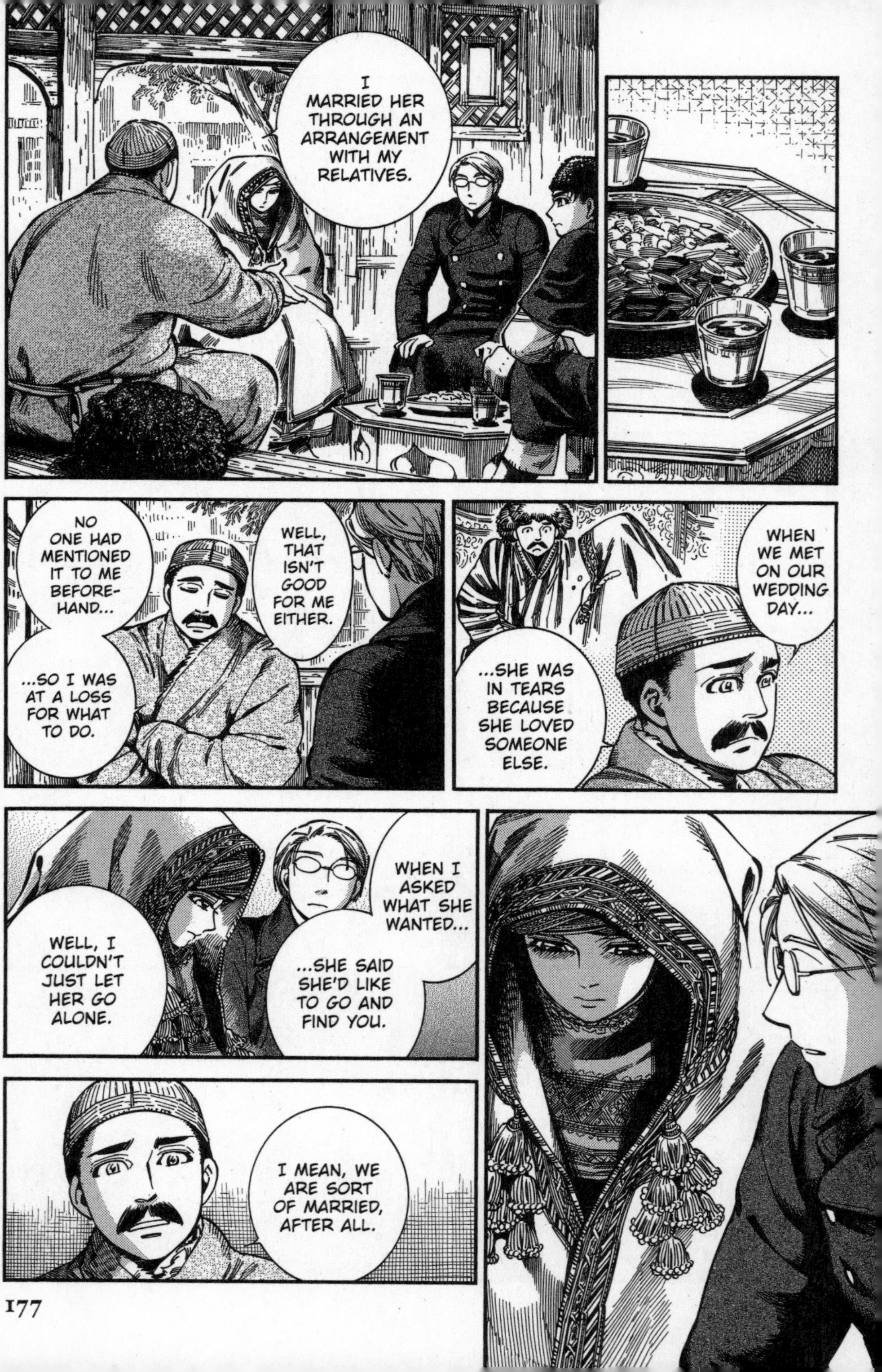
I MARRIED HER THROUGH AN ARRANGEMENT WITH MY RELATIVES.
WHEN WE MET ON OUR WEDDING DAY...
...SHE WAS IN TEARS BECAUSE SHE LOVED SOMEONE ELSE.
WELL, THAT ISN'T GOOD FOR ME EITHER.
NO ONE HAD MENTIONED IT TO ME BEFORE-HAND...
...SO I WAS AT A LOSS FOR WHAT TO DO.
WHEN I ASKED WHAT SHE WANTED...
...SHE SAID SHE'D LIKE TO GO AND FIND YOU.
WELL, I COULDN'T JUST LET HER GO ALONE.
I MEAN, WE ARE SORT OF MARRIED, AFTER ALL.

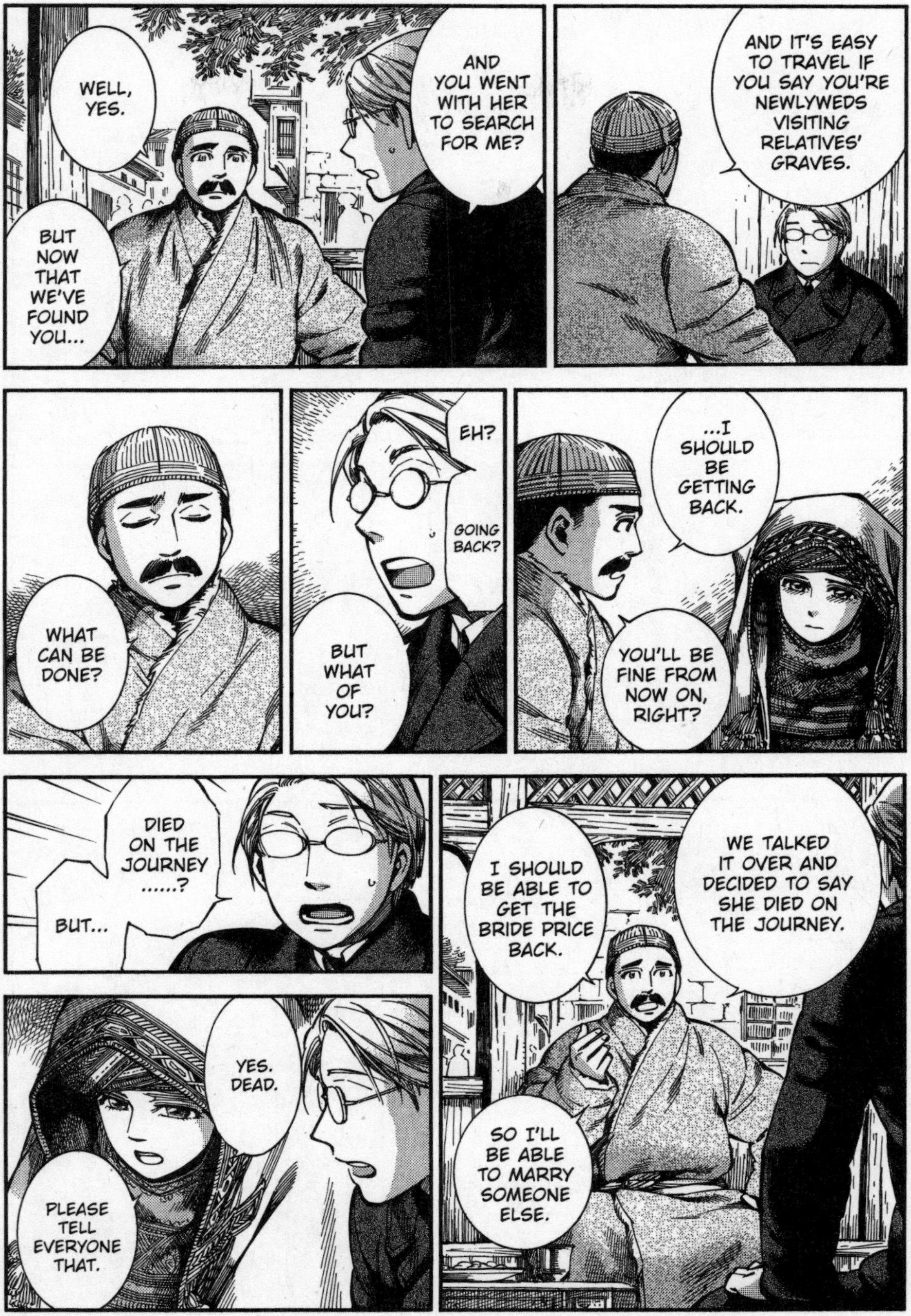
AND IT'S EASY TO TRAVEL IF YOU SAY YOU'RE NEWLYWEDS VISITING RELATIVES' GRAVES.
AND YOU WENT WITH HER TO SEARCH FOR ME?
WELL, YES.
BUT NOW THAT WE'VE FOUND YOU...
...I SHOULD BE GETTING BACK.
YOU'LL BE FINE FROM NOW ON, RIGHT?
EH?
GOING BACK?
BUT WHAT OF YOU?
WHAT CAN BE DONE?
WE TALKED IT OVER AND DECIDED TO SAY SHE DIED ON THE JOURNEY.
I SHOULD BE ABLE TO GET THE BRIDE PRICE BACK.
SO I'LL BE ABLE TO MARRY SOMEONE ELSE.
DIED ON THE JOURNEY ......?
BUT...
YES. DEAD.
PLEASE TELL EVERYONE THAT.

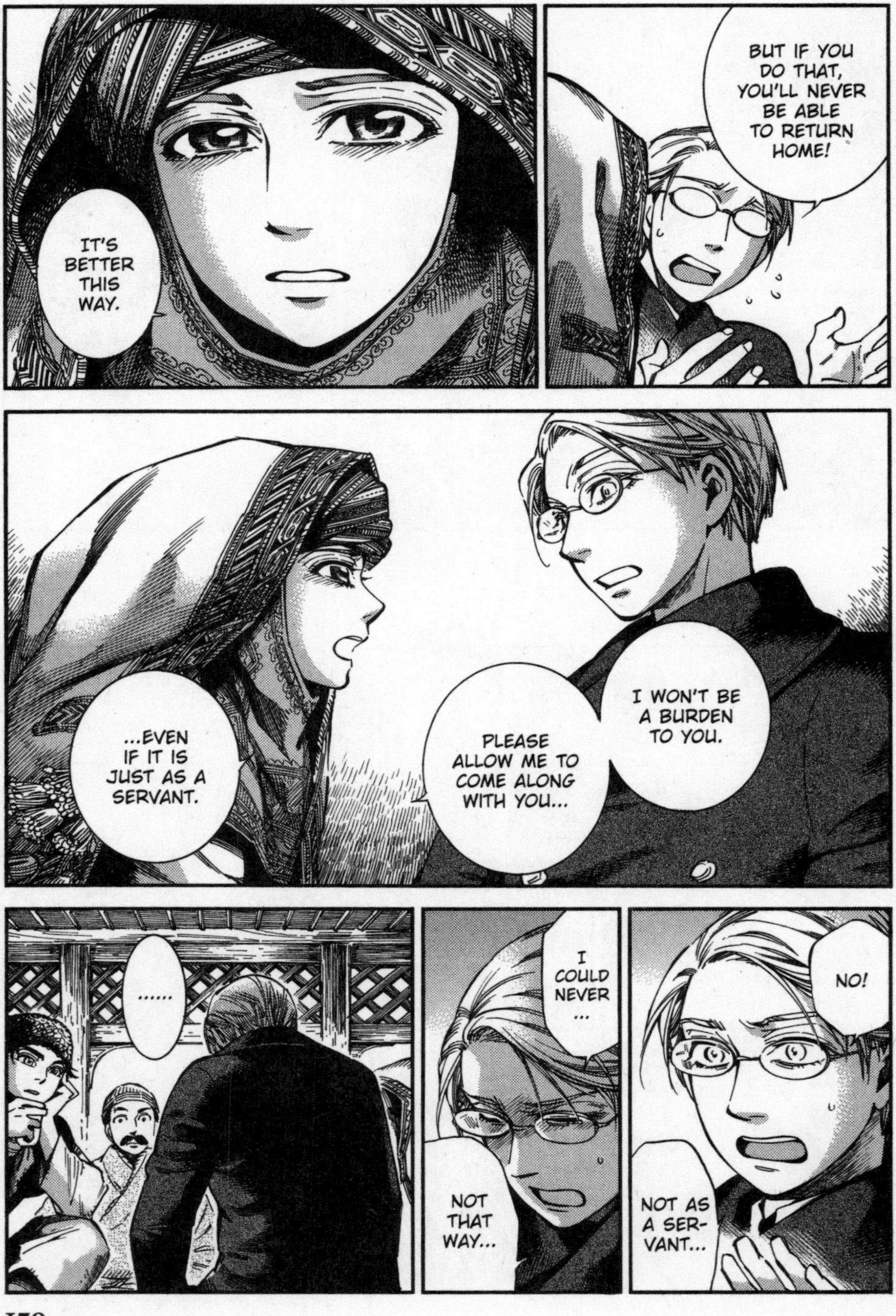
BUT IF YOU DO THAT, YOU'LL NEVER BE ABLE TO RETURN HOME!
IT'S BETTER THIS WAY.
I WON'T BE A BURDEN TO YOU.
PLEASE ALLOW ME TO COME ALONG WITH YOU...
...EVEN IF IT IS JUST AS A SERVANT.
NO!
NOT AS A SER-VANT...
I COULD NEVER ...
NOT THAT WAY...
......

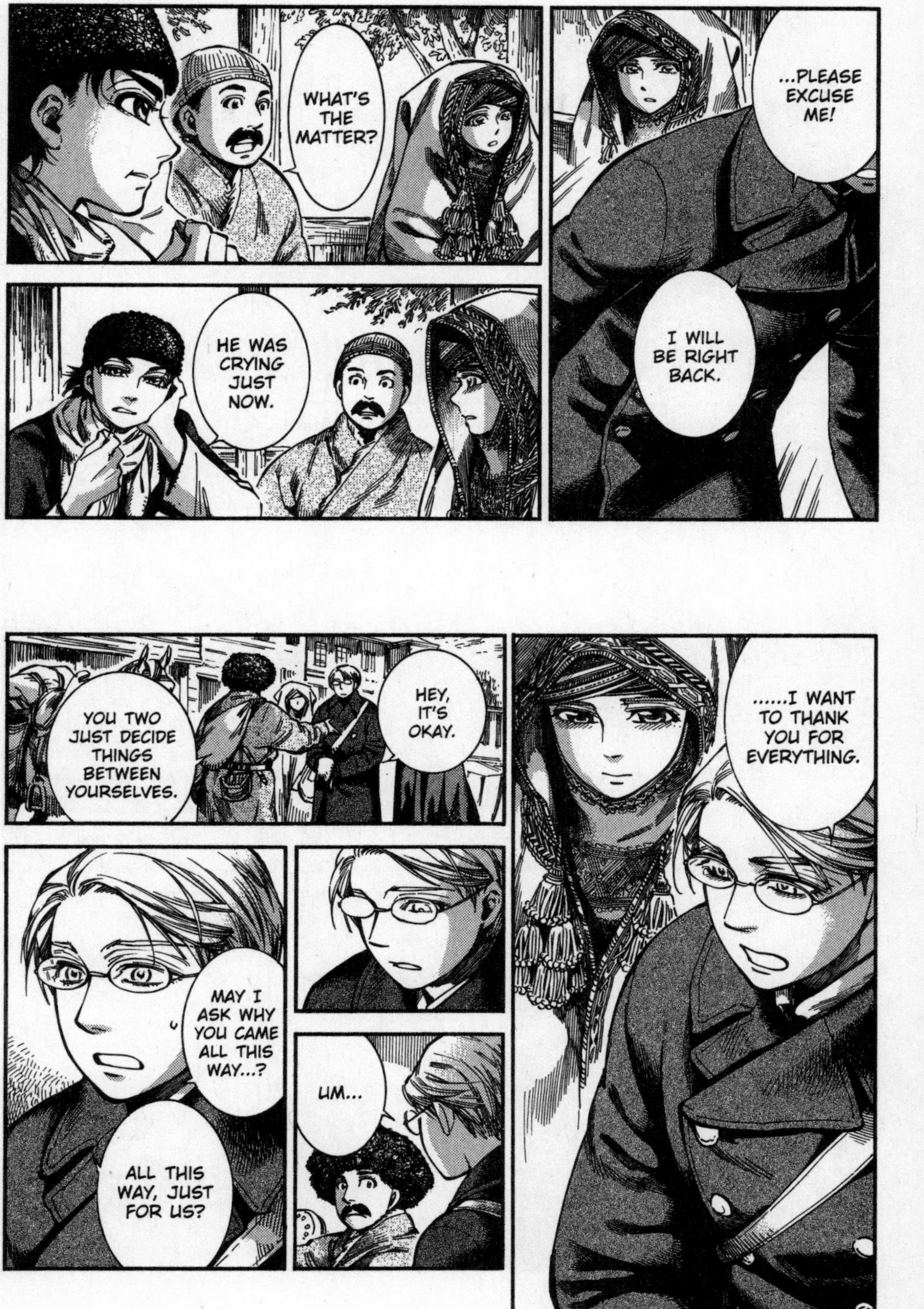
...PLEASE EXCUSE ME!
I WILL BE RIGHT BACK.
WHAT'S THE MATTER?
HE WAS CRYING JUST NOW.
......I WANT TO THANK YOU FOR EVERYTHING.
HEY, IT'S OKAY.
YOU TWO JUST DECIDE THINGS BETWEEN YOURSELVES.
UM...
MAY I ASK WHY YOU CAME ALL THIS WAY...?
ALL THIS WAY, JUST FOR US?

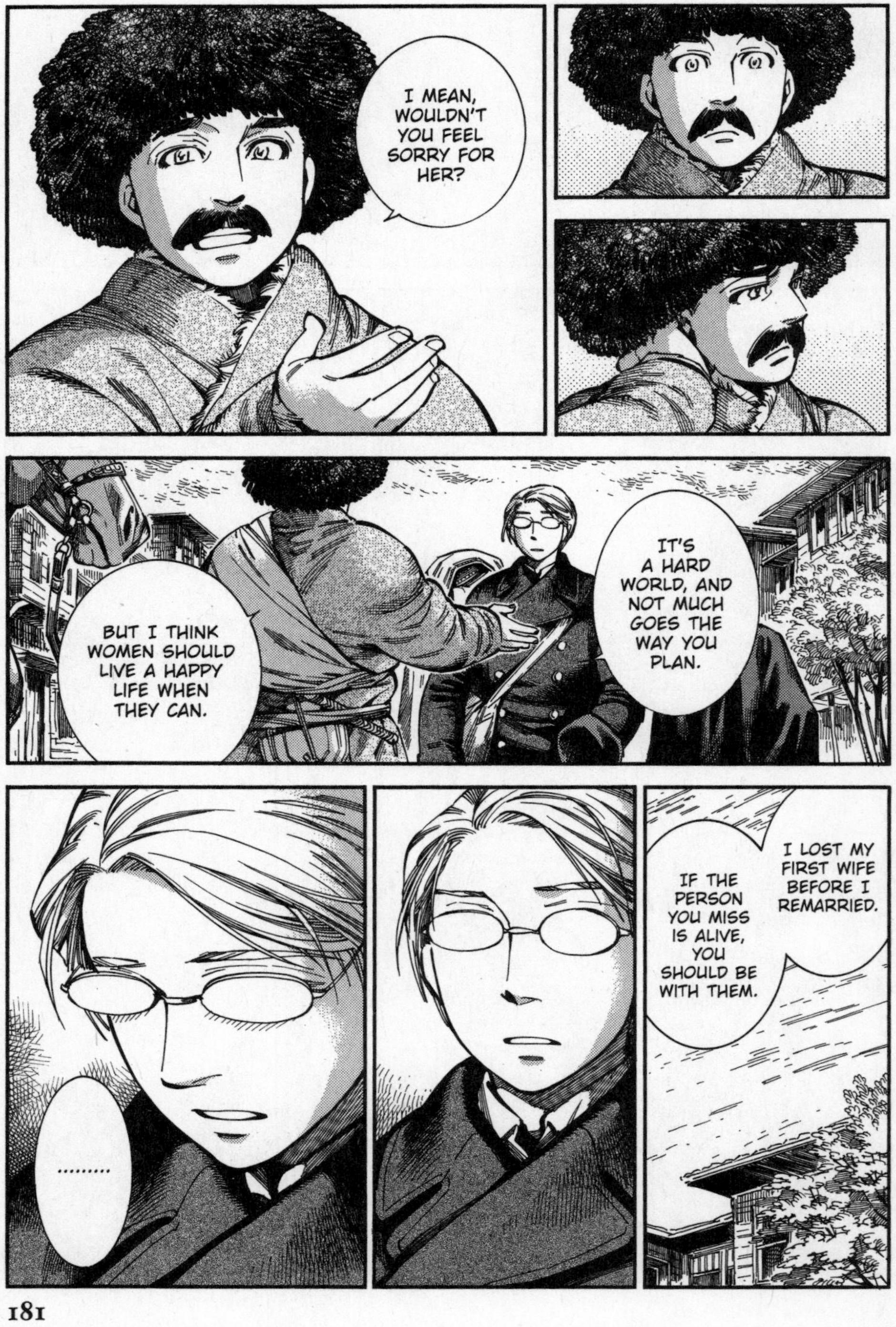
I MEAN, WOULDN'T YOU FEEL SORRY FOR HER?
IT'S A HARD WORLD, AND NOT MUCH GOES THE WAY YOU PLAN.
BUT I THINK WOMEN SHOULD LIVE A HAPPY LIFE WHEN THEY CAN.
I LOST MY FIRST WIFE BEFORE I REMARRIED.
IF THE PERSON YOU MISS IS ALIVE, YOU SHOULD BE WITH THEM.
....

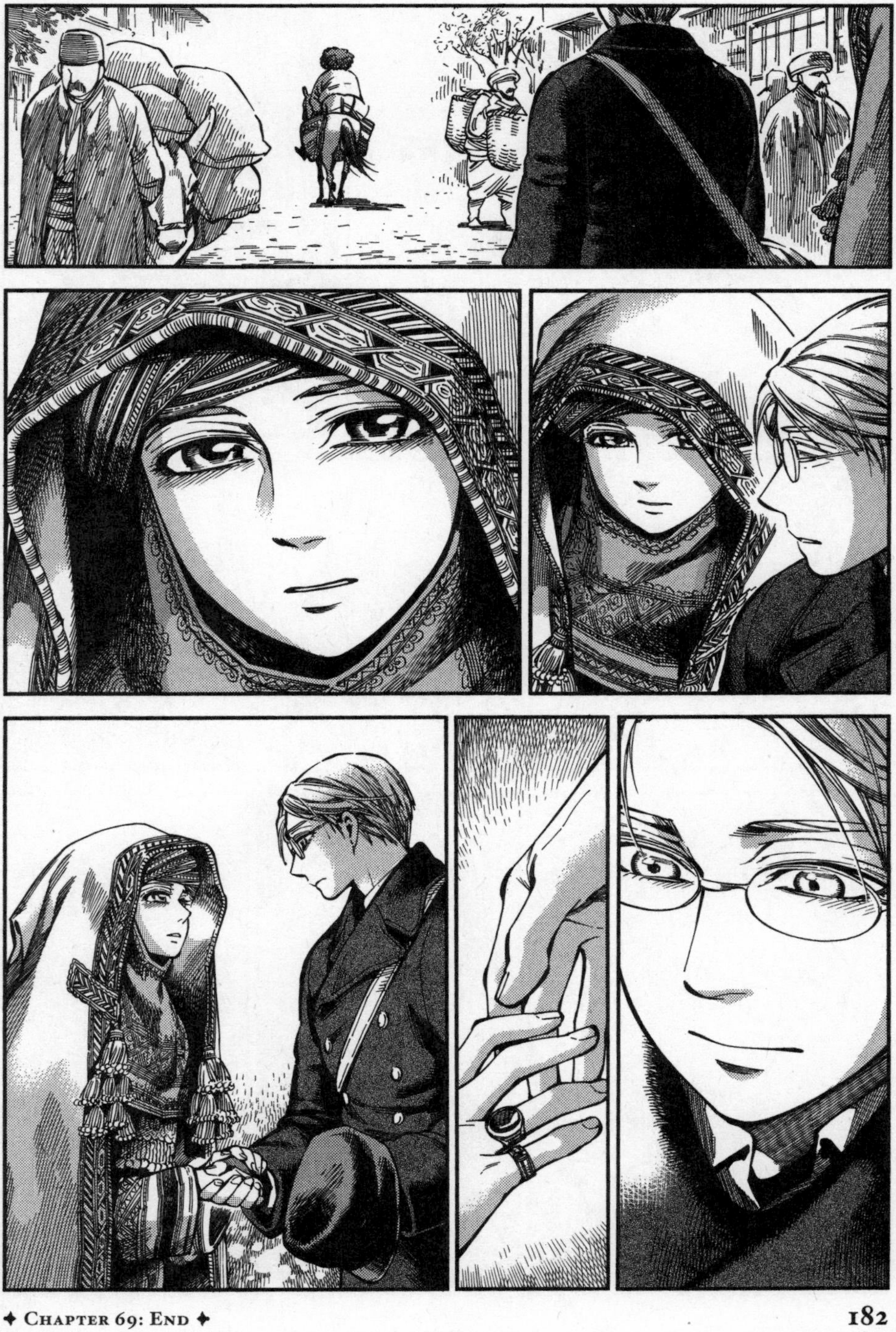

AFTERWORD

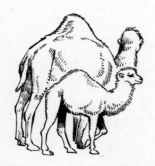

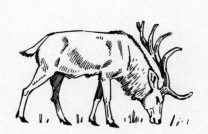

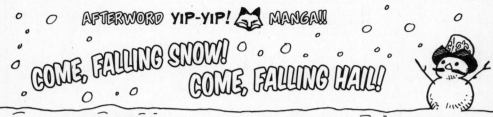

AFTERWORD YIP-YIP! MANGA!!
COME, FALLING SNOW! COME, FALLING HAIL!
AND WITH THAT, HELLO, EVERYONE! IT'S ME, KAORU MORI!
AND A BRIDE'S STORY HAS REACHED ITS TENTH VOLUME!
THIS VOLUME DESCRIBES THE WINDS OF THE HIGH COUNTRY IN WINTER!
AND FALCONRY!
GOLDEN EAGLES ARE SO COOL!
THEY'RE AMAZING!
YOU KNOW, IT CROSSES MY MIND EVERY TIME...
I'M SORRY!
I'M WRITING THESE STORIES BECAUSE I LOVE ANIMALS...
I REALLY DO LOVE RABBITS AND SNAKES AND FOXES AND DEER!
...BUT ALL OF THE GREAT ANIMALS I DRAW END UP GETTING HUNTED OR EATEN. IT BREAKS MY HEART!
NOW, ABOUT THE SNOW...
THERE'S NOTHING TO DRAW!!
BUT LET'S JUST PUT THAT ASIDE.
IT'S JUST HER USUAL ILLNESS.
THE AMOUNT OF SNOWFALL IS DIRECTLY RELATED TO THE AMOUNT OF RAINFALL...
THE INLAND IS VERY DRY.
...SO IT'S DOUBTFUL THE HIGH PLAINS OF CENTRAL ASIA WOULD GET DEEP SNOW LIKE THAT.
STILL, IT'S SO COLD!
WINDCHILL
IF YOU EXPOSED YOUR BODY TO IT, YOU COULD KISS THE LAND OF THE LIVING GOOD-BYE!
INCREDIBLY COLD!
-15°C
THE LOCALS ARE USED TO IT, THOUGH.
IT HAPPENS EVERY YEAR.

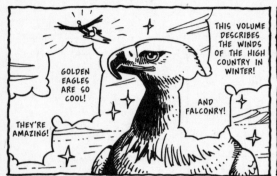

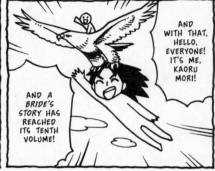

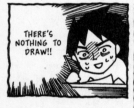

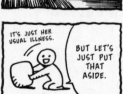

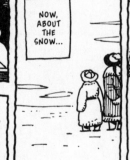

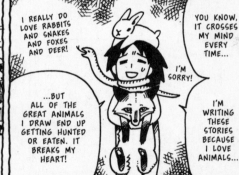

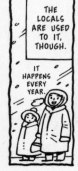

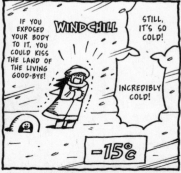

NOTE: THE AFTERWORD TITLE REFERS TO ANOTHER FAMOUS JAPANESE SONG FOR CHILDREN. THE LYRICS CELEBRATE WINTER AND CALL FOR THE SNOW AND HAIL BECAUSE IT GIVES A HAT TO THE MOUNTAINS. IT ALSO NOTES HOW THE DOGS PLAY IN THE SNOW WHILE THE CAT CURLS UP UNDER THE KOTATSU (TABLE WITH A HEATER).

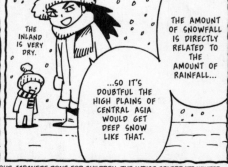

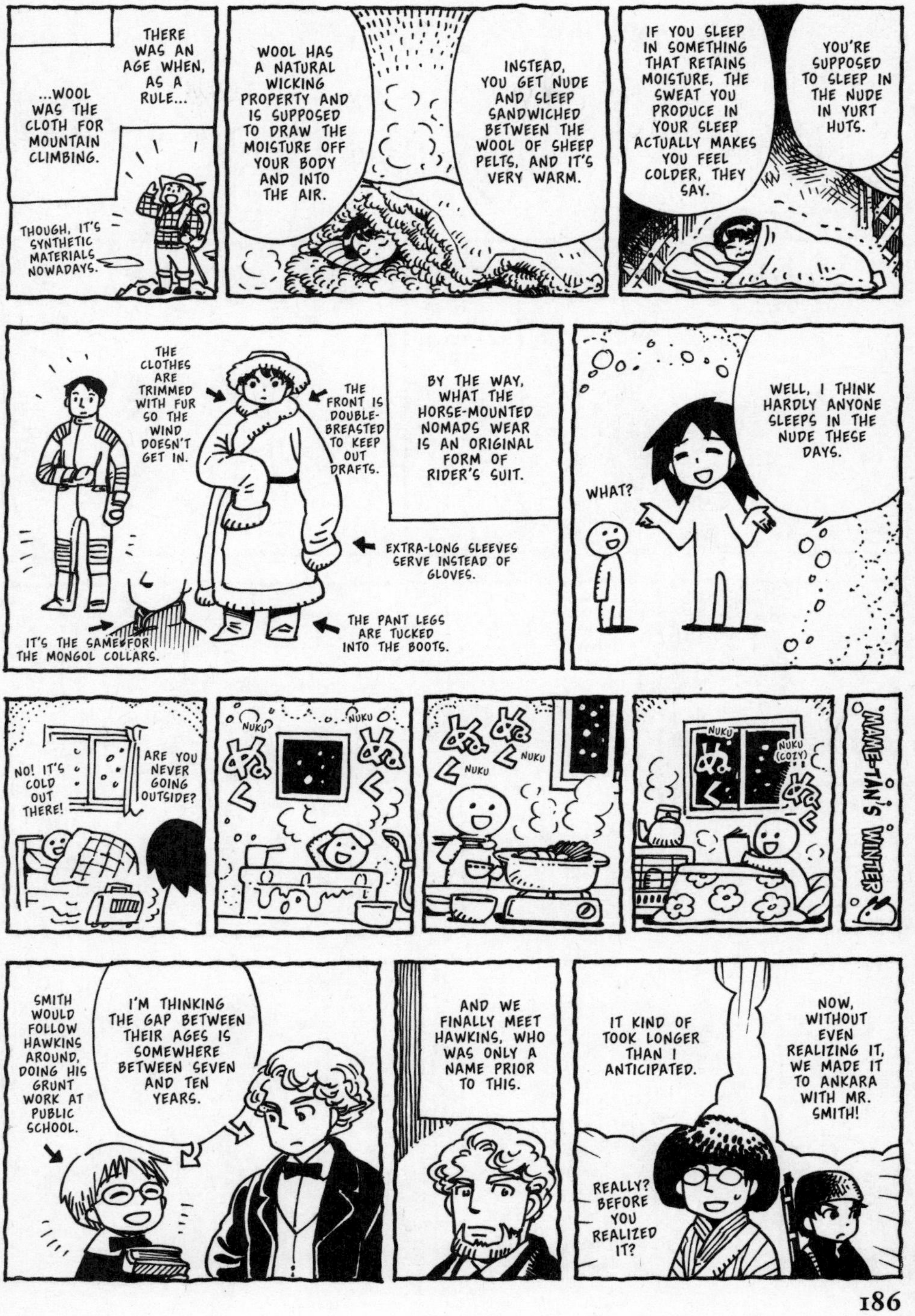
YOU'RE SUPPOSED TO SLEEP IN THE NUDE IN YURT HUTS.
IF YOU SLEEP IN SOMETHING THAT RETAINS MOISTURE, THE SWEAT YOU PRODUCE IN YOUR SLEEP ACTUALLY MAKES YOU FEEL COLDER, THEY SAY.
INSTEAD, YOU GET NUDE AND SLEEP SANDWICHED BETWEEN THE WOOL OF SHEEP PELTS, AND IT'S VERY WARM.
WOOL HAS A NATURAL WICKING PROPERTY AND IS SUPPOSED TO DRAW THE MOISTURE OFF YOUR BODY AND INTO THE AIR.
THERE WAS AN AGE WHEN, AS A RULE...
...WOOL WAS THE CLOTH FOR MOUNTAIN CLIMBING.
THOUGH, IT'S SYNTHETIC MATERIALS NOWADAYS.
WELL, I THINK HARDLY ANYONE SLEEPS IN THE NUDE THESE DAYS.
WHAT?
BY THE WAY, WHAT THE HORSE-MOUNTED NOMADS WEAR IS AN ORIGINAL FORM OF RIDER'S SUIT.
THE FRONT IS DOUBLE-BREASTED TO KEEP OUT DRAFTS.
THE CLOTHES ARE TRIMMED WITH FUR SO THE WIND DOESN'T GET IN.
EXTRA-LONG SLEEVES SERVE INSTEAD OF GLOVES.
THE PANT LEGS ARE TUCKED INTO THE BOOTS.
IT'S THE SAME FOR THE MONGOL COLLARS.
NAME-TAN'S WINTER
NUKU (COZY)
NUKU
NUKU
NUKU
NUKU
NUKU
ARE YOU NEVER GOING OUTSIDE?
NO! IT'S COLD OUT THERE!
NOW, WITHOUT EVEN REALIZING IT, WE MADE IT TO ANKARA WITH MR. SMITH!
IT KIND OF TOOK LONGER THAN I ANTICIPATED.
REALLY? BEFORE YOU REALIZED IT?
AND WE FINALLY MEET HAWKINS, WHO WAS ONLY A NAME PRIOR TO THIS.
I'M THINKING THE GAP BETWEEN THEIR AGES IS SOMEWHERE BETWEEN SEVEN AND TEN YEARS.
SMITH WOULD FOLLOW HAWKINS AROUND, DOING HIS GRUNT WORK AT PUBLIC SCHOOL.

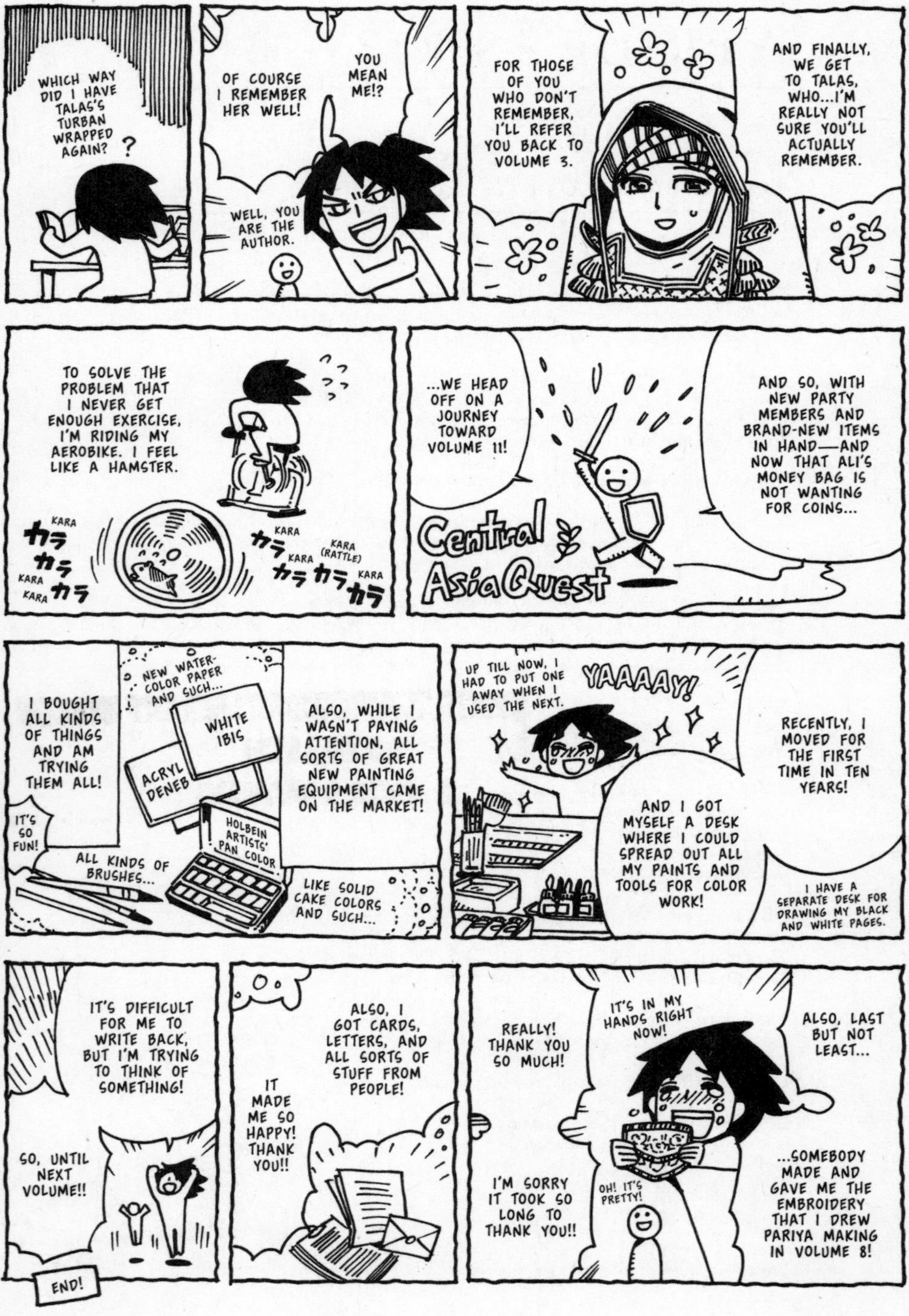
AND FINALLY, WE GET TO TALAS, WHO...I'M REALLY NOT SURE YOU'LL ACTUALLY REMEMBER.
FOR THOSE OF YOU WHO DON'T REMEMBER, I'LL REFER YOU BACK TO VOLUME 3.
YOU MEAN ME!?
OF COURSE I REMEMBER HER WELL!
WELL, YOU ARE THE AUTHOR.
WHICH WAY DID I HAVE TALAS'S TURBAN WRAPPED AGAIN?
?
AND SO, WITH NEW PARTY MEMBERS AND BRAND-NEW ITEMS IN HAND—AND NOW THAT ALI'S MONEY BAG IS NOT WANTING FOR COINS...
...WE HEAD OFF ON A JOURNEY TOWARD VOLUME 11!
Central Asia Quest
TO SOLVE THE PROBLEM THAT I NEVER GET ENOUGH EXERCISE, I'M RIDING MY AEROBIKE. I FEEL LIKE A HAMSTER.
カラ KARA
カラ KARA
カラ KARA (RATTLE)
カラ KARA
カラ KARA
カラ KARA
カラ KARA
RECENTLY, I MOVED FOR THE FIRST TIME IN TEN YEARS!
YAAAAY!
UP TILL NOW, I HAD TO PUT ONE AWAY WHEN I USED THE NEXT.
AND I GOT MYSELF A DESK WHERE I COULD SPREAD OUT ALL MY PAINTS AND TOOLS FOR COLOR WORK!
I HAVE A SEPARATE DESK FOR DRAWING MY BLACK AND WHITE PAGES.
ALSO, WHILE I WASN'T PAYING ATTENTION, ALL SORTS OF GREAT NEW PAINTING EQUIPMENT CAME ON THE MARKET!
NEW WATER-COLOR PAPER AND SUCH...
WHITE IBIS
ACRYL DENEB
I BOUGHT ALL KINDS OF THINGS AND AM TRYING THEM ALL!
HOLBEIN ARTISTS' PAN COLOR
LIKE SOLID CAKE COLORS AND SUCH...
ALL KINDS OF BRUSHES...
IT'S SO FUN!
ALSO, LAST BUT NOT LEAST...
IT'S IN MY HANDS RIGHT NOW!
REALLY! THANK YOU SO MUCH!
...SOMEBODY MADE AND GAVE ME THE EMBROIDERY THAT I DREW PARIYA MAKING IN VOLUME 8!
OH! IT'S PRETTY!
I'M SORRY IT TOOK SO LONG TO THANK YOU!!
ALSO, I GOT CARDS, LETTERS, AND ALL SORTS OF STUFF FROM PEOPLE!
IT MADE ME SO HAPPY! THANK YOU!!
IT'S DIFFICULT FOR ME TO WRITE BACK, BUT I'M TRYING TO THINK OF SOMETHING!
SO, UNTIL NEXT VOLUME!!
END!

A BRIDE'S STORY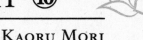

Kaoru Mori

Translation: William Flanagan

Lettering: Abigail Blackman

A BRIDE'S STORY Volume 10 © Kaoru Mori 2018
First published in Japan in 2018 by KADOKAWA CORPORATION, Tokyo.
English translation rights arranged with KADOKAWA CORPORATION, Tokyo through Tuttle-Mori Agency, Inc., Tokyo.

English translation © 2018 by Yen Press, LLC

Yen Press
1290 Avenue of the Americas
New York, NY 10104

Visit us at yenpress.com
facebook.com/yenpress
twitter.com/yenpress
yenpress.tumblr.com
instagram.com/yenpress

First Yen Press Edition: November 2018

Yen Press is an imprint of Yen Press, LLC. The Yen Press name and logo are trademarks of Yen Press, LLC.

The publisher is not responsible for websites (or their content) that are not owned by the publisher.

Library of Congress Control Number: 2012450076

ISBNs: 978-1-9753-2798-9 (hardcover)
        978-1-9753-5632-3 (ebook)

10 9 8 7 6 5 4 3 2 1

WOR

Printed in the United States of America

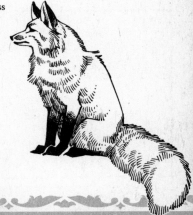